THE SIX
SACRED STONES

MATTHEW
REILLY

PAN BOOKS

First published 2007 by Macmillan
an imprint of Pan Macmillan Australia Pty Limited, Sydney

First published in Great Britain 2007 by Macmillan

This edition published 2010 by Pan Books
an imprint of Pan Macmillan, a division of Macmillan Publishers Limited
Pan Macmillan, 20 New Wharf Road, London N1 9RR
Basingstoke and Oxford
Associated companies throughout the world
www.panmacmillan.com

ISBN 978-1-4472-3915-4

A CIP catalogue record for this book is available from
the British Library.

Printed and bound by CPI Group (UK) Ltd, Croydon, CR0 4YY

Visit **www.panmacmillan.com** to read more about all our books
and to buy them. You will also find features, author interviews and
news of any author events, and you can sign up for e-newsletters
so that you're always first to hear about our new releases.

THE SIX SACRED STONES

Matthew Reilly is the Australian-born author of best-selling novels *Contest*, *Ice Station*, *Temple*, *Area 7*, *Scarecrow*, *Seven Ancient Wonders* and *The Six Sacred Stones*, which reached the *Sunday Times* top-ten best-seller list. He wrote his first two books while studying law at the University of New South Wales, and now writes full-time, producing novels and screenplays and creating television series. The author lives in Sydney.

Also by Matthew Reilly

For John Schrooten
A great and true friend

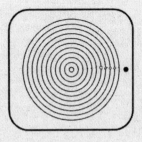

The Mystery of the Circles

A MORTAL BATTLE,
BETWEEN FATHER AND SON,
ONE FIGHTS FOR ALL,
AND THE OTHER FOR ONE.

ANONYMOUS (FROM AN INSCRIPTION FOUND
IN A 3,000-YEAR-OLD CHINESE SHRINE IN
THE WU GORGE, CENTRAL CHINA)

ANY SUFFICIENTLY ADVANCED
TECHNOLOGY IS INDISTINGUISHABLE
FROM MAGIC.

ARTHUR C. CLARKE

THE END OF ALL THINGS IS NEAR.

1 PETER 4:7

INTRODUCTION

THE DARK CEREMONY

12:00 MIDNIGHT

20 AUGUST, 2007

LOCATION: UNKNOWN

In a dark chamber beneath a great island in the most distant corner of the world, an ancient ceremony was under way.

A priceless gold stone—pyramidal in shape, with a crystal at its peak—was set in place.

Then an ancient incantation, unheard for thousands of years, was uttered.

No sooner had the words been spoken than a great purple beam blasted down from the star-filled sky and lit up the pyramidal capstone.

The only witnesses to this ceremony were five angry men.

When it was over, the leader of the group spoke into a satellite radio: 'The ritual has been performed. In theory, the power of Tartarus has been broken. This must be tested. Kill one of them tomorrow in Iraq.'

The next day, on the other side of the world, in war-torn Iraq, an Australian special forces soldier named Stephen

Oakes was shot dead by insurgents. Ambushed in his jeep at a security checkpoint, he was ripped apart by an overwhelming wave of gunfire from six masked attackers. His body was riddled with over two hundred bullet holes. His attackers were never found.

That an allied soldier should die during the occupation of Iraq was nothing new. Already over 3,200 American servicemen had been killed there.

What was unusual about this death was that it had been an *Australian* who had been killed.

For curiously, since March 2006, there had not been a single Australian death in combat in any conflict around the world.

But with the death of Specialist Steve Oakes on August 21, 2007, the uncanny luck of Australian troops came to a bloody and conclusive end.

The day after that, an encrypted message was handed to one of the most powerful men in the world.

It read:

```
SECURE TRANSCRIPT 061-7332/1A
CLASS LEVEL: ALPHA-SUPER
FOR A-1'S EYES ONLY
22-AUG-07
BEGIN SECURE MESSAGE:
```

Note death of Australian specialist Oakes in Iraq. The power of Tartarus has been nullified. Someone has the other capstone.

The game is back on.

Now we must find the Stones.

END SECURE MESSAGE.

THE SIX SACRED STONES

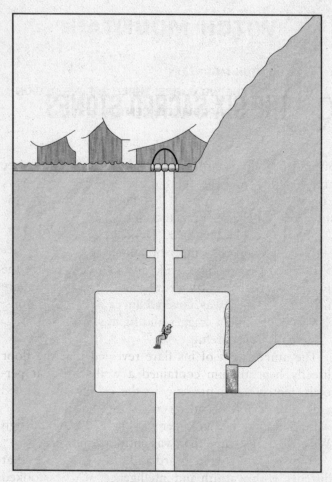

THE ENTRY CHAMBER

PROLOGUE

WITCH MOUNTAIN

 WITCH MOUNTAIN
OFF THE WU GORGE, THREE GORGES REGION
SICHUAN PROVINCE, CENTRAL CHINA
1 DECEMBER, 2007

Sitting in a sling harness suspended from a long rope and hanging in near total darkness, Professor Max Epper cracked the top off his flare, illuminating the subterranean chamber around him.

'Oh my . . .' he breathed. 'Ooooh, *my* . . .'

The chamber was simply breathtaking.

It was a perfect cube, wide and high, cut out of the living rock, perhaps fifty feet to a side. And every square inch of its walls was covered in carved inscriptions: characters, symbols, images and figures.

He had to be careful.

The amber light of his flare revealed that the floor directly beneath him contained a well-shaft that perfectly matched his opening in the ceiling. It yawned wide, a dark hole of indeterminate depth.

In some circles, Max Epper was known by the call-sign 'Wizard', a nickname that was entirely appropriate.

With a flowing white beard and watery blue eyes that glistened with warmth and intelligence, at 67 he looked like a modern-day Merlin. A professor of archaeology at Trinity College, Dublin, it was said that, among other feats, he had once been part of a secret international team that had located—and re-erected—the Golden Capstone of the Great Pyramid at Giza.

Swinging to the floor of the chamber, Wizard unclipped himself and gazed in awe at the text-covered walls.

Some of the symbols he recognised—Chinese characters and even a few Egyptian hieroglyphs. This was not unexpected: long ago, the owner and designer of this tunnel system had been the great Chinese philosopher, Laozi. In addition to being a venerated thinker, Laozi had been a great traveller and was known to have ventured as far as Egypt in the 4th century BC.

In pride of place in the exact centre of the feature wall was a large raised relief that Wizard had seen before:

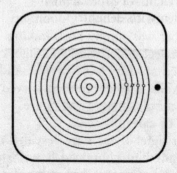

Known as the Mystery of the Circles, it had not yet been decoded. Modern observers guessed it to be a representation of our solar system, but there was a problem with this analysis: there were too many planets circling the central Sun.

Wizard had seen the Mystery of the Circles perhaps a dozen times around the world—in Mexico and Egypt, even in Wales and Ireland—and in various forms: from crude scratchings on bare rock walls to artistic carvings over ancient doorways, but none of those renderings was anywhere near as beautifully and elaborately carved as this one.

This specimen was dazzling.

Inlaid with rubies, sapphires and jade, each of its concentric circles was rimmed with gold. It glittered in the glare of Wizard's high-powered flashlight.

Directly beneath the Mystery of the Circles was a thin doorway of sorts: perhaps two feet wide and six feet high, but shallow, recessed a couple of feet into the solid stone wall. It reminded Wizard of a coffin standing vertically, embedded in the wall. Strangely its rear wall was *curved*.

Carved above it was a small symbol that made Wizard's eyes widen with delight:

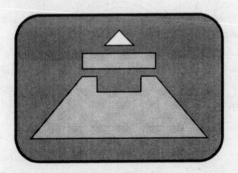

'The symbol for Laozi's Stone . . .' he breathed. 'The Philosopher's Stone. *My God.* We've found it.'

Surrounded by this repository of ancient knowledge and priceless treasure, Wizard pulled out a high-tech Motorola UHF radio and spoke into it: 'Tank. You aren't going to believe this. I've found the antechamber and it's positively stunning. It also contains a sealed doorway which I assume gives access to the trap system. We're close. Very close. I need you to come down here and—'

'*Wizard,*' came the reply. '*We just got a call from our lookout at the docks down on the Yangtze. The Chinese Army is snooping around. Gunboat patrol, nine boats, heading into our gorge. They're coming this way.*'

'It's Mao. How could he have found us?' Wizard said.

'*It may not be him. Could just be a regular patrol,*' the voice of Yobu 'Tank' Tanaka said.

'Which could actually be worse.' Chinese military patrols were notorious for roughing up archaeological expeditions in these parts in search of petty bribes.

'How long have we got till they get here?' Wizard asked.

'*An hour, maybe less. I think it would be wise for us to be gone by the time they arrive.*'

'I agree, my old friend,' Wizard said. 'We'd better hurry. Get down here and bring some more lights. Tell Chow to fire up his computer: I'm going to get started recording images and transmitting them up to him.'

The underground chamber in which Wizard found himself was situated in the Three Gorges region of China, in an area that very much suited him.

This was because the Chinese character *wu* means 'wizard' or 'witch' depending on the context—and it was used often in the names of the area's features: Wu Gorge, the second of the famous Three Gorges; Wushan, the ancient walled fortress-town that once sat on the banks of the Yangtze; and of course Mount Wushan, the colossal two-mile-high peak that towered above Wizard's chamber.

Translation: Witch Mountain.

The Wu Gorge area was renowned for its history—shrines, temples, carvings like the Kong Ming Tablet, and rock-cut caves like the Green Stone Cavern—nearly all of which had now been submerged beneath the waters of the 350-mile-long lake that had formed behind the gargantuan walls of the Three Gorges Dam.

The area was also known, however, for certain *unusual* events.

The Roswell of China, for hundreds of years it had been the site of numerous strange sightings: unexplained celestial phenomena, swarms of shooting stars and aurora-like apparitions. It was even claimed that on one gruesome day in the 17th century the clouds over Wushan had rained *blood*.

The Wu Gorge area certainly had a history.

But now in the 21st century, that history had been drowned in the name of progress, swallowed by the waters of the Yangtze as the great river backed up against the largest structure ever built by mankind. The Old Town of Wushan now lay 300 feet beneath the waves.

Fast-flowing tributaries that had once gushed into the Yangtze via spectacular side-gorges had also been humbled by the expanding Dam Lake—what had once been dramatic 400-foot-high whitewater ravines were now just regular hundred-foot-high gorges with placid water at their bases.

Small stone villages that had once sat on the banks of these little rivers, already far removed from the outside world, had now disappeared completely from history.

But not from Wizard.

In one partially flooded gorge, deep within the mountains to the north of the Yangtze, he had found an isolated mountain hamlet built on higher ground and in it the entrance to this cave system.

The hamlet was primitive and ancient, a few huts constructed of irregular stones and tilting thatch roofs. It had been abandoned three hundred years ago and the locals thought it haunted.

Now, thanks to the ultra-modern dam a hundred miles away, the deserted hamlet was flooded to knee-height.

The entrance to the cave system had been neither guarded by booby traps nor heralded by elaborate gates. It was, rather, its very ordinariness that had kept it secret for over two millennia.

Wizard had found the entrance inside a small stone hut that backed onto the base of the mountain. Once inhabited by the great Chinese philosopher, Laozi—the inventor of Taoism and the teacher of Confucius—this unassuming little hut possessed within it a stone well with a raised brick rim.

And at the bottom of that well, concealed beneath a layer of foul black water, was a false floor—and underneath that false floor, had been this magnificent chamber.

Wizard got to work.

He pulled a powerful Asus laptop from his backpack and connected it to a high-res digital camera and started clicking away, taking shots of the chamber's walls.

As the camera gathered its images, a rapid-fire series of computations took place on Wizard's computer screen.

At work was a translation program—a complex database that had taken Wizard years to compile. It featured thousands of ancient symbols, from many countries and cultures, and their accepted translations. It could also perform 'fuzzy' translations, a kind of best guess when a symbol's meaning was ambiguous.

Every time a symbol was captured on the digital camera, it was scanned by the computer and a translation found. For example:

石头寺

ELEMENT TRANSLATIONS: *shi tou* (stone) *si* (temple)
FULL SEQUENCE TRANS: 'The Temple of Stone'
FUZZ TRANS POSSIBILITIES: 'Stone shrine', 'Stone Temple of
the Dark Sun', 'Stonehenge' (Match Ref. ER:46-2B)

Among the other glyphs and reliefs on the walls,
the computer found Laozi's most famous philosophical
invention, the Taijitu:

The computer translated: 'Taijitu; Ref. *Tao Te Ching*.
Western colloq. ref: "Yin–Yang". Common symbol for
the duality of all things: opposites possess small traits of
each other: e.g. in the good there is some evil and in the
evil there is some good.'

On other occasions, the computer found no prior
record of a symbol:

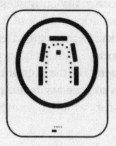

NO IMAGE MATCH.

SEQUENCE TRANS:

UNKNOWN

NEW FILE CREATED

In these cases it created a new file and added it to the database, so that if the symbol in question was ever found again, the database would have a record of it.

Either way, Wizard's computer whirred, absorbing the images hungrily.

After a few minutes of this scanning, one particular translation caught Wizard's attention. It read:

THE 1ST PILLAR* MUST BE INLAID
EXACTLY 100 DAYS BEFORE THE RETURN.

THE PRIZE SHALL BE KNOWLEDGE**.

_____

AMBIGUOUS TERMS:

* 'bar', 'diamond block'
** 'wisdom'

'The First Pillar . . .' Wizard breathed. 'Oh my goodness.'

Ten minutes later, as Wizard continued to feed more photos into his computer, a second figure descended into the chamber.

It was Tank Tanaka, a stocky Japanese professor from the University of Tokyo, Wizard's research partner on this project and long-time friend. With soft brown eyes, a kind round face and wisps of grey at his temples, Tank was the professor every history student wanted.

As he swung himself to solid ground, Wizard's computer pinged loudly, alerting them to a new translation.

The two old professors peered at the screen. It read:

THE COMING OF RA'S DESTROYER

THE COMING OF RA'S DESTROYER
SEES THE STARTING* OF THE GREAT MACHINE**
AND WITH IT THE RISE OF THE SA-BENBEN.

HONOUR THE SA-BENBEN,
KEEP IT CLOSE, KEEP IT NEAR,
FOR IT ALONE GOVERNS THE SIX
AND ONLY THE EMPOWERED SIX CAN
PREPARE THE PILLARS AND
LEAD YOU TO THE SHRINES AND THUS
COMPLETE THE MACHINE
BEFORE THE SECOND COMING.***

THE END OF ALL THINGS IS NEAR.

AMBIGUOUS TERMS:

 * 'commencement' or 'trigger' or 'set off'
 ** 'Mechanism' or 'World'
 *** 'the Return'

MATCH REFERENCE:

Ref XR:5-12 Partial inscription found at
Zhou-Zu Monastery, Tibet (2001)

'The *Sa*-Benben . . . ?' Tanaka said.

Wizard's eyes went wide with excitement. 'It's a little-used name for the uppermost and smallest piece of the Golden Capstone of the Great Pyramid. The entire Capstone was called the *Benben*. But the top piece is special, because unlike the other pieces, which are all trapezoidal in shape, it's a mini-pyramid and so, essentially, a small Benben. Hence the name, Sa-Benben. The Eastern name for it is a bit more dramatic: they call it the Firestone.'

Wizard gazed at the symbol above the translation. 'The Machine . . .' he whispered.

He scanned the translation carefully, saw the match reference at the end of the entry. 'Yes, yes, I've seen this before. It was on a cracked stone tablet unearthed in northern Tibet. But because of the damage to the tablet, only the first and third lines were readable: "The coming of Ra's Destroyer" and "And with it the rise of the Sa-Benben." But this is the full text. This is *momentous*.'

Wizard began muttering quickly to himself: 'Ra's Destroyer is Tartarus, the Tartarus Sunspot . . . But

Tartarus was averted . . . Only . . . only what if the Tartarus Event *started* something else, something we didn't anticipate . . . And if the Firestone governs the six sacred stones, empowers them, then it's fundamental to everything . . . to the Pillars, to the Machine and to the Return of the Dark Sun—oh dear Lord.'

He snapped up, his eyes wide.

'Tank. The Tartarus Event at Giza was connected to the Machine. I never suspected . . . I mean, I should have . . . I should have seen it all along but I—' A frantic look crossed his face. 'When did we calculate the Return?'

Tank shrugged. 'Not until next year's vernal equinox: 20 March, 2008.'

'What about the placing of the Pillars? There was something here about the First Pillar. Here it is: "The 1st Pillar must be inlaid exactly 100 days before the Return. The Prize shall be *knowledge*."'

'One hundred days,' Tank said, calculating. 'That's . . . damn . . . December 10th *this* year—'

Wizard said, 'Nine days from now. Good God, we knew the time was approaching, but this is—'

'Max, are you telling me that we only have nine days to set the First Pillar in position? We haven't even *found* the First Pillar yet . . .' Tank said.

But Wizard wasn't listening any more. His eyes were glazed, staring off into infinity.

He turned. 'Tank. Who else knows about this?'

Tank shrugged. 'Only us. And, I guess, anyone else who has seen this inscription. We know of the tablet in Tibet, but you say it was only partial. Where did it end up?'

'The Chinese Cultural Relics Bureau claimed owner-ship of it and took it back to Beijing. It hasn't been seen since.'

Tank scanned Wizard's frowning face. 'Do you think the Chinese authorities have found the other pieces of the cracked tablet and put it back together? You think they already know about this?'

Wizard stood suddenly.

'How many gunboats did you say are coming up this river gorge?'

'Nine.'

'Nine. You don't send nine gunboats on a routine patrol or a shakedown. The Chinese know, and they're coming for us now. And if they know about this, then they know about the Capstone. Damn! I have to warn Jack and Lily.'

He hurriedly pulled a book from his backpack. Oddly, it wasn't a reference book of any kind, but rather a well-known paperback novel. He began flipping pages and writing numbers down in his notebook.

When he was done, he grabbed his radio and called up to their boat topside.

'Chow! Quickly, take this message down and post it immediately on the noticeboard.'

Wizard then relayed a long series of numbers to Chow. 'Okay, that's it, go! Upload it now—now, now, now!'

A hundred feet above Wizard, a battered old river barge bobbed among the half-submerged huts of the ancient mountain village. It lay at anchor alongside the stone hut that gave entry to the underground chamber.

Inside its main cabin, an eager grad student named Chow Ling hurriedly tapped out Wizard's code, posting it on—of all things—a website devoted to the *Lord of the Rings* movies.

When he was done, he called Wizard on the radio. 'Code has been sent, Professor.'

Wizard's voice came through Chow's headset: *'Thank you, Chow. Good work. Now I want you to forward every image that I've sent up to you to Jack West via email. Then delete them all from your hard-drive.'*

'Delete them?' Chow said in disbelief.

'Yes, all of them. Every last image. As much as you can before our Chinese friends arrive.'

Chow worked fast, tapping keys feverishly, forwarding and then deleting Wizard's incredible images.

As he tapped away on his computer, he never saw the first People's Liberation Army gunboat glide by behind him, cruising down the submerged street of the village.

A harsh voice over a loudhailer made him jerk up: *'Eh! Zou chu lai dao jia ban shang! Wo yao kan de dao ni. Ba shou ju zhe gao gao de!'*

Translation: 'Hey! Come out onto the deck! Remain in plain sight! Hold your hands up high!'

Deleting a final image, Chow did as he was told, kicked back from his desk and stepped out onto the open foredeck of his barge.

The lead gunboat towered above him. It was a modern one, fast, with camouflaged flanks and a huge forward gun.

Chinese soldiers with American-made Colt Commando assault rifles lined its deck, their short-barrelled guns pointed at Chow.

That they held modern American weapons was a bad sign: it meant that these soldiers were elite troops, special forces. Ordinary Chinese infantrymen carried clunky old

Type 56 assault rifles—the Chinese rip-off of the AK-47.

These guys weren't ordinary.

Chow raised his hands—a bare second before someone fired and the entire front half of his body exploded with bloody holes and he was hurled backwards with violent force.

Wizard keyed his radio-mike.

'Chow? Chow, are you there?'

There was no reply.

Then, abruptly, the harness that until now had hung suspended from the well-hole in the ceiling went whizzing back up into the hole like a spooked snake, hauled up by someone above.

'Chow!' Wizard called into his radio. 'What are you—'

Moments later, the harness came back into view . . .

. . . with Chow on it.

Wizard's blood turned to ice.

'Oh, dear me, no . . .' he rushed forward.

Almost unrecognisable from the many bullet wounds, Chow's body came level with Wizard.

As if on cue, the radio suddenly came to life.

'*Professor Epper*,' a voice said in English. '*This is Colonel Mao Gongli. We know you are in there and we are coming in. Try nothing foolish or you will meet the same fate as your assistant.*'

The Chinese troops entered the chamber quickly, abseiling down drop-ropes with clinical precision.

Within two minutes, Wizard and Tank were surrounded by a dozen men with guns.

Colonel Mao Gongli entered last of all. At fifty-five years of age, he was a portly man but he stood with perfect poise, ramrod straight. Like many men of his generation, he'd been patriotically named after Chairman Mao. He had no operational nickname except the one his enemies had given him after his actions at Tiananmen Square in 1989 as a major—the Butcher of Tiananmen, they called him.

Silence hung in the air.

Mao stared at Wizard with dead eyes. When at last he spoke, he did so in clear, clipped English.

'Professor Max T. Epper, call-sign Merlin, but known to some as Wizard. Canadian by birth, but resident Professor of Archaeology at Trinity College, Dublin. Connected with the rather unusual incident that took place atop the Great Pyramid at Giza on March 20, 2006.

'And Professor Yobu Tanaka, from the University of Tokyo. Not connected with the Giza incident, but an expert on ancient civilisations. Gentlemen, your assistant was a gifted and intelligent young man. You can see how much I care for such men.'

'What do you want?' Wizard demanded.

Mao smiled, a thin joyless smile.

'Why Professor Epper, I want *you*.'

Wizard frowned. He hadn't expected that answer.

Mao stepped forward, gazing at the grand chamber around them. 'Great times are upon us, Professor. In the coming months, empires will rise and nations will fall. In times such as these, the People's Republic of China needs knowledgeable men, men like you. Which is why you work for me now, Professor. And I'm sure that with the right kind of persuasion—in one of my torture chambers—you are going to help me find the Six Ramesean Stones.'

FIRST ORDEAL

THE FLIGHT OF THE FIRESTONE

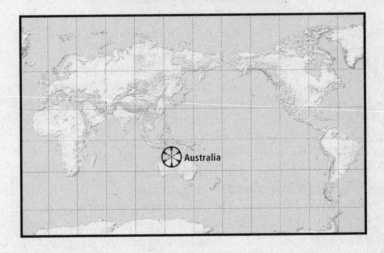

Australia

AUSTRALIA
1 DECEMBER, 2007
9 DAYS BEFORE THE 1ST DEADLINE

On the day his farm was attacked with overwhelming force, Jack West Jr had slept in till 7:00 a.m.

Normally he got up around six to see the dawn, but life was good these days. His world had been at peace for almost eighteen months, so he decided to skip the damn dawn and get an extra hour's sleep.

The kids, of course, were already up. Lily had a friend over for the summer holidays, a little boy from her school named Alby Calvin.

Noisy and excited and generally up to mischief, they'd played non-stop for the past three days, exploring every corner of the vast desert farm by day, while at night they gazed up at the stars through Alby's telescope.

That Alby was partially deaf meant little to Lily or to Jack. At their school in Perth for gifted and talented students, Lily was the star linguist and Alby the star mathematician and that was all that mattered.

At 11, she now knew six languages, two of them ancient and one of them sign language—it had been easily acquired, and was actually something that she and Jack had done together. Today the end-tips of her beautiful long black hair were coloured electric-pink.

For his part, Alby was 12, black, and wore large thick-lensed glasses. He had a cochlear implant, the miraculous technology that allowed the deaf to hear, and spoke with a slightly rounded inflection—signing was still necessary for those times when he needed to understand extra emotion or urgency in a matter—but deaf or not, Alby Calvin could rumble with the best of them.

West was standing on the porch with his shirt off, sipping a mug of coffee. His left arm glinted in the morning sun—from the bicep down, it was made entirely of metal.

He gazed out at the wide desert landscape, hazy in the morning light. Of medium height, with blue eyes and tousled dark hair, he was handsome in a rugged kind of way. Once upon a time, he had been ranked the fourth-best special forces soldier in the world, a lone Australian on a list dominated by Americans.

But he was no longer a soldier. After leading a daring ten-year mission to acquire the fabled Golden Capstone of the Great Pyramid from the remains of the Seven Wonders of the Ancient World, he was now more a treasure hunter than a warrior, more skilled at skirting booby-trapped cave systems and deciphering ancient riddles than killing people.

The adventure with the Capstone, which had ended atop the Great Pyramid, had forged West's relationship with Lily. Since her parents were dead, Jack had raised her—with the help of a truly unique team of international soldiers. Soon after the Capstone mission had concluded, he had formally adopted her.

And since that day nearly two years ago, he had lived out here in splendid isolation, away from missions, away from the world, only travelling to Perth when Lily's schooling required it.

As for the Golden Capstone, it sat in all its glory in an abandoned nickel mine behind his farmhouse.

A few months back, a newspaper article had troubled West.

An Australian special forces trooper named Oakes had been killed in Iraq, shot to death in an ambush, the first Australian battle casualty in *any* conflict in nearly two years.

It bothered West because he was one of the few people in the world who knew exactly why no Australian had been killed in battle these past eighteen months. It had to do with the Tartarus Rotation of 2006 and the Capstone: thanks to his performance of an ancient ritual back then, West had assured Australia invulnerability for what was supposed to be a very long time.

But now with the death of that soldier in Iraq, that period of invulnerability appeared to be over.

The date of the man's death had struck him: 21 August. It was suspiciously close to the northern autumnal equinox.

West himself had performed the Tartarus ritual atop the Great Pyramid on March 20, 2006, the day of the *vernal* equinox, the spring day when the Sun is perfectly overhead and day equals night.

The vernal and autumnal equinoxes were twin celestial moments that occurred at opposite times of the year.

Opposites but the same, West thought. *Yin and yang.*

Someone, somewhere, had done something around the autumnal equinox that had neutralised Tartarus.

West was disturbed from his reverie by a small brown shape cutting across his view to the east.

It was a bird, a falcon, soaring gracefully across the dusty sky, wings wide. It was Horus, his peregrine falcon and loyal companion. The bird landed on the railing next to him, squawking at the eastern horizon.

West looked that way just in time to see several black dots appear in the sky there, flying in formation.

About five hundred kilometres away, near the coastal town of Wyndham, military exercises were under way, the biennial *Talisman Sabre* exercises that Australia held with America. Large in scale, they involved all sections of both nations' armed forces: navy, army and air force.

Only this year, *Talisman Sabre* came with a twist: for the first time ever, China was participating. No one was under any illusions. Under the chaperoning of neutral Australia (it had significant trade links with China and longstanding military links with the US), China and America, the two biggest kids on the block, were sizing each other up. At first, the US hadn't wanted China's participation, but the Chinese had exerted some considerable trade pressure on Australia to be involved and the Australians had begged the US to allow it.

But happily, West thought, these weren't matters that concerned him any more.

He turned to watch Lily and Alby scamper around the barn, kicking up matching dust-trails, when the computer in his kitchen pinged.

Ping, ping, ping, ping.

Emails.

Lots of them.

Jack stepped inside, still gripping his coffee, and checked the monitor.

Over two *dozen* emails from Max Epper had just come in. Jack clicked on one, and found himself staring at a digital photo of an ancient carved symbol. Chinese, by the look of it.

'Oh, Wizard,' he sighed. 'What's happened now? Did you forget to take your extra hard-drive again?'

Wizard had done this before. He needed to back something up but had forgotten to take a second hard-drive, so he'd emailed his photographs to Jack for safe-keeping.

With a groan, Jack clicked over to the Internet and brought up a *Lord of the Rings* chatroom, punched in his ID tag: STRIDER101.

A little-used noticeboard came up. This was how he and Lily communicated with Wizard: through the anonymity of the Internet. If Wizard was sending a bulk block of emails, then he'd probably also sent an explanatory message via the chatroom.

Sure enough the last message left on the noticeboard was from GANDALF101: Wizard.

West scrolled down to view the message, expecting to see the usual bashful apology from Wizard . . .

. . . only to be surprised by what he saw.

He saw numbers.

Lots of numbers, interspersed with parentheses and forward slashes:

(3/289/-5/5) (3/290/-2/6) (3/289/-8/4) (3/290/-8/4) (3/290/-1/12)
(3/291/-3/3) (1/187/15/6) (1/168/-9/11)

(3/47/-3/4) (3/47/-4/12) (3/45/-163) (3/47/-1/5)
(3/305/-3/1) (3/304/-8/10)
(3/43/1/12) (3/30/-3/6)
(3/15/7/4) (3/15/7/3)
(3/63/-20/7) (3/65/5/1-2)
(3/291/-14/2) (3/308/-8/11) (3/232/5/7) (3/290/-1/9)
(3/69/-13/5) (3/302/1/8)
(3/55/-4/11-13) (3/55/-3/1)

Jack frowned, concerned.

It was a coded message from Wizard, a special code known only to the members of their trusted inner circle.

This was serious.

Jack quickly grabbed a paperback novel from the nearby bookshelf—the same novel that Wizard had used to compose the message in China—and began flicking pages, unravelling the coded communication.

He jotted down words underneath each numerical reference until at last he had the full message and his blood ran cold:

(3/289/-5/5) (3/290/-2/6) (3/289/-8/4) (3/290/-8/4) (3/290/-1/12)
GET   OUT   GET   OUT   NOW!

(3/291/-3/3) (1/187/15/6) (1/168/-9/11)
GRAB   FIRE   STONE

(3/47/-3/4) (3/47/-4/12) (3/45/-163) (3/47/-1/5)
AND   MY   BLACK   BOOK
(3/305/-3/1) (3/304/-8/10)
AND   RUN

(3/43/1/12) (3/30/-3/6)
NEW   EMERGENCY

(3/15/7/4) (3/15/7/3)
VERY   DANGEROUS

(3/63/-20/7) (3/65/5/1-2)
ENEMIES   ARE COMING

(3/291/-14/2) (3/308/-8/11) (3/232/5/7) (3/290/-1/9)
WILL   MEET   YOU   AT

(3/69/-13/5) (3/302/1/8)
GREAT   TOWER

(3/55/-4/11-13) (3/55/-3/1)
THE WORST IS COMING

'Holy shit . . .' Jack breathed.

He snapped to look back out the kitchen window, saw Lily and Alby still playing out by the barn. Then he saw the hazy orange sky beyond them, glorious in the morning sun—

—as it began to fill with falling figures, dozens and dozens of them, figures that issued blooming parachutes above them, slowing their falls.

Paratroopers. Hundreds of paratroopers.

Coming for his farm.

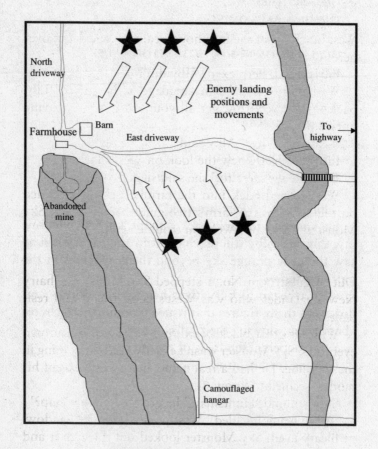

THE ATTACK ON JACK'S FARM

West burst out of the farmhouse, calling, 'Kids! Get over here! Quickly!'

Lily turned, perplexed. Alby did too.

West motioned in sign language as he spoke: 'Lily, pack a suitcase! Alby, get all your stuff! We're leaving in two minutes!'

'Leaving? Why?' Alby said.

Lily, however, knew the look on West's face.

'Because we have to,' she said/signed. 'Come on.'

West rushed back into the farmhouse and pounded on the doors of the farm's two guest rooms. 'Zoe! Sky Monster! Wake up! We're in trouble again!'

Out of guestroom No. 1 stepped Sky Monster, a hairy New Zealander who was West's good friend and resident pilot.

With his great black beard, pot belly, and overgrown eyebrows, Sky Monster wasn't exactly pretty first thing in the morning. He had a real name, but no one except his mother seemed to know it.

'Not so loud, Huntsman,' he growled. 'What's up?'

'We're being invaded.' West pointed out the window.

Bleary-eyed, Sky Monster looked out through it and saw the swarm of falling parachutes filling the morning sky. His eyes sprang wide. '*Australia* is being invaded?'

'No, just us. Just this farm. Get dressed and then get down to the *Halicarnassus*. Prep her for immediate lift-off.'

'Gotcha,' Sky Monster hurried away, just as the door to guestroom No. 2 opened, revealing a far more pleasant sight.

Zoe Kissane emerged from her room, dressed in a spare pair of West's pyjamas. With sky-blue eyes, shortish blonde hair and a lightly freckled face, she was a true Irish beauty. She was also on leave from the Sciathan Fhianoglach an Airm, the famed crack commando unit of the Irish Army. A veteran of the Capstone adventure, she and West were close, and—some said—getting closer. The end-tips of her blonde hair were also electric-pink, the remains of a hair session with Lily the previous day.

She opened her mouth to speak, but West just pointed out the window.

'Well, you don't see that every day,' she said. 'Where's Lily?'

Jack ducked into his room, snatching stuff from all sides: a canvas miner's jacket, a fireman's helmet, and a double-holstered gunbelt that he strapped round his waist. 'Getting her things. Alby's with her.'

'Oh God, Alby. What will we—'

'We take him with us.'

'I was going to say, what will we tell his mother? "Hi, Lois, yes, the kids had a great summer, outran an invading force of paratroopers."'

'Something like that,' Jack said, dashing into his study and emerging a moment later with a large black leather folder.

Then he hurried past Zoe, heading down the hallway to the back door of the farmhouse. 'Get your things and corral the kids. We're leaving in two minutes. I have to get the top piece of the Capstone.'

'The *what*—?' Zoe asked but West had already dashed out into the sunlight, the screen door clapping shut behind him.

'And grab the codebooks and computer hard-drives, too!' came his distant shouting voice.

A moment later, Sky Monster came bustling out of his guestroom, buckling his belt and holding his pilot's helmet. He too shoved past Zoe—with a gruff 'Mornin', Princess'—before stomping out the back door.

And suddenly Zoe woke up to the situation.

'Holy shite,' she hurried back into her room.

Jack West hustled across the backyard of his farmhouse and dashed inside the entrance to an old abandoned mine set into a low hill there.

He hurried down a dark tunnel, guided by the pen-light attached to his fireman's helmet, until after about a hundred metres he came to a larger space, a wide chamber containing . . .

. . . the Golden Capstone.

Nine feet tall, glittering and golden, the great mini-pyramid that had once sat atop the Great Pyramid at Giza possessed an authority, a presence, that humbled Jack every time he saw it.

Arrayed around the Capstone were several other artefacts from his previous adventure, artefacts that were all in some way related to the Seven Wonders of the Ancient World: the Mirror from the Lighthouse at

Alexandria, the head of the Colossus of Rhodes.

On occasion, Jack would come here and just sit and stare at the priceless collection of treasures assembled in the cavern.

But not today.

Today he grabbed an old stepladder and climbed up alongside the Capstone and carefully removed its uppermost piece, the only piece that was itself a pyramid, the Firestone.

The Firestone was small, its square base perhaps as wide as a hardback book. At its summit was a tiny clear crystal, an inch wide. All the other pieces of the Capstone possessed similar crystals in their centres, all seven of which lined up in a row when the Capstone was assembled.

West tucked the Firestone into his rucksack and hurried back out the exit tunnel.

As he ran down it, he triggered several black boxes mounted on wooden supports along the way—red lights blinked on. At the last support beam, he switched on a final box and grabbed a remote handheld unit that had lain on top of the box for just this occasion.

Then West was out, back in the morning sunshine, standing before the entrance to the old mine.

'I never wanted to do this,' he said sadly.

He hit 'DETONATE' on the remote. Muffled sequential booms thudded out from the mine tunnel as each charge detonated, the innermost charges going off first.

Then, with a great rushing *whoosh*, a billowing cloud of dust came blasting out from the mine's entrance. As the last charge exploded, it caused a landslide to cascade down from the low hill above the mine entrance, a loose body of rubble, sand and rocks.

Jack turned and ran back toward the farmhouse.

If he'd had time to look back, he would have seen the great dustcloud settle. Once the dust had completely come to rest, all that remained in its place was a hill—a plain ordinary rock-and-sand-covered hill no different from any of the others in the surrounding area.

Jack returned to the farmhouse in time to see Sky Monster zoom off in a pick-up truck, heading south for the hangar.

The parachutes were still falling from the sky, many of them close to the ground now. There were literally hundreds of them, some obviously bearing armed men, while others were larger chutes carrying oversized objects: jeeps and trucks.

'Mother of God . . .' Jack whispered.

Zoe was pushing Lily and Alby out the back door of the farmhouse, with a computer hard-drive tucked under one arm.

'Did you grab the codebooks?' West called.

'Lily's got 'em!'

'This way, to the barn!' West waved them to follow.

The four of them ran together, two adults, two children, struggling with either backpacks or essential gear, with Horus flying above them.

As he ran, Alby saw West's guns.

West noticed the shocked look on the boy's face. 'It's okay, kid. This sort of thing happens to us all the time.'

West came to the barn's huge door, ushered the others inside before he peered out after Sky Monster's pick-up as it sped south alongside a spur of hills, kicking up a thick dustcloud behind it—

But then a parachutist cut off his view of the truck, a fully-equipped Chinese trooper who hit the dusty ground and rolled skilfully, slewed his chute and quickly pulled out an automatic rifle.

Then he started running directly for the farmhouse.

Another man landed behind him. Then another, and another.

West swallowed. He and the others were cut off from Sky Monster. 'Damn it, damn it,' he breathed.

Then he ducked inside the barn as over a hundred more paratroopers hit the ground on every side of his farm.

The East Drive

Moments later, the barn doors blasted open and two compact all-wheel-drive vehicles boomed out from it.

They looked like something out of a *Mad Max* movie.

They were modified Longline 'Light Strike Vehicles', or LSVs—ultralight two-seater dune buggies with chunky all-terrain tyres, high-tolerance wishbone suspension, and sleek bodies made only of rollbars and struts.

Jack and Alby were in the first car; Zoe and Lily in the second.

'Sky Monster!' Jack called into the radio-mike wrapped around his throat. 'We're cut off from you! We're going to have to meet you at the highway! We'll take the east drive and the river crossing.'

'*Copy that,*' Sky Monster's voice replied. '*The highway it is.*'

'*Jack,*' Zoe's voice came in. '*Who are these people and how the hell did they find us?*'

'I don't know,' Jack said. 'I don't know. But Wizard knew they were coming. He sent us a warning—'

Just then, a storm of bullets chewed a line across the dirt road in front of Jack's car. Jack yanked his steering wheel hard over, blasted through the dustcloud.

The shots had come from a big all-terrain vehicle thundering in from the desert plain to the north.

It was a distinctive six-wheeled vehicle, a WZ-551 armoured personnel carrier built by the Chinese North Industries Corporation for the PLA. Featuring heavy armour and a French-made Dragar turret on its top, it had a box-shaped body and a flat prow-like nose that sloped backwards underneath it. The Dragar turret boasted a brutish 25mm cannon and a 7.62mm co-axial machine gun.

It was the first of many APCs coming from the north. Jack counted seven . . . nine . . . eleven vehicles behind it, plus even more smaller ones, jeeps and trucks, all over-flowing with armed troops.

It was the same from the south: men and vehicles had touched down there, discarded their chutes, and were now coming north toward the east drive.

An armada of vehicles coming right at them, from both the north and the south.

Zoe's voice: '*Jack! Those APCs look Chinese!*'

'I know!'

He keyed his radio scanner, picked up the broadcast frequency for the *Talisman Sabre* exercises. A voice was shouting: '*Red Force Three! Come in! You are way off course for this drop! What the hell are you guys doing!*'

Clever, West thought. His attackers had made this look like an exercise drop gone wrong.

He evaluated his options.

The east drive led to the Fitzroy River, a north–south running river that was currently full, it being the wet season. A single bridge spanned it. Beyond that river was an old highway which—at one straight section—doubled as West's own private runway.

If his cars could make it across the river before these inrushing forces cut them off, they could make it to the highway, where they'd rendezvous with Sky Monster.

But a quick glance at the twin columns coming at him from the north and the south revealed a simple mathematical truth: it was going to be close.

West's LSV roared down the dusty east drive.

In the passenger seat, Alby gripped the rollbar, his eyes wide with terror.

West glanced over at the little boy.

'Bet you never experienced anything like *this* at another kid's house over the summer!'

'Nope!' Alby shouted over the whipping wind.

'You a boy scout, Alby?'

'Yes!'

'And what's the boy scout motto?'

'Be prepared!'

'Absolutely! Now, young man, you're gonna find out why you're not allowed to play on the cattle crossings or the bridge.'

The two LSVs whipped down the dusty road—with their twin hordes of pursuers closing in from either side, converging on them in a V-shaped formation. Giant clouds of dirt rose behind the two incoming forces.

'Zoe! Swing in front!' West called.

Zoe obeyed, pulled her car in front of West's, just as the two cars zoomed over a cattle grid.

As his LSV shot over the grille, however, West swung

left, plowing right into a low sign-post that read 'CATTLE CROSSING'.

The post—unknown to the casual observer—was equipped with a tripwire that snapped as the LSV shot over it, triggering a concealed mechanism that launched a hundred six-pronged nails onto the roadway behind the fleeing car.

Alby turned, saw the star-shaped nails bounce down onto the road, fanning out all across it, just as the first pursuing jeep—the men on it firing hard—drove right into the field of nails.

Blasting puncture noises ripped the air as all four of the jeep's tyres blew and the vehicle skidded and then flipped, spraying men in every direction.

A second jeep suffered a similar fate, but the rest skirted the nail-field, bouncing around the suspect section of road.

Alby watched them crash before turning to face West, who shouted over the wind, 'Be prepared!'

Alby then swung back to see the trailing APCs, slower than the jeeps, reach the nails—with their runflat tyres they just thundered right over them, impervious to damage.

Chasing. Pursuing. Hunting.

As she drove, Zoe continued to monitor the airwaves with her car's radio scanner. A moment after the two jeeps crashed, it picked up voices speaking in Mandarin over a secure military frequency.

'Jack!' she called into her own mike. 'I got the bad guys on UHF 610.15!'

In his car, Jack switched to that channel and heard

the voices of his enemy speaking Mandarin:

'*Heading east in two cars—*'

'*Ground Force Seven is in pursuit—*'

'*Ground Force Six is going for the bridge—*'

'*Command. This is Ground Force Two. We're right on their tail. Please repeat capture instructions—*'

A new voice came on the line, a calmer one, one possessing clear authority.

'*Ground Force Two, this is Black Dragon. Capture instructions are as follows: priority one is the Firestone; priority two, the girl and West, both are to be captured alive if possible. Any other captives are to be executed. There can be no witnesses to our doings here.*'

Hearing this, West snapped to look over at Alby. Then he looked forward at Zoe, driving the lead car.

It was one thing to know that if everything ended badly, you were safe, but it was another thing entirely to know that those dear to you were not.

'*You hear that?*' Zoe said over the radio.

'Yep,' West said, his jaw tightening.

'*Please get us out of here, Jack.*'

As Jack and Zoe's cars sped away to the east, a Chinese command APC was arriving at Jack's farmhouse, flanked by several escort jeeps.

As it skidded to a halt, two men stepped out of it, one Chinese, the other American. While the Chinese man was clearly older, both bore the rank of major on their collars.

The Chinese major was *Black Dragon*, the owner of the voice on the airwaves. Officious and intense, Black Dragon was known for his cold methodical efficiency; he was a man who got the job done.

The younger American with him was tall and broad, powerful, and he wore the customised uniform of a US Army Special Forces operator. He had a sharp-edged crew-cut and the unblinking eyes of a psychopath. His call-sign: *Rapier*.

'Secure the farmhouse,' Black Dragon ordered the nearest unit of paratroopers. 'But be wary of any improvised devices. Captain West is clearly a man who prepares for eventualities such as this.'

Rapier said nothing. He just stared intently at the abandoned farmhouse, as if absorbing every feature of it.

The River Crossing

The bridge was up ahead now, maybe two kilometres away—an old wooden single-lane bridge.

West saw it come into view, just as three APCs and five Chinese jeeps skidded to a halt in front of it, blocking the way. A roadblock.

They'd got there first.

Damn.

The lead APC lowered its turret-mounted cannon ominously.

At that exact same moment, four Chinese jeeps caught up with West's cars from behind, two to each side.

The soldiers on the jeeps looked angry as all hell and, buffeted and jostled by the uneven terrain, they tried to aim their rifles at West's tyres.

'*Jack!*' Zoe called over the radio. '*Jack . . . !*'

'Stay on the road! Whatever you do, stay on the road till you reach the windmills!'

Two skinny windmills flanked the road up ahead, halfway between them and the bridge.

An explosion boomed out behind Jack's LSV—barely a metre behind it—tearing a crater from the road. A shot from the APC's cannon.

'Sheesh,' Jack turned to Alby. 'Do me a favour, kid. Try not to tell your mother about this part of your stay.'

Zoe's car came to the windmills flanking the roadway, shoomed between them, closely followed by Jack and Alby's LSV—still harried by the four Chinese jeeps.

Jack cut through the windmills, while the jeeps took

them differently: one jeep swung onto the road proper and sped between the windmills, while the three others went wider, whipping around the *outside* of the windmills and—

Suddenly the first such jeep dropped from view. As did the jeep travelling immediately behind it *and* the one that had sped around the windmill on the other side of the road.

The three jeeps just fell out of sight, as if they had been swallowed by the earth.

In fact, that was exactly what had happened. They had fallen into Indian tiger traps—large concealed holes in the ground next to the windmills, designed by Jack for an escape just like this one.

'Zoe! Quickly! Let me pass, then drive exactly where I do!'

Jack zoomed past Zoe's car and then abruptly shot left, off the road and out onto rough scrubland. Zoe followed him, swinging her LSV left, chased now by the sole surviving Chinese jeep.

Bouncing over the scrub, the river up ahead, the roadblock off to their right.

'*Exactly* where I drive!' West repeated into his mike.

He swept down an embankment toward the Fitzroy River—a suicidal course. There was no way he could possibly cross the fast-flowing waters of the river in his low-slung LSV.

But into the river he went. At full speed.

The LSV plunged into the Fitzroy, kicking up spectacular fans of spray on either side as it sheared right through the water, unusually shallow water, across an uncommonly smooth section of riverbed: a concealed concrete ford.

As Jack's LSV skipped out the other side of the river, roaring up the far bank with a metre-high jump, Zoe's car hit the near edge of the stream, at the same time as the last Chinese jeep came alongside it.

Zoe hit the ford, following Jack's path exactly. But the pursuing jeep didn't, and the ford was deliberately narrow, a submerged concrete bridge only one car-width wide, and thus the Chinese jeep nosedived into the water and came to a jarring splashing halt, while Zoe's LSV just continued on, bouncing safely up the far side.

Seeing the two LSVs successfully cross the river to the north, the Chinese troops blocking the bridge leapt into their jeeps and APCs, and started across the bridge in pursuit.

Only for the bridge to collapse completely beneath the first jeep.

Amid a tangled mess of—pre-cracked—wooden beams and struts, the jeep tumbled down into the river, leaving the remaining vehicles bunched up behind the void, now with no bridge to cross.

They hurried for the ford, but by the time they found it and negotiated its narrow span, Jack's two escape cars were already speeding onto the highway.

The Escape Plane

While Jack and Zoe had been fleeing east, tripping nail-traps and racing over concealed river crossings, Sky Monster had been busy, too.

He'd arrived in his pick-up at the very south of the farm, where he disappeared inside a cabin set into the hillside, a hillside which—when seen from up close—was actually a giant camouflage-netted structure.

A hangar.

And in it was a giant black 747.

If one looked closely at the plane's underbelly, one could still make out an inscription in Arabic: 'PRESIDENT ONE—AIR FORCE OF IRAQ: HALICARNASSUS'.

It was a plane that had once lived in a secret hangar outside Basra, one of several such 747s that had lain in secret locations around Iraq, ready to whisk Saddam Hussein to safe havens in East Africa in the event of an invasion. Saddam, it turned out, had never been able to use this particular plane. But in 1991, cornered by enemy forces and abandoned by his own men, Jack West Jr had.

It was now his plane, the *Halicarnassus*.

*

The *Halicarnassus* rumbled out of its hangar and down a wide dirt taxiway which itself crossed the flowing Fitzoy River via a second submerged concrete ford a few kilometres south of the rigged bridge.

Once over its ford, Sky Monster brought the big 747 left onto the highway, pointing north.

The giant plane thundered up the desert highway, a great black behemoth speeding along the shimmering blacktop, until Sky Monster saw the two LSVs of Jack and Zoe swing out onto the bitumen a few hundred metres in front of him.

A ramp at the rear of the *Halicarnassus* lowered to the roadway, kicking up sparks as it did so, and—with the great plane still moving at considerable speed—the two LSVs swung in behind it and zoomed up the ramp into its belly, closely followed by the tiny shape of Horus.

Once the second car was inside and firmly tied down with a crank-harness, the ramp was raised and the plane sped up and hit take-off speed and slowly, gracefully, lifted off the empty desert highway, leaving the farm—now crawling with Chinese cars and troops—in its wake.

West strode into the cockpit of the *Halicarnassus*.

'We're not outta this yet, Boss,' Sky Monster said. 'I got incoming bogies. Four of them. Look like J-9 Interceptors. Chinese Mig variants.'

West charged back into the main cabin, where Zoe was buckling in the kids.

'Zoe,' he said. 'To the guns.'

Moments later, he and Zoe were harnessed into the

Halicarnassus's wing-mounted gun turrets. The plane also had revolving guns on its roof and underbelly that Sky Monster could control from the cockpit.

'*They can't blow us out of the sky, can they?*' Sky Monster asked over the intercom. '*They'd destroy the Firestone.*'

'It's made of almost solid gold,' West replied. 'It'd survive just about anything except a total fuel fire. If I were them, I'd shoot us down and expect to find it in the wreckage.'

'*Great. Here they come . . .*'

Four Chinese J-9 Interceptors blasted across the sky in pursuit of the *Halicarnassus*, screaming low over the desert, unleashing their missiles.

Four small aerial darts zoomed out from their wings, spiralling smoke-trails extending out behind them.

'Launch countermeasures!' West called.

'*Launching countermeasures!*' Sky Monster reported back.

He punched some buttons and immediately several chaff bombs sprang out from the underbelly of the *Hali*.

Three of the missiles took the bait, and detonated harmlessly against the fake targets.

West himself nailed the fourth and last one, blowing it to pieces with his cannon.

'Sky Monster! Hit the deck! Rawson's Canyon! Let's throw the line and hope Super Betty still works! Go! Go! Go!'

The *Halicarnassus* banked and dived, swooping for the flat desert floor. Two of the Interceptors took off in pursuit, the other two staying high.

The *Halicarnassus* came to a rocky canyonland, a wide dry plain flanked by low mesas and hills. It shot into Rawson's Canyon, a long thin chute-like canyon that ended at a narrow aperture between two mesas. Technically this was all Army land, but no one except Jack West Jr had set foot out here in years.

The *Halicarnassus* zoomed low through the canyon, barely a hundred feet off the ground, chased by the two Chinese Interceptors.

The fighters fired their guns.

Jack and Zoe blazed back from their revolving turrets.

Tracers sizzled through the air between the chased and the chasers, the landscape whizzing by in a blur of speed.

Then Zoe got a bead and hammered the left-hand Interceptor with a wave of tracers that entered it square in its intakes. The J-9 shuddered instantly, belching black smoke, before it wobbled in the air and lurched dangerously to the left, popped its ejection seat and smashed at 800 km/h into the canyon wall.

The remaining fighter kept firing, but Sky Monster kept banking within the confines of the narrow canyon and the bullets sizzled past the speeding black plane, nicking its wingtips but hitting nothing of value.

Then the *Halicarnassus* hit the end of the canyonway and blasted through the narrow exit, just as Jack called: 'Sky Monster! Call in Super Betty! Now!'

And—*bam!*—Sky Monster punched a switch on his console marked: 'LAUNCH SUP BET'.

*

A hundred feet below and behind him, the solenoid on a large explosive that had sat undisturbed on the desert floor for many months tripped.

The explosive was a large RDX one, based on the principle of the Bouncing Betty landmine. Once triggered, it set off a preliminary blast that launched the main bomb a hundred feet into the air.

Three seconds later, the main charge went off, just like a Bouncing Betty, only much bigger. Plane-sized. And filled with shrapnel.

The Super Betty.

A giant star-shaped blast exploded in the air behind the fleeing *Halicarnassus*, right in the path of the second speeding Interceptor.

Shards of shrapnel assaulted the fighter jet head-on, smacking against its cockpit canopy, lodging in its reinforced glass, creating a hundred spiderwebs. More shards slammed into the J-9's air intakes, ripping apart the innards of the plane.

The pilot's ejection was followed by the fighter's full-scale explosion. Dead Interceptor.

'I hadn't checked on Betty for months,' West said. 'Glad she still worked.'

The *Hali* soared up into the sky.

Where the last two Interceptors were waiting.

By now, Sky Monster had taken them north-west, towards the coast, and as the *Halicarnassus* left the mainland of Australia and shot out over the Indian Ocean, the two Interceptors engaged it.

Missiles, guns: they gave it everything they had.

West and Zoe returned fire with equal violence until

finally West nailed one Interceptor with his cannon and . . . went dry.

'Right side gun is out!' he called into the intercom. 'How're you travelling, Zoe?'

'*Still got a few rounds left,*' she said as she fired at the last J-9. '*But not many—shit! I'm out, too!*'

They were out of ammo and there was still one bad guy left.

'Uh, Huntsman . . . !' Sky Monster called expectantly. 'What are we gonna do now, throw rocks?'

Jack stared at their remaining pursuer—the Interceptor hovered in the sky behind them, waiting, watching, holding back a little, as if it sensed something was wrong.

'Shit. Shit, shit, shit,' he muttered.

He unbuckled himself from his gun-chair and hurried back into the main cabin, thinking fast.

Then it hit him.

He keyed his headset radio. 'Sky Monster. Take us vertical. As vertical as you can go.'

'What? What are you doing?'

'I'll be in the rear hold.'

Sky Monster pulled back on the yoke and the *Halicarnassus* went nose-up into the sky.

Climbing, climbing, climbing . . .

The Interceptor gave chase, zooming upwards after it.

Battling the slope, Jack staggered into the rear hold, clipped a safety rope to his belt, and opened the rear loading ramp.

Air rushed into the hold, and beyond the entryway, he

saw the Interceptor immediately behind them—beneath them—framed by the deep blue ocean.

It fired.

Sizzling-hot tracer bullets *entered* the hold, smacking into the girders all around Jack—*sping!-sping!-sping!*—just as he kicked a release lever—the release lever that held his LSV harnessed in place.

The springloaded harness retracted instantly, whip-snapping away, and the light strike vehicle rolled out the back of the plane and fell out into the sky.

Seen from the outside, it must have looked very odd indeed.

The *Halicarnassus* soaring upwards with the J-9 behind and below it, when suddenly the LSV—an entire car—came dropping out of the *Hali* and . . .

. . . sailed *past* the J-9, the Chinese fighter banking at the last moment, just getting out of the way.

Its pilot grinned, proud of his reflexes.

Reflexes, however, that weren't fast enough to evade or avoid the second LSV that came tumbling out of the *Halicarnassus*'s rear hold a moment later!

The second falling LSV smashed squarely into the fighter's nose, causing the whole Interceptor to just drop out of the sky. It plummeted down to the ocean, ejecting its pilot a moment before it and the car entered the water with twin gigantic splashes.

High above it, the *Halicarnassus* righted itself, retracted its rear ramp and flew off to the north-west, safe and away.

'*Huntsman*,' Sky Monster's voice came over the intercom. '*Where to now?*'

Standing in the hold, Jack recalled Wizard's message. 'WILL MEET YOU AT GREAT TOWER.'

He keyed the intercom. 'Dubai, Sky Monster. Set a course for Dubai.'

Back at West's farm, Chinese troops stood guard at every gate.

The two majors, Black Dragon and Rapier, waited formally on the front porch as a helicopter touched down on the dusty turnaround in front of them.

Two figures emerged from the chopper, an older American man shadowed by his bodyguard, a twenty-something US Marine of Asian-American extraction.

The older man walked casually up onto the porch, unchecked by any of the guards.

No-one dared stop him. They all knew who he was and the considerable power he wielded.

He was a Pentagon player, an American colonel in his late 50s, and he was fit, extremely fit, with a barrel chest and hard blue eyes. His hair was blond but greying, his features weathered and creased. In stance and bearing, he could have passed for Jack West twenty years from now.

His Marine bodyguard, ever alert, went by the call-sign *Switchblade*. He looked like a human attack dog.

Black Dragon greeted the senior man with a bow.

'Sir,' the Chinese major said. 'They have escaped. We brought enormous force and executed our landings perfectly. But they, well, they were—'

'They were prepared,' the senior man said. 'They were prepared for this eventuality.'

He strolled past the two majors and entered the farmhouse.

He ambled slowly through West's abandoned home, taking it in, pausing every so often to examine some trinket closely—a framed photograph on the wall of West with Lily and Zoe at a waterslide park; a ballet trophy on a shelf that belonged to Lily. He lingered longest over a photo of the Great Pyramid at Giza.

Black Dragon, Rapier and the bodyguard, Switchblade, followed him at a discreet distance, waiting patiently for whatever instructions he might have.

The senior man picked up the photo of West, Lily and Zoe at the waterslide park. The three of them appeared happy, smiling for the camera, grinning in the sunshine.

'Very good, Jack . . .' the senior man said, staring at the photo. 'You got away from me this time. You're still wary enough of the world to have a getaway plan. But you're slipping. You detected us late and you know it.'

The senior man gazed at the smiling faces in the photo and his lip curled into a snarl. 'Oh, Jack, you've become domesticated. Happy, even. And *that* is your weakness. It will be your downfall.'

He dropped the photo, let it shatter against the floor, then turned to the two majors:

'Black Dragon. Call Colonel Mao. Tell him we have not yet acquired the Firestone. But that need not stop him from advancing at his end. Tell him to commence his interrogation of Professor Epper, with extreme prejudice.'

'As you command,' Black Dragon bowed and stepped a few yards away to speak into his sat-phone.

The senior man watched as he did this. After a

minute or so, Black Dragon hung up and returned. 'Colonel Mao sends his regards and says that he will do as you order.'

'Thank you,' the senior man said. 'Now, if you wouldn't mind, Black Dragon, shoot yourself in the head.'

'What!'

'Shoot yourself in the head. Jack West escaped because of your hamfisted assault. He saw you coming and so got away. I cannot tolerate failure on this mission. You were responsible and so you must pay the ultimate penalty.'

Black Dragon stammered. 'I . . . no, I cannot do tha—'

'Rapier,' the senior man said.

Quick as a whip, the big man named Rapier drew his pistol and fired it into the Chinese major's temple. Blood sprayed. Black Dragon collapsed to the floor of Jack West's living room, dead.

The senior man hardly even blinked.

He turned away casually. 'Thank you, Rapier. Now, call our people at Diego Garcia. Tell them to initiate blanket satellite surveillance of the entire southern hemisphere. Target is an aerial contact, Boeing 747, black with stealth profile. Use all aerial signatures to locate it: transponder, contrail wake, infra-red, the lot. Find that plane. And when you do, let me know. I'm eager to reunite Captain West with his Jamaican friend.'

'Yes, sir,' Rapier hurried outside.

'Switchblade,' the senior man said to his bodyguard. 'A moment alone, please.'

With a deferential nod, the young Asian-American Marine left the room.

Alone now in the living room of West's farmhouse, the senior man pulled out his own sat-phone and dialled a number: 'Sir. It's Wolf. They have the Firestone and they're running.'

As all this was going on in Australia, other things were happening around the world:

In Dubai, a middle-aged American cargo pilot staying overnight in the Gulf city was being brutally strangled in his hotel room.

He struggled against his three attackers, gasping and thrashing, but to no avail.

When he was dead, one of his attackers keyed a cell phone. 'The pilot is prepared.'

A voice responded: '*West is en route. We'll keep watching him, and tell you when to proceed.*'

The dead pilot's name was Earl McShane, from Fort Worth, Texas, a cargo hauler for the TransAtlantic Air Freight company. He was not a particularly noteworthy individual: perhaps the biggest thing he'd done in his life was after 9/11 when he had written to his local newspaper denouncing 'the dirty Muslims that done this' and demanding revenge.

At the same time, in rural Ireland—County Kerry, to be exact—a crack force of twelve men in black were advancing stealthily on an isolated farmhouse.

Within seven minutes it was all over.

They had achieved their goal.

All six of the guards at the farmhouse had been liquidated, and in the attackers' midst as they left the darkened farmhouse was a small boy named Alexander, aged eleven.

As for the *Halicarnassus*, it shot across the Indian Ocean, heading for the Persian Gulf.

But it didn't fly there directly. It took a circuitous route that included an overnight stop at a deserted airfield in Sri Lanka, just in case the Chinese had anticipated their escape route.

It meant that they approached Dubai in darkness, late in the evening of 2 December.

Inside the *Halicarnassus*, all was quiet and still. Only a few lights were on. The two kids were asleep in the bunkroom of the plane, Zoe had nodded off on a couch in the main cabin and Sky Monster was up in the cockpit, staring out at the stars, his face illuminated by the instrument dials.

In a study at the rear of the plane, however, one light was on.

The light in Jack West's office.

Ever since they had taken off from Sri Lanka—the first time he had truly felt out of reach—Jack had been reading intently from the black folder he had grabbed just before leaving his farm: an old leather binder crammed with notes, clippings, diagrams and photocopies.

This was Wizard's 'black book', the one Wizard had instructed Jack to take.

And as he read it, Jack's eyes grew wide with wonder. 'Oh my God, Wizard. Why didn't you tell me? *Oh. My. God . . .*'

A MEETING OF NATIONS

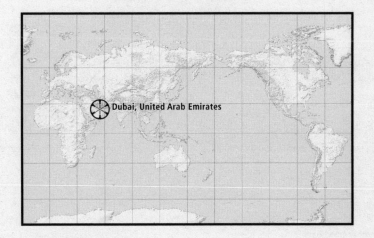

Dubai, United Arab Emirates

DUBAI, UNITED ARAB EMIRATES
2 DECEMBER, 2007
8 DAYS BEFORE THE 1ST DEADLINE

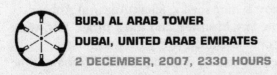
The Burj al Arab is one of the most spectacular buildings in the world.

Shaped like a gigantic spinnaker, it is stunning in almost every respect. Eighty-one storeys tall, it houses the world's only 7-star hotel. On its 80th floor, jutting out from beneath a revolving restaurant, is a huge helipad practically designed for photo opportunities: Tiger Woods once hit golf balls from it; Andre Agassi and Roger Federer once played tennis on it.

It is the most recognised structure of the most modern Arab nation on Earth, the United Arab Emirates.

A great tower, some would say.

The great tower, Wizard would say.

Soon after their arrival in Dubai—the *Hali* had landed at a military airbase—West and his group were flown by helicopter to the Burj al Arab, where they were accommodated in no less than the Presidential Suite, a vast and plush expanse of bedrooms, sitting rooms and lounge rooms that took up the entire 79th floor.

This royal treatment was not unwarranted. The Emirates

had been a partner in West's initial adventure with the Golden Capstone, an adventure that had seen a coalition of small nations take on—and prevail against—the might of the United States and Europe.

One of the most heroic members of West's team on that mission had been the second son of one of the Emirates' most senior sheiks, Sheik Anzar al Abbas.

West, Zoe, Sky Monster, and most of all, Lily, were always welcome in Dubai.

Alby, needless to say, was impressed. 'Whoa . . .' he said, gazing out the windows at the stunning view.

Lily just shrugged. She'd stayed here before. 'I get dibs on the double bed!' she yelled, racing into a bedroom.

The doorbell rang, despite the fact it was almost midnight.

West opened the door to reveal—

—Sheik Anzar al Abbas and his entourage.

With his great beard, round belly, deeply etched olive skin, and dressed in a traditional desert robe and head-scarf, the regal old sheik could have stepped straight out of *Lawrence of Arabia*.

'The hour is late and Captain Jack West Jr arrives in haste,' Abbas said in his deep voice. 'I sense trouble.'

West nodded grimly. 'Thank you once again for your hospitality, Lord Sheik. Please, come inside.'

Abbas entered, his robe flowing, followed by his six attendants. 'My son, Zahir, sends his regards. He is cur-rently working as a senior instructor at our special forces training facility in the desert, teaching our best fighters many of the strategies you taught him. He begged me to inform you that he is on his way at all possible speed.'

West walked with the sheik. 'I fear the circumstances are grave, far graver than ever before. Where once we banded together to fight against the desires of selfish men, now, if Wizard's research is correct, we face a far more sinister threat. Wizard hasn't arrived here yet, but I imagine he'll enlighten us further when he gets here.'

Abbas's eyes flickered. 'You do not know?'

'Know what?'

'What has happened to Max Epper, the Wizard.'

Jack froze. 'What's happened?'

'We picked it up from Chinese satellite radio chatter last night. Wizard was arrested twenty-four hours ago by Chinese forces not far from the Three Gorges Dam. I fear he won't be coming here anytime soon.'

Jack could only stare.

'Wizard left this file at my home,' he said, once he and the sheik were settled in one of the sitting areas of the suite. Zoe and Sky Monster were there, too, along with Lily and the rather confused Alby.

Significantly, Sheik Abbas's entourage had been left in an outer room.

'The file summarises his research into a set of six stones called the Ramesean Stones and their relation-ship with six oblong blocks known as the Pillars of the World, or sometimes, the Pillars of Vishnu.'

'Vishnu?' Abbas said, recognising the word. 'As in . . .'

'Yes,' West said. 'As in "I am Vishnu, Destroyer of the World." The study of the Ramesean Stones was Wizard's life's work. Our ten-year mission to locate the Seven Wonders of the Ancient World and through them the Golden Capstone was merely a side-mission for him. This is the study that has consumed his entire life.

'And now he's been arrested in China at the same time Chinese forces attacked my supposedly secret farm in Australia. The Chinese know. About his work *and* that we have the Firestone, the top piece of the Capstone.'

Abbas frowned. 'The Capstone has greater significance? Beyond the Tartarus Event?'

'From what I read last night, more significance than we can possibly imagine,' West said. 'The striking of the Capstone by the Sun during the Tartarus Rotation was just the beginning.'

At that moment, West seemed to retreat into himself, thinking in silence. Then he said, 'I need more time to examine Wizard's work and to make some calls. After that we have to convene a meeting. A new meeting of concerned nations. Give me a day to study all this and then let's gather here for what might be the most important meeting in the history of mankind.'

West spent the whole of the next day reading and sorting through Wizard's voluminous notes.

Names were scattered among Wizard's writing, of which West knew some but not others.

Tank Tanaka, for instance, he knew. Tank was Wizard's long-time Japanese colleague; West had met him on numerous occasions.

Others he only knew slightly, like 'the Terrible Twins', Lachlan and Julius Adamson, a pair of mathematical geniuses from Scotland who had studied under Wizard in Dublin. Fast-talking, exuberant and much-loved by Wizard, the twins operated as one brain, and taken together they were arguably the most formidable non-computerised mathematical force in the world. In their spare time, they liked to beat Vegas casinos at the blackjack tables simply by 'doing the math'.

One summary sheet that Wizard had prepared commanded most of Jack's attention. It was virtually a representation of Wizard's thoughts, a mixture of diagrams, lists and handwritten notations by the old professor:

REWARDS
(according to Rameses II at Abydos)

1. KNOWLEDGE
2. HEAT
3. SIGHT
4. LIFE
5. DEATH
6. POWER

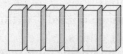

THE SIX PILLARS

- Oblong uncut diamonds;
- Must be '_cleansed_' by the Ph's Stone before they can be placed in the Machine;
- Whereabouts? The Great Houses of Europe; Perhaps the 'Five Warriors'???

THE GREAT MACHINE

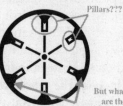

Pillars???

But what are the TRIANGLES then?

MUST HAVE BOTH THE SA-BENBEN **AND** THE PHILOSOPHER'S STONE! THEY ARE CENTRAL TO EVERYTHING!!

The Sa-Benben (a.k.a. 'The Firestone')

Interacts uniquely with each of the Six Ramesean Stones:

1. <u>Philosopher's</u>: cleanses Pillars.
2. <u>Stonehenge</u>: gives location of vertices of the Great Machine.
3. <u>Delphi</u>: allows one to see the Dark Sun.
4. <u>Tablets</u>: contain the final incantation.
5. <u>Killing</u>: gives dates by which Pillars must be laid.
6. <u>Basin</u>: unknown.

Rate of approach must be calculated. Call the Twins!

$16,467 \times 365.25$
Mean V = 125,445 km/s
Max output in 1962 was 10.57
But in 1991 was 10.72. Growing.

TITANIC SINKING & RISING (DEC 2007) CONNECTION? POSSIBLE SIGHTING OPPORTUNITY?

WRONG!

Faberge Egg - Newton's alchemical work
The Ness spring...?
Equinox/Easter '08

West recognised a few of the terms on the sheet, like the Sa-Benben, Firestone and Abydos.

Abydos was a little-known but hugely important Egyptian archaeological site. It had been sacred to the ancient Egyptians from the very beginning to the very end of their civilisation, spanning some 3,000 years. It bore temples belonging to Seti I and his son, Rameses II, and contained some of the earliest shrines in Egypt.

Jack had also seen the Mystery of the Circles before, but had no clue what it meant.

Other things, however, were completely new to him.

The 'Great Machine'.

The Six Pillars. That they might be oblong-shaped uncut *diamonds* was certainly intriguing.

The obscure references to Fabergé Eggs, Easter and the sinking of the *Titanic* at the bottom of the page—well, they completely baffled him.

And, of course, the unusual diagrams scattered all over it.

He used this sheet as his central reference point and read on.

Elsewhere among Wizard's notes, he found some digital photos of stone carvings written in a language he had not seen since the Seven Wonders mission.

It was an ancient script known only as the Word of Thoth—named after the Egyptian god of knowledge.

Mysterious and obscure, it was a language that defied translation even by modern supercomputers. Indeed, its cuneiform-like strokes were often thought to contain secret mystical knowledge.

Historically, only one person in the world could read

it: the Oracle of the Siwa Oasis in Egypt. This person—magically, it seemed—was born with the ability to read the Word of Thoth. A long line of Oracles had existed right up to the present day, and although it was unknown to her teachers and friends at school, Lily was one of them.

She was the daughter of the last Oracle at Siwa, a foul spoilt man who had died shortly after her birth.

Most unusually for an Oracle, though, Lily was a twin. As Jack had discovered during the Capstone mission, she had a brother named Alexander—like his father, a disagreeable, spoilt boy—who could *also* read the Word of Thoth. After that mission, Alexander had been spirited away to a quiet life in rural Ireland, in County Kerry.

Jack got Lily to translate many of the Thoth inscriptions in Wizard's notes. Many were nonsensical to Jack, while some were just plain weird: for instance, one Thoth carving stated that the ancient Mesopotamian city of Ur, famous for its huge ziggurat, was an exact replica of 'the Second Great Temple-Shrine', whatever that was.

Jack also showed Lily one prominent Word of Thoth carving from Wizard's notes:

Lily looked at the complex array of symbols and shrugged, translating it in seconds. 'It says:

With my beloved, Nefertari,
I, Rameses, son of Ra,
Keep watch over the most sacred shrine.
We shall watch over it forever.
Great sentinels,
With our third eyes, we see all.'

'With our third eyes?' Jack frowned.

'That's what it says.'

'Nefertari was the favourite wife of Rameses II,' Jack said. 'And together they keep watch over the most sacred shrine, whatever that is. Thanks, kiddo.'

Lily smiled. She loved it when he called her that.

Later that evening, the outer door to the Presidential Suite opened and Lily rushed into the arms of the man standing in the doorway. 'Pooh Bear! Pooh Bear! You came!'

The man was a shorter, younger version of Sheik Abbas. He was the great sheik's second son, Zahir al Anzar al Abbas, call-sign *Saladin*, but renamed by Lily *Pooh Bear*. Short, rotund and bushy-bearded, he had a voice as big as his heart—and that was *big*.

With him was a taller man, thinner, with skeletal features: a master-sniper once known as *Archer*, now *Stretch*, having also been rechristened by Lily.

Israeli by birth, Stretch had once been a member of the Mossad, but after a certain . . . conflict . . . with them during the Capstone chase, he was now *persona non grata* in Israel. In fact, it was known that the Mossad had put a price on his head for his actions back then.

Greetings were exchanged with Zoe, Sky Monster and, when they finally extracted him from his study, West.

Lily said to Pooh Bear, 'And this is my friend, Alby. He's a whiz at maths and computers.'

'It's a pleasure to meet you, Alby,' Pooh Bear roared. 'I hope your intentions with my little Lily are pure. No, let me put that another way: if you break her heart, boy, I'll hunt you down to the ends of the Earth.'

Alby gulped. 'We're just friends.'

Pooh Bear smiled, winking at Lily. 'So, young Alby, are you joining us on this endeavour?'

Lily said, 'Alby's parents are currently in South America and out of phone contact. Alby was supposed to be staying with us at the farm. Now I guess he's staying with us wherever we go.'

'So, Huntsman!' Pooh Bear exclaimed. 'What ails you this time?'

'It could be bad, Pooh. Really bad. Tartarus has been neutralised, and some people want the Firestone badly. We barely got away at all.'

'They found you in Australia?'

'Yes. I've called a meeting, one that will bring the original team back together. Fuzzy is the last one. He's on his way from Jamaica.'

'And Wizard?'

'He's out of the picture for the moment, but he's sent me enough information to make a start. With Lily's help I've managed to decipher a few of his recent discoveries.'

Pooh looked at Lily. 'Is that so? How many are you up to now, young one?'

'Five, plus sign language.'

'Good girl,' he said. 'Never stop learning. Never stop honing your gift.'

Pooh turned back to West, his face serious. 'My father sends a message. At tomorrow's meeting there will be a few other countries represented. Some not from the original seven. Word has got out, it seems.'

West frowned. This was moving too fast, at a pace beyond his control. It was as if he was still trying to catch up himself.

He pulled out several copies of a five-page summary he'd found amid Wizard's notes and handed them out to the others.

'This is a summary I'll be giving to everyone at the meeting tomorrow. It's about Wizard's work. Read it beforehand. It'll be less astonishing that way.'

Then, looking at them all—his old friends, friends who had bonded over the course of a long, hard and at times seemingly impossible mission—he smiled.

'I'm glad you're all here for this one.'

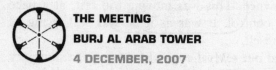

THE MEETING
BURJ AL ARAB TOWER
4 DECEMBER, 2007

The next day, as each delegation arrived at the Presidential Suite, they were handed the five-page briefing.

It was a peculiar array of national representatives.

Of the original seven nations who had sponsored West's initial quest to locate the Golden Capstone, only four were present now: Australia (West), Ireland (Zoe), the UAE (Pooh Bear) and New Zealand (Sky Monster).

Canada's Wizard was missing in China.

Spain, having lost a man during the first mission, had declined to send a representative to this one. And Jamaica's man, Fuzzy, was uncharacteristically late.

'We're still waiting for Fuzzy and a few others,' West said. 'So, please, while you wait, acquaint yourself with the briefing material.'

They did so.

The briefing was headed: 'The Six Ramesean Stones and the Pillars of the World':

THE SIX RAMESEAN STONES AND
THE PILLARS OF THE WORLD
by Professor Max T. Epper,
Trinity College, University of Dublin

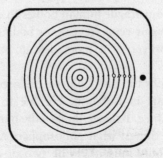

The Mystery of the Circles

The end of the world has preoccupied humanity for as long as humanity has existed.

For Hindus, Vishnu will destroy the Earth. Christians fear the Apocalypse prophesied in the final books of the Bible. No less than St Peter himself famously wrote, 'The end of all things is near.'

I fear it may be nearer than we think.

The Marriage of Light and Dark

Our small planet does not exist in a void.

It exists in concert with our Sun and the other planets of our solar system.

Certain ancient civilisations knew about these relationships: the Maya, the Aztecs, the Egyptians, even the Neolithic peoples of Britain; all of them saw patterns in the night sky.

And as I myself discovered during the Tartarus Event of 2006, our Earth is directly linked to our Sun.

Our Sun begets life. It provides the light that sparks photosynthesis and the temperate warmth that allows our fragile human bodies to exist without the blood in our veins freezing or boiling.

This, however, is a more delicate situation than many realise.

To paraphrase the Chinese philosopher, Laozi, nothing exists in isolation. For life to exist, there must be *balance*. Balance implies the harmonic existence of *two* things, what philosophers call 'Duality'.

But not only must there be two of everything— man, woman; heat, cold; light, darkness; good, bad—but *inside* the good there must be some bad, just as inside the bad, there must be some good. This has never been better displayed than in the famous Taijitu, the Yin–Yang.

So what does this concept of duality mean in the context of our solar system? It means this:

Our Sun does not exist alone.

It has a twin, an opposite, an invisible body of dark matter known as a 'zero-point field'. This spherical field roams through the outer regions of our solar system like a moving black hole, not so much possessed of negative energy as *no energy* at all. It absorbs light. It is indescribably cold. It breaks down oxygen at the molecular level. It is, in short, a variety of energy that is anathema to life as we know it.

And if this zero-point field—this Dark Sun, if you will—ever sweeps into our solar system, it will destroy all life on Earth.

Observe the image at the beginning of this article. It is a carving found all over the world from Abu Simbel in Egypt to Newgrange in Ireland to Peru in South America.

It is called 'the Mystery of the Circles'.

A quick glance at it leads the observer to conclude that it depicts our solar system, with the Sun at the centre, orbited by nine planets.

Not so.

If you look closely, you will see that the Mystery of the Circles contains *ten* planets orbiting a central Sun. It also features—somewhat mysteriously—a strange black orb sitting outside the orbits of the ten planets, equal in size to the central Sun.

It is my belief that the Mystery of the Circles is indeed a depiction of our solar system, but not as we see it today. It is a picture of our solar system as it was a long time ago.

Forget the planets for a moment and keep your eyes on the black orb hovering outside the circles.

This must be the focus of our inquiry.

For it represents our Sun's dark twin, and it now approaches, bringing with it our destruction.

The Machine

But a mechanism has been put in place to allow us to avert our destruction.

Unfortunately the knowledge crucial to our salvation—to the operation of this 'Machine'—which was known to the ancients, has long since been lost through wars, dark ages, witch-hunts and holocausts.

However, great men and women throughout history have held pieces of this knowledge: Laozi and his famous student, Confucius; Rameses II, the mighty pharaoh, and his priest–builder, Imhotep II;

Cleopatra VII, the doomed Egyptian queen; the great Mayan ruler, King Pakal; and in more recent times, Isaac Newton, in his obsessive search for the secrets of alchemy.

In all their writings, there is one common feature. The Machine is always represented by this image:

What the image actually means, though, remains elusive.

The Six Ramesean Stones

Of all the impressive individuals who have known about this Machine, it is Rameses II—greatest of all the pharaohs, greater even than Khufu, builder of the Great Pyramid—who has left us the most information about it and indeed identified the key to solving the mystery:

The Six Sacred Stones.

Six stones which, in his honour, we now call the Ramesean Stones. They are:

1. The Philosopher's Stone
2. The Altar Stone of the Temple of Ra's Dark Twin (Stonehenge)

3. The Twin Tablets of Thutmosis
4. The Killing Stone of the Maya
5. The Seeing Stone of the Southern Tribe (Delphi)
6. The Basin of Rameses II

In his temple at Abydos in a remote corner of southern Egypt—not far from his famous list of 76 pharaohs carved into a wall—Rameses left a tablet mentioning the 'Six Guidestones of Ra's Dark Twin'.

Now while it is not impossible that Rameses could have seen all of these stones, it is unlikely. It *is* believed, however, that all six of the stones resided at one time in Egypt, even the Stonehenge and Mayan ones. Whatever the case, Rameses does seem to have been in possession of some advanced knowledge about them, and of all the pharaohs he alone committed that knowledge to writing.

These guidestones, he said, once 'impregnated by the Sa-Benben' would provide 'the necessary wisdom' when 'Ra's Dark Twin returned to wreak his vengeance on the world'.

As you can imagine, for many years this confounded Egyptologists. *Ra* was the Sun. Who or what, then, was *Ra's Dark Twin*? Another Sun?

It took the technological wizardry of modern astronomy to find it: the Dark Sun now approaching our solar system.

So what do the Six Ramesean Stones do? Why did Rameses call them *guidestones*?

Simple: they guide us to the Machine.

And the Machine saves our planet.

We thought our troubles were over when we erected the Capstone atop the Great Pyramid, but no, we were only completing a necessary precondition for this, the main event: we 'charged' the Sa-Benben.

And so now the Sa-Benben has been charged by the Sun. As such it is ready to interact with the Six. It is my belief that when the Sa-Benben comes into contact with each Sacred Stone, that Stone will provide a unique insight into the coming of the Dark Sun and the Earth-saving operation of the Machine.

The end of all things is near . . .

. . . but it's not over yet.

A door slammed somewhere. The assembled delegates looked up from their reading.

'Ah-ha! My son!' Sheik Abbas leapt up from his chair and embraced the handsome young man who had entered the room.

He was Captain Rashid Abbas, commander of the UAE's elite First Commando Regiment. The sheik's first son, he was a strikingly handsome man: with a chiselled jaw, dark Arabian skin, and deep blue eyes. His call-sign was typically grand: *The Scimitar of Allah*, or just *Scimitar* for short.

'Father,' he said, embracing Abbas warmly. 'Forgive my lateness, but I was waiting on my friend here.'

Scimitar indicated his companion—who had entered the room almost invisibly, outshone by Scimitar's luminous presence. He was a delicate, precise fellow, with a bald head and a long rat-like nose. His shifting eyes swept the room, taking in everything, tense and edgy, suspicious.

Scimitar said, 'Father, allow me to introduce Abdul Rahman al Saud from the Kingdom of Saudi Arabia, from their esteemed Royal Intelligence Service. His call-sign: *Vulture*.'

Vulture bowed to Sheik Abbas, low and slow.

Lily disliked Vulture on sight. His bow was too low, too obsequious, too deliberate.

As for Scimitar, she had seen him once or twice before—and then, as now, she noticed that Pooh Bear retreated into a corner of the room at the arrival of his handsome older brother. It seemed to Lily that the presence of his dashing brother clearly affected the younger and fatter Pooh Bear.

It made her dislike Scimitar, too.

Jack was also disturbed, but for different reasons. While he had expected Scimitar, he had not expected him to bring a Saudi spy along, the first of Sheik Abbas's uninvited guests.

'Vulture?' he said. 'Not the Blood Vulture of Abu Ghraib prison fame?'

Vulture visibly stiffened. So did Scimitar.

During the official investigation into the atrocities at the notorious Iraqi prison, it emerged that Saudi intelligence agents had carried out torture activities that American soldiers were forbidden to do. One such Saudi intelligence agent had performed acts of torture so shockingly brutal that he had earned the nickname 'Blood Vulture'.

'I visited that prison on several occasions, Captain West,' Vulture said in a low voice, his eyes locked on Jack's, 'but not at the times the depravities took place.'

'I will personally vouch for this man,' Scimitar said irritably. 'We have been through much together, over two Gulf Wars and more in between. The rumours of Abu Ghraib are unfounded lies. He is practically my brother.'

At that, Lily saw Pooh Bear lower his eyes.

Vulture said, 'I bring information that I am sure will be useful to you and your cause. For instance, I know the plans of the Chinese.'

That got West's attention. 'You do?'

The phone rang. Zoe got it, turned to West: 'Jack. It's the hotel manager. He says there are a couple of people downstairs who would like an audience with you. He says they're American.'

Moments later, the door to the suite opened to reveal two men: one a tall grey-haired gentleman in a suit; the second a younger man dressed in plain clothes that scarcely disguised his military physique. A soldier.

From his chair, Sheik Abbas recognised the older man. 'Why, Attaché Robertson! What are you—?'

Jack remained standing between the two Americans and the meeting, blocking the way. 'Names. Now.'

The older gentleman didn't flinch an inch. 'Captain West, my name is Paul Robertson, special attaché to the US Ambassador here in the United Arab Emirates. This is Lieutenant Sean Miller, from the United States Marine Corps, call-sign *Astro*. We're here to express our country's . . . concern . . . at recent Chinese actions, both military and archaeological, and hopefully assist you in some way.'

Special attaché, Jack thought, *meant CIA agent*.

'And how can you help me?' he asked.

Jack's relations with the United States of America were somewhat strained. His mission to locate the Seven Ancient Wonders had been in direct opposition to an influential group of Americans known as the Caldwell Group, who at the time had had the ear of the President. There had been some deaths involved, including people dear to Jack.

Robertson remained impassive, a cool customer. 'We know, for instance, where the Chinese are keeping your friend, Professor Epper.'

West stepped aside immediately. 'Come on in. Take a seat.'

At that very moment a windowless Boeing 767 cargo plane took off from Dubai International Airport.

On its flanks were emblazoned the words: 'TRANS-ATLANTIC AIR FREIGHT'.

Its listed pilot: Captain Earl McShane.

And so now the representatives of six nations sat arrayed around the Presidential Suite of the Burj al Arab: Australia, Ireland, New Zealand, the Emirates, Saudi Arabia and the United States of America.

'You've all read the briefing document,' West said. 'Here is the translation of a carving that I received from Wizard in China just before he was captured by Chinese forces.'

West distributed a new three-page handout. On the first sheet was Wizard's translation from China:

<u>THE COMING OF RA'S DESTROYER</u>

THE COMING OF RA'S DESTROYER
SEES THE <u>STARTING</u>* OF THE GREAT <u>MACHINE</u>**
AND WITH IT THE RISE OF THE SA-BENBEN.
HONOUR THE SA-BENBEN,
KEEP IT CLOSE, KEEP IT NEAR,
FOR IT ALONE GOVERNS THE SIX
AND ONLY THE EMPOWERED SIX CAN
PREPARE THE PILLARS AND
LEAD YOU TO THE SHRINES AND THUS

COMPLETE THE MACHINE
BEFORE THE SECOND COMING.***

THE END OF ALL THINGS IS NEAR.

AMBIGUOUS TERMS:

* 'commencement' or 'trigger' or 'set off'
** 'Mechanism' or 'World'
*** 'the Return'

MATCH REFERENCE:

Ref XR:5-12 Partial inscription found at
Zhou-Zu Monastery, Tibet (2001)

West said, 'As you'll see, this decryption refers to a Great Machine and the importance of the Sa-Benben. "The Second Coming" to which it refers is the coming of the Dark Sun.'

'This Dark Sun, or Star, this bringer of the Apocalypse, why have astronomers not seen it before now?' Sheik Abbas asked.

'According to Wizard,' West said, 'it exists on a light spectrum unknown to humanity, so we can't see it through any of our telescopes, in any spectra, like infra-red or ultra-violet or UVB. Its presence has only been verified by what it *blocks* from our view.

'From what I've read, it seems to roam the outer reaches of our solar system in a hyper-elongated elliptical orbit. When it comes near, which is not very often, about once every six million years, Jupiter's movement shields us from it, blocks us from its deadly radiation. But even if this didn't happen, you couldn't see this Dark Sun with the naked eye.

'In any case, it's close now and this time—apparently—it will emerge from behind Jupiter, and that's when things get really ugly. That's when its constant discharge of radiation-like zero-point energy will wash over our planet, killing every living creature on it—unless we can rebuild this Machine. The Machine, apparently, sends out a balancing response that counters the Dark Sun's energy stream, saving the Earth. It always comes back to balance, to harmony.'

'Come *on*, Jack,' Zoe said. 'Listen to yourself. Are you seriously saying that there is some kind of evil celestial orb out there bent on destroying the Earth?'

'It's not evil, Zoe. It just is. Call it anti-matter, call it a singularity, call it a moving black hole. In the end, it is a net-negative void. A dense moving hole in the air. It's not evil and it doesn't hate us. We're just in its way.'

Stretch said, 'And yet some*where*, some*time*, some*one* built a Machine here on Earth that is some*how* connected to this Dark Sun. Are you talking about advanced technology, Jack? Alien technology?'

Jack bowed his head. 'I don't know. Wizard doesn't say.'

Vulture mused aloud: '"Any sufficiently advanced technology is indistinguishable from magic." Arthur C. Clarke.'

'So how do we rebuild this Machine?' Sheik Abbas asked. 'And why does China have such a keen interest in doing so by itself? Surely, even the Chinese would realise that a united global coalition would be the best vehicle to achieve this?'

'As always, Lord Sheik, you go directly to the heart of the matter,' West said. 'Please turn to the second sheet of your handout.'

They all did so. On it was a photocopy of Wizard's summarising page:

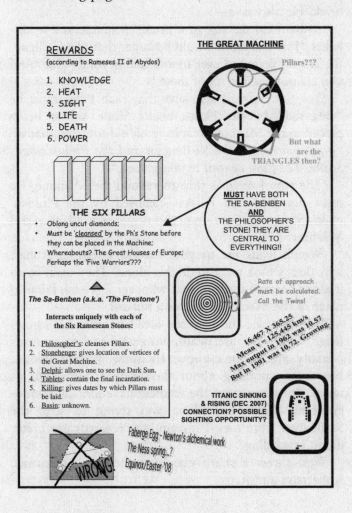

REWARDS
(according to Rameses II at Abydos)

1. KNOWLEDGE
2. HEAT
3. SIGHT
4. LIFE
5. DEATH
6. POWER

THE GREAT MACHINE

Pillars???

But what are the TRIANGLES then?

THE SIX PILLARS

- Oblong uncut diamonds;
- Must be '*cleansed*' by the Ph's Stone before they can be placed in the Machine;
- Whereabouts? The Great Houses of Europe; Perhaps the 'Five Warriors'???

MUST HAVE BOTH THE SA-BENBEN **AND** THE PHILOSOPHER'S STONE! THEY ARE CENTRAL TO EVERYTHING!!

The Sa-Benben (a.k.a. 'The Firestone')

Interacts uniquely with each of the Six Ramesean Stones:

1. <u>Philosopher's</u>: cleanses Pillars.
2. <u>Stonehenge</u>: gives location of vertices of the Great Machine.
3. <u>Delphi</u>: allows one to see the Dark Sun.
4. <u>Tablets</u>: contain the final incantation.
5. <u>Killing</u>: gives dates by which Pillars must be laid.
6. <u>Basin</u>: unknown.

Rate of approach must be calculated. Call the Twins!

16,467 X 365.25
Mean v = 125,445 km/s
Max output in 1962 was 10.57
But in 1991 was 10.72. Growing.

TITANIC SINKING & RISING (DEC 2007) CONNECTION? POSSIBLE SIGHTING OPPORTUNITY?

WRONG!

Faberge Egg - Newton's alchemical work
The Ness spring...?
Equinox/Easter '08

West directed them to the centre of the page. 'To your first question, Sheik: how do we rebuild the Machine? Observe the six Pillars drawn by Wizard and described as "oblong uncut diamonds". Elsewhere in his notes, he states that these Pillars are each about the size of a brick. He also says—'

'A diamond the size of a brick?' Scimitar said in disbelief. 'Just one alone would be larger than the Cullinan, the largest diamond ever found, and beyond value. And you claim there are *six* of these.'

'Yes, six. Wizard also says that each Pillar must be "cleansed" by the Philosopher's Stone before being placed in the Machine, inspiring his exhortation that we "*must* have both the Sa-Benben *and* the Philosopher's Stone. They are central to everything.*"

'The way I see it is this: to rebuild the Machine, we must place the six Pillars—cleansed by the Philosopher's Stone—in position in this mysterious all-powerful Machine.

'Which leads me to your second question, Abbas: why does China want to do this alone? They want to go it alone because it seems that whoever sets each Pillar in place in the Machine receives a *reward*.

'You can see the rewards listed by Wizard: knowledge, heat, sight, life, death, power. What these rewards actually are, I don't know. I assume Wizard knows, but there's nothing about their actual nature in his notes. But given what the Chinese have already done— grabbing Wizard in China and trying to steal the Sa-Benben from me—I imagine the rewards are pretty damn rewarding.'

West threw a sharp glance at the two Americans, Robertson and Astro.

Robertson cleared his throat. 'I am not privy to my country's research on this matter, so please don't even ask me about that. But yes, the United States is unwilling to allow China to obtain the benefits you so describe.'

'We'll be wanting to talk to *someone* about your country's research soon,' West said pointedly.

'Wait, wait, wait,' Zoe said. 'I need to backtrack a bit. The Six Ramesean Stones plus the Sa-Benben give us *information* about this Machine. The Philosopher's Stone, once charged by the Sa-Benben, *cleanses* the Six Pillars, which then have to be placed *in* the Machine. So what is this Machine? And how big can it be?'

West tapped the image that signified the Machine:

After reading Wizard's notes these last couple of days, he'd been thinking about the Machine a lot: about this image and Wizard's scribblings around it.

At last he said, 'Wizard doesn't say what or how big the Machine is. But I have a theory.'

'And?'

West turned to face Zoe. 'I think "the Machine" is another name for our planet.' He pointed at the image: 'This circle is Earth. And these dark triangles are sites located around the Earth, six sites at which the six Pillars—properly "cleansed" or activated—must be set in place, thus restoring the Machine to working order before the Dark Sun emits its fatal burst.'

'Good God . . .' someone said.

'Yes. And if we don't rebuild this Machine by the appointed time, our planet will be destroyed. People, the end of the world really is nigh.'

Sheik Abbas breathed, 'The end of the world . . .'

He glanced around the room—only to see that the American, Robertson, was unmoved by Jack's conclusion; likewise Scimitar and his Saudi companion, Vulture.

Jack said, 'You'll recall that in his article, Wizard mentioned the black orb depicted in the Mystery of the Circles. He suggested that it was a Dark Star, a twin of our own Sun, its opposite. He also mentioned that the Mystery of the Circles depicts our solar system with ten planets instead of nine.'

'Yes . . .'

'Today, our solar system possesses nine planets plus an asteroid belt between Mars and Jupiter. But this may not always have been so. Later in his article, Wizard postulates that that asteroid belt between Mars and Jupiter *was once a very small planet* not unlike our own. Now. If a planet were to be somehow destroyed, its pieces would coalesce into a floating belt of asteroids similar to the one found between Mars and Jupiter.'

There was silence in the room.

'Yes,' Jack said, reading their thoughts. 'This has happened before.'

*

'Ladies and gentlemen,' he went on, 'we need to pool our resources and fight this menace. We need to restore this Machine before that Dark Star arrives.

'But at the moment there are too many pieces of this puzzle missing, such as *when* this Dark Star will arrive and thus the time by which the Machine must be rebuilt. Wizard knows many of the answers to these questions, but I imagine your own researchers know some of them, too. And that's not even mentioning the rewards and China's interest in this situation and whatever she might know.'

Jack eyed the group arrayed before him. 'I need to know what you all know.'

There was an uncomfortable silence. It was time for some of them to reveal their secrets.

Someone coughed, clearing his throat.

It was the Saudi spy, Vulture.

'My family, the High House of Saud, possesses one of these Pillars you describe,' he said. 'It is indeed a large uncut diamond, oblong in shape, translucent to look at, yet still breathtaking to behold. We have held it for generations, always in a secure place. Other identical diamond Pillars are held by the two great European houses of Saxe-Coburg-Gotha and Oldenburg. I cannot, however, vouch for the whereabouts of the remaining three.'

'Thank you,' Jack said, nodding.

The American 'attaché' Robertson cleared *his* throat. 'I am authorised to disclose that the United States of America has in its possession one of the Ramesean Stones you describe: the Killing Stone of the Maya. I am also authorised to make this Stone available to any multi-national effort to combat the arrival of the Dark Sun.'

Other minor pieces of information were offered, but after all was said and done, it appeared that the single greatest source of wisdom on the matter of the Machine, the Stones and the Pillars, was Professor Max T. Epper.

'We have to get Wizard back from the Chinese,' Jack said. 'Mr Robertson. It's time for you to pay your entry fee.'

Robertson said, 'Professor Epper is being held at Xintan Prison, a remote facility in the mountains of Sichuan Province in central China. He is classified as a D-class prisoner: high-value but subject to vigorous interrogation.'

'You mean torture,' Pooh Bear said.

Scimitar added, 'Xintan is a fortress. No man who has entered it against his will has ever left it alive.'

'That's about to change,' West said.

Vulture backed up Scimitar. 'One does not just walk into the torture wing of Xintan Prison and stroll out again. It is beyond fortified. It is impregnable.'

Robertson spoke formally: 'The United States would have serious reservations about participating in any incursive act against China, especially one that would appear so aggressive. If Lieutenant Miller here were captured on Chinese soil during such a raid, it would be on the front page of every newspaper in the—'

'Then don't come,' Stretch said from the side of the room. A veteran of the first mission, Stretch was still seriously wary of these apparently well-meaning intruders.

Jack said, 'We'll handle those logistics when we come to them. Is there anything more? Anyone else have anything to offer?'

The room was silent.

The meeting was over—

But then a hand went up, timidly, hesitantly. A little hand, in the back of the room.

Alby.

Paul Robertson turned and said, 'Well, if we're taking questions from children now, my time here is over. I have things to do.'

Jack wasn't so dismissive. In fact, he found it quite courageous of Alby to raise his hand, given the company around him.

'What is it, Alby?'

'I think I can help you with something on Wizard's note page,' the little boy said, signing at the same time.

'What exactly?' Jack was surprised that Alby was using sign language, since it wasn't really necessary here.

'Here,' Alby said. 'Where he says "*Titanic sinking—Dec 2007 & Titanic rising.*" It's not a reference to *Titanic*, the boat. It means the sinking and rising of Saturn's moon, Titan, behind the planet Jupiter. Titanic Sinking and Titanic Rising are terms used by astronomers to describe it. It's pretty rare, but when Jupiter and Saturn are in alignment—which they will be until next March—it occurs twice a week.'

'And exactly when will Earth, Jupiter and Saturn be in alignment again?' Zoe asked.

Alby shrugged. 'Maybe three, four hundred years.'

Abbas coughed. 'This is significant.'

'You bet it is,' Jack glanced at Alby—only to find Alby staring intently back at him, right in the eye. The boy signed: *There's also something else.*

Jack nodded in understanding—*later*—before saying to the group: 'Thank you, Alby. That's a great contribution, and something I imagine Wizard will be able to clarify.'

Beside Alby, Lily gave her friend a proud nudge.

At that moment, two things happened: the doorbell rang and Sheik Abbas's phone buzzed. The old sheik answered it quietly while Jack went to the door.

At the door was a hotel clerk, bearing a package for Jack—a designer hatbox, of all things. On it was a card: '*For Jack West. From Jamaica.*'

Jack frowned as he opened the box and when he saw its contents, he froze in horror, his face draining of blood. 'Oh, no. Fuzzy . . .'

Inside the box was a severed human head.

The severed head of his Jamaican friend, and veteran of the Capstone mission, V.J. Weatherly, call-sign *Fuzzy*.

At exactly the same moment, Abbas frowned into his phone. 'Good God. Call the hotel. Order it evacuated. *Now!*'

Everyone in the room spun as the old bearded sheik ended the call and looked up.

'We have to leave this building immediately. It's about to be struck by an aeroplane.'

Jack blinked, put the lid back on the hatbox before anyone else saw what was inside it. '*A wha*—?'

Then a klaxon sounded.

A hotel alarm.

Red emergency lights blazed to life as a voice came over the internal PA system, speaking first in Arabic, then in English: '*Would all guests please evacuate the hotel. This is an emergency. Would all guests please evacuate the hotel and convene out by the parking lot.*'

Everyone exchanged worried glances as the voice went on in other languages.

And then other phones started ringing.

First Robertson's, then Vulture's.

'What is it?' Jack asked Abbas.

The sheik's face was white. 'They say a plane that took off a short time ago from Dubai International has departed from its flightplan and deviated from the regular flight corridor. It's headed this way, toward this building.'

Jack froze. 'This can't be a coincidence. Everybody out! Now! We'll rendezvous at the *Halicarnassus*! Move!'

Everyone cleared the room—Abbas was whisked outside by his minders; Robertson went out all by himself. The Marine, Astro, stayed, saying to Jack: 'How can I help?'

Jack was already springing into action. 'Zoe! Pooh Bear! Get the kids outta here! I've got to grab Wizard's stuff. Stretch, help me out! Lieutenant'—he said to Astro—'you can help, too. I could use an extra pair of hands.'

It was then that West looked out through the wide panoramic windows of the Presidential Suite.

And his jaw dropped.

He saw a Boeing 767 cargo jet banking across the sky and then levelling out on a dead-straight flightpath that would end at the Burj al Arab Tower.

'Oh, crap,' he breathed.

If you could have seen it up close, you would have made out the words 'TRANSATLANTIC AIR FREIGHT' on the side of the speeding cargo plane.

And although the pilot listed on its flightplan was Earl McShane, it wasn't Earl McShane who sat at the controls. It was a lone man who was prepared to die—for a matter of honour.

The 767 zeroed in on the tower.

In the hotel, people were running every which way.

Every elevator was jammed to overflowing. The fire escape stairs were filled with fleeing guests, some in tuxedos, others in their pyjamas.

Up on the helipad, high above the world, a helicopter lifted off and powered away from the building.

The PA blared: '*This is an emergency. Would all guests please evacuate the hotel . . .*'

Zoe and Pooh Bear burst out of the fire escape into the wide lobby of the hotel, gripping Lily and Alby by the hand.

'This is crazy,' Zoe whispered. 'Just crazy.'

They dashed outside into the morning sunshine, into the massing crowd.

*

Up in the Presidential Suite, Jack, Stretch and Astro were the last ones left.

They were packing frantically, gathering together all of Wizard's notes and books in a few sportsbags.

When at last they had everything, they ran from the suite, West coming last of all, peering back out the window in time to see the cargo plane looming large *right outside it*.

Then the plane dipped below the windowline and a moment later Jack felt the building shudder in a way he wished he'd never feel again.

Seen from the outside, the speeding 767 hit the Burj al Arab Tower about two-thirds of the way up its side, around the 50th floor.

The entire plane instantly burst into a billowing fireball, a flaming meteor that spewed out the other side of the waterfront tower.

The building shuddered violently and tottered, belching a great plume of smoke, eerily reminiscent of the World Trade Center towers on 9/11 in that terrible hour before they fell.

'We're cut off!' Stretch called from the entrance to the fire stairs. 'We can't get down!'

West spun. The world around him was literally crumbling. The tower was swaying. Black smoke rose past the windows, blotting out the sun.

'Up,' he said. 'We go up.'

*

Minutes later, the three of them burst out onto the helipad of the burning Burj al Arab Tower.

The coastline of Dubai stretched out before them—a dead-flat desert plain meeting the aqua waters of the Persian Gulf. The Sun was blood red in colour, veiled by the smoke.

'This is outrageous!' Astro yelled.

'Welcome to my world,' West called back as he flung open the door to a supply shed situated at the edge of the helipad.

Suddenly, the building rocked. Girders shrieked.

'Huntsman! We don't have much time!' Stretch yelled. 'This building is going to fall any second!'

'I know! I know!' West was rummaging around inside the shed. 'Here!'

He hurled something out through the doorway and into Stretch's arms: a pack of some sort.

A parachute.

'Safety precaution for a helipad this high up,' West said, emerging with two more parachutes. He flung one to Astro. 'Again, welcome to my world.'

They strapped the chutes on and hurried to the edge of the helipad, railless and dizzyingly high, eighty storeys above the ground.

The building's steel skeleton shrieked once more. The air around it began to shimmer in the heat. It was about to collapse—

'Jump!' West called.

And they did, together, the three of them basejumping off the burning building, plummeting through the shimmering sky, the building beside them blurring with speed—

—a bare instant before the whole top third of the

Burj al Arab Tower came free from the rest of the building and toppled off it!

The building's great spire, its helipad and its top thirty floors all tipped as one, falling sideways like a slow-falling tree, folding at the point where the plane had hit it, before tearing free of the main structure and falling off it, chasing the three tiny figures that only an instant before had leapt off the helipad.

But then abruptly three parachutes blossomed to life above the three figures and they sailed clear of the peak of the tower. They flew away to landward as the now upside-down spire of the building came crashing down into the sea with a momentous ear-splitting smash.

The incredible sight would appear in newspapers around the world the following day, images of the half-standing tower.

The culprit: an angry American loner, Earl McShane, seething for revenge after 9/11. Hell, he'd even written to his local paper after September 11 calling for vengeance.

And so he'd decided to exact his own form of revenge on an Islamic country in exactly the same way the Islamist terrorists had attacked America: by flying a plane into their biggest, most well-known tower.

Thankfully, all the papers reported, owing to the professionalism of the hotel staff, their flawless evacuation procedures and their rapid—almost forewarned—response to the news of the incoming cargo plane, not a single person was killed in the fiendish attack.

In the end, the only life McShane took was his own.

*

Naturally, in the hours following the event, all air traffic in the region was grounded pending further notice.

The skies above the Emirates remained eerily empty for the entire next day, all flights cancelled.

Except for one.

One plane that was given permission to take off from a high-security military airbase on the outskirts of Dubai.

A black 747, heading east, for China.

The first plane out the following day was a private Lear jet belonging to Sheik Anzar al Abbas, carrying three passengers—Zoe, Lily and Alby.

After a quick exchange between West and Alby on the tarmac of the military base the previous day, it was decided that the team would split here, with Zoe and the two children heading in the opposite direction: for England.

SECOND ORDEAL

THE CHINESE BREAKOUT

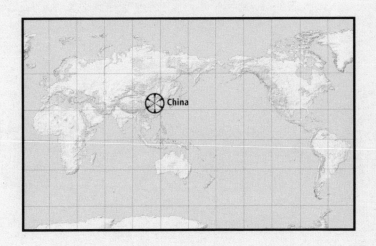

CHINA
5 DECEMBER, 2007
5 DAYS BEFORE THE 1ST DEADLINE

AIRSPACE OVER SOUTH-WESTERN CHINA

The *Halicarnassus* soared over the Himalayas and entered Chinese airspace.

Its black radar-absorbent paint and irregular multi-angled flanks would ensure that it did not show up on any local radar systems. These features, however, would not protect it from being spotted by other, more advanced, satellite-based systems.

Not long after their take-off from Dubai, Jack had turned to his two newest team members, the American Marine, Astro, and the Saudi spy, Vulture: 'Okay, gentlemen. Time to show me what you know. The subject is Xintan Prison.'

The young American lieutenant replied with a question of his own. 'Are you sure this is a wise course of action? You seem to work just fine without this Wizard guy. Why not go straight for the Stones and the Pillars? Going after Wizard will only serve to antagonise the Chinese.'

Jack said, 'I only know what Wizard has told me or written down. The vast stores of knowledge in his brain on this subject are the only thing that'll successfully get us through this. That alone is worth antagonising China for. There's also another reason.'

'And that is . . . ?'

'Wizard is my friend,' Jack said flatly. *Just as Fuzzy was my friend, and look at what happened to him. Jesus.*

'And you'd risk our lives and our nations' reputations just to save your friend—'

'Yes.' Jack didn't even blink. The image of Fuzzy's head in that box flashed through his mind, a friend he hadn't been able to save.

'That's some loyalty you have there,' Astro said. 'Will you risk all that for *me* if I get into trouble?'

'I don't know you that well yet,' Jack said. 'I'll let you know later, if you survive. Now. The prison.'

Vulture unfolded some maps and satellite photos he'd brought from Saudi Intelligence. 'The Chinese are keeping Professors Epper and Tanaka at the Xintan Hard Labor Penal Facility, a Grade 4 penitentiary in the remote western region of Sichuan Province.

'Xintan is a special facility reserved for political prisoners and maximum security inmates. Its prisoners are used to dig the tunnels and high passes for China's high-altitude train lines, like the Qinghai–Tibet Railway, the so-called "Roof of the World" railway. The Chinese are the best railroad builders on Earth—they've built tracks over, under and through the most mountainous terrain on the planet, many of them connecting the mainland provinces to Tibet.'

At this point, Pooh Bear's brother, Scimitar, joined in. 'They're using the new railways to flood Tibet with Chinese workers. Trying to wipe out the local population by sheer weight of numbers. It's a new form of genocide. Genocide by overwhelming immigration.'

Jack assessed Scimitar. He could not have been more unlike his younger brother. Where Pooh Bear was rotund, bearded and earthy, Scimitar was lean, cleanshaven and cultured. He had pale blue eyes, olive skin, and an Oxford accent. The classic modern Arabian prince. Jack noticed that he had put China's railway-building into a political context.

'In any case,' Vulture said, 'building the railways is very dangerous work. Many prisoners die doing it and they're just buried in the concrete. Epper, however, was taken to Xintan because it features an interrogation and debriefing wing.'

'Torture chambers?' West asked.

'Torture chambers,' Vulture said.

'Xintan is notorious for its torture wing,' Astro said. 'Falun Gong devotees, student protesters, Tibetan monks. All have been "re-educated", as the Chinese put it, at Xintan. The thing is, by virtue of its unusual terrain, Xintan is uniquely positioned to be a perfect interrogation facility. You see, Xintan is built on top of not one but two adjacent mountain peaks known as "The Devil's Horns".

'Xintan One, the main prison, is located on the primary peak and is entered via a high-altitude railway line that passes directly into the prison via a huge iron gate.'

'Sounds like Auschwitz,' Stretch said.

'Similar, but not entirely,' Astro said. 'After dropping off its cargo of new prisoners at the main prison, the railway line continues *all the way through* Xintan One, emerging from another gate at the far end. There the railway line crosses a long bridge and arrives at Xintan Two, the smaller wing, the torture wing, situated atop its own peak. The railway enters Xintan Two via a third massive gate and there it ends. Apart from that gate, there is no exit from Xintan Two.'

'Like Auschwitz,' Stretch said again.

'In this respect, yes it is, Jew,' Vulture said.

Sitting nearby, Pooh Bear looked up sharply. 'Vulture.

I honour you as my brother's friend. I would ask then that you honour my friend. He is known as Cohen, Archer or Stretch. You will not call him Jew again.'

Vulture bowed low in apology, again in his slow calculating way—which bespoke insult as much as it did regret. 'I humbly beg your pardon.'

Astro broke the awkward silence with more information: 'According to our intelligence, the Chinese also have a chase copter at Xintan in the event someone does escape.'

'What kind of chase copter?' Jack asked, cocking his head.

'A big motherfucking Hind gunship,' Astro said, 'the kind of helicopter you don't mess around with. Captain West, it's said that the prisoners in Xintan One can hear the screams from the torture victims across the valley in Xintan Two. If there's one complex in China you don't want to be in, it's Xintan Two. No one has ever escaped from it alive.'

'Ever?'

'Ever,' Astro said.

That had been several hours ago.

Now as they entered Chinese airspace, Scimitar charged into West's office and said: 'Huntsman! We just got something from the Americans. NSA intercept. The Chinese are moving your friend Wizard *today*. In one hour.'

West leapt out of his chair.

The news was bad. Very bad.

Wizard and Tank were being transferred from Xintan Two to Xintan One. From there, they were to be taken by train under armed guard to Wushan. Their presence had been demanded by Colonel Mao Gongli himself.

'What time?' West said, entering the main cabin.

'The train leaves Xintan Two at noon!' Astro called from his seat at a wall-console.

'Could they know we're coming?' Scimitar asked.

West was thinking exactly the same thing.

'It's certainly possible,' Vulture said. 'After Captain West's rather noisy escape from Australia three days ago and yesterday's plane crash in Dubai, they could well believe we're up to something.'

Scimitar said, 'But surely the Chinese can't believe anyone would seriously consider storming Xintan.'

'Sky Monster!' West called to the ceiling. 'ETA on Xintan?'

Sky Monster's voice came back over the intercom: *'It'll be close, but I think I can get you there by noon.'*

'Do it,' West called.

This was happening a lot faster than he'd anticipated. He'd expected to have more time to create a plan.

He stepped over to the central table, stared at Astro's maps of the mountaintop Xintan complex. 'The internal transfer is the weak point. The bridge between Xintan One and Xintan Two. That's where we can get them.'

'The bridge?' Astro said, coming over. 'Maybe you didn't hear us right, Captain. That bridge is *inside* the complex. Wouldn't it be better to try to grab Epper and Tanaka later, when they're travelling on the train outside the prison perimeter?'

West was gazing at the maps, formulating a plan. 'No. They'll assign extra guards for the external leg, probably Army troops, but for the internal transfer, they'll only use prison guards, regular prison guards.'

Jack bit his lip. 'It won't be pretty—in fact, it'll be downright ugly if it works at all—but that's our opening, that's where we can snatch them.'

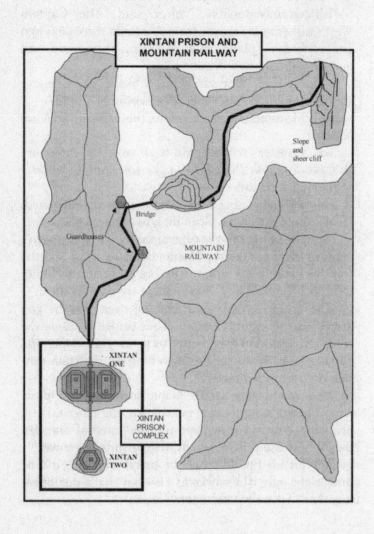

XINTAN PRISON AND MOUNTAIN RAILWAY

Slope and sheer cliff

Bridge

Guardhouses

MOUNTAIN RAILWAY

XINTAN ONE

XINTAN PRISON COMPLEX

XINTAN TWO

The two grey concrete structures sat atop their adjoining mountain peaks like twin castles in a fantasy world, gazing out over the mountain wilderness, high above the cloud layer.

The larger structure, Xintan One, was five storeys tall, bulky and fat. It sat lazily on its peak, bulging over the precipices, as if some god had just dropped a slab of plasticine onto the summit from a great height. Built almost entirely of dirty grey concrete—Communism's contribution to architecture—it possessed four high towers soaring into the sky.

The smaller structure, Xintan Two, lay to the south of its big brother. It was only three storeys tall and had just one tower. But its compact size only seemed to make it harsher, more confident in its authority. It didn't need to be big to be feared.

Connecting the two wings was a long arched railway bridge, about a kilometre in length and spanning a jagged valley gorge hundreds of feet deep. Today, that gorge was obscured by a layer of low clouds that wound its way between the mountains like a river.

High and isolated, and silent save for the whistling of the mountain wind, the scene might have been beautiful if it weren't for the stench of death and despair that surrounded the place.

At precisely 12 noon, the great iron gates of Xintan Two rumbled open to reveal the prison train.

With black iron flanks and reinforced grilles on every window except for those on the engine cars at either end of the five-carriage-long train, it looked like a ferocious armoured beast. Held back at the threshold of the gate, it snorted like a bull, expelling steam, its forward engine growling.

The two prisoners were loaded into the middle car of the train.

They were dressed in rags and blindfolds, and they shuffled rather than walked, their arms and legs bound in chains. There were only the two of them—Wizard and Tank.

Stony-faced prison guards surrounded them, twelve in total, the standard number for an internal transfer. All the guards were aware that two entire platoons of Chinese Army troops were waiting at Xintan One to accompany the prisoners on their external journey.

Wizard and Tank were placed in the third carriage where their leg-irons were padlocked to ringbolts in the floor.

Then the sliding door to their carriage clanged shut and a whistle blew and the armoured train moved out, expelling more steam, so that as it emerged from the gates, it looked like a great evil thing emerging from the depths of Hell itself.

*

The train commenced its short journey across the long arched bridge, looking tiny against the wild mountains of China, just as two bird-like objects appeared in the sky above it, descending fast, objects that as they came closer lost their bird-like appearance and took on the appearance of men . . . two men dressed in black with wings on their backs.

Jack West Jr shot down through the air at bullet speed, a high-altitude facemask covering his face, a pair of ultra-high-tech carbon-fibre wings, called Gullwings, attached to his back.

The Gullwings were an FID—a fast-insertion device— developed by Wizard for the US Air Force many years ago. Fast, silent and stealthy, they were essentially one-man gliders which also possessed small compressed-air thrusters to enable gliding for sustained periods. In the end, the USAF had decided against using them, but Wizard had retained several prototypes which West kept on the *Hali* for situations like this.

Zooming down through the sky alongside West, similarly garbed, was Stretch.

Both men were armed to the teeth, with many holsters packed with pistols, submachine-guns and grenades and, in Stretch's case, one compact Predator anti-tank rocket launcher.

The prison train thundered across the long high bridge.

A kilometre away, the great behemoth of Xintan One loomed before it, the railway tracks ending at a solid hundred-foot-high concrete wall fitted with not a single aperture except for the imposing iron gate.

But as the train whipped across the long bridge, closing in on Xintan One, the two winged figures swooped in low over it, travelling horizontally above the five armoured carriages, moving gradually forward till they flew only a few feet above the front-most carriage, the engine car.

Their arrival went unseen by anyone, the guards at Xintan One having long grown complacent with the internal leg of the journey. After all, there had never been an escape in the prison's history. As such, no one was actually assigned to watch the train during the bridge crossing.

Once the two flying figures had reached the engine car, gliding low over it, West and Stretch retracted their wings and dropped to the roof of the engine, landing perfectly on their feet.

They had to move fast. By now the train had covered almost two-thirds of its short journey and the gates of the main facility rose large before them.

West drew his two Desert Eagle pistols and leapt down onto the nose of the engine car and proceeded to blow out its two drivers' windows.

The windows shattered and he swung in through one, landing inside the driver's compartment.

Both drivers—Chinese Army men—shouted and reached for their guns. They never got to them.

Stretch swung inside the driver's compartment to find the drivers dead and West taking the controls of the train.

'Predator,' West called above the wind now screaming in through the shattered windshield.

Stretch loaded his anti-tank rocket launcher, then

shouldered it, aiming it out the broken front windows.

'Ready!' he called.

Then, right on cue, the iron gates of Xintan One cracked open, ready to receive the transfer train.

At which point, West jammed forward on the throttle.

As the gates rumbled open, the two platoons of Chinese Army troops waiting on the receiving platform of Xintan One turned, expecting to see the armoured train engaging its brakes, disgorging steam and generally slowing.

What they saw was the exact opposite.

The armoured train *burst* in through the great gateway at full speed, accelerating through the tight confines of the archway and blasting past the siding.

Then a finger of smoke shoomed out from the shattered forward windshield of the engine car—the smoketrail of a Predator anti-tank missile, a missile that cut a beeline for . . .

. . . the other gate of Xintan One.

The outer gate.

The Predator missile *slammed* into the iron gate and exploded. Smoke and dust billowed out in every direction, engulfing the receiving platform, obscuring everything.

The huge iron outer doors buckled and groaned, their centre sections twisted and loosened, which was all West needed, for a moment later his train thundered into them at phenomenal speed and crashed right through them, flinging them open, hurling them from their massive hinges, before the train itself rushed out into grey daylight, racing away from the mountaintop prison, running for all it was worth.

At first, the Chinese were just stunned, but their response when it came was fierce.

Within four minutes, two compact helicopters—fast-attack Russian-built Kamov Ka-50s, otherwise known as Werewolves—rose from within Xintan One and took off after the runaway train.

Another minute later, a much larger helicopter rose from within Xintan Two. It was also Russian-made, but of far higher quality. It was an Mi-24 Hind gunship, one of the most feared choppers in the world. Bristling with cannons, gunpods, chem-weapons dispensers and rockets, it had a unique double-domed cockpit. It also possessed a troop hold, which today bore ten fully armed Chinese shock troops.

Once clear of the prison's walls, the Hind lowered its nose and thundered off in pursuit of West's fleeing train.

The final aspect of the Chinese response was electronic.

The Xintan complex possessed two outer guardhouses situated on the mountain railway a few miles north of the prison, guardhouses that the train would have to pass by.

Frantic phone calls were made to the guards posted at both guardhouses, but strangely no reply came back from either one.

At both outposts the scene was the same: all the guards lay on the floor, out cold, their hands bound with flex-cuffs.

West's people had already been there.

The armoured train whipped through the mountains at breakneck speed, a rain of snow rushing in through its shattered forward windows.

It roared past the first guardhouse, crashing through its boomgate as if it were a toothpick.

Stretch drove, eyeing the landscape around them—snow-covered mountainside to the left, a sheer thousand-foot drop to the right.

The train rounded a left-hand spur and suddenly the second guardhouse came into view, plus a long soaring iron bridge beyond it.

'Huntsman! I've got a visual on the outer bridge!' Stretch called.

West had been leaning up and out through the shattered windshield, setting up some kind of mortar-type device and peering behind them, back at the prison complex. He ducked back inside.

'We got choppers on our tail. Two attack birds and one big bastard Hind—'

'*Three* choppers?' Stretch turned. 'I thought Astro said they only kept one chase copter at Xintan, the Hind?'

'Looks like his intelligence was two choppers short,' West said wryly. 'I hope that's the only thing he got wrong. Too late to worry about it now. The rotor net is mounted and in your hands. Just get us to that bridge before somebody on that Hind figures out who we are and decides it's worth blowing the bridge to stop us. Keep me posted. I've got work to do.'

West then grabbed a microphone from the dash, keyed the train's internal intercom and began speaking in Mandarin: 'Attention all guards aboard this train! Attention! We are now in command of this vehicle. All we want are the prisoners—'

In the five regular carriages of the train, every one of the Chinese guards looked up at the voice coming in over the PA.

Among them, one other face snapped up and gasped, the only one to recognise the voice.

Wizard. He was bloody, bruised and beaten. But his eyes lit up at the sound of his friend's voice. 'Jack . . .' he rasped.

'—*We mean you no harm. We understand that many of you are just doing your job, that you are men with families, children. But if you get in our way, know this: harm will come to you. We will be coming through the train now, so we give you a choice: lay down your weapons, and you will not be killed. Raise your weapons against us and you will die.*'

The intercom clicked off.

Up in the driver's compartment, West threw open the interconnecting door between the engine car and the first carriage.

Then, holding an MP-7 submachine-gun in one hand

and a Desert Eagle in the other, he entered the prison train.

The three guards in the first carriage had heeded his warning.

They stood backed up against the walls, their Type-56 rifles at their feet, their hands raised. West moved warily past them, his guns up, when suddenly one of the guards whipped out a pistol and—

Blam!

The guard was blown back against the wall of the carriage, nailed by West's powerful Desert Eagle.

'I *told* you not to raise your weapons,' he said to the others in a low voice. He jerked his chin at a nearby cell: 'Into the cage, now.'

The four guards in the second carriage were smarter. They'd set a trap. First, they'd cut the lights, darkening the carriage; and second, they'd concealed one of their men in the ceiling *above* the interconnecting doorway while the others feigned surrender to West.

West entered the carriage, rocking with the motion of the train, to see three of them holding up their hands and crying 'Mercy! Mercy! Don't shoot us!', diverting his attention from the man hidden in the shadows above the door.

Then, completely unseen by West, the concealed man extended his arm, aiming his gun at West's head from directly above—

—and suddenly West looked up, too late—

—just as the entire carriage rocked wildly, pummelled

from the outside by a ferocious burst of supermachine-gun fire.

The chase copters had arrived and had started firing on the speeding train!

The guard above him was thrown from his perch above the door and, missing West by inches, hit the floor with a clumsy thud.

Then the other three guards drew *their* weapons and the darkened carriage erupted in strobe-like flashes of gunfire, with Jack West Jr in the middle of it all, firing in every direction with both of his guns—side-stepping to one side then firing left, right and down—until at the end of it all when darkness had returned and the smoke had cleared he was the only one left standing.

He moved grimly onward: next carriage.

The prisoner carriage.

At the same time, outside, the two chase helicopters from Xintan had caught up with the runaway train and were assaulting it with a hail of bulletfire from their strut-mounted 30mm guns.

Stretch brought the train past the second guardhouse, smashing through its boomgate before racing out onto the long swooping bridge that led to the rest of the mountain railway.

Onto the bridge, totally exposed.

One chase chopper swooped low over the train's engine car—just as Stretch triggered the mortar-like device on its bonnet.

The device went off with a muffled whump, propelling something into the air high above the speeding train.

It was a wide nylon net with heavy weighted bearings at every corner. It fanned out above the engine car like a giant lateral spiderweb—a spiderweb that was designed to bring down helicopters.

The net entered the rotor blades of the lead chopper and instantly got entangled.

The rotors caught horribly and with a jerk, stopped, and suddenly the banking helicopter became a forward-moving glider with the aerodynamics of a brick.

It sailed down into the ravine below the bridge, falling down and down and down before it hit the bottom with a tremendous explosion.

Stretch left the controls of the train for a moment to grab his Predator rocket launcher and insert a final rocket-propelled grenade into it.

When he returned to the controls, he found himself staring at the huge Chinese gunship, the Hind, hovering off to the side of the long swooping bridge, flying parallel to his engine car.

'Oh shit,' Stretch breathed.

The Hind loosed a single rocket from one of its side-mounted pods—a missile aimed not at the train, but rather at the *bridge*; a missile that would stop West from snatching Wizard and Tank. That a few guards would also be lost was clearly of no concern to the Chinese generals who had ordered the missile launch.

'Fuck me . . .' Stretch keyed his radio: 'Huntsman! They're going to take out the bridge . . .'

'*Then drive faster*,' came the reply.

'Right!' Stretch hit the gas, pushing the train's throttle as far forward as it would go.

*

The missile from the Hind struck the bridge right in its middle, in the latticework of struts that formed the apex of its arch, a bare second after the speeding train had shot over that point.

The detonation of the missile sent a shower of iron girders and beams raining down into the ravine.

But the bridge held . . . for the moment.

The train sped across it, a hundred yards from the other side and the shelter of a tunnel there.

There came an almighty groan. The distinctive groan of iron girders bending.

Then, in almost glorious slow motion, the great bridge began to sway, and rock, and from the middle outward, it began to drop in pieces into the ravine.

It was an incredible sight.

The slowly collapsing bridge, falling away in its centre, while the armoured train—*still on it*—sped off its eastern end, chased by the disintegrating bridge.

But the train was just a fraction too fast.

It shot off the end of the bridge and disappeared into the waiting tunnel a bare second before the rails behind its final carriage—the rear-facing second engine—dropped away into the ravine, disappearing forever.

Inside the train, Jack came to the third carriage, the prisoner car, just as all the lights abruptly went off.

The guards here weren't going to give up without a fight and now in the darkness of the tunnel, the interior of the prison train was enveloped in near total blackness.

Snapping the night-vision goggles on his helmet into place, Jack entered the prisoner car, seeing the world in phosphorescent green, and he beheld . . .

. . . two burly Chinese guards holding both Wizard and Tank in front of their bodies with guns held to each of the blindfolded professors' heads. Neither of the guards wore night-vision goggles and they stared wildly into the darkness—they didn't need NVGs to kill their hostages.

When they heard the heavy interconnecting door open, one of them yelled, 'Drop your weapon or we blow their—'

Ba-blam! Two shots.

Both guards dropped. Matching holes in their faces.

Jack never even broke his stride.

The other two guards in the carriage weren't so bold and Jack quickly herded them into a spare cell before sealing the rear door of the carriage with an axe—he didn't want any more enemies bothering him.

Then he slid to Wizard's side, snatched away the blindfold, and gazed in horror at his battered friend. 'Wizard, it's me. Jesus, what did they do to you . . .'

The old man's face was a mess of cuts and peeled skin. His arms and chest bore the distinctive scars of electric shock equipment. His long white beard was matted with dried blood.

'Jack!' he sobbed. 'Oh, Jack. I'm sorry! I'm so sorry to have brought this on you! I thought I'd die here! I never thought you would come for me!'

'You'd do the same for me,' Jack said, glancing at the thick ringbolts holding Wizard's and Tank's leg-irons to the floor. 'Don't celebrate too soon. We're not out of this yet.'

Jack then extracted a handheld blowtorch from his utility belt, fired it up, and went to work.

The train zoomed through the tunnel.

As it did so, the remaining chase copter flew ahead, gunning for the tunnel's exit further round the mountain.

It beat the train there, steadying itself in a deadly hover just out from the tunnel's mouth, cannons ready and aimed at the oncoming engine car.

But before the train emerged from the tunnel, something else did.

A Predator missile.

It lanced out from the tunnel's mouth, a dead-straight tail of smoke issuing out behind it, before it ploughed into the hovering copter, blasting it to a million pieces, blowing it out of the sky.

Then the train roared out of the tunnel and swung hard left, following the mountain railway on its course.

But the meanest pursuer of all still remained.

The Hind gunship.

It chased Stretch around every bend, paralleling the fleeing train, harrying the engine car mercilessly with withering fire.

Before suddenly, all the gunfire stopped.

Stretch frowned, confused.

What the—?

Thumps on the roof.

Then before he knew what was happening, a dark figure swung in through one of the shattered forward windows and into the driver's compartment!

Two boots slammed into his chest, knocking him to the floor.

Damn it! I was stupid! he realised as he tumbled. *They're guards—from the back carriages of the train. Must've crawled forward along the roof . . .*

The first guard to land inside the cabin drew his pistol, only for Stretch to kick him viciously—square on the kneecap—breaking it backwards, causing the man to howl out in pain, giving Stretch the second he needed to draw his own gun and fire it once, twice, three times into the man's chest—

More thumps on the roof.

Stretch stood—just in time to see three more pairs of boots jump down onto the bonnet of the engine car, blocking his view of the track ahead: a long, straight section of track that ended at a sharp left-hand curve. Beyond that curve was a steep downward slope of densely packed snow.

'Huntsman!' he called into his radio-mike. 'How's it going back there?'

'*I've found Wizard and Tank. Just have to cut them free.*'

'I got overwhelming company up here, about to storm my position! They came over the roof, from the rear carriages! I have to launch us now!'

'*Do it,*' West's voice was calm. '*Then get back here.*'

'Right.'

Stretch knew what he had to do.

He jammed the throttle fully forward—and the train sped up markedly. Then he wedged a grenade between the throttle and the brakes and pulled the pin.

This was now a one-way ticket.

He dashed back into the the train itself, slamming the interconnecting door behind him—

—just as the grenade exploded, ripping the controls to shreds—

—a moment before the entire driver's compartment was shredded by a volley of bullets and three more guards swung in through the forward windows.

They entered with their guns up, their leader—an older man, more seasoned than the others, more battle hardened, the Captain of the Guard—looking pissed as hell at this brazen assault on his train.

The train was now rocketing along the high-altitude railway, all-but out of control and heading for the sharp left-hand bend that it couldn't possibly take at this speed.

Stretch burst into the third carriage, the prisoner carriage, where he saw West kneeling beside Wizard and Tank, blowtorch flaring.

Tank was free, but West was still cutting through the leg-irons fastening Wizard to the floor.

The Captain of the Guard stormed angrily into the first carriage, not caring for the runaway state of the train—unable to slow it, he was going after the intruders.

He found two of his men huddled in a cell there and heard their pathetic excuses, before he put a bullet in each of their heads for cowardice.

Then he moved on, hunting.

West's blowtorch blazed away as it carved through Wizard's chains.

'How long?' Stretch asked anxiously.

'Almost there . . .' West said, his face illuminated by the blowtorch's magnesium glare.

The rocking motion of the train was getting wilder.

'We don't have much track left, Jack . . .'

'Just . . . another . . . second . . .'

The door to their carriage burst open—revealing the Captain of the Guard!

Stretch spun.

West spun.

The Captain of the Guard stood in the doorway, grinning. He gripped his gun tighter.

But he needn't have, because it was already too late.

For just then, the runaway train hit the bend.

The speeding train hit the alpine curve going way too fast.

Derailment.

The forward engine car jumped the tracks, bumping roughly over them before skidding out onto the steeply sloping plain of snow beyond the curve.

The rest of the great black train followed the engine car, leaping off the rails before also sliding out onto the snow-plain.

The engine car skidded down the slope, its forward grille grinding into the powder, the rest of the train snaking along behind it like a twisted accordion, the whole crashing mess turning laterally as it slid until the entire train was sliding *in reverse* down the slope and headed inexorably toward the bottom, where there was nothing but a bare cliff-edge and a thousand-foot drop.

And circling above all this was the Hind gunship.

Inside the train, the world spun crazily.

The shocking jolt of their derailment had sent the

Captain of the Guard flying sideways, slamming into the right-hand wall of the carriage. Then the inertia of the train's lateral spin as it slid down the slope—at first forwards, now backwards—pressed him into it.

West and Stretch were better prepared: they'd grabbed hold of the nearest cell-bars at the first bump and it still took all of their strength to stay upright during the crazy bouncing of the derailment—Stretch grabbing Tank, West clutching Wizard.

Yet still, in its own out-of-control way, this was part of West's plan. He'd planned to crash here. To end up on this snow-plain with the train buried in the deep snow.

Because he still needed something.

He still needed the Chinese to—

But then with shocking suddenness something happened that West *hadn't* planned.

The train went over the edge at the base of the snow-slope.

Unfortunately, the snow hadn't quite been deep enough, its slick icy base causing the snake-like train to slide *all the way* down the snow-plain to the very edge.

Now travelling backwards, the rear engine car went over the edge first, its weight pulling first one, then two, then three carriages over with it—

West felt it coming an instant before it happened.

Felt the distinctive *tug* of the train's last three cars— the engine car and the last two regular carriages—going over the precipice a moment before his own carriage lurched sickeningly and . . .

'Grab something!' he yelled to the others, including Wizard who was still not yet free of his ringbolts.

Their carriage went over the edge.

The world went vertical.

Anything not nailed down dropped the length of the carriage, including one of the Captain of the Guard's men.

With a cry, the hapless fellow fell the full vertical length of the carriage, hitting the heavy iron door at the bottom with a foul cracking noise.

The Guard Captain and his remaining companion had quicker reflexes: as the carriage fell, they both discarded their guns in favour of having free hands, and rolled into a nearby cell at the top end of the now-vertical carriage.

West and Stretch grabbed the bars of the nearest cell, holding onto Wizard and Tank, before—*smack*—their carriage's fall was arrested.

Somehow, the entire train had stopped its plunge down the cliff-face, coming to a jarring, crunching halt.

Although they couldn't see it, the train's lead engine car had rammed up against a large boulder at the edge of the precipice and lodged there, holding fast, holding the entire train suspended beneath it, dangling over the thousand-foot drop!

West quickly took in their new predicament: he, Stretch, Wizard and Tank were halfway down the vertical carriage. The Guard Captain and his buddy were up near the top, resting against the now-horizontal wall of their cell, not far from the interconnecting door that led upward to safety.

A grinding groaning sound.

With a jerk the entire train dropped a metre. Chunks of snow rained past the barred windows. The upper engine was slipping, one metre at a time.

West exchanged a look with Stretch.

Then another groan, but a different kind: the sound of a metal coupling straining under the weight of the dangling train.

'We're gonna fall,' West said to Stretch. '*Up! Now!*'

'What about you?' Stretch nodded at Wizard's ring-bolt. The old man's leg-irons were still chained to it.

'Just go!' West said. 'I'm not leaving him! Go! Someone has to get out of here alive!'

Stretch didn't bother to argue. He just grabbed Tank and started hauling him up the carriage, using the bars of the cells as ladder rungs.

They climbed up the left-hand side of the carriage's central aisle—passing the Guard Captain as he emerged from his cell on the right, dazed and gunless.

West went back to work on Wizard's chains with his blowtorch. He had to do this fast.

Another grinding groan. More snow sailed past the window.

The train dropped another metre.

The blowtorch cut further through the chains before— *shwack!*—the flame sizzled through the final section of chain and Wizard was free.

'Come on, old buddy,' West said. 'We gotta move.'

They looked up to see Stretch and Tank disappear through the interconnecting door at the top of the carriage—but also in time to see the Guard Captain step across their line of sight, staring daggers at West, blocking the way.

'This way,' West said, leading Wizard down.

'Down?' Wizard asked.

'Trust me.'

They came to the bottom door of the third carriage just as another metallic groan squealed out from nearby and—*crack*—the coupling connecting their car to the carriage beneath them broke loose and the bottom two carriages of the train, plus the rear engine car, just fell away into the void.

The three cars fell forever, soaring silently down into the great mountain chasm before they smashed violently against the jagged rocks at the base of the ravine, the engine car exploding in a cloud of flames and black smoke.

'No time to waste,' West said to Wizard. 'This way.'

Dangling by their fingertips, they swung out along the underside of their carriage, their feet hanging a thousand feet above the world, before they turned upward, climbing *up the outside* of the third suspended prison car, using any and every protrusion on it as a handhold—the bars on the windows, hinges, handles, anything.

Up the side of the third carriage they went, moving quickly, Jack helping Wizard. They reached the gap between this carriage and the next one just as the Guard Captain and his companion did—moving inside the train—and so Jack and Wizard just kept on moving, scaling the exterior of the second carriage as quickly as they could until they reached its summit and clambered onto its flat upper surface—

—just in time to see the Guard Captain climb up into the safety of the next (and last) carriage above them, his junior companion still waiting to climb up after him.

It was at that moment that the Captain saw West—and something evil gleamed in his eye.

He reached for the coupling, despite the fact that his own man was still standing on the lower carriage. The junior guard yelped 'No!' when he saw what was going to happen but West just moved, leaping for a grille on the upper carriage, calling to Wizard as he did so: 'Max! Jump for my legs!'

Wizard jumped immediately, reaching for Jack's waist as—

The Guard Captain disengaged the coupling.

The second carriage dropped instantly.

It took the junior guard with it, his wide eyes receding into the chasm, his mouth open in a silent scream all the way down.

But West and Wizard were still in the game: West now dangling from the bottom of the first carriage, with Wizard hanging *from his belt!*

'Max, quick, climb up my body!' West yelled, as Wizard quickly and clumsily climbed up the length of West's frame, at one point using the folded carbon-fibre wings on Jack's back for handholds.

The look on the Guard Captain's face said it all. He was furious. He wouldn't let that happen again.

He ducked back inside the carriage and started climbing—fast.

Jack knew what was happening instantly.

It was now a race to the next coupling.

'Go, Jack! Go!' Wizard yelled. 'I'll catch up!'

West charged up the outer wall of the final carriage, while the Guard Captain raced up its internal aisle.

They both moved quickly, clambering up the vertical carriage.

'Stretch!' West called into his radio as he climbed. 'Where are you!'

'*We're up, on the precipice, but we got a prob*—'

West knew what that problem was. He could see it.

The Hind chopper was hovering directly above him, a short way out from the clifftop, not far from the sharply tilted engine car hanging out over the edge—waiting for them, if they made it up.

Stay alive, he thought. *As long as you're alive, you have a chance.*

Up he climbed, up the outside of the vertical carriage, moving like a monkey.

Then he rose over the final lip and stood . . . just as the Guard Captain emerged from the doorway there.

Jack had beaten him in this race, got there first by a bare two seconds. He stepped forward to unleash a fierce kick at the Guard Captain—

Only to see a gun appear in the Captain's hand.

Jack froze as the realisation dawned on him: that was why he'd beaten the Captain in their race. The Guard Captain had taken a moment to grab a loose gun on the way up.

Aw, shit . . . Jack thought. *Shit, shit, shit.*

He stood there, frozen on the horizontal end section of the upturned carriage, the beating wind from the helicopter hammering his clothes. Without thinking, he raised his hands.

'You lose!' the Guard Captain spat in English, grinning, as Wizard's face popped up over the edge behind Jack's boots and saw the situation.

The Captain jammed back on the hammer of his gun.

'Wizard . . .' Jack said. 'It's time to fly.'

Then, just as the Guard Captain pulled the trigger on his gun, quick as a flash, Jack's raised hands grabbed the safety rod on the coupling above his head and disengaged it—

—causing *their own carriage* to drop away from the engine car, with them and the Guard Captain on it!

The Guard Captain's eyes boggled. Jack had just condemned them *all* to death.

The carriage fell fast. Down the side of the massive cliff.

The grey rock wall blurred with speed as the iron prison car fell past it.

But as the carriage fell, Jack was all action. He grabbed Wizard and pulled him into a bearhug, yelling 'Hold on to me!' as he pressed something on his chest armour and suddenly his Gullwings sprang out from the compact unit on his back and instantly the two of them soared away from the falling armoured carriage, at first flying downwards at incredible speed before swooping up in a graceful glide, leaving the Guard Captain to fall the rest of the way by himself, screaming all the way to his death.

With Wizard hanging from his chest, Jack caught an upward thermal draught, and they glided away from the mountain railway and the twin mountain peaks that housed Xintan Prison.

'Astro?' West said into his mike. 'We're gonna need a pick-up further down the railway. How about near that farm we saw earlier?'

'*Roger that, Huntsman,*' came the reply. '*Just gotta grab Stretch first. Then we'll come get you.*'

Stretch stood on solid ground, knee-deep in snow, with the weary Tank beside him, alongside the engine car of the prison train, tilted on the edge of the precipice, the only carriage still remaining.

Unfortunately, hovering in the air in front of them was the Hind gunship, looming large.

A voice over its loudhailer commanded in English: '*You two! Remain where you are!*'

'Whatever you say,' Stretch said.

The Hind landed on the snow-plain, its rotors kicking up a mini-blizzard.

Ten Chinese troops rushed out of its hold, dashing through the billowing snow, quickly forming a ring around Stretch and Tank.

Sitting in the chopper's cockpit, the Hind's two Chinese pilots saw Stretch raise his hands a moment before the mini-blizzard shrouded the entire scene in white.

Which was why the pilots never saw the snow-plain around their gunship come alive, three ghost-like figures rising from beneath it, dressed in white camouflage gear and bearing MP-7 submachine-guns: Astro, Scimitar and Vulture.

The three white-clad men took the unguarded chopper easily and once they had it, Vulture aimed its huge six-barrelled cannon at the ten-man Chinese team on the ground and demanded over the loudhailer that they drop their weapons. Needless to say, they complied.

*

Minutes later, the Hind's crew and troops stood shivering on the snow-plain, dressed only in their undergarments, their helicopter lifting off without them—flown by Astro and Scimitar, with Vulture manning the main cannon and Stretch and Tank safely in the hold.

It was the final piece of Jack's plan: they'd needed the Hind to land here—so they could steal it for the next part of their mission in China.

AN ANCIENT MYSTERY

THE SALISBURY STONES

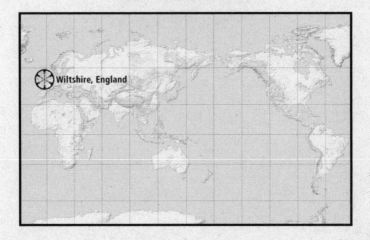

Wiltshire, England

SALISBURY PLAIN, ENGLAND
5 DECEMBER, 2007
5 DAYS BEFORE THE 1ST DEADLINE

SALISBURY PLAIN, ENGLAND
5 DECEMBER, 2007, 3:05 A.M.

The rented Honda Odyssey zoomed along the A303, alone in the night.

In the glare of a bright full moon, endless fields of Wiltshire farmland stretched away to the horizon on either side of the highway, bathed in eerie blue light.

Zoe drove, with Lily and Alby beside her.

In the back of the people-mover sat the two young men who had met her and the kids at Heathrow: the totally unique Adamson brothers, Lachlan and Julius.

Identical twins, they were both tall and lean, with friendly freckled faces, carrot-orange hair and thick Scottish accents.

Both wore simple T-shirts, one black, the other white. Lachlan's black shirt read, somewhat enigmatically: 'I HAVE SEEN THE COW LEVEL!' while Julius's white one proclaimed: 'THERE IS NO COW LEVEL!'

They also had a habit of finishing each other's sentences.

'Zoe!' Lachlan had exclaimed on seeing her.

'It's great to see you again!' Julius said. 'Hey, this sounds like a secret mission.'

'*Is* it a secret mission?' Lachlan asked.

Julius: 'If it is, don't you think Lachy and I should have codenames, you know, like Maverick or Goose?'

'I'd like to be called Blade,' Lachlan said.

'And I'd like Bullfighter,' Julius said.

'Blade? Bullfighter?'

Julius said, 'Pretty rugged and heroic, huh? We've been thinking about this while we've been waiting for you.'

'Clearly,' Zoe said. 'How about Tweedledum and Tweedledee? Romulus and Remus?'

'Aw, no! Not twin codenames,' Lachlan said. 'Anything but twin names.'

'Sorry, boys, but there's only one rule when it comes to call-signs.'

'And that is?'

'You never get to pick your own,' Zoe smiled. 'And sometimes your nickname can change. Look at me, I used to be known as Bloody Mary, until I met this little one.' A nod at Lily. 'And now everyone calls me Princess. Be patient, you'll get call-signs when the occasion calls for it. Because, yes, this mission is about as secret as it gets.'

Now, speeding west along the A303, they were heading for a place that of all people Alby had led them to.

The military airbase outside Dubai. Two days previously. Just after Earl McShane's cargo plane had smashed into the Burj al Arab.

Jack West had stood on the tarmac, crouched low over Alby and Lily, while armed men and CIA agents calling themselves attachés spoke into cell phones, a

REWARDS
(according to Rameses II at Abydos)

1. KNOWLEDGE
2. HEAT
3. SIGHT
4. LIFE
5. DEATH
6. POWER

THE GREAT MACHINE

Pillars???

But what are the TRIANGLES then?

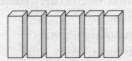

THE SIX PILLARS

- Oblong uncut diamonds;
- Must be '*cleansed*' by the Ph's Stone before they can be placed in the Machine;
- Whereabouts? The Great Houses of Europe; Perhaps the 'Five Warriors'???

MUST HAVE BOTH THE SA-BENBEN **AND** THE PHILOSOPHER'S STONE! THEY ARE CENTRAL TO EVERYTHING!!

The Sa-Benben (a.k.a. 'The Firestone')

Interacts uniquely with each of the Six Ramesean Stones:

1. <u>Philosopher's</u>: cleanses Pillars.
2. <u>Stonehenge</u>: gives location of vertices of the Great Machine.
3. <u>Delphi</u>: allows one to see the Dark Sun.
4. <u>Tablets</u>: contain the final incantation.
5. <u>Killing</u>: gives dates by which Pillars must be laid.
6. <u>Basin</u>: unknown.

Rate of approach must be calculated. Call the Twins!

16.467×365.25
Mean $v = 125.445$ km/s
Max output in 1962 was 10.57
But in 1991 was 10.72. Growing.

TITANIC SINKING & RISING (DEC 2007) CONNECTION? POSSIBLE SIGHTING OPPORTUNITY?

Faberge Egg - Newton's alchemical work
The Ness spring...?
Equinox/Easter '08

WRONG!

black pillar of smoke rising into the sky above the Burj al Arab in the distance.

'Talk to me, Alby,' Jack had said.

During the meeting, Alby had deciphered one of Wizard's more obscure notes: the reference to the 'Titanic Sinking and Rising'. But he had hinted to Jack that there was more to it.

Alby said, 'I also know what one of the symbols on Wizard's summary sheet means.'

Jack had pulled out the summary sheet.

'The symbol at the bottom right,' Alby said. 'Next to the "Titanic Sinking" reference.'

'Yes . . .' West had said.

'It's not a symbol. It's a diagram.'

'Of what?'

Alby had looked up at West seriously. 'It's a diagram of the layout of Stonehenge.'

STONEHENGE

The Honda crested a rise, and without warning the cluster of great stones came into view.

Zoe inhaled sharply.

Of course she had been here before, several times. Everyone in the UK had. But the scale of the site, the sheer *bravura* of it, always took her by surprise.

Stonehenge.

Quite simply, Stonehenge was stunning.

A source of fascination to her for a long time, Zoe knew all the myths: that this ring of towering stones was an ancient calendar; or an ancient observatory; that the bluestones—the smaller two-metre-high dolerite stones that formed a horseshoe-shaped arc *within* the far more famous trilithons—had been brought to the Salisbury Plain around the year 2700 BC by some unknown tribe from the Preseli Hills *over 240 kilometres away* in distant Wales. To this day, many believe that the bluestones, even on bitterly cold winter days, remain warm to the touch.

It would be another 150 years, around 2570 BC, before the spectacular trilithons were raised around this mini-henge of bluestones. But the date is important: in 2570 BC the Egyptian pharaoh Khufu was completing his famous work on the Giza plateau in Egypt, the Great Pyramid.

Over the years, Zoe knew, cosmologists and astrologers had tried to link Stonehenge with the Great Pyramid, but without success. The only confirmed link was the closely matching dates of their construction.

Other peculiarities of Stonehenge intrigued her.

Like the rare green cynobacterium that grew on the great trilithons themselves. A variety of lichen, it was a true oddity, an uncommon hybrid of algae and fungus that grew only on exposed coastlines—yet Stonehenge was eighty kilometres from the nearest sea, the Bristol Channel. The moss-like substance gave the stones a mottled, uneven aspect.

And then, of course, there were the unexplained theories about the site's location: the unique way the Sun and Moon rise over the 51st parallel; and the unusually high number of neolithic sites running the length of the British Isles on the same degree of longitude as Stonehenge.

In the final analysis, only one thing about Stonehenge could be said with any degree of certainty: for over 4,500 years it had withstood the ravages of wind, rain and time itself, offering a multitude of questions and very few answers.

'Okay,' Zoe said as she drove. 'How are we going to tackle this? Thoughts, anyone?'

'Thoughts?' Lachlan said. 'How about this: that there's *no precedent* for what we're about to do. Over the years, scholars and wackos have linked Stonehenge with the Sun and the Moon, with virgins and druids, with solstices and eclipses, but never with Jupiter. If

Wizard's hypothesis is correct and this Firestone is the real deal, then we're going to see something that hasn't been seen for over 4,500 years.'

Julius said, 'Can I add that the good folk at English Heritage don't look kindly on people who step over the rope at Stonehenge and walk among the stones, let alone lunatics like us wanting to perform ancient occult rituals. There'll be security guards.'

'Leave the guards to me,' Zoe said. 'You just handle the occult ritual.'

The twins pulled out Wizard's notes again, gazed at the diagram of Stonehenge:

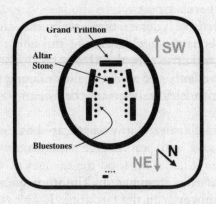

'In his notes, Wizard says that the Ramesean Stone at Stonehenge is the Altar Stone,' Julius said. 'But what about the Grand Trilithon? It's the signature element of Stonehenge.'

'No, I'd go with the Altar Stone, too,' Lachlan said. 'It's the focal point of the structure. It's also made of bluestone, laid at the same time as the original ring of bluestones, so it's older than the trilithons. And fortunately for us, it's still there.'

Over four-and-a-half millennia, Stonehenge had been pilfered by locals searching for stones to use as walls or as millstones. Nearly all the bluestones of the henge were gone. The bigger trilithons had survived— at over six metres tall (seven in the case of the Grand Trilithon) they had just been too big for the local peasants to move.

Lachlan turned to Alby: 'What do *you* reckon, kid?'

Alby looked up, surprised to be asked his opinion. He had thought that, as kids, he and Lily were just being brought along for the ride, assigned to Zoe to be kept safe.

'Well?' Lachlan said expectantly. 'Jack West thinks you're a clever one and Jack's a notoriously hard judge. And Zoe here doesn't hang out with losers—I mean, hey, look at us.'

Lily raised an eyebrow at that.

Julius added, 'And weren't you the one who figured out the connection between the Titanic Rising and Stonehenge?'

Alby swallowed. Lily smiled at him reassuringly. She had long ago become used to this kind of adult treatment.

'I, well,' Alby stammered. 'The stone we're after has to fit some way with the Firestone. I can't see the Firestone fitting onto the Grand Trilithon in any practical way. But the Altar Stone, if re-erected, would be at the very heart of the structure. The other thing to remember is the rising of Titan to the north-east—'

'Ah, yes, yes. Good point,' Julius said.

They had gone through this earlier.

As Alby had explained briefly at the meeting in Dubai, the Titanic Rising and Sinking occurred only when the Earth, Jupiter and Saturn were in alignment, something that occurred approximately once every 400 years, and which—clearly by no coincidence—was happening right now.

The 'rising' of Saturn's largest moon, Titan, actually preceded the passage of Saturn itself, rising up from behind the great hulking mass of Jupiter. Soon after this rising, Saturn would sink again behind Jupiter. Due to each planet's angled orbit around the Sun—its ecliptic—this upward–downward motion occurred eight times in the month that the planets remained aligned.

Seen from Stonehenge, first Jupiter would appear on the north-eastern horizon, then Titan, then Saturn.

'So why is this Titanic Rising so important?' Zoe asked. 'What does Titan or Jupiter or Saturn have to do with the Sa-Benben and the Dark Star?'

'The connection with the Sa-Benben is straightforward,' Julius said. 'It's the connection between Stonehenge and the Great Pyramid that people have been searching for for centuries. Our theory is simple: the Pyramid is a temple to our Sun. Stonehenge is a temple to the Dark Sun.'

'And the two are most certainly linked geographically,' Lachlan added. 'You know how the bluestones were brought to the Salisbury Plain from the Preseli Hills in Wales?'

'Yes, Lachlan,' Zoe said patiently. 'I *do* have two degrees in archaeology. I just didn't do the subjects on Crazy British Neolithic Cosmology that you obviously majored in.'

'Then you know about the rectangle formed by the four original Station Stones that once surrounded Stonehenge?'

'Yes.'

'I don't,' Lily said.

To illustrate, Lachlan opened a book, showing Lily a picture of Stonehenge's layout. Arrayed around the circular henge in a perfect rectangle were four stones known as the 'Station Stones'. They formed a 5:12 rectangle.

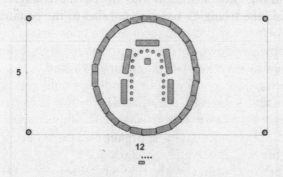

Lachlan said, 'Now, if you draw a diagonal across that rectangle, simple Pythagorean math tells us that the resulting right-angled triangle is a 5:12:13 triangle.'

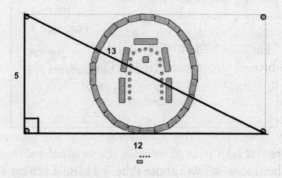

He drew a triangle on the picture with a pencil.

'Following me?' he said.

'So far,' Lily said.

'Nice triangle, isn't it?'

'I guess.'

Lachlan then pulled out a map of the United Kingdom. He indicated Stonehenge at the bottom of the map, and then drew the same 5:12:13 triangle on the map using Stonehenge as the tip of the triangle and keeping the triangle's baseline parallel to the equator.

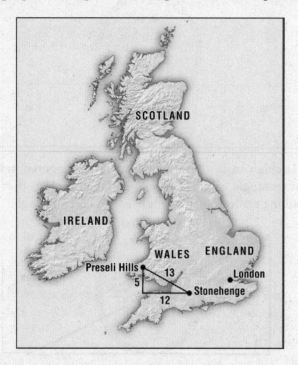

'The 5:12:13 triangle reveals the original location of the bluestones in Wales: the Preseli Hills,' Lachlan said. 'This is pretty exceptional geography for a primitive tribe. It's *so* exceptional that some believe the ancients had outside help.'

'I thought you were going to prove a link between Stonehenge and the Great Pyramid,' Zoe said.

Lachlan smiled. He winked to Lily. 'Remember how I said it was a nice triangle?'

'Yeah . . .'

'Well, if you extend the hypotenuse of this wonderful triangle like this . . .'

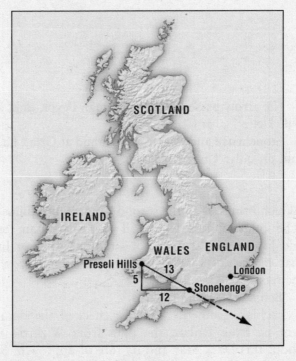

'. . . see what it runs through.'

Lachlan turned to a map of the world and did precisely that.

'No way . . .' Lily said, when she saw the finished product.

The arrow passed directly through Egypt, right at the Nile Delta . . . at Giza.

'Stonehenge and the Great Pyramid at Giza,' Lachlan said proudly. 'United at last.'

'Which brings us to the second connection,' Julius said. 'The connection between all this and Titan, Saturn and Jupiter. You see, it's not Titan or Saturn or Jupiter that matters. It's what lies hidden *behind them* that matters.'

'Behind them?' Lily asked.

Lachlan grinned. 'Yes. We checked the data you sent us from Dubai, the data from Wizard's notes about this Dark Star and its rate of approach. Seems it's coming at us from *behind* Jupiter. Thus the importance of this celestial event, the rising of Saturn behind Jupiter. It is, to put it simply, beyond value, because it will allow us, for the very first time, to see this fearsome Dark Star.'

'How?' Zoe asked, turning in the driver's seat. 'I thought we couldn't see it in our light spectrum.'

'Well, we won't see *it*, we'll see the dark space that it occupies,' Julius said. 'Now, are you familiar with the concept of space–time?' Julius asked.

'Or more specifically the *curvature* of space–time,' Lachlan added.

'Yes, good clarification, brother,' Julius said.

'Thank you.'

'More or less,' Zoe said. 'The gravitational pull of a planet *bends* the space around it. I once heard it compared to a stretched-out rubber sheet with marbles placed on it . . .'

'That's right,' Lachlan said, 'and each marble makes a slight depression in the rubber sheet, indicating the curvature of space–time. So if you were in a spaceship travelling past these planets, your trajectory will actually bend as you pass each planet, unless of course you apply more power.'

'Yes . . .'

Julius said, 'Well, it's the same with light. Light bends, too, as it passes through the gravitational fields of planets and stars.'

Lachlan: 'And big planets like Jupiter bend it more than small planets like Mercury.'

'Correct,' Julius said. 'So tonight, as we look out at Jupiter from Stonehenge, and see Saturn rise behind it, we will, if only for a moment, thanks to the peculiar bending of light around those two planets, get a glimpse of the section of space hidden *behind* Jupiter.'

Zoe frowned. 'And if the Sa-Benben is set in place at that time—positioned atop the Ramesean Stone of Stonehenge—what happens then?'

Julius looked at Lachlan.

Lachlan looked at Julius.

Then they both turned to face Zoe and shrugged together.

'That,' Julius said, 'is what we're going to find out.'

The car sped into the night.

STONEHENGE
5 DECEMBER, 2007, 3:22 A.M.

They parked on the gravel shoulder a few hundred yards from the henge.

The moon shone down on the wide plain like a great spotlight, illuminating the relentlessly flat landscape all the way to the horizon.

Stonehenge stood at the junction of the A303 and a smaller road.

Two security guards stood near the great shadowy stones, silhouettes in the moonlight. They saw the Honda stop, but did not investigate: travellers from London often stopped to gaze at the stones while they stretched their legs.

Zoe stepped closer, to within fifty metres of the two guards and then quickly raised a boxy gun-like object fitted with a handgrip and trigger, aimed it at the guards and called, '*Hey!*'

The guards looked over.

Zoe pulled the trigger. There was an instantaneous flash from her device accompanied by a deep sonic *whump*, and immediately the two guards dropped to the ground like marionettes whose strings had been cut, out cold.

'What *the hell* was that!' Julius asked, coming up alongside Zoe.

'And where can we get one!' Lachlan added.

'LaSon-V stun gun,' Zoe said. 'It's a non-lethal incapacitator. Laser flash accompanied by a sonic charge. Originally designed for use on planes by sky marshals to subdue hijackers without the risk of shooting out a window and disrupting cabin pressure. The sonic charge would usually be enough to knock out an aggressive attacker, but the laser flash blinds them too. No after-effects except for a splitting headache. Some people think this is what was used to disorient Princess Diana's driver just before her fatal car crash.'

'Okaaaay . . .' Julius said. 'On that cheery note, let's get to work.'

A gap was cut in the wire fence surrounding the henge and Zoe and the twins quickly rolled a handcart packed with equipment through it, followed by the kids.

They came to the stones and paused for a moment, awed.

The towering pillars of rock soared into the sky above them, looming large in the moonlight—powerful, ominous, *ancient*. The biggest of them, the lone pillar of the Grand Trilithon, rose to a massive 7.9 metres, a conical stone 'tongue' at its peak indicative of the lintel that had once lain across its top.

'What time is the "Titanic Rising?"' Zoe asked.

'Jupiter should already be on the horizon,' Alby said, setting up a serious-looking telescope on the grass among the stones. 'Titan will rise over it at 3.49 a.m., Saturn two minutes later, then, as it rises, a gap will appear between Saturn and Jupiter.'

'And that's when we see our Dark Star.'

'Correct.'

Zoe checked her watch. It was 3:25. 'Let's move. We've got twenty-four minutes.'

By the light of a penlight, Julius examined a more recent plan of Stonehenge, showing the layout of the stones that still stood:

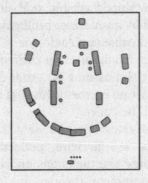

'Three of the five central trilithons are still intact,' he said. 'One upright from the Grand Trilithon still stands, and one upright down here, at the bottom right. Might be an issue.'

'What about the Altar Stone?' Lachlan said.

'It's fallen.'

'Which one is it?' Zoe asked.

'This one,' Lachlan hustled among the towering stones, came to a fallen one, a great horizontal slab, half-buried in the grass within the central ring of stones. It was about eight feet long, slim and lean. A small rectangular hole in the earth lay next to it.

Lachlan examined one of its ends and called, 'It's got

a depression in it! Square in shape. Maybe twenty by twenty centimetres.'

'That would match the Sa-Benben,' Zoe said.

She stared at the horizontal slab, amazed at what she was about to say: 'Okay, then. Let's re-erect it.'

They moved quickly but gently, not wanting to damage the 4,500-year-old stones.

Slings were wrapped around the Altar Stone and it was gently lifted by an A-frame pulley system fitted with a diesel-powered cable spooler.

While this was going on, Lily cleared out the hole in the ground near the base of the Altar Stone. Alby was training his telescope on the north-east horizon.

'I see Jupiter!' he called.

Through his telescope, he saw a small orange dot hovering on the horizon, perfectly aligned with Stonehenge's outer ring of lintels and its famous Heel Stone.

'Hurry!' Zoe called to the twins.

'I am not going to hurry with a national treasure,' Julius said indignantly.

Slowly, very slowly, the spooler reeled the great stone slab upward, pulling it vertical until—*whump*—Julius jumped at the sound—it slid abruptly downwards, slotting into the hole where over four thousand years ago it had originally stood.

Zoe checked her watch.

3:48 a.m.

One minute to go.

*

It was then that she removed something from her backpack.

The top piece of the Golden Capstone.

The Sa-Benben.

The Firestone.

It was stunning to behold. It glimmered in the night, its golden sides shining, its crystalline peak sparkling.

Zoe climbed a stepladder and stood at the top of the now-erect Altar Stone.

She saw the depression in the flat top of the stone, saw that, yes, it matched the size of the Firestone's base perfectly.

'All right, then . . .' she said softly to herself. 'The Great Pyramid and Stonehenge. Let's see what you got.'

With great reverence, she placed the square-based Firestone in the matching recess of the Altar Stone and suddenly, the Altar Stone took on a wholly new appearance: it looked like a mini-obelisk, surrounded by the trilithons of the henge, guardians in the night.

Her watch hit 3:49.

'I see Titan . . .' Alby said.

Through his high-powered telescope, the greatest moon of Saturn appeared as barely a dot behind the large orange orb that was Jupiter. It rose behind it, looking like a very dim star.

A minute passed. The twins hit 'RECORD' on some digital video cameras they'd set up around the henge. They held ready in their hands still cameras as well.

Another minute passed.

'And I see Saturn . . . *wow*!'

A larger dot rose up behind Jupiter, moving ever-so-slowly, its rings barely apparent, before it cleared the horizon of Jupiter and a gap appeared between the two planets.

At which point Stonehenge, silent and mysterious for over forty-five centuries, suddenly and spectacularly came to life.

An invisible light-force shot over the horizon from the Dark Sun, lanced over the Heel Stone in a dead-straight line, shot through the outer circle of lintels before it *slammed* into the Firestone sitting atop the central Altar Stone.

The Firestone blazed to life.

Brilliant purple light flared around it, illuminating the ring of trilithons in an unearthly glow.

Then shafts of this purple light—bright, strong shafts of the stuff, six of them—lanced outwards from the Firestone like the spokes of a wheel and *hit* some of the uprights of the trilithons.

Zoe and the others could only stare in stunned awe at the lightshow, a lightshow that had not been seen for over 4,500 years.

And then something else happened.

The lichens on the surface of the trilithons—the strange algae-fungus that had no business existing this far inland—began to glow a pale green.

And suddenly, as this faint glowing of the lichens combined with the cracks and indentations of the stone uprights themselves, *images* began to form on the trilithons, images that hadn't been discernible before.

Zoe stared in wonder.

The images on the trilithons looked strangely familiar, kind of like the continents of Earth—but not *exactly* like them. They were somehow different, the familiar coastlines warped. A couple of the trilithons depicted what appeared to be the *edges* of continents.

Before   *During*

'It's the world,' Lachlan breathed. 'They all combine to create a map of the Earth, millions of years ago.'

'*What?*' Zoe whispered, not realising that she was whispering.

Lachlan nodded at the glowing images in the stones: 'They're the continents of our planet. They're in their current positions, but before rising oceans gave them their current coastlines. Whoever built this, built it a *long* time ago.'

Zoe swung back to gaze at the glowing images on the stones, and saw that he was right.

There was Africa . . .

And that looked a little like Asia . . .

The stone depicting Africa was pierced by two of the laser-like purple light-shafts: one shaft penetrating it near the northern end, the second shaft hitting it at the very southern tip.

'You're getting all this?' Zoe called.

The twins were indeed clicking away on their digital cameras, taking photos of the illuminated stones and light-shafts. At the same time, their video cameras also captured it all.

'What about those two?' Zoe asked, indicating the two uprights that appeared to depict the edges of continents.

'Oceans, I guess,' Julius said, 'but it's hard to tell which ones, given the altered coastlines. The world has three main oceans, the Pacific, Indian and Atlantic Oceans. A third ocean might have been on one of the fallen uprights. Which makes sense. No one has ever figured out why Stonehenge has ten uprights. This would explain it: seven continents and three oceans.'

Zoe blinked.

Holy, holy shit . . .

Then Alby called, 'She's sinking! Saturn's sinking!'

A moment later, everything went dark.

The Firestone's purple light went out and the great stone circle was dark once more.

Zoe gazed at the twins and the kids. 'Bet you haven't seen that before. Come on,' she hurriedly re-erected her stepladder, heading for the Firestone. 'We're done. Lachlan, Julius: lower the Altar Stone, put it back exactly where you found it. Then we have to motor. Wizard and Jack are not gonna believe this.'

When the two security guards awoke two hours later, groggy and dazed, they found Stonehenge undamaged, seemingly untouched.

There were several sets of footprints among the central stones, suggesting unusual activity, but nothing was missing. Except for the hole that had once housed the Altar Stone—it had been cleared of dirt—everything, thankfully, was where it should be.

The next day there would be reports from locals of a glowing purple light emanating from the area, but they were quickly dismissed. Every year there were at least a dozen UFO sightings over Salisbury Plain and numerous other crackpot claims.

And so as dawn came, Stonehenge stood once again, tall and silent, maintaining its centuries-old watch over the ancient landscape.

THIRD ORDEAL

JACK WEST JR AND THE PHILOSOPHER'S STONE

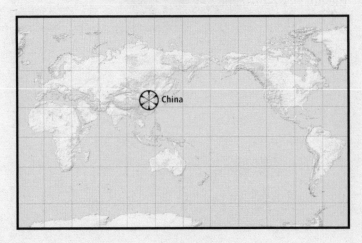

CHINA

5 DECEMBER, 2007

5 DAYS BEFORE THE 1ST DEADLINE

SICHUAN MOUNTAINS, CHINA
5 DECEMBER, 2007, 1735 HOURS

Around the same time Zoe and the twins were watching the wondrous lightshow at Stonehenge, Jack and Wizard were soaring over the wild, rugged mountains of central China in the hold of their stolen Hind helicopter, aware that a sizeable portion of the Chinese People's Liberation Army—some 1.2 million men—were at that very moment mobilising to hunt them down.

With them were Stretch, Astro, Scimitar, Vulture and the injured Tank Tanaka.

Sky Monster had taken the *Halicarnassus* south, just over the Burmese border, where he waited patiently for the extraction call.

'It is absolutely imperative that we get the Philosopher's Stone,' Wizard said to Jack when they were alone in a corner of the hold. He munched hungrily on some food while he put on clean clothes.

'I got that impression from your notes,' Jack said. 'That's where we're going right now. It's also why we needed to get this helicopter.'

Jack told Wizard about the meeting in Dubai, about the new coalition of nations helping them in this quest—including America and Saudi Arabia—and most importantly, what they had so far deduced from Wizard's research.

'But I need to know more, Max,' he concluded. 'Your notes were good, but we could only piece together so much.'

'Yes, yes . . .'

'For instance, the part where you said the Sa-Benben and the Philosopher's Stone were central to everything. Why?'

Wizard's head snapped up. 'Good God, Jack, you didn't bring the Firestone with you, did you? We can't allow our enemies to have both it and Laozi's Stone.'

'No, I didn't,' Jack said. 'Zoe has it. In England. She's gone to Stonehenge with the Firestone, the twins and the kids.'

'You got in touch with the twins? Oh, *excellent*,' Wizard said, sighing deeply. 'And Stonehenge. Stonehenge and the Sa-Benben. But, wait, it must be done during the Titanic Ris—'

'Got it covered.'

Wizard stared off into space, smiled. 'I only wish I could have been there to see it. I'm glad you figured that out.'

'Wasn't me. It was Lily's friend, Alby.'

'Ah, Alby. Smart boy. And such a good friend to Lily. As things get more difficult, she will need companions like him . . .' Wizard's voice trailed off, his eyes glazing over into a deep sadness.

As he spoke, Jack scanned the torture scars on the old man's face, the bruises and gashes, the dried blood on his beard. Wizard had been through the wringer in that prison.

'Oh, Jack,' Wizard said. 'The situation is dire. Most dire. It's like nothing we've ever encountered before.'

'Tell me.'

'The world has reached a critical stage in its existence. A turning point has come, a *testing* point, a time at which the Earth can either renew itself or be destroyed. The Tartarus Rotation was just the beginning, merely the first step in a far larger drama.'

'The coming of this Dark Sun?' Jack prompted.

'The coming of the Dark Sun is only part of it. There are many unexplained things in our world, Jack, and with the coming of the zero-point field, this Dark Sun, many of them will reveal their true purpose. The Great Pyramid and its Capstone are just the start. Stonehenge. Nazca. Easter Island. It all comes together now, with the coming of the Dark Sun. A coalescence of ancient things. But the greatest thing to fear, as always, is man himself.'

'Why?'

Wizard said, 'Let me backtrack.'

He grabbed a sheet from his notes, indicated a picture on it that Jack recalled seeing before:

Wizard said, 'This is the common symbol for the Great Machine. Now, as you deduced correctly from my notes, the Machine is simply our planet. As the image shows, at six locations around our planet are six underground shrines, pyramidal in shape and inverted, but gigantic, and all pointing down toward the centre of the Earth. Note the downward-pointing pyramids in the picture, with the white rectangular pillars sticking out of them.

'While the Machine is depicted in this image as a flat two-dimensional structure, we should picture it three-dimensionally, with the six *vertices* situated just below the Earth's surface, arrayed around the spherical planet. Like this.'

Wizard drew a rough sketch:

'Now, at each of these locations, a *cleansed* pillar must be set in place, the pillars being small oblong-shaped uncut diamonds whose whereabouts are largely unknown.'

'Not totally unknown,' Jack said. 'We're working on that.'

'Oh, good. Now, let me come to the Ramesean Stones, and the most unique part that they play in this challenge. We call them "Ramesean" stones but their true name is actually "Guidestones". The Six Guide-stones of Ra's Dark Twin. For when each comes into contact with the Sun-charged Sa-Benben, they reveal something about this Machine.

'For instance, at Stonehenge: when the Sa-Benben is placed atop the guidestone there at the rising of Saturn over Jupiter, the *locations* of the six vertices will be revealed. How this actually occurs at the site of Stonehenge, I don't know. Hopefully, Zoe now does.'

'And the Philosopher's Stone?' Jack asked.

Wizard again riffled through his notes, came up with another image:

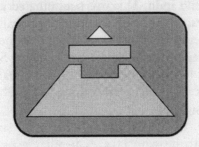

'This is a carving of Laozi's Stone,' Wizard said, 'otherwise known as the Philosopher's Stone. Note the pyramidal capstone hovering above it and the rectangular recess in it.

'To cleanse a pillar, one needs three things: the Sa-Benben, the Philosopher's Stone, and one of the pillars. You place the pillar inside the recess in the Philosopher's Stone, close the lid, and then place the charged Sa-Benben on the lid. The pillar is thus cleansed and is then ready for placement in one of the six vertices.'

'Which is why the Sa-Benben and the Philosopher's Stone are central to everything . . .' Jack said, understanding.

'Correct. The next most important Ramesean Stone is the Killing Stone of the Maya: when united with the Sa-Benben, it will specify the astronomical dates by

which the pillars must be set in place at the vertices.
Now, I already understand that the placing of the six
pillars is divided into two distinct timeframes—the first
two pillars must be set in place within the next week or
so; the remaining four must be placed later, about three
months from now, just before the equinox on March 20,
2008, when the Dark Sun will make its long-awaited
return.'

Jack's mind spun. This was sounding very big indeed:
stars, stones, pillars, vertices, astronomical dates. In a
vague corner of his mind he recalled that the Americans
had said they possessed the Mayan Killing Stone.

Clearing his head, he brought Wizard back: 'So why
in all this is *man* the greatest thing to fear?'

Wizard sighed.

'Because of the rewards,' he said simply. 'The
rewards. "To he who lays each pillar goes a fabulous
reward." So it is said on the walls of Abydos. It was
there that I found the six rewards listed underneath a
carving of Rameses II and his father, Seti I—a carving
that scholars have long dismissed as a mere adornment.
The six rewards were listed as: *knowledge, heat, sight,
death, life* and *power*.'

Wizard's face went grim. 'Jack. What the rewards are
exactly, no one knows, but by all accounts, they are of
immense value. For instance, I believe *heat* is a fabulous
power source, an unending power source; and *knowledge* is some great insight that we are yet to discover.'

Jack listened intently to what Wizard was saying.
Power sources, great knowledge. Suddenly the US–Saudi
interest in the success of his mission made more sense,
not to mention China's grab for the Firestone at his
farm.

Wizard said, 'Given these stakes, and the arrival of this Dark Sun and the possible end of our world, I can see nations taking great risks to acquire and then place these pillars. And if history teaches us nothing, it teaches us this: where items of great worth are at stake, men will do anything to possess them.'

Just then, the cargo hold was plunged into red emergency lighting, a buzzer sounding repeatedly. The intercom over Jack's head crackled.

'*Huntsman, we're coming up on the Wu Gorge system,*' Astro's voice said. '*ETA is nine minutes and we're about to pop up on their radars like a big friggin' Christmas light. I hope you're right about this.*'

'Come on,' Jack said, standing. 'We'd better suit up. The target is guarded and we're on top of the local Most Wanted List, so we'll be going in hard and going in fast. Just stay close to me. It's time for us to finish what you started, it's time to get the Philosopher's Stone.'

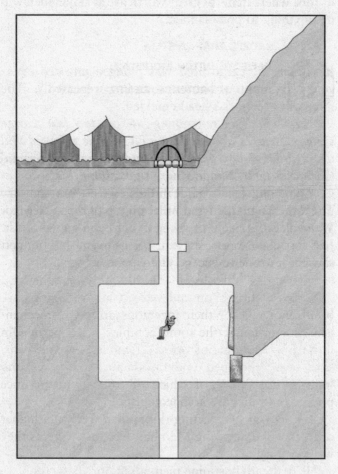

THE ENTRY CHAMBER

Colonel Mao Gongli swore loudly.

In the four days since he'd captured Max Epper and sent him off to Xintan for interrogation, his force of Chinese troops had made little headway through the underground tunnel system that protected Laozi's legendary stone.

Chiefly, their progress had been hindered by numerous anti-intruder devices: booby traps.

Mao cursed himself. He should have known better.

For over three thousand years, Chinese tombs have been renowned for their ingenious protective mechanisms: for instance, the tomb complex of Emperor Qin in Xi'an—the home of China's famous terracotta warriors—was equipped with automatic crossbows and 'murder holes', out of which oil and liquid tar once poured onto unwary archaeologists.

But the traps protecting this system were of a higher order, beyond anything Mao had seen, as clever as they were vicious.

He'd already lost nine men, all in horrific ways.

The first three to die had not got past the very

first threshold of the trap system: the cylindrical doorway set into the wall. The doorway had rotated abruptly, trapping each man inside it . . . before dropping a foul-smelling, skin-searing yellow liquid from its hollow ceiling onto the trapped man, a liquid Mao now knew to be a primitive form of sulphuric acid.

So his men had blown open that door with C-2 plastic explosive and entered an inner chamber, the only exit from which was a low pipe-like tunnel on the far side.

Thus the next man to die had been lying on his stomach, belly-crawling through the pipe, when he had been *skewered through the fucking heart* by an iron spike that had risen up from an innocuous-looking hole in the floor. It had slowly and painfully penetrated the man's entire body, punching out through his back.

Two more men had suffered a similar fate—from other holes in the floor of the tunnel—before Mao's chief lieutenant had hit upon the idea of pouring quick-setting cement into the murderous holes, plugging them up.

And so cement was sent for—it would ultimately come from the Three Gorges Dam a hundred miles away—and after a two-day wait, they passed through the pipe tunnel.

But still they lost men in the *next* chamber: a long and magnificent downward-sloping hallway that was lined with silent terracotta statues on both sides.

Here one of Mao's troopers had died when a terracotta warrior with a wide yawning mouth had suddenly vomited a spray of liquid mercury into the hapless trooper's face. The trooper had screamed horribly as the mercury stuck to his eyeballs. The thick liquid clogged every pore of his face, slowly poisoning his very blood. He died in agony, hours later.

More quick-setting cement was brought in.

It was poured into the mouth of the offending terracotta warrior, stopping it up. Planning to do the same at every other statue in the hall, Mao's men had moved on.

Only for another trooper to be killed almost immediately when the second terracotta warrior statue shot a crossbow bolt out of its *eye-socket* into his eye.

As a third soldier poured cement into the adjoining statue, he managed to dodge that statue's lethal defence-mechanism: a primitive fragmentation charge, set off by a small amount of gunpowder hidden within the statue's eyes. A volley of tiny lead ball-bearings had blasted out from the statue's eye-sockets, narrowly missing the Chinese soldier but causing him to lurch backwards—

—and slip on the wet floor of the sloping passageway and slide out of control down its full length before he just *fell off* the bottom end of the passageway—dropping into darkness, disappearing from his teammates' view. They soon discovered that he had fallen into a deep and dark underground chasm at the end of the passageway, a chasm of unknown depth.

And they hadn't got beyond that chasm.

Which was why, earlier that morning, word had been sent to Xintan, demanding that Wizard and Tank be brought back to see if they might reveal the secrets of Laozi's trap system.

The Submerged Village

The four Chinese sentries left up on the surface of the trap system all looked skyward at the sound of an approaching helicopter, their alertness slackening when they saw that it was one of their own: a Hind gunship with PLA markings.

The big chopper landed on a floating helipad nestled among the half-submerged stone huts, blowing debris and spray through the alleyways of the ancient village.

The sentries ambled over to the chopper, their rifles slung lazily over their shoulders—only to see the side door of the gunship whip open and all of a sudden find themselves staring at the wrong ends of some Type-56 assault rifles and MP-7 submachine-guns.

Dressed in the Chinese Army uniforms of the helicopter's crew, Jack West Jr and his team had arrived.

The Entry Chamber

There were two more low-ranking Chinese sentries in the entry chamber—the same chamber that Wizard had marvelled at only four days previously, before he had been captured by Mao, before Mao had murdered his gentle assistant, Chow.

Suddenly an odd-looking silver grenade came flying down into the entry chamber from the well-shaft.

The grenade bounced on the floor of the chamber, missing the wide hole in its centre, but causing the two sentries to turn.

It went off.

A sun-like flash filled the ancient room, astonishingly bright, and both sentries fell to their knees, clutching their eyes, screaming, blinded, their retinas nearly burned clean off. The blindness wouldn't be permanent, but it would last for two whole days.

Then Jack came swinging out of the entry shaft, swooping down into the chamber, his boots thumping hard against the stone floor, his gun raised.

He keyed his radio. 'Guards are down. Chamber is clear. Come on down.'

It was only then that he noticed the bodybags.

There were nine of them: containing the soldiers the Chinese had lost inside the trap system.

As Wizard and the others joined him in the chamber—Stretch binding and gagging the two whimpering guards, Wizard gasping at the stench of the bodybags—Jack examined the entry chamber's feature wall.

He beheld the magnificent jewel-encrusted carving of the Mystery of the Circles, ten feet wide and stunning.

And directly below it: a thin recessed doorway with curved walls. Above the doorway was a small inscription of the Philosopher's Stone just like the one he'd seen earlier, complete with the Sa-Benben hovering over it:

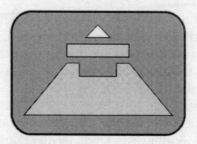

The curved cylindrical doorway was roughly the size of a coffin, and on one side of it there were three cast-iron levers and the Chinese symbol for 'dwelling':

The ceiling of this tiny space was crudely stopped up with concrete—presumably plugging a pipe out of which fell some horrific liquid.

'Not exactly elegant,' Jack said. 'But effective.'

Wizard shook his head. 'This system was designed by the great Chinese architect, Sun Mai, a contemporary of Confucius and, like him, once a student of Laozi. Sun Mai was a brilliant craftsman, a man of rare flair. He was also a castle-builder, fortifications and the like, so he was well-suited to this task. And how does Mao tackle him? With concrete. *Concrete.* Oh, how China has changed over the centuries.'

'The trap system,' Jack said seriously, gazing at the darkness beyond the open doorway-recess. 'Any research? Like the trap order?'

'You cannot study this system's traps beforehand,' Wizard said. 'It possesses multiple thresholds, through which one passes by answering a riddle *in situ*.'

'Riddles *in situ*. My favourite . . .'

'But riddles related to the works of Laozi.'

'Oh, even better.'

Wizard examined the concreted doorway and the chamber beyond it, then he nodded at the bodybags. 'It seems our Chinese rivals have met with some considerable difficulty. If they'd asked me the right questions during my interrogation, I might have been more helpful.'

'So what's the trick?' West said.

Wizard smiled. 'What is Laozi's most well-known contribution to philosophy?'

'The Yin–Yang.'

'Yes. The concept of *duality*. The idea that there are two of everything. Elemental pairs. Good and evil, light and dark, and all that. But there's more to it: every pair is *connected*. In the good, there is some evil, and in the evil, some good.'

'Which means . . .' Jack prompted.

Wizard didn't answer. Let him figure it out for himself.

' . . . if there's two of everything, then there are two entrances to this system,' Jack said.

Wizard nodded. 'And?'

Jack frowned. 'The second entrance is *connected* to this entrance?'

'Well done, my friend. Full marks.'

Wizard strode to the wide circular well-shaft in the floor, the one that matched the entry shaft in the ceiling, and peered down into it.

'There is indeed a second entrance to this trap system. Down there.'

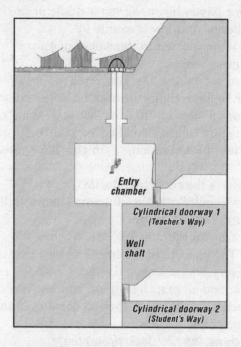

Wizard said, 'The tunnel system branching off this chamber is called the Teacher's Way. A second tunnel system situated below us is called the Student's Way.'

'So how are they connected?'

'Simple. They must be tackled simultaneously. Two people, one in each tunnel, moving alternately through their respective traps, each disabling the other's traps.'

'You have got to be kidding me . . .' Jack had survived many trap systems over the years, but he had never encountered anything like this.

'It's the ultimate trust exercise,' Wizard said. 'As I set

off in the upper tunnel, I trigger a trap. That trap is nullified not by me, but by *you* in the lower tunnel. My life is in your hands. Then the opposite occurs—you trigger a trap, and I must save you. This is why our Chinese friends are experiencing such difficulty in there. They don't know of the lower route. So they use concrete and brute force, and in the typical Chinese way'—he nodded at the bodybags—'they just weather the losses and make very inefficient progress. They'll eventually get through, but it will cost them many lives and much time.'

Jack bit his lip, thinking. 'All right then. Stretch. You take Scimitar, and find the lower entrance. I'll enter through here with Astro and Wizard. Tank, you stay here with Pooh Bear. Keep in radio contact with Vulture up in the chopper, because I suspect we'll be needing a rapid evac. All right, everyone. Buckle up. We're going in.'

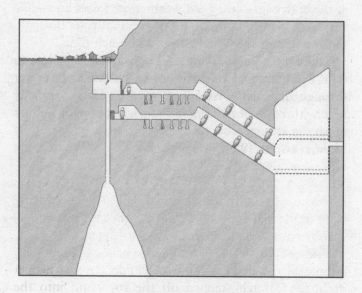

**LAOZI'S TRAP SYSTEM
ENTRY TUNNELS**

The Cylindrical Doorway (Lower)

Minutes later, Stretch's voice came over West's earpiece: *'We've found the second entrance. About sixty feet below you. Thin doorway, cut into the wall of the shaft. Identical to yours. But intact. No concrete clogging its upper recess.'*

'Step into it,' West instructed.

Down in the shaft, Stretch and Scimitar were hanging from individual ropes in front of a thin recessed doorway hewn into the wall of the vertical shaft.

The shaft itself dropped away beneath them into infinite black, depth unknown. Guided by his helmet flashlight, Stretch stepped off the rope and into the doorway . . .

. . . only to see the entire doorway suddenly rotate around him on its axis, its curved walls spinning ninety degrees so that the entry gap was sealed, and he found himself trapped in the coffin-sized recess, bounded on every side, with nowhere to go.

Claustrophobia gripped him. His rapid breathing echoed in his ears. His flashlight's glow was too close against the tight walls.

Then something gurgled in the void above him and Stretch's blood went cold.

'Er, Jack . . .'

Up in the doorway of the Teacher's Way, Jack assessed the three cast-iron levers in the wall, one on top of the other, next to the Chinese symbol for 'dwelling': none of the levers bore *any* marks or carvings; they were completely plain.

'*Er, Jack . . .*' came Stretch's voice. '*Whatever you have to do up there, please do it soon . . .*'

'Pull the bottom lever,' Wizard said. 'Now.'

Jack yanked on the bottom lever—

—and at the same moment, down in Stretch's route, a slab of stone slid across the ceiling and the cylinder rotated another ninety degrees, and suddenly, Stretch saw a new chamber on the other side, a cube-shaped stone room.

He quickly stepped out of the deadly cylinder-doorway and said, 'I'm through. Thanks, guys. Scimitar, your turn.'

In the upper tunnel, Jack turned to Wizard: 'How did you know?'

Wizard said, 'Famous quote from Laozi. "In thinking, keep to the simple. In conflict, be fair and generous. In dwelling, live close to the ground." Since our clue was "Dwelling", I picked the lever that was closest to the ground.'

'Nice.'

After getting Scimitar through the same way, Jack,

Wizard and Astro just stepped through their open entry door, its trap disabled by the concrete of Mao's troops.

The Crawling Tunnel

Both sets of men were now met by identical cube-shaped rooms.

Four life-sized terracotta warriors—all magnificently detailed—stood in the corners of each room. In West's room, their mouths had been plugged with cement, while in Stretch's they yawned wide, revealing only darkness within.

'Don't step near the statues,' Wizard warned.

On the far side of each room was a low tunnel at floor level. Barely two feet square and pipe-like, it was the only exit from the stone room.

Jack peered into his: it stretched for about a hundred metres, maybe more. Along its length were numerous tennis-ball-sized holes cut into the floor, all of which had been filled with concrete.

'Spike holes,' Wizard said. 'Stretch?'

'*We got a tunnel down here, low to the ground, looks long, and it appears we can only get through it by crawling on our stomachs. Lots of holes in its floor.*'

Jack said, 'Careful with those holes. Iron spikes.'

Wizard found an inscription above his tunnel, this time accompanied by a single lever that could be pushed up or down. The inscription read:

'Genius,' Wizard said. 'It's the Chinese symbol for *genius.*'

At either extremity of the lever were two images: above it was a carving of a beautiful tree, below it was a picture of a very plain seed.

'Ah . . .' Wizard said, nodding. '"To see things in the seed, that is genius." Another maxim of Laozi. Pull the lever down, Jack.'

West did so.

'Okay, Stretch, you should be safe,' Wizard said into his radio-mike.

'*Should* be safe?' Scimitar scowled, looking at Stretch. 'This whole situation troubles me greatly.'

'It's a trust exercise. It's only troubling if you don't trust your friends.'

Scimitar eyed Stretch for a long moment. 'My sources tell me it was the Old Master himself who put that massive price on your head.'

Stretch froze at the name. The 'Old Master' was the nickname of a Mossad legend, General Mordechai Muniz, a former head of the Mossad who many said, even in retirement, was still the most influential figure in the organisation; the puppet-master who pulled the strings of those ostensibly in charge.

'Sixteen million dollars,' Scimitar mused. 'A good price, one of the highest ever. The Old Master wants to make an example of you.'

'I chose loyalty to your brother over loyalty to the Mossad,' Stretch said.

'And perhaps this is why you have become such friends. My brother thinks too often with his heart and not his head. Such thinking is foolish and weak. Look where it has got you.'

Stretch thought about Pooh Bear up in the entry-chamber. 'I would lay down my life for your brother, because I believe in him. But you do not. Which makes me wonder, first son of the Sheik, what do you believe in?'

Scimitar did not answer that.

Shaking his head, Stretch crouched and entered the low tunnel, belly-crawling through it. It was a tight journey, claustrophobic in the extreme. The tight wet walls brushed against his shoulders.

Then he slithered over the first hole in the floor, and he held his breath, waiting for—

—but nothing sprang up from it.

Scimitar followed close behind him and the two of them wriggled along the tunnel until they emerged into standing room once more, finding themselves at the top of a steep, downward-sloping hallway.

On the wall behind them, above the exit to the low tunnel, was a lever just like the one West had pulled, with the Chinese symbol for *knowledge* alongside it.

Above this lever was a picture of an ear; below it, a picture of an eye.

Stretch relayed this to Wizard and West.

'*The correct answer is the ear*,' Wizard replied. '*Since you're in the Student's Way, your riddles are Confucian, Laozi's most talented and trusted student. Confucius said, "I hear and I know, I see and I remember." Knowledge is then hearing. As for us, once again, thanks to Mao's concreters, we don't need your help on this one.*'

The Grand Hall of the Warriors

It took them a while, but soon West's team was through their low tunnel. Now, like Stretch and Scimitar, they stood at the top of a magnificent downward-sloping hallway.

It was absolutely beautiful—with soaring corbelled ceilings at least twenty feet high and lined with gigantic warrior statues, each one seven feet tall and bearing a weapon of some kind.

The hallway seemed to stretch for over a hundred metres, sloping sharply downward but with no stairs to get a foothold, delving deep into the bowels of the Earth. The floor was wet and slippery. Battery-powered lamps left by Mao's men lined the walls like dim runway lights.

Distantly, West heard something coming from the end of his superlong tunnel.

Voices.

Accompanied by the movement of lights and glowsticks.

It was Colonel Mao and his men, held up at a trap at the bottom end of the tunnel.

They'd caught up.

Astro came up beside West and they peered together down into the darkness, in the direction of the voices.

Without a word, Astro held up a grenade, this one with a yellow stripe on it.

West turned, saw it. 'Do I even want to know what's in this one?'

'CS-II. Variety of tear/nerve gas, with covering smoke,' Astro said. 'It's a little stronger than the usual kind of CS gas you use in hostage situations. Designed for situations like this, where you need to get past an enemy force holding an entryway but don't necessarily want to kill them. Although if you want to do *that*—'

'Tears and unconsciousness will be fine, Lieutenant,' West said. 'I don't like killing someone if I don't have to. Max, oxygen kit.'

At this point, Jack grabbed his trademark fireman's helmet and attached its full facemask and oxygen kit. The others did the same.

Moments later, three of Astro's yellow-striped grenades came bouncing down the hallway and entered the midst of Mao's Chinese force gathered at its base, at the edge of the abrupt vertical drop there.

Flash—bang!

Hissing gas and dense smoke engulfed the dozen or so Chinese troops. They instantly began coughing and gagging, their eyes watering uncontrollably.

Through this hazy gas-filled environment, three figures moved like ghosts.

Wearing full-face oxygen masks and moving quickly, Jack, Astro and Wizard slipped between the screaming Chinese as they fell to the floor, losing consciousness—although Jack did take the opportunity to give Colonel Mao a sharp blow with the butt of his Desert Eagle on the way past, breaking the Chinese commander's nose and dropping him.

Then he came to the spot where the hallway's floor just fell away into nothingness.

'Mother of God . . .' he breathed.

Mao and his men had set up a diesel generator and some arc lights to illuminate the area, and now, in the haze of the gas, the vast space that opened up before Jack took on a mystical, almost otherworldly appearance.

A vast chasm dropped away in front of him—perhaps thirty metres across and of unknown depth. On its far side was a sheer polished stone wall. This wall was literally covered in round holes, hundreds of them laid out in a grid, each about the size of a human hand.

And in the exact centre of the wall was a small square tunnel, heading deeper into the mountain.

Standing on the edge of the chasm, Jack kicked a dropped Chinese gun over the edge.

It sailed down into the darkness.

Silence as it fell.

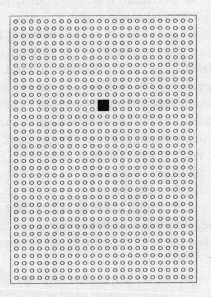

Long silence.

Then, finally, a distant *clunk-splonk*.

'Whoa . . .' West whispered.

'*Jack!*' a voice called both in his earpiece and from somewhere nearby. '*Down here!*'

West looked down, and saw Stretch and Scimitar poking their heads out from an identical ledge sixty feet *below* his.

The only walkways connecting their tunnels to the magnificent dotted wall were a pair of narrow ledges— one for each hallway: West's higher one ran along the short *left*-hand connecting wall; Stretch's lower one ran along the *right*-side one.

Along each narrow ledge were more of the hand-sized holes—handholds, Jack guessed, but lethal ones.

Each hole, he noticed, every single one, had a small carved Chinese symbol above it.

'Classic Chinese tomb trap,' Wizard said. 'The easy way to spot a grave-robber in ancient China was to spot the guy with the missing hand. Those are hand-chopping holes. Some have grips inside them, to help you climb. All the others have springloaded scissor-blades. If you know which ones are safe, you get across. If you don't, you lose a hand and in all likelihood fall to your death.'

'What's the clue?' West said.

'It's here,' Wizard went to a panel on the wall. He translated it aloud: '"Here, where two paths will become one, the teacher becomes the student and the student becomes the teacher." A subtle but deadly change. Our riddle is now Laozian.'

At the bottom of the panel was another cryptic carving:

'"The greatest treasure,"' Wizard translated. 'What, according to Laozi, was the greatest treasure?' he asked aloud. 'Ah . . .'

He recalled the old philosopher's axiom in his mind:

Health is the greatest possession,
Contentment the greatest treasure,
Confidence the greatest friend,
Non-being the greatest joy.

'It's contentment,' he said to Jack.

Sure enough, one of the handholes on the left-hand ledge bore the symbol for contentment—和豆炭粪—above it. So did the third one, and the fifth and several more.

'Go!' Wizard said. 'Go! Go! Go!'

Wasting no time and trusting his friend, Jack plunged his hand into the first hole . . .

. . . and found a handgrip.

Then he was off, out along the ledge, above the bottomless black of the subterranean chasm.

Stretch called in: '*We got an inscription, too: "The noblest path to wisdom."*'

Following close behind Jack, Wizard said, 'That's an easy one. Look for the Chinese symbol for *reflection*. It's a Confucian saying: "There are three paths to wisdom: first, by reflection, which is noblest; second, by imitation, which is easiest; and third, by experience, which is the bitterest."'

After Wizard described it, Stretch said, '*Got it. It's above every second or third handhole.*'

'Use only those holes, Stretch,' Jack said. 'If you use any of the others, you'll lose a hand. See you on the other side.'

At length, Jack came to the great pockmarked wall itself, and saw that again every single hole had a symbol carved above it.

It made for a bamboozling sight, and to the uninitiated, it would have seemed totally incomprehensible.

But following the holes that bore the symbol for

contentment, he found a continuing path that ended at the square hole in the centre of the polished wall.

Free-climbing across the sheer slippery wall, high above the deep black chasm below it, he traced a winding path from the left, while Stretch and Scimitar followed a similar trail from their ledge on the lower right:

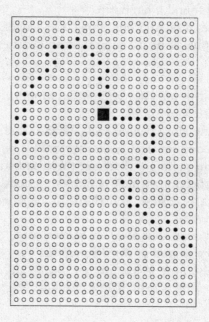

And all the while, Mao and his crew lay on the floor of the hallway, a few of them groaning weakly on the edge of consciousness.

Jack, Wizard and Astro came to the square hole, where they were soon joined by Stretch and Scimitar.

'Looks like we go together from here,' Jack said.

He cracked a glowstick and tossed it into the dark

hole, revealing another ultra-long tunnel, square-shaped this time, big enough to crawl through and stretching away into distant darkness.

'What choice do we have?' he said to no one.

And so he hoisted himself up and climbed into the square hole and guided by his helmet flashlight and another glowstick, disappeared into the passage.

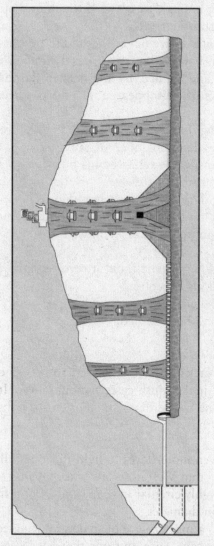

THE CAVERN OF THE TOWER

The Cavern of the Tower

After crawling for about two hundred metres, Jack emerged in a dark chamber of some kind, where he could stand easily. He removed his breathing mask.

For some reason, however, his flashlight couldn't penetrate the darkness around him. He could see a lake of some kind immediately in front of him, but no walls. Only black, infinite black. It must have been a large space.

He cracked a glowstick, but it revealed little more.

So he fired his flare-gun . . .

. . . and beheld the space in which he stood.

'Hoo-ah . . .' he breathed.

In his time, Jack West Jr had seen some big caverns, including one in the south-eastern mountains of Iraq that had housed the fabled Hanging Gardens of Babylon.

But even that cavern paled in comparison to this one.

It took seven more flares to light this one fully.

The cavern that West now saw was *immense*—utterly immense; roughly circular in shape and at least five hundred metres in diameter.

It was also a masterpiece of structural engineering: it was a natural cave, sure, but one that had been shaped by the work of men—tens of thousands of men, Jack guessed—to be even more impressive than nature had originally made it.

Nine towering pillars of stone held up the cavern's soaring ceiling. They had clearly once been limestone stalactites that, over thousands of years, had eventually met their matching stalagmites on the floor of the cavern, forming into thick roof-supporting columns. But somewhere in history, a Chinese work-army had shaped them into beautifully decorated columns, complete with faux guard balconies.

But it was the column in the very centre of the cavern that dominated the scene.

Thicker than the others and entirely man-made, it looked like a glorious tower, a great twenty-storey fortified tower, reaching all the way to the cavern's superhigh ceiling, where it joined with it.

It was easily the most intricately decorated of all the columns: it bore many balconies, doorways, archer slits, and at its base, four sets of rising stone stairs leading to four separate stone doorways.

Surrounding the tower and each of the other columns was a wide perfectly still lake of a dark oil-like liquid that was certainly not water. It glinted dully in the light of West's flares. Stretching across it, from West's position all the way to the tower in the middle of the cavern, was a long series of seven-foot-high stepping stones—a bridge of sorts, but one which no doubt possessed its own nasty surprises.

'Liquid mercury,' Astro said, raising his gas-mask to briefly sniff the lake's fumes. 'You can tell by the odour. Highly toxic. Clogs your pores, poisons you right through the skin. Don't fall in.'

As he rejoined West and the others, Wizard recited:

'In the highest room of the highest tower,
In the lowest part of the lowest cave,
There you will find me.

'From Confucius,' he said. 'Third book of eternal maxims. I never really understood it till now.'

Near their position, a red-and-black cast-iron archway spanned the first stepping stone. Carved into it was a message in ancient Chinese script:

A journey of a thousand miles
Begins with a single step.
So too this final challenge
Begins, and ends, with a single step.

Wizard nodded. 'Appropriate. "Every journey begins with a single step" is a quote attributed to both Laozi *and* Confucius. Historians are unsure which of them came up with it. So here, where their two paths merge fully into one, there is just one quote.'

'So what's the catch?' Scimitar asked.

West eyed the stepping stones, the tower and the great cavern, the intent of it all becoming clear.

'It's a time-and-speed trap,' he said softly.

'Oh, God, you're right,' Wizard said.

Astro frowned. 'A what? What's a time-and-speed trap?'

'A big one,' Wizard said.

'That usually begins with a single step,' West added. 'Your first step sets off the trap. Then you have to get in and out before the trap completes its sequence. You need accuracy *and* speed to get through it. I imagine that as soon as one of us steps on the first stepping stone, the sequence is set off.' He turned to Wizard. 'Max?'

Wizard thought for a moment. '"In the highest room of the highest tower in the lowest part of the lowest cave." I imagine it's up there, in the highest room of that tower. I think we need your skill and speed from here, Jack.'

'That's what I figured,' West said wryly.

He removed his heavy garments, until all he wore was his T-shirt, cargo pants, boots, and the lower half of his gas-mask, leaving his eyes clear. His metal left arm glinted in the dull light. He put his fireman's helmet back on his head and gripped a climbing rope in one hand. He also kept his gunbelt with its twin holsters on.

'He's going alone?' Scimitar asked, surprised, and perhaps a little suspiciously.

'For this test, the most important thing is speed,' Wizard said, 'and in places like this, there's no man in the world faster than Jack. From here, he must go alone. He's the only one who can.'

'Yeah, right,' West said. 'Stretch, if it looks like I'm in trouble, back-up would be appreciated.'

'You got it, Huntsman.'

Then Jack turned to face the long line of stepping stones stretching out toward the colossal tower.

He took a deep breath.

Then he ran, out onto the first stepping stone.

The Run

No sooner had his foot hit the first stepping stone than things began moving all around the immense cavern.

First, a line of stalactites in the ceiling of the cavern—each the size of a man—began dropping from their places, raining down on the stepping stones, inches behind the running figure of Jack West.

Jack bolted, arms and legs pumping, moving rapidly across the high stones, seven feet above the mercury lake as *boom!-boom!-boom!* the pointed missiles rained down behind him, some hitting the raised stepping stones, others splashing into the lake around him. But he outran the rain of sharpened stones.

The flurry of stalactites was also highly distracting, designed to force an error from the intruder, but Jack kept concentrating as he ran, holding his nerve for the two-hundred-metre-long dash.

He hit the stairs at the base of the tower at a sprint, clambered up them two-at-a-time, came to a high arched doorway . . . just as a mini-waterfall of amber-coloured acid came splashing down across its threshold.

Jack dived under it, somersaulting into the tower a split-second ahead of the skin-searing acid.

He turned to look behind him—and saw the long

line of high stepping stones *all slowly begin to lower into the lake*!

'Oh that's just nasty . . .'

At their rate of descent, he reckoned he had about four minutes till they were completely submerged under the mercury lake, cutting off his only means of escape.

'*Jack . . . !*' Wizard called urgently.

'I see them!'

He looked upward and by the light of his helmet flashlight saw that the tower was completely hollow: a soaring cylindrical well-shaft rising ominously into darkness above him, with ladder-like hand- and foot-holds cut into one side.

Breathing hard, he climbed up the ladder-holds, noticing some small man-sized recesses along the way. Curiously, carved above each recess was the Chinese symbol for 'sanctuary'.

A groaning noise made him look up.

The distinctive grinding sound of rolling rock, then a faint *whistling* . . .

Jack swung into the nearest recess just as—*whoosh*—a two-ton boulder came plummeting down the hollow shaft, filling it completely from wall to wall, whipping by Jack in his tiny recess, missing his nose by millimetres.

Once it was past him, Jack resumed climbing, and on two more occasions he dived into other 'sanctuary' recesses just before more boulders rained past him, preceded only by the telltale groaning.

'Why do these guys have to be so protective of their treasures . . .' he muttered.

But then, after a minute of climbing, he came to the top of the tower, to the point where it merged with the ceiling of the supercavern, and found himself entering a space just above the cavern's roof.

He rose up into a beautiful square chamber, not unlike the entry chamber back near the surface.

Intricately carved reliefs lined the walls: carvings of the Mystery of the Circles and the symbol that represented the Machine, and against one wall, above a low darkened alcove: an image of the Philosopher's Stone.

There were other carvings, including one of four throned kings sitting shoulder-to-shoulder and flanked by five standing warriors, but Jack ignored them.

He crossed to the alcove and beheld within it a small stone altar on which stood one of the most beautiful, most exquisite, most magnificent artefacts he had ever seen in his life.

The Philosopher's Stone.

It wasn't very big, but the simple purity of its design commanded respect.

Its sides were perfectly lacquered in the ancient Chinese way—the shiny black flanks were of a deep, deep black and were lined with red. Flecks of gold peppered the red lining.

Made of two pieces, the Stone's body section was trapezoidal in shape, with a rectangular void cut into the top surface. Its second piece, the lid, was smaller, a perfectly smooth square block, and—Jack noticed—exactly the same size as the base of the Firestone.

Peering into the alcove, Jack saw that its roof was hollow, like a chimney above a fireplace, so with a quick lunge, he reached in and snatched Laozi's Stone and dived out of the alcove—

—a bare second before the alcove—but not the Stone's altar—was drenched in a waterfall of pouring sulphuric acid that drained away through a grate in its floor.

Jack hurried away from the alcove, stuffing the venerable Stone into his rucksack and began his breakneck return journey.

Down the hollow core of the tower, ducking into its recesses as more boulders rained down—more now than before; it was as if the trap system knew the Stone had been taken and was doing everything it could to stop the fleeing thief.

Jack clambered down the handholds in the wall, came to the bottom just as another boulder came shooting down the shaft.

He jumped into the main doorway, whose acid curtain had stopped by now, where he briefly glimpsed the lowering stepping stones leading back across the lake, when suddenly the boulder came whistling past, clipping his shoulder, causing him to lose his balance and to his horror, he fell, snatching desperately for a handhold but finding none, and so Jack dropped, into the darkness of the well-shaft at the base of the tower—

Only for a hand to snatch his wrist and clamp tightly around it.

Hanging from the hand, West looked up to see Stretch's sweat-streaked face.

'Your back-up has arrived, Captain West,' Stretch said grimly. 'Come on. One more sprint to go.'

They emerged from the tower to see the stepping stones now only one foot above the surface of the mercury lake and lowering fast.

'Go!' Stretch yelled.

They raced out across the mercury lake, moving step for step, almost perfectly in time, springing from stone to stone, all while the stones kept lowering.

With ten metres to go, the stones hit the waterline and Stretch called, 'Keep going! Suck it in, Jack! Suck it in!'

Jack was almost out on his feet, exhausted, his heart pounding loudly inside his head, lactic bile rising in his throat, breathing through his half-mask in deep rasping heaves.

Then his feet splashed in mercury and, with a terrible sense of helplessness, he felt himself begin to stumble and knew there was nothing he could do about it—he was going to fall face-first into this mercury lake, three steps short of safety!

Staggering and breathless, he toppled forward—only to feel Stretch spring up alongside him, loop an arm under his armpit and drag him over the last three steps until they both went sprawling onto solid ground, sliding to a halt on their bellies right at Wizard's feet.

'Goodness gracious me!' Wizard blurted, helping Jack to his feet.

Sweating and gasping and held up only by Wizard and Stretch, Jack sucked in air by the gulpful.

When at last he could speak again, he uttered two glorious words: 'Got it.'

Jack and his team would be out of China by the end of the day, having left the trap system via the lower route—thus avoiding Mao's men—and rendezvousing with the *Halicarnassus* at the Burmese border.

Once they were safely back on board the *Hali*, Wizard and Tank were sent straight to the infirmary to be treated by Stretch.

Sky Monster said to Jack: 'Huntsman. I just got a call from Zoe. She said the mission at Stonehenge was *very* successful. Says she has a ton of data that Wizard will want to see.'

'Excellent,' Jack said, his clothes still covered in blood, grime and splashes of mercury. 'Set a course for England and call Zoe back. Tell her to send through any images she thinks we need to see beforehand.'

'Assembly point?'

'Tell her we're coming to her, time and location to be advised. We're going to have to take the long route.'

'Roger that.'

'Astro, call your American bosses and get them to send the Killing Stone of the Maya to England. And if they know the location of any of the Pillars— which I'm pretty sure they do—tell them to bring those, too.'

'Got it.'

'Oh, and tell our CIA friend, Robertson, that we need him to pull some strings with America's old friends, the House of Saxe-Coburg-Gotha, and get them to bring their Pillar.'

'The House of Saxe-what?' Astro was confused.

'He'll understand.'

'Okay . . .' Astro said, heading for a comms console.

Jack turned to Vulture, sitting nearby. 'I'm also gonna need the House of Saud's Pillar, Vulture.'

Vulture stood. 'I knew you had a reputation for daring, Captain, but this, this borders on rank impudence. You really *are* a bold one.'

'Yeah, real bold.' West headed aft in the direction of his quarters. 'Now, if nobody minds, I'm going to boldly take a shower and then I'm going to boldly hit the sack. Wake me when we hit Eastern Europe.'

A few minutes later, Jack was all cleaned up and lying in his bunk, eyes open in the darkness, when something occurred to him.

He keyed the intercom button above his bunk.

'*Yes, Huntsman?*' Sky Monster's voice said from the cockpit.

'Have you spoken to Zoe yet?'

'*Just finished talking to her a second ago.*'

'Can you call her back for me and tell her to pass on this message to Lily: "Daddy says, I love you and I miss you. Goodnight."'

'*Sure, bro.*'

Jack clicked off the intercom and within seconds he was lost in a deep, deep sleep.

He dreamed of many things—memories mostly, some

of them happy, others horrific—but most of all, he dreamed of Lily, of her bright smiling face and the home they'd made together in the remote north-west corner of Australia . . .

A GIRL
NAMED LILY

PART III

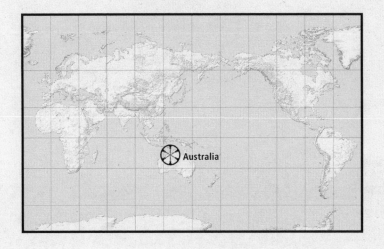

Australia

AUSTRALIA
MARCH 2006–DECEMBER 2007
THE MONTHS AFTER TARTARUS

GREAT SANDY DESERT
NORTH-WESTERN AUSTRALIA
MARCH 2006–DECEMBER 2007

In the months after the Tartarus Rotation of March 2006, Jack West's team returned to their countries of origin—with the exception of Stretch, since his home nation, Israel, had declared him *persona non grata* after his actions during that mission. He variously stayed with Jack, Wizard and Pooh Bear.

Reports had to be filed, careers had to be restarted. After all, it was not exactly common for a professional soldier to disappear on a ten-year mission, and such an absence had to be explained to the various bureaucracies. Backdated promotions, for instance, were given to all of them.

Naturally, this disbanding of the team had an effect on Lily, for that team of soldiers was the closest thing to family she had ever known.

She felt like Frodo at the end of her favourite book, *The Lord of the Rings*. Having completed a huge Earth-changing mission, now they all had to return to normal life—and how could normal life ever satisfy someone who had participated in such an adventure? Worse, how did you deal with *ordinary people* who didn't— couldn't—know of the great deeds you'd done on their behalf?

Fortunately, the team came to visit her and Jack at the farm often; and once she got her own cell phone—a big day—Lily kept in touch with them by SMS. And of course, whenever it could be arranged, she went to visit them: seeing Pooh Bear in Dubai, Fuzzy in Jamaica, Wizard all over the place, and Zoe in Ireland.

Zoe.

Lily's favourite times, of course, were Zoe's visits to Australia. But at first this had been difficult, since an insensitive lieutenant-colonel in the Irish Army—ignorant of the heroic role she had played in the Seven Wonders mission—had insisted she retrain and be regraded in the Sciathan Fhianoglach an Airm.

Ordinary people, Lily sighed. *Urgh*.

Naturally, Jack was aware of this. Indeed, sometimes he felt the same way himself.

The solution was simple.

They had to find new challenges to occupy them.

Which was okay for him, Lily thought, as Wizard would often send him queries and conundrums via email. Things like: 'Jack, can you look up the Neetha Tribe for me, from the Congo?' Or: 'Can you get an authoritative translation of Aristotle's Riddles?' Or: 'Can you find out the names of all the Bird-Men of Easter Island?'

But then, just when she had been at a loss for interesting challenges, Jack had provided Lily with a startling new one that she had not been prepared for:

School.

*

Since schools were kind of hard to come by in the northern deserts of Australia, Lily was sent to a prestigious boarding school for gifted children in Perth.

But prestigious or not, kids are kids, and for a little girl who had grown up as an only child among crack troops on an isolated farm in Kenya, school proved to be a confusing and tough experience.

Of course, Jack had known this would be the case— but he also knew that it was necessary.

Just how tough it had been, however, became clear at his first parent–teacher meeting.

Dressed in jeans and a jacket that concealed his muscular physique and workgloves that hid his artificial left hand, Jack West Jr—commando, adventurer, and owner of two masters degrees in ancient history—sat in a low plastic chair at a tiny plastic desk in front of Lily's personal guidance adviser, a bespectacled woman named Brooke. A 'guidance adviser', Jack was told, was simply a teacher assigned to monitor Lily's overall progress at school.

Brooke's long list of comments made Jack smile behind his concerned exterior:

'Lily has been embarrassing her Latin teacher in class. Correcting her in front of the other students.

'She's scoring excellently in all her subjects, averaging over 90 per cent, but I get the feeling that she can do better. She seems only to be doing what is necessary to get a tick, not what she is truly capable of. Our syllabus is the most advanced in the country, yet she seems, well, bored.

'She's very choosy when it comes to friends. She hangs

out with Alby Calvin, which is great, but from what I've seen she appears to have no female friends at all.

'Oh, and she made young Tyson Bradley cry by bending his wrist backwards with a strange grip. The school nurse says she almost broke his arm.'

Jack knew about that one.

Young Tyson Bradley was a little ratbastard and garden-variety bully, and one day he'd tried to bully Alby into giving up his lunch money.

Lily had intervened, and when Tyson had reached out for her throat, she had grabbed his wrist and twisted it inside-out, forcing Tyson to his knees, almost breaking his wrist—exactly as West had trained her to do.

Young Tyson had not bothered Alby or Lily again.

It was at that parent–teacher night that West had first met Alby's mother, Lois Calvin.

A sweet, timid woman from America, she was living in Perth with her mining executive husband. Anxious and nervous, she worried constantly about her gifted son.

'That awful sportsmaster just terrorises him,' she complained to Jack over coffee. 'I honestly don't see why a gentle boy like Alby should have to play a sport. What if he gets a knock to the head? My son can do amazing things in mathematics—things his teachers couldn't even *dream* of doing—and that could all be ruined by a single head injury in a soccer game. But that horrible sportsmaster insists that sport is compulsory and I can't persuade him to excuse Alby.'

Lois was a lovely woman and she clearly adored Alby, but Jack felt she must be exaggerating things—until later that evening when he himself met the sportsmaster, Mr Naismith.

Mr Todd Naismith was a great hulking man who wore too-tight tennis shorts and a polo shirt that accentuated his thick biceps. To a kid, he would have appeared gigantic. To Jack, he was just a bigger version of Tyson Bradley—an adult bully.

The big sportsmaster seemed to assess West's size and stature as he sat down. He pulled out Lily's file, absently tossing a softball in his spare hand as he did so.

'Lily West . . .' he said, perusing the file. 'Ah, yes. How could I forget. She refused to participate in a game of dodgeball one day. Said it was a stupid game and that I was a "dumb jock-moron who didn't know anything about the real world", if I recall correctly.'

Oh dear, Jack had thought. *He hadn't heard about this.*

'Geez,' he said. 'I'm really sor—'

'Not much of an athlete, your girl,' Mr Naismith went on anyway, bringing Jack up short. 'But her teachers tell me she's a bright one. Now booksmarts are one thing, and sure, this school focuses on the academic. But between us, I like sports. You know why I like 'em?'

'I can't imagine—'

'Because they engender a team mentality. *Team.* The idea of selflessness. If the chips were down and their backs were to the wall, would Lily stand up and put herself on the line for her friends? I would, and I know I would, from my experiences in sport.'

Jack felt his jaw begin to grind, knowing full well what Lily had done on behalf of dipshits like this guy.

'Is that so?' he said slowly.

'It sure is,' Naismith kept tossing his ball and—

Quick as a whip, Jack snatched the softball in mid-air and held it in his gloved left hand between their faces, his ice-cold blue eyes levelled at the big sportsmaster's.

'Mr Naismith. Todd. My daughter, she's a good kid. And I have no problem with her conceptions of loyalty and team spirit. I apologise for any offence she might have caused you. She gets her stubbornness from me. But then—'

West squeezed the softball with his mechanical left hand . . . and with a soft *crunch*, cracked it to pieces, stringy pieces that fell through his fingers to the floor, the ball's leather cover sliding limply after it.

Mr Naismith's eyes went wide, his previous confidence vanishing in a second.

'—perhaps you should try appealing to her on a more intellectual level. You might get a better response that way. Oh, and, Mr Naismith—Todd—if her little friend, Alby Calvin, doesn't want to play soccer, don't make him. You're making his mother nervous. That'll be all.'

With that, Jack left, leaving Todd Naismith sitting there with his mouth open.

And so Lily lived for holidays and weekends, when she could return to the farm and meet up with her old friends.

Wizard's visits were a highlight, although as the months went by, they became less frequent. He was at work, he said, on a very important project, one that he had been working on his whole life.

Lily was thrilled to read his notes, filled as they were with ancient mysteries and symbols, and on a few occasions, she even helped Wizard translate some carvings that were written in the Word of Thoth, an ancient language that only she and one other person in the world could decode.

Twice Wizard brought his research partner Tank Tanaka to the farm.

Lily liked Tank. Clever, cuddly and fun, on his second visit he brought Lily a toy from his native Japan, a little robot dog built by the Sony Corporation, called Aibo. Lily quickly renamed the dog Sir Barksalot and equally quickly set about using him to terrorise Horus. A quick tweak from Wizard enhanced Sir Barksalot's infra-red motion sensors—making him bark if he detected movement, even in the dark. It made for great games of 'spotlight' with Alby, with the goal being to belly-crawl past the hyper-alert robot dog.

Tank also had a tattoo on his right forearm that intrigued Lily: it depicted a Japanese character hidden behind the flag of Japan. Ever curious about languages, she tried to look it up one day on the Net, but she couldn't find it anywhere.

But there was something else that struck Lily about Tank: there was a tremendous *sadness* to him, a blankness in his eyes that Lily detected on their very first meeting.

When she asked him what was wrong, he answered by telling her about his childhood:

'I was a small boy, about your age, when my country went to war against America. I lived in Nagasaki, a beautiful city. But when the war turned for my country and the American Air Force started bombing our cities at will, my parents sent me away, to live with my grandparents in the countryside.

'My parents were in Nagasaki the day the Americans dropped their terrible bomb on that city. My parents were never found. They'd been obliterated, reduced to dust.'

Lily knew exactly what it meant to lose your parents—she had never known either of hers—and so a special bond had developed between her and Tank.

'I'm not very old,' she said solemnly, 'but one of the biggest things I've learned in life is this: while it can never replace the real one, you can make a new family with your friends.'

Tank had looked at her kindly, his eyes moist. 'You are most wise for one so young, little Lily. I wish I saw the world as you do.'

Lily didn't quite understand Tank's final comment, but she just smiled anyway. He seemed to like that.

After each of Wizard's visits the whiteboard in West's study would be overflowing with notes.

After one such visit, it had this on it:

THUTHMOSIS V

Renegade priest of Akenaten regime; monotheist; Rival of Rameses II; exiled by him under threat of execution.

Note Egyptian name-element "**mosis**" meaning "son of" or "born of"; this element is usually followed by a *theorific*, or divine, element.

So: "mosis" or "moses" or "meses" = "son of"; Rameses = Ra-moses = son of Ra. Thuthmosis = Thoth-moses = son of *Thoth!*

WHEREABOUTS OF TWIN TABLETS OF THUTHMOSIS

Who knows!!
Temple of Solomon →
arca foederis →
Menelik → **Ethiopia**

Templar quest to Ethiopia in 1280 A.D. →
Churches of Lalibela?
Templar symbols all over them.
Are the Tablets in Ethiopia?

NEETHA TRIBE

- *Remote tribe from Democratic Republic of the Congo/Zaire region; warlike; much-feared by other tribes; cannibals;*
- *Congenital deformities in all members, variety of Proteus Syndrome (bony growth on skull, similar to Elephant Man);*

- Found by accident by HENRY MORTON STANLEY in 1876; Neetha warriors killed seventeen of his party; Stanley barely escaped alive; years later, he tried to find them again, but could not locate them.

- Possibly the same tribe encountered by the Greek explorer HIERONYMUS during his expedition into central Africa in 205 B.C. (Hieronymus mentioned a tribe with terrible facial deformities in the jungles south of Nubia. It was from the Neetha that he stole the clear spherical orb that was later used by the Oracle at Delphi.)

- BEST-KNOWN EXPERT: DR DIANE CASSIDY, Anthropologist from USC. But her whole 20-man expedition went missing in 2002 while searching for the Neetha in the Congo.

- Cassidy found this cave painting in northern Zambia and attributed it to ancestors of the Neetha:

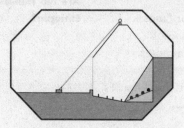

- Seems to depict a hollowed-out volcano with the Delphic Orb at the summit but its meaning is unknown.

And finally, the entries that intrigued Lily the most:

EASTER ISLAND (a.k.a. 'RAPA NUI': 'THE NAVEL OF THE WORLD') CO-ORDS: 27°09'S, 109°27'W	ARISTOTLE'S RIDDLES

EASTER ISLAND (a.k.a. 'RAPA NUI': 'THE NAVEL OF THE WORLD') CO-ORDS: 27°09'S, 109°27'W

BIRD-MAN CULT ('TANGATA MANU')

- Annual competition, held near Rano Kau, the southernmost volcano of Easter Is, whereby a young champion would compete on behalf of his chieftain;

- Each champion had to swim to islet of Motu Nui, grab the first tern egg of the season and then return across the shark-infested waters. The winner's sponsor became Bird-Man, or Chief of Chiefs, for the next year.

ARISTOTLE'S RIDDLES

Series of strange axioms left by Aristotle as 'life-guidance' for his students.

Aristotle's authorship of them is disputed, since they find no correlation elsewhere in his works. They begin with:

What is the best number of lies?
(One, since to support one lie means telling more)

What is the best number of eyes?
(Again, one, after the All-Seeing Eye of Egypt)

What is the best life to live?
(The afterlife—key source of Christian theology)

What is the direction of Death?
(West—Egyptian origin)

Lily particularly loved to read through West's books on Easter Island, she could stare for hours at the great statues, the famous *moai*, that gazed out over the barren landscape of that distant island, the most remote on Earth.

It was not uncommon for West to find her asleep in the corner of his office, an open book lying across her lap. On those occasions he would gently pick her up, carry her to her room, and put her to bed.

The introduction of Alby to Lily's life brought not only fun and good times, but also new reading material.

While Lily had been a long-time fan of *The Lord of the Rings*, it was Alby who introduced her to a boy wizard named Harry Potter.

Lily devoured the Harry Potter series and constantly re-read them. In fact, whenever she travelled—either back and forth to school, or overseas to visit her Cap-stone teammates—the entire Harry Potter series always went with her. Always.

But as ever, the greatest source of mystery to Lily—even now after he had adopted her—was Jack West Jr.

During her adventure with the Seven Wonders, Lily had learned a lot about Jack—except when it came to his family.

She remembered once overhearing Zoe and Wizard talking about his father.

Apparently, Jack West Sr was American, and he and Jack didn't get along. To anger his father—who wanted him to join the US military—Jack had become a member of the Australian Army, based on his mother's nationality.

So one day, over breakfast, Lily asked him straight out, 'Daddy? Do you have a family?'

Jack smiled. 'Yes. I do.'

'Brothers or sisters?'

'One sister.'

'Older or younger?'

'Older. By two years. Although . . .'

'Although what?'

'Although, she's not older than me anymore. Her name was Lauren. She's no longer older than me because she died when she was thirty.'

'Oh. How did she die?' Lily asked.

'She was killed in a plane crash,' Jack's eyes became distant. 'An airliner accident.'

'Were you close?'

'Sure we were,' Jack said, perking up, returning from his memories. 'She even married my best friend, a Navy guy named J.J. Wickham.'

'What about your parents?'

'They divorced when Lauren and I were in our teens. My mother was a high school teacher. History. A smart and quiet woman. And my dad, well—'

Lily waited, holding her breath.

West stared off into space for a moment. 'He was with the US Army, met my mum while out here on exercises. He was on the fast track up the promotions ladder and always wanting to go higher. Ambitious. He was also intelligent, really intelligent, but conceited about it—he looked down on anyone who didn't know as much as he did, talked down to them, including my mother. Which was why they split in the end. She won't see him now.'

'Do you keep in touch with her?' Lily had never met Jack's mother.

Jack laughed. 'Of course I do! It's just that . . . she doesn't want my father to know where she is, so I only see her rarely. I was actually going to ask you if you wanted to join me the next time I visited her. She's very keen to meet you.'

'Is she? I'd love to!' Lily exclaimed, but then she frowned: 'What about your dad? Do you ever see him?'

'No,' Jack said firmly. 'We never really got along. In fact, I can honestly say I don't ever want to see him again.'

Despite the fact that Jack was no longer on active service, the military never quite went away.

On one occasion in late 2006, an Australian general came to visit Jack at the farm and asked him lots of questions about the Capstone mission.

The general also asked Jack if he knew the whereabouts of someone called the Sea Ranger.

This Sea Ranger, Lily gleaned, was a modern-day pirate of some sort, cruising the east coast of Africa in some kind of boat.

Jack told the general he hadn't seen the Sea Ranger in years.

But the thing about Jack that was of most interest to Lily was his relationship with Zoe.

When Zoe was finally able to come to Australia more often, Lily was thrilled—especially when she could see how close Zoe and Jack were becoming.

They would smile when they talked on the balcony or went for walks together at sunset.

Lily also enjoyed doing girly stuff with Zoe—painting toenails, doing each other's hair, dyeing their end-tips in matching electric-pink—but more than anything else, she loved how Zoe made Jack happy.

She once asked Zoe if she was in love with Jack. Zoe had just smiled. 'I've loved him from the first moment I met him. But, well—'

'But what?' Lily had asked gently but Zoe didn't reply, she just stared off into space, her eyes moist with tears.

Lily let it go, but more than once she imagined Jack and Zoe getting married, and it made her happy because then Zoe would officially be her mum.

*

Christmas 2006 was an occasion Lily would remember for a long, long time.

She and Jack spent it in Dubai, at the Burj al Arab tower, with all the members of the team that had found the Seven Wonders and the Capstone.

Pooh Bear and Stretch were there, as was Fuzzy, having come all the way from Jamaica. Zoe and Sky Monster, Wizard and Tank.

The whole family, back together again. Lily loved it.

She spent much of the next week with Pooh Bear and Stretch, visiting Pooh's father's palace.

There she met Pooh's older brother, Scimitar, but he talked to her like she was a child, so she didn't like him too much.

What she *did* like was Pooh's demolition shed out beyond the mansion's stables. An explosives expert, Pooh had all manner of blasting supplies there. He even showed Lily a strange foam-like epoxy that Wizard had given to him: it was called Blast-Foam and it came from the famous Sandia Laboratories in the US. You sprayed foam from a small canister around a live grenade and it could *absorb* the blast of the grenade.

He also showed Lily how to use C-2 plastic explosive—a small-radius/high-impact explosive used by archaeologists on delicate sites. It could blast away tight sections of rock but not damage nearby relics.

'It can also blow locks,' Pooh Bear whispered to Lily. 'Which is why Huntsman always keeps a little wad of it in a compartment in his artificial arm, and why I keep some in this'—he indicated the ornamental bronze ring that kept his massive beard in check. 'Don't leave home without it.'

Lily grinned. Pooh Bear was cool.

A week later, the team celebrated the New Year on the rooftop helipad of the Burj al Arab tower, watching a fireworks display in the Arabian sky alongside many of Sheik Abbas's powerful friends and associates.

Despite the fact that she should have been in bed, Lily snuck out in her gown and slippers and watched the gathering from the storage shed on the helipad.

The women wore sparkling dresses—even Zoe, who Lily thought looked just beautiful—and all the men wore smart dinner suits or Arabian-style robes. Even Jack wore a tux, which Lily found very funny. It didn't suit him at all and he seemed very uncomfortable in it, but it did make him look very handsome.

Arriving late at the New Year's celebration, just before midnight, had been Jack's brother-in-law, J.J. Wickham.

Wickham was a few years older than Jack and seriously good looking, with short brown hair and a rough unshaven jaw; a sexy guy. All the women on the pad cast sideways glances at him as he walked by.

Accompanying Wickham was an exceedingly tall and skinny black man named Solomon Kol. His skin was a deep, deep black and his eyes were kind. He walked with a long loping stride and stood with a stoop, as if to diminish his considerable height.

Lily stared at the two men, frowning, struck by a strange feeling of recognition. She felt she had seen both of them before but couldn't remember where.

'Why if it isn't the Sea Ranger!' Pooh Bear exclaimed, clasping Wickham's hand warmly.

'Hey, Zahir,' Wickham said quietly. 'Sorry, it's Pooh Bear now, isn't it?'

'It is indeed and it is a name I wear with pride. 'Tis a great honour to be renamed by young Lily. I hope you have that honour one day.'

Lily smiled inwardly. She just loved Pooh Bear.

'Wick,' Jack said, coming over. 'Glad you could make it. And Solomon, my old friend, how are you?'

The giant African smiled broadly. 'We miss you in Kenya, Huntsman. You must visit again soon. Magdala misses young Lily terribly. She yearns to see how she has grown.'

'Oh, she's grown all right,' Jack said. 'And she's hiding right now in the shed over there. Lily! You can come out now.'

Lily emerged, head bowed, in her gown and slippers.

Jack put a hand on her shoulder. 'Lily, I'm not sure if you remember Solomon. He used to live next door to our farm in Kenya, and would come over often. He now looks after it for us, just in case we ever return.'

'My, my, you have grown, little one,' Solomon said. 'Soon you will be as tall as me!'

Wickham was also gazing down at Lily, but silently, sadly.

Then he turned to Jack: 'I can't stay long. Got the Man on my tail again. But thought I'd swing by and say hi.'

Jack said, 'They came asking about you last month. Arms smuggling. Said you grabbed an American weapons shipment by mistake.'

'Oh, it wasn't a mistake. I knew exactly what it was,' Wickham said. 'And I knew exactly where those weapons were heading.'

'Be careful, Wick,' Jack said. 'One man's crusader is another man's pirate.'

'They're calling me a pirate now?'

'You keep grabbing CIA weapons shipments to African warlords and soon you're gonna have the whole Seventh Fleet combing the Indian Ocean for your ass.'

'Bring it on,' Wickham said. 'The American military can be beaten. I mean, hell, look at what *you* did and you're a chump!'

Jack smiled. 'Watch yourself is all I'm saying.'

'I will. Call me if you're ever in Zanzibar,' Wickham said. 'Buy you a beer.'

Then the midnight fireworks started going off. Seen from the helipad of the Burj al Arab, they were simply spectacular. The assembled crowd oohed and aahed as the desert sky lit up in a million colours.

But when Lily turned back from the dazzling fireworks display, J.J. Wickham was gone.

A few days later, when they were alone, Lily asked Jack about him.

'He's a good man,' Jack said. 'A decent man who got court-martialled by the US Navy for doing the right thing.'

'What did he do?'

'It was more what he *didn't* do. Wick was the XO on

a submarine in the US Navy, a little Sturgeon-class sub operating out of Diego Garcia, the US base in the Indian Ocean, doing patrols off eastern Africa.

'Anyway, a few years after the *Black Hawk Down* incident in Somalia, his boat intercepted an unregistered Kilo-class submarine en route to the private dock of a Somali warlord: Russian pirates in an old Russian sub, smuggling arms. Wick's captain ordered him to take a boarding party onto the Kilo and sail it back to Diego Garcia.

'When he got on board the Kilo, however, Wick found a dozen crates of American Stinger missiles and one very pissed off CIA agent. Turned out the CIA was in the process of destabilising East Africa by arming *all* the warlords.'

'So what did he do?' Lily asked.

'Wick did what he'd been ordered to do. With a small team, he secured the Russian pirates, took command of the Russian sub and began sailing it back to Diego Garcia.

'But halfway there, he got a priority signal from Naval HQ, telling him to hand the sub back to the CIA man and forget he'd ever seen it.

'Wick was stunned. The bigshots back home were actually *supporting* this operation. So he made a decision. He figured enough was enough, and since he no longer had a family to worry about, he'd do something. And so he stopped the sub in the middle of the Indian Ocean, threw all its crew—including the enraged CIA man—into a liferaft and set them adrift.

'Knowing a court-martial would follow, he offered all his men on board the sub the opportunity to leave— indeed, he encouraged them to do so, to think of their careers. Most did and he set them adrift as well, in life-rafts with homing beacons.

'And so with a skeleton crew Wick *kept* the Russian submarine and has been using it ever since, conducting his own private patrols off the coast of Africa, using several old World War II submarine refuelling stations as his bases. He was court-martialled for desertion and disobeying a direct order *in absentia*, and sentenced to 25 years in a military prison. There's still an outstanding warrant for his arrest.'

'So is he a pirate?'

'To the people of Africa, he's a hero, the only guy who stands up to the warlords, by intercepting their arms shipments. He also brings the people food, free of charge and obligation. They call him the Sea Ranger. Unfortunately, he steals much of the food from western cargoes, so the US and British navies call him a pirate.'

Lily frowned. 'When I saw him on New Year's Eve, he seemed, I don't know, familiar. Like I'd seen him before.'

'That's because you have seen him before.'

'I have? When?'

'When you were very young and we were living in Kenya. You were just a toddler and Wick had only just started sailing his own private submarine. He was on the run, so I let him hide out with us for a while.

'He played hide-and-seek with you, peek-a-boo, that sort of thing. You loved it. Now that you're officially my daughter, he's officially your uncle. He lives mostly on the island of Zanzibar, off the Kenyan–Tanzanian coast. But wherever he is and wherever we are, we'll always be family.'

*

And so life went on for Lily—at the farm with Jack and at school with Alby, and with Zoe and Wizard when they came to visit—until that fine summer's day when the sky above the farm filled with parachutes.

THE SECOND MEETING

LOCATING
THE TEMPLE
SHRINES

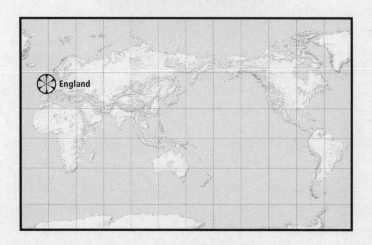

ENGLAND
9 DECEMBER, 2007
1 DAY BEFORE THE 1ST DEADLINE

'Daddy!'

Lily leapt into West's arms as he strode into the central lab of the submarine base, K-10, having taken three full days to get to England.

Situated on a windswept island in the mouth of the Bristol Channel, K-10 had been a refuelling and repair station for US naval vessels in the Second World War. After the war, as a gesture of thanks to the Americans, the British had allowed them to keep using the island. To this day it has remained a US base on British soil.

In the American classification system, it is a Level Alpha base, the highest security level, and along with Diego Garcia in the Indian Ocean, is the only base outside of continental America to maintain and store SLBMs—submarine-launched ballistic nuclear missiles.

About a dozen people milled around the high-tech lab: Zoe and the kids; the twins in their 'Cow Level' T-shirts; two Saudi commandos, guarding a small velvet case between them—Vulture went directly to them; and Paul Robertson, the American diplomat/spy they'd met in Dubai, who had arrived with a larger Samsonite trunk.

When Lily saw Wizard—his welts and cuts still pink—she released Jack and threw her arms around the old man.

Jack went straight to Zoe. 'Hey. So?'

'We've been busy while we were waiting for you. The data from Stonehenge is absolutely mind-blowing.'

Jack glanced at Robertson. 'He brought the Killing Stone of the Maya?'

'Arrived about an hour ago all by himself. With the Mayan Stone in his big case.'

'He didn't bring a Pillar, too?'

'No. He said America didn't possess one.'

'Hmmm. What'd he say about the Saxe-Coburg Pillar?'

'Apparently a member of no less than the British Royal Family is coming here, bringing it. Mr Robertson certainly has some pull.'

'You bet he does. What about the Saudi goon squad over there?' Jack said.

'They brought the Pillar of the House of Saud, complete with a couple of armed guards.' Zoe shifted hesitantly. 'Jack, can we really trust these guys?'

'No,' Jack said. 'Not a bit. But right now, they're being uncommonly helpful and we need that help. The big question will come later—how loyal will they be then? For now, just keep one hand on your gun.'

At that moment, the outer doors to the central laboratory opened and a very attractive young woman strode in, accompanied by two burly bodyguards whom Jack immediately picked as British SAS men.

Paul Robertson exclaimed, 'Ah! Iolanthe! I was wondering if they would send you . . .'

He air-kissed the young woman's cheeks. Jack noticed that she held in her hands a purple velveteen case the size of a jewellery box—or a Pillar.

Lily gazed at the woman in dumbstruck awe: she was *beautiful*. Perhaps 35, she had shoulder-length black hair which seemed professionally groomed, perfect make-up with the most exquisitely sharpened eyebrows, and striking green eyes—penetrating eyes that seemed to miss nothing.

Most of all, however, this young woman just had a confidence about her: an easy yet absolute belief in her own right to be here. She dominated the room instantly. Lily had never seen anything like it before.

Paul Robertson performed the introductions. 'Ms Iolanthe Compton-Jones, may I present to you Captain Jack West.'

Jack noted that in his introduction, Robertson had presented *Jack* to *her*, a formality of diplomatic etiquette that implied this woman was Jack's superior.

Iolanthe Compton-Jones shook his hand with a firm grip. As she did so, she appraised him, and smiled at what she saw.

'The Huntsman,' she said, relishing the word. 'Your reputation precedes you.'

'Ms Compton-Jones.'

'Call me Iolanthe. I am the Official Keeper of the Royal Personal Records for the House of Windsor, a position that has existed for nearly seven hundred years and which can only be held by a blood relative of the monarch.'

'And then only by a talented one,' Robertson added. 'One in whom the Queen has the utmost confidence.'

Iolanthe ignored the compliment and handed West her velveteen box. 'I was instructed to give this to you personally.'

He opened the box to reveal the Pillar inside it.

Jack suppressed a gasp.

It was the first time he had seen one of these fabled Pillars and its magnificence took him by surprise.

Resting in a fitted velvet hollow inside the box, it was an uncut diamond the size and shape of a house-brick. But it wasn't shiny like any diamond he had seen before. Rather it was cloudy, translucent, more like a piece of ice than a diamond. Nevertheless it was still breathtaking.

Robertson said, 'Princess Iolanthe is the emissary of the House of Windsor in this matter.'

'*Princess* Iolanthe?' Lily blurted. 'You're a real princess?'

Iolanthe turned and saw Lily as if for the first time. She smiled kindly and crouched down in the most ladylike manner Lily had ever witnessed. 'Why, hello there. You must be Lily. I've heard a lot about you. You're practically royalty yourself and from a far older line than I. It's a pleasure to make your acquaintance.'

They shook hands. Lily blushed, twirling her pink-tipped hair nervously.

'And yes, I suppose technically I am a princess,' Iolanthe said. 'I am a distant member of the Royal Family, second cousin to Princes William and Harry.'

'No *way* . . .'

Beside Lily, Zoe rolled her eyes, at which point Iolanthe noticed her.

'And who might you be?' she enquired politely.

'Zoe Kissane, Irish commandos. No royal blood, I fear.'

Lily jumped in quickly. 'Zoe's a princess, too, you know. Well, her *nickname* is Princess.'

'Is that so?' Iolanthe said, glancing at the pink end-tips of Zoe's blonde hair, before saying, deadpan, 'How positively quaint.'

Jack saw Zoe's eyes flash and he quickly jumped in.

'As you of all people should know, Iolanthe, names are important,' he said. 'One can do many things with a name, including hiding one's past. Today, you've brought us your family's Pillar, an object it has held far longer than it has held its current name.'

Now Iolanthe's eyes flashed, seeing where he was going with this.

Jack turned to Lily. 'You see, the House of *Windsor*—the name by which the world knows the British Royal Family—has only existed since 1914. But while the name is young, the House is old, very old. Once known as the House of Tudor, then Stuart, in the 1800s it became known as the House of Saxe-Coburg-Gotha, a very Germanic name that not only betrayed the British Royal Family's strong links to European royalty but which also became most embarrassing during the First World War. To save face, the British Royal Family changed their moniker, naming themselves after their favourite manor, Windsor.'

'You're named after a *house*?' Lily asked incredulously.

Iolanthe clenched her jaw. 'The handsome Captain is indeed correct.' Then in a lower voice: 'He is also clearly loyal to his people'—a nod at Zoe. 'Once again, your reputation precedes you, Captain.'

Jack nodded. The unspoken battle for control of this room was over.

And so he turned to the rest of the gathered crowd: 'Okay, people. Let's do this. Let's all open our treasure chests.'

The base had several examination labs, two of which— Labs 1 and 2—were sterile rooms, with two-way observation windows in their walls.

In Lab 1, Wizard had set up the Philosopher's Stone on a workbench.

In Lab 2, the second clean room, the Killing Stone of the Maya was also placed on a bench. Chunky and solid, with a triangular void on its uppermost side—a void which had once perfectly matched a triangular head-chopping blade—and with rather frightening Mayan inscriptions of human sacrifice all over it, it resonated with menace.

Last of all, in Lab 3, the twins had set up several data projectors ready to roll their startling footage from Stonehenge.

Taking the Firestone from Zoe, West said, 'Before we cleanse any Pillars, we need to know where and when they have to be placed. We start in Lab 3. Lachlan, Julius. You're on.'

The lights went out in Lab 3, and as the assembled audience watched in silent awe, Julius and Lachlan played back the video footage of their spectacular ritual at Stonehenge.

Purple light played over Jack's face as he saw the Firestone burst to life in the midst of the dark circle of ancient stones.

Julius commentated: 'Note the shapes on the stones, formed by the indentations, the lichens and the Firestone's light. We'll look at those shapes in more detail later, but for now—'

At that moment, the Firestone let loose its six shafts of purple light, sending the laser-like beams into some of the uprights of the henge, one after the other.

And then it was over—Stonehenge was plunged back into darkness—and Julius stopped the playback and projected some digital snapshots onto the screen.

'Okay,' he began. 'Now let's go through it all a little more methodically. This is how one of the trilithons looked before the lightshow . . .'

He flashed up a digital still:

'During the ritual, however, as the light-beams from the Firestone hit it and the lichens came to life, it appeared like this:

'Note the right-hand upright,' Lachlan said. 'And see how the outline of the African continent can be clearly discerned. You can even seen the Mediterranean Sea at the top. The Red Sea, which only flooded in recent geological times, is not yet in existence.'

Lachlan quickly outlined the twins' theory that the shapes on the stones represented the continents and oceans as they existed millions of years ago, before the melting of the ice caps and the worldwide rising of sea levels had produced the present coastlines.

'What about the outline on the left-hand upright?' Paul Robertson asked from the darkness.

Julius said, 'That one's more difficult. As you can see, it only depicts a sliver of land on the right and at the top, so we're guessing that it depicts a section of ocean, but we haven't figured out which one yet.'

Lachlan went on. 'You will further see on the right-hand upright, three luminous little star-like objects. These are the points at which the shafts of light struck the upright. We have numbered them 1, 2 and 4—while No. 6, as you'll see, is on the left-hand upright. This is the order in which the light-shafts hit the stones of the henge.'

'The order in which the Pillars must be placed,' Wizard said.

'Yes,' Julius said. 'That's right. That's what we think.'

'I'm glad my years of studying this matter meet with your approval, Julius,' Wizard said with a half-smile.

'Oh, yeah, sorry,' Julius said. 'Here's the other trilithon that was hit by light-shafts 3 and 5:

'Again, we are still working on the exact locations of these points. As you can see, the coastlines are exceedingly old—representing the Earth as it was millions of years ago—and so don't match any existing coastlines. So, like the previous example, we do not yet have a match for these locations.'

Lachlan took over. 'In any case, according to Professor Epper's research, each of these sparkling points represents a vertex, or corner, of a giant six-pointed Machine—'

Julius said: '—Think of two pyramids sitting base-to-base, forming a diamond within the Earth's spherical shape.'

Wizard interrupted. 'Point of clarification, boys. They represent no less than the locations of six great *temple-shrines*, underground structures of a magnificence that we cannot even begin to contemplate. It is at each of these temple-shrines that a cleansed Pillar must be placed.'

Julius nodded. 'Yes, sorry, good point that.'

'So where are they?' Paul Robertson asked gruffly. 'The first one looks like it's somewhere in Egypt . . .'

'That's not a bad guess,' Lachlan said. 'The African ones are the easiest to figure out, thanks to the relative stability of the continent's shape over the millennia. GPS-imaging and satellite photography have proved to be very helpful.'

'Not to mention Google Earth,' Julius added.

'Oh yes, Google Earth, too,' Lachlan said. 'In the end, according to the data, the first site lies in Southern Egypt, not far from the Sudanese border. *But . . .*'

'But what?' Scimitar asked warily.

Julius winced. 'But there's a problem with our analysis. We've run the data over and over again, and one issue remains. This first site, it seems, lies underneath a lake.'

'A lake?' Vulture said.

'Yes, Lake Nasser, in the deep south of Egypt,' Lachlan said. 'One of the largest lakes in the world.'

Julius said, 'And sadly, that's as precise as we can be from the available data. We're not sure how you find the exact location of the temple-shrine if it's underwater, let alone its entrance.'

A general murmur of disappointment went through the room, and the twins—Lily saw—seemed a little embarrassed not to have done better. She felt for them.

But then a voice spoke up from the darkness.

The voice of Jack West Jr.

'Which *end* of the lake was it?'

'The southern end,' Lachlan said.

Jack nodded. 'Thank you, gentlemen. Well done. I think I know where the first temple-shrine is.'

'Where?' Vulture asked quickly.

'Yes, where?' Iolanthe snapped around in her chair.

Jack stood up, examining the image on the screen closely.

'Lake Nasser is not a natural lake,' he said, gazing at the picture of the first trilithon. 'Technically, it's part of the Nile. It's an artificial lake that formed behind the Aswan High Dam in 1971; stretches for about two hundred miles to the south. It could easily have covered the entrance to an ancient subterranean structure.

'The dam was also built by the Soviets, after the US pulled out at the last minute,' a glance at Paul Robertson. 'Its construction was a Cold War battlefield for Egypt's allegiance. After much initial excitement and promise-making, during which the Americans did extensive surveying of the area, the US suddenly decided that they didn't want to go ahead with the project. Maybe their surveyors just didn't find what they were looking for.'

Paul Robertson was poker-faced.

Jack looked directly at him, 'You guys have been at work on this Dark Sun project for a long time.'

Robertson shrugged. 'We all have our secrets.'

Jack's gaze lingered on him before he went on, grabbing a sheet from Wizard's black folder and placing it on the projector:

'This is a scan from Wizard's notes. It's a carving from the sarcophagus of Rameses II, written in the Word of Thoth. Translated by my learned colleague'—a nod to Lily—'it reads:

With my beloved, Nefertari,
I, Rameses, son of Ra,
Keep watch over the most sacred shrine.
We shall watch over it forever.
Great sentinels,
With our third eyes, we see all.

'"With our third eyes, we see all." That line didn't make sense to me until now.'

Astro said, 'What are you saying?'

'At the extreme southern end of Lake Nasser stands one of Egypt's greatest monuments, the four colossal seated statues of Rameses II at Abu Simbel. Each one is over twenty *metres* tall. Gigantic.

'Back in Rameses's time, they sat on the banks of the Nile at the border of Egypt and Nubia as a warning to any would-be intruders: "This is how powerful the King of Egypt is. Think twice before you enter our lands."

'Abu Simbel, as it's called, is also the most distant monument in Egypt—its distance from the major Egyptian centres of Thebes and Cairo is astonishing, making it the subject of much speculation. Why build such a dazzling monument so far from the centres of your civilisation?

'The thing is,' Jack said, 'there's a *second* set of statues at Abu Simbel, about a hundred metres from the four well-known ones of Rameses. It's a smaller rock-cut temple dedicated to his favourite wife, Nefertari. That second temple features some giant statues of Nefertari, all of which *also* gaze out over the lake.

'These two sets of immense statues are still there today, sitting on the banks of the Nile, now Lake Nasser. But they don't just keep watch over an old border. According to this carving from Rameses's own sarcophagus, they keep watch over *the most sacred shrine*. The temple-shrine.'

A hush fell over the room as the magnitude of what he was saying set in.

'So how do these statues reveal the shrine's location?' Vulture asked.

'With their third eyes,' Jack said, smiling.

'Oh, Jack . . .' Wizard said. 'You're a genius.'

'What? What do you mean?' Scimitar said.

Jack's eyes glowed as he spoke. 'I imagine if we go to Abu Simbel and carefully calibrate the *eyelines* from the third eye of each set of statues—of Rameses and of Nefertari—the meeting point of those eyelines will be the location of the first temple-shrine.'

The Killing Stone of the Maya

The group moved on to Lab 2, to where the Killing Stone of the Maya sat on its workbench. They all filed into the observation room that looked into the lab.

Leading the way, Wizard said, 'In addition to the locations of the temple-shrines, we need to know the *dates* by which the Pillars must be placed in them.

'Now, in Laozi's entry chamber in China, Tank and I discovered this reference to the laying of the first Pillar:

THE 1ST <u>PILLAR</u> MUST BE INLAID
EXACTLY 100 DAYS BEFORE THE RETURN.

THE PRIZE SHALL BE <u>KNOWLEDGE</u>.

'We had previously calculated the Return—being the full return of the Dark Sun, when its orbit brings it to

the outer reaches of our solar system—to be the day of
next year's vernal equinox, March 20, 2008. Working
backwards then, we deduced that the first Pillar—duly
cleansed—must be set in place by December 10, this
year, by the light of the Dark Sun, which means during
a Titanic Rising.'

'December 10,' Stretch said drily. 'Tomorrow.'

'Yes.'

'Cutting it a little close, aren't we?'

Wizard shrugged as he headed for the door. 'When
ancient knowledge is lost, sometimes it is never found in
time. We've been very lucky so far. Tank and I were aware
of the 2008 deadline, so we thought we had more time
than this. We were surprised that the laying of the first two
Pillars was required so soon, and so far in advance of the
latter four. Jack? Do you have the Firestone?'

Jack produced the Firestone from its pack, handed it
to Wizard.

The old professor then stepped out of the observation
room and into an airlock-type doorway, emerging inside
Lab 2, now alone with the Killing Stone.

Everyone watched intently through the two-way window as Wizard brought the little golden pyramid over to
the Killing Stone. Two HDV video cameras whirred in
the silence, recording the scene through the glass. Four
more were inside the lab with Wizard, filming the Killing Stone from every angle.

The two stones could not have been more different—the Firestone was ultrasmooth, gold and glittering;
the Killing Stone rough and scratched, with dry maroon
stains all over it.

And yet somehow they seemed connected. Fashioned
by the same maker.

One of the two flat sections on the upper surface of the Killing Stone bore a shallow square-shaped recess that perfectly matched the base of the Firestone.

'*Okay,*' Wizard's voice said over the speakers in the observation room, '*I am now going to set the Firestone atop the Killing Stone . . .*'

Slowly and with great reverence, he held the Firestone above the recess in the Killing Stone . . .

. . . and then he lowered the pyramidion onto it.

As he gazed through the two-way window, Jack found himself holding his breath.

The Firestone slotted into the recess perfectly, now married to the Killing Stone.

Wizard stepped back.

Nothing happened.

And then the crystal on the Firestone's peak began to glimmer.

An ominous humming began to thrum from the paired stones.

Wizard's eyes went wide.

Then, abruptly, the humming stopped.

Silence.

No one moved.

But then, in beautiful silence, some symbols on the Killing Stone—individual symbols mixed among the dozens of others carved into it—began to glow dazzling white, one after the other.

One symbol would glow brightly—in total silence— before it went dull again and another shone to life, and another, and another.

A sequence of some kind.

As it played out, the twins jotted down each symbol as it glowed.

'*Numbers and Mayan epochs*,' Wizard said over the intercom. '*Only the numerical symbols for dates are glowing. Crucial dates.*'

The sequence went for about forty seconds, before the glowing subsided and both ancient stones resumed their normal appearance once again.

Half an hour later, after Wizard, Tank and the twins had watched and re-watched the video footage of the event and crunched the numbers, Wizard announced, 'The date from Laozi's chamber is correct. The first Pillar must be set in place during the Titanic Rising just before dawn tomorrow, the 10th of December. The second Pillar must be laid a week from now, on December 17, again during a Titanic Rising.'

'Can you be absolutely sure of your calculations?' Robertson asked.

Tank said, 'Yes, the Mayan calendar has long been synchronised with our own. It is one of the easier primitive calendars to calculate.'

'What about the other four dates?' Robertson asked.

'They are all some way off,' Wizard said, 'three months from now, clustered around the ten days immediately before the Return itself in late March 2008. It seems we face two separate periods of intense activity, one now, one later. If we survive the placing of the first two Pillars over the coming week, we get a period of relief, a hiatus, before in three months' time we face another flurry of activity requiring the placing of four Pillars in the space of ten days.'

Jack said, 'So unless we get it right this week, we don't even get to play next year?'

'That is correct,' Wizard said.

There was a silence as everyone present took this in.

'Okay, then . . .' Jack said. 'Our next step is to cleanse the Pillars we have. Which brings us to the last lab.'

The Philosopher's Stone

Last of all, the group moved into Lab 1, where the
Philosopher's Stone sat proudly and silently on its
workbench.

Once again, the larger group remained in an observation room while Wizard, Vulture and Stretch entered
the lab itself: Wizard carrying the Firestone; Vulture
bearing the velvet case containing the Saudi Pillar; and
Stretch carrying Iolanthe's velveteen case with the British Pillar.

Again, cameras recorded everything.

And although no one noticed it, a security camera
inside the observation room was observing *them*.

In a darkened room elsewhere on the island base,
others were watching.

*

In the lab, Vulture opened his velvet case, and placed his family's Pillar on the workbench. Stretch did the same with Iolanthe's, so that the two Pillars stood side by side.

They were almost identical: two brick-sized blocks of uncut diamond, extraordinary in size, hazy and translucent.

As Jack knew, all diamonds looked this way until they were cleaved by an expert and polished to sparkling brilliance.

He also knew that these two raw diamonds far exceeded any diamond previously found on Earth.

The largest diamond ever found was the Cullinan, a huge gem found in South Africa in 1905. Cut into nine smaller gems, labelled Cullinan I to IX, its largest gem—the Cullinan I—was the size of a baseball and now formed part of the British Crown Jewels.

It was only then that Jack noticed something else about these Pillars. Most peculiarly, each of the Pillars possessed an oval-shaped *void* in its core, a little round chamber that appeared to contain a liquid of some sort.

A clear, colourless liquid.

'But how can that be—?' he whispered.

'It can't be explained,' Iolanthe said from beside him. 'It defies explanation.'

'What can't be explained?' Lily asked.

Jack said, 'Diamonds are made from carbon that has been crystallised under intense pressure and heat. This makes a diamond one of the hardest and most dense substances known to man.'

Zoe added, 'The word *diamond* itself comes from the Greek, *adamas*, and its equivalent in Latin, *diamas*, meaning—'

'Unconquerable,' Lily said.

Jack said, 'Which means that a true diamond, so violently compressed during its formation, should *never* have any kind of void inside it, let alone one that's filled with liquid.' He keyed the intercom. 'Vulture. Do you have any idea what kind of liquid is inside the diamond?'

From inside the lab, Vulture replied: 'An analysis by our scientists suggests that it is a form of liquid helium known as helium-3, He-3.'

Lachlan Adamson whispered, 'A substance not found on Earth. Although it was found in solid form on the Moon. *Apollo 15* brought some back.'

'Very curious,' Jack said.

There was one other thing about the two Pillars that he noticed. On the uppermost flat end of each was a marking.

On Vulture's it was a single horizontal line: –

On Iolanthe's, there were four.

Even Jack could count in Thoth: these were the First and Fourth Pillars.

Inside the lab, Wizard approached the Philosopher's Stone, carrying the Firestone. Then, reverently, he slotted the Firestone into the flat square section on top of the Philosopher's Stone's lid.

It clicked into place.

'Okay,' he nodded to Vulture. 'Place your Pillar inside the Philosopher's Stone.'

Vulture stepped forward and held his oblong diamond block above the rectangular slot in the Philosopher's

Stone. The dimensions of the slot matched those of the Pillar exactly.

With both hands, Vulture lowered the Pillar horizontally into the slot until it rested on its side, its long flat upper surface lying flush with the rim of the slot.

Then he stepped away and, with Wizard, gently picked up the lid and—with the Firestone now incorporated into it—slowly lowered the lid back into position, covering the Pillar.

Jack watched intently.

Beside him, so did Paul Robertson and Iolanthe.

The lid slotted into place, concealing the Pillar.

Now the two pieces of the Philosopher's Stone were one—with the charged Firestone crowning it and with the Saudi Pillar within it.

All the watchers waited in silence.

No-one knew what this so-called 'cleansing' would entail—

A blinding flash of light startled them all.

It flared out from the slit between the lid of the Philosopher's Stone and its trapezoidal base, and yet it easily illuminated the entire lab.

The watchers stepped back, shielding their eyes.

The dazzling white light continued to blaze out from within the Philosopher's Stone. Some incredible kind of transformation was taking place inside it.

The crystal at the peak of the Firestone flared like a purple beacon.

From beside West, Tank spoke quietly: 'Throughout the ages, the Philosopher's Stone has always been associated with transformation. Some say that it can perform the act of alchemy, or as scientists would say today, elemental transmutation—Isaac Newton was notoriously obsessed with this property. Others have claimed that it can change water into an elixir that can grant long life. Always the key word has been *change*. Incredible, astonishing change.'

Then as suddenly as it had appeared, the blazing light from the Philosopher's Stone went out, as did the purple light atop the Firestone.

Silence again. Normal light.

Everyone blinked.

In the lab, the Philosopher's Stone sat still, lifeless, yet somehow it radiated energy, power.

Wizard and Vulture then used some tongs to gently lift away its lid.

The lid came clear . . .

. . . to reveal the Pillar still nestled within the Stone.

Wizard lifted the Pillar from its slot and gasped.

Whereas before the diamond Pillar was cloudy and translucent, now it was perfectly clear, like polished glass or crystal. And the liquid trapped inside it, which had previously been colourless, was now a vivid shiny silver.

The First Pillar had been transformed.

It had been cleansed.

'We've got no time to waste,' Jack said, striding through the corridors of the base. 'We have to get this cleansed Pillar to the temple-shrine at Abu Simbel by dawn.'

Hustling to keep up, Iolanthe said, 'Captain! Captain, please! There are other issues about the Pillars that I must discuss with you.'

'You can discuss them on the way to Egypt,' Jack said, heading for the door.

'I'm going with you?'

'She's going with us?' Zoe asked.

'She is now.'

Things started moving very quickly.

In a hangar near the base's runway, the *Halicarnassus* stood in all its glory, black and huge, bathed in arc lights.

The doors to the hangar parted and a chill Atlantic storm rushed in, rain and wind lashing the nose of the plane.

Jack's team hot-footed it across the hangar floor to the airstairs leading up to the 747.

The trusted regulars: Wizard, Zoe, Pooh Bear, Stretch.

And the new players: Vulture, Scimitar, Astro and now Iolanthe.

And the kids: Lily and Alby. This time, Jack decided, they'd come with him. In Egypt, the home of the Word of Thoth, he had a feeling he might need Lily's linguistic skills.

The only ones *not* going were Tank and the twins, Lachlan and Julius Adamson. They would stay here on Mortimer Island and continue their studies, searching for the locations of the other temple-shrines.

In an office elsewhere on the island base, the American colonel known as Wolf watched the eleven members of West's Abu Simbel team arrive at the *Halicarnassus* on a closed circuit TV monitor.

Flanking him, as always, were his two junior men, Rapier and Switchblade.

The door behind them opened, and Paul Robertson entered.

'What do you think, Colonel?' he asked.

At first, Wolf didn't reply. He just kept watching Jack on the monitor.

'Judah was right,' he said at last. 'West is good. He puts together puzzles very well—Abu Simbel was smart. He's also slippery. He got the better of Judah at Giza and escaped Black Dragon's attack in Australia.'

'Iolanthe?' Robertson asked.

'She is to be watched like a hawk,' Wolf said. 'They might appear helpful now, but the Great Houses of Europe only ever act in their own interests. They have their own agenda here. Make no mistake, the Royals will abandon us the instant it suits them.'

'Do you want me to give Astro or Vulture any special instructions?' Robertson asked.

'As far as Astro is concerned, definitely not. At this stage, his actions must be completely unconnected to us. Astro must be completely ignorant of his role in this, otherwise West will almost certainly find him out. As for the Saudi, he knows we're watching.'

'What about this mission to Abu Simbel to place the First Pillar?' Robertson said. 'Should we step in?'

Wolf thought about that for a moment.

'No. Not yet. It's not the first reward that interests us. It's the *second*. Thus we have an interest in Captain West succeeding in placing this First Pillar. We can also learn from his experience.'

Wolf turned to Robertson, his blue eyes glinting. 'Let young West lay this one, and when it is done, grab the little fuck and all his people and bring them to me.'

Lashed by the driving rain, the *Halicarnassus* lifted off from Mortimer Island in the Bristol Channel.

As it banked round on a heading that would take it to Egypt, another encrypted signal went out from the island base, but not one related to Jack or Wolf or even Iolanthe. To those who could decrypt it, the message read:

FIRST PILLAR SUCCESSFULLY CLEANSED.
WEST GOING TO ABU SIMBEL IN
SOUTHERN EGYPT TO SET IT IN PLACE.
DO WHAT MUST BE DONE.

FOURTH ORDEAL

THE FIRST VERTEX

Abu Simbel, Egypt

ABU SIMBEL, EGYPT
10 DECEMBER, 2007
THE DAY OF THE 1ST DEADLINE

TEMPLE OF RAMESES II AT ABU SIMBEL

TEMPLE OF NEFERTARI AT ABU SIMBEL

The *Halicarnassus* soared toward southern Egypt, zooming through the night sky, racing the coming dawn.

Despite the late hour, there was activity going on all over the plane: Jack and Iolanthe checking the layout of Abu Simbel and its surrounds; Wizard, Zoe and Alby doing mathematical and astronomical calculations; while Lily, Stretch and Pooh Bear studied Lake Nasser.

'So,' Jack said, coming over to Wizard's desk, 'when exactly do we need to have the Pillar in place?'

Wizard tapped some astronomical charts with his pen. 'Again, everything depends on Jupiter. According to these charts, the Titanic Rising will occur at 6:12 a.m. local time, just around dawn.

'It'll be difficult to see Jupiter due to the light of the rising Sun—so we'll have to use an infra-red telescope. The duration of the Rising will also be shorter than the one Zoe saw at Stonehenge because we're on a different latitude—at the high latitude of Stonehenge, the Firestone received a flat, almost tangential blow from the Dark Sun. But at Abu Simbel we'll be a lot closer to the Equator and thus more perpendicular to the Dark Sun, so we'll receive a more direct hit from it. Which means it'll be shorter, lasting about a minute.'

Jack nodded. '6:12 it is then.'

Wizard asked, 'How are you going with the location of the temple-shrine?'

'I think we have a candidate.'

Jack turned a book around for Wizard and the others to see. It showed the two massive temples dedicated to Rameses II and his wife Nefertari at Abu Simbel.

The larger temple featured four twenty-metre-high figures of Rameses, all seated on thrones, while the façade of the second temple—one hundred metres from the first—featured six ten-metre-high figures: four of Rameses and two of his favourite wife, Nefertari. Both sets of statues gazed out over Lake Nasser at a curious collection of pyramid-shaped islands that jutted above the flat surface of the lake.

'What we have to remember about Abu Simbel,' Jack said, 'is that it does not stand where it originally stood. When the Soviets built the Aswan High Dam in the 1960s, they knew that the lake it created would cover the statues. So UNESCO had the statues of Abu Simbel moved to higher ground, block by block, piece by piece. They erected the statues on higher ground, in almost exactly the same alignment as they originally stood.'

'*Almost* exactly the same alignment?' Astro said, alarmed. 'You mean the statues aren't correctly aligned anymore? If they're not—'

'They're a couple of degrees out,' Jack said calmly. 'But the discrepancy is known, so we can account for it. You can see the difference in this picture: the original and present-day positions of the statues.'

'They don't look so big,' Astro said.

'Trust me. They're big.'

The plane flew south.

At one point on its journey, Iolanthe disappeared into the aft crew quarters to get changed into something more rugged.

As soon as she was gone, Vulture spun to face West. 'Huntsman. A moment with you. Can the British Royal be trusted?'

Jack turned, gazing at the rear section of the plane.

'Not at all,' he said. 'She's here to represent her family, her Royal House, just as you are here representing yours, the Kingdom of Saudi Arabia—so I guess I trust her about as much as I trust you. Right now, we're useful to her and she's useful to us. But the moment we cease to be useful, she'll cut us loose.'

'Or cut our throats,' Zoe said.

The American Marine, Astro, frowned, confused. 'I'm sorry, but what are you talking about?

Great Houses? Royal Houses?'

Stretch said, 'When we ventured out to locate the Seven Wonders of the Ancient World, we did so in competition with the United States on the one hand, and Old Europe on the other—France, Germany, Italy, Austria. The Catholic Church, knowledgeable in ancient matters, also formed part of this Old Europe coalition.'

'Think of it as Old Money versus New Money,' Jack said. 'America is New Money, recently attained and acquired. Europe is Old Money, wealth that is acquired through heredity, land ownership, family name. Remember Jane Austen: a gentleman does not work, he receives income from his lands.'

Astro reddened. 'I didn't read Jane Austen in high school . . .'

Stretch said, 'While we like to think of Europe today as a patchwork of modern democracies run by and for the people, this is an illusion. Almost 55 per cent of mainland Europe is owned by three families: the Saxe-Coburgs of the United Kingdom—which, through war and marriage, acquired the lands of the old Habsburg family of Austria-Germany—the Romanovs of Russia, and the Oldenburgs of Denmark, the canniest and most cunning royal line in history. Through multiple royal marriages, Danish blood runs thick through nearly all the Houses of Europe, and thus the Danish royal family controls a quarter of continental Europe all by itself.'

'The Romanovs of Russia?' Astro said. 'I thought the Russian royal family was executed out of existence in 1918 by the Soviets.'

'Not at all,' Stretch said. 'Two of the royal children survived, Alexei and one of the girls. And royals do not like to see other royals deposed—they look after their own. The surviving Romanov children of Tsar Nicholas II were sheltered by the Danish royal family in Copenhagen and ultimately married off to well-bred families. While they might not use formal royal titles like *Tsar* any more, the Romanov line certainly still exists, just out of popular sight.'

Stretch then turned an eye to Vulture, who was sitting a little too silently in the corner. 'There is, of course, one other rather old Royal House that holds much sway in the world today: the House of Saud in Arabia. But it is not held in high esteem by the Great Houses of Europe— since its rise from obscurity in the 1700s, it has always been seen by the European Houses as a quaint band of tribesmen merely affecting royal traits. Even the discovery of oil in Arabia in the twentieth century, by which the Saudis gained enormous wealth and power, did not gain for them the respect they so desired.'

'Old Money only respects Old Money,' Jack said.

Vulture said nothing, but the look in his eyes suggested that he agreed.

'So, these Royal Houses, what's their link to the Machine?' Astro asked.

'Think of royalty throughout history,' Wizard said, 'going all the way back to primitive tribes. What made one tribal family worthy of greater respect than all the other families of the tribe?'

'Strength. Their ability to fight on behalf of the tribe.'

'Sometimes, yes,' Jack said. 'But not always.'

Astro shrugged. 'What else is there, then?'

Wizard said, 'More often it was the family *that held some kind of sacred talisman* that was regarded as the head family of the tribe. It might be a mace, or a crown, or a holy stone. The ability to fight was often collateral to the ability to maintain possession of a sacred object.'

Jack said, 'Macbeth slays Duncan and takes his mace, thus Macbeth, as holder of the mace, becomes king.'

Wizard said, 'And the Three Great Houses of Europe have always held something that has made them *greater* than other noble households . . .'

'Pillars,' Astro said, getting it.

'Exactly,' Wizard said, 'and the knowledge that goes with them: hereditary knowledge, passed down from generation to generation, about the use and purpose of those Pillars.'

Jack added, 'And the fact that our Princess Iolanthe is the current Keeper of the Royal Personal Records means that she's a key holder of that knowledge.'

Astro said, 'So if there are only three European Houses, does that mean they only have three Pillars?'

'I believe so,' Wizard said. 'But—'

'—but that doesn't mean we don't know where the other three are,' Iolanthe said from the doorway at the rear of the main cabin.

Everyone spun.

Iolanthe was the picture of calm and not, it seemed, the least bit offended that they had been talking about her behind her back.

Now dressed in a cream jacket, Oakley boots and slim cargo pants, she strolled back into the cabin and slid onto a spare couch.

'If I may contribute to the discussion,' she said. 'Throughout history, commoners have actively *sought* someone to look up to. Someone of higher birth, of noble blood, of superior sensibility. Royalty. Those who would willingly undertake an obligation to keep safe both the people and certain important objects. And because royalty are known to subscribe to a higher standard of honour, they are trusted to do so.

'The common folk, on the other hand—knowing in their hearts that they themselves are too fickle, too greedy, to stay true to any such notion of honour—seek a family of renown who will. Thus the strong rule and the weak get ruled over, by their own choice. It is the natural order of things. It has been so since humans began to walk upright.'

Lily gazed at Iolanthe closely.

The strong rule, and the weak get ruled over. She had heard those words before: uttered by a deranged Vatican priest named Francisco del Piero, the man who had raised her twin brother, Alexander, to be a despotic and cruel ruler.

Wizard had heard those same words, and he too gazed at Iolanthe with watchful eyes.

Astro said, 'If people love royalty so much, why is democracy so embraced then? Look at America.'

Iolanthe snuffed a laugh. 'Look at America? Why, Lieutenant, for the last two hundred years, your country has been steadily and unequivocally marching toward monarchy.

'The problem is, your rulers have no talisman, no treasure, to hold on behalf of the people. So you get bold usurpers seeking to create a kingdom: Kennedy's father, Joseph, wanted to establish a line of Kennedy presidents: John then Robert then Edward. In recent years, the Bush family—aided by its friends in the House of Saud—has succeeded in creating a lineage, and indeed plans to install a third Bush on the throne. But it has no talisman, and thus no kingdom. Although perhaps when this adventure is over, it will, and thus it will take a seat at the table with the Great Houses of Europe.'

Jack said, 'So right now in this race we have: us, the good guys, aided by the New Money wannabes from Saudi Arabia and America; you, the royal dynasties of Europe; and China, aided by who-knows-who. So where do, say, the United Arab Emirates fit into this world view?'

'Newer Money, that's all,' Iolanthe said. 'A puny desert tribe that only recently found itself sitting on massive oil reserves.' She shrugged apologetically at Pooh Bear and Scimitar. 'No offence.'

Pooh Bear growled, 'Ma'am, in the words of my young friend, Lily, get bent.'

Scimitar just bowed. 'We take no offence at all, madam.'

Jack said, 'So what about other countries? Like Australia, for instance.'

'Still a colony of Britain,' Iolanthe said dismissively.

'China?'

'A nation of corrupt officials and a billion ignorant rural peasants. Fat, slow and bloated. By the time it advances to the level of the West, we will have reached Mars.'

'Africa?'

'The slavelands of the world. Useless now, as it has already been thoroughly plundered. Nowadays African nations are like whores, willing to sell themselves and their armies to anyone with hard currency.'

'Japan?'

'An interesting case, for the Japanese stand *sui generis* in our world, in a category of their own. Even the most humble commoner there has a deep sense of honour. But their pride is their weakness. Japan is the most racist nation on Earth: the Japanese sincerely believe themselves to be superior to all other races. This got them into trouble in World War II.'

'But Japan has a royal family,' Zoe said. 'The oldest continuous royal line in the world.'

'This is true,' Iolanthe said. 'It is old and noble and not nearly as weak as it pretends to be. Japan's capitulation at the end of the Second World War almost saw the first modern destruction of a legitimate royal family. The Americans humiliated Hirohito but they did not disempower him. Because they were unable to find his talisman.'

Jack frowned at that. This was something new to him. He leaned forward.

'And that talisman was . . . ?'

' . . . something which I am not inclined to tell you about just yet, my dashing Huntsman.' Iolanthe gave Jack a mischievous sexy grin. 'You may have to employ other methods to prise that little secret from me—maybe you could *romance* it out of me. Alternatively, you could just ask your American colleague here,' a nod at Astro.

Jack raised an eyebrow at Astro. 'Well?'

'Search me,' Astro said.

Iolanthe said, 'In any case, while they might protest otherwise and say that they have moved on, the Japanese have not forgotten the profound slur of World War II. And such a prideful people hold a very long grudge. You turn your back on Japan at your peril.'

For a moment, no one said anything.

'The world is a complex place,' Iolanthe said softly, almost to herself. 'Wars are won and lost. Empires rise and fall. But through all of recorded history, power has *always* been in a state of flux, ever transferred from one empire to the next: from Egypt to Greece and then to Rome; or more recently, from France under Napoleon to the British Empire to the current American dominance. But now—with the igniting of the Machine—it will be different. The transfer of power will cease. For now is the one and only time in history where total and absolute power will come to rest, forever, in the hands of one nation.'

A couple of hours later, the main cabin of the plane was dark and silent.

The only person still at work in it was Jack, poring over a map of Africa by the light of a desk lamp, with Horus perched on his chairback. All the others had gone aft to get some sleep before the big day ahead—except for Lily; she lay fast asleep on the couch beside Jack.

Horus squawked.

Jack looked up to see Iolanthe standing in the doorway to the main cabin, dressed in a loose tracksuit, her hair tousled from sleep.

'Command is lonely,' she said.

'Sometimes.'

'I was told you inspire loyalty in those who follow you.' Iolanthe sat down.

'All I do is let my people think for themselves. Seems to work.'

Iolanthe watched him for a moment, eyeing him closely in the darkness, as if assessing this strange being named Jack West Jr.

'Few people can think for themselves,' she said.

'*All* people can think for themselves,' Jack said quickly.

'No. Not true. Not all of them can,' she said softly, looking away.

Jack said, 'You mentioned before that you might know the whereabouts of the *other* Pillars . . .'

Iolanthe was roused from her reverie and she smiled at him, raising an eyebrow. 'I might.'

'It's just that we have this Saudi Pillar, marked with a single dash, and your one, marked with four dashes, indicating that they're the First and Fourth Pillars. We'll be needing the second one soon, within the week.'

'*If* we survive today.'

'Let's be optimistic and assume we will,' West said. 'Where is it?'

Iolanthe stood, touching her upper lip with her tongue. 'According to my sources, the Second Pillar is to be found in the jungles of central Africa, zealously and jealously guarded by the same tribe that has held it for over three thousand years, the Neetha.'

'I've researched the Neetha. Cannibals. Nasty.'

'Captain, *nasty* does not even begin to describe the Neetha. Nor does cannibal. *Carnivore* would be better. Ordinary cannibals kill you before they eat you. The Neetha do not give you that dignity.

'It's believed that a thousand Rwandan refugees fleeing the genocide in 1998 got lost in the jungle and stumbled upon the grounds of the Neetha. Not a single one of them emerged. To enter the Neetha's territory is to enter a spider's web.'

'Another question,' Jack said. 'What do you know about the last Ramesean Stone, the Basin of Rameses II? Wizard doesn't know where it is.'

'Nobody knows where it is,' Iolanthe said simply. 'The Basin long ago disappeared from history.'

'Do you know what it does?'

'No. Not a clue.' Iolanthe turned to go.

'I don't trust you, you know,' Jack said after her.

'Nor should you,' she said, not turning around. 'Nor should you.'

She left the room. Jack continued with his reading.

Neither he nor Iolanthe had noticed that Lily had awoken during their conversation.

And heard every word.

An hour later, the cabin lights throughout the plane came on and a tone beeped over the intercom.

'*Rise and shine, people!*' Sky Monster's voice called cheerfully. '*Jack, I've spotted a stretch of highway about forty klicks west of Abu Simbel. Nothing there but desert. Can't land on the northern highway: there are several convoys of tourist coaches coming down it—they set out early each day from Aswan to get to Abu Simbel just after dawn. The western road should be long enough to act as a runway and far enough out to allow us to get in and out without anyone noticing.*'

'Thanks, Monster,' Jack said, standing. 'Take us in.'

ABU SIMBEL

SOUTHERN EGYPT

In the pre-dawn light, the enormous statues of Rameses the Great loomed like giants frozen forever in stone.

They towered above West's team and their vehicles, dwarfing them.

Whereas Zoe had used silent non-lethal force to subdue the guards at Stonehenge, here Jack had not been so subtle. The two Egyptian Department of Antiquities guards who had been on patrol at the popular tourist site had quickly surrendered when they found themselves staring down the barrels of four submachine-guns. Now they lay bound and gagged in their guardhouse.

Jack stood before the four statues of Rameses, while Wizard stood a hundred metres away in front of the smaller temple of Nefertari. The whole team was here except for Sky Monster and Stretch—they'd remained on the *Halicarnassus* and now circled high overhead, keeping watch over the landscape and waiting for the extraction call.

'Rangefinders,' Jack commanded, and two laser range-finders were brought out, one for each set of statues.

'Is that going to be a problem?' Zoe said, nodding at the second of the four statues of Rameses II. Sometime in the distant past, its head had fallen off.

'No,' West said. 'In ancient Egypt, they counted from left to right. The "third eye" will be on that one,' he pointed at the statue second from the right.

Helped by Pooh Bear, Astro abseiled down from the rocky overhang above the statue in question, clutching one of the rangefinders in his free hand.

Over at the Nefertari temple, Scimitar did the same, aided by Vulture: there the 'third eye' was also on the second statue from the right, a statue of Nefertari.

As they roped into position, West turned and gazed out over Lake Nasser.

The great lake stretched away to the horizon, dark and silent, possessed of that unnatural calm found only in man-made lakes. A low fog hovered over it.

The opposite shore swung around in a long curve, and rising up out of the lake in front of this shoreline, Jack could just make out a series of pyramid-shaped islands.

At the base of many of those islands and all along the old shoreline, Jack knew, were all manner of hieroglyphic carvings that UNESCO had not been able to save from the rising waters. Just like the Three Gorges Dam in China.

Astro and Scimitar were in position.

The great stone head in front of Astro was simply huge, even larger than he was.

'Mount the rangefinders in the eye sockets,' West instructed. 'Make sure they're precisely aligned with the statues' sightlines.'

Astro did so—likewise, Scimitar at his statue—using

clamps to secure his rangefinder to the eye socket of his statue.

Once they were done, West got them to adjust the devices slightly, two degrees to southward—to account for the slight repositioning of Abu Simbel by UNESCO.

'Okay, turn them on.'

The rangefinders were switched on—

—and suddenly two dead-straight red laser-lines lanced out from the third eye sockets, shooting out over the lake, slicing through the fog, disappearing into the near distance—

—only to converge at a point about two kilometres away, at one of the small pyramidal rock islands jutting up out of the waters of Lake Nasser not far from the opposite shore.

'Oh my goodness,' Wizard breathed. 'We found it.'

Two Zodiac speedboats were immediately inflated and launched into the water.

Vulture and Scimitar were left on the shore as a rear-guard while Jack and the others shoomed off in the two speedboats.

Within ten minutes, the two Zodiacs arrived at the pyramidal island, shrouded by fog.

The semi-submerged snouts of dozens of Nile croco-diles could be seen nearby, forming a wide circle around the two boats, their eyes glinting in the team's flash-lights, staring at these intruders.

As it drew near, Zoe peered up at the rocky island. At the waterline, its flanks were sheer, almost vertical, while further up they tapered to a more gentle slope.

'The surface looks almost hand-carved,' she said.

'Like someone *chiselled* the rock island into the shape of a pyramid.'

Wizard said, 'Archaeologists have long pondered the shape of these islands, back when they were just hills, before the lake rose. But, no, tests have proved that they were not carved in any way. This is just their natural shape.'

'Weird,' Lily said.

'Hey! I've got a sonar reading . . .' Astro called from his Zodiac, on which was all manner of depth-sounding and ground-penetrating radar devices.

'No, wait,' he sighed. 'It's nothing. Living signature. Something down on the bottom. Probably just a croc—hold on, this is better, GPR has found a void in the base of the island directly beneath us. Sonic resonance confirms it. Looks like a horizontal tunnel of some kind, delving into the island.'

'Bring the boats together,' Jack ordered, 'and anchor us to the base of the island. Then bring out the air-chute and the docking door. Astro, Pooh Bear—get your tanks on. You've got the job of sealing the entrance.'

Twenty minutes later, a strange contraption sat in between the two anchored Zodiacs: a hollow inflatable rubber tube that dived down into the water like an open-topped vertical pipe.

Astro and Pooh Bear—in full scuba gear and bearing harpoon guns for the crocs—splashed backwards into the inky water, flashlights on.

Thirty metres underneath the boats, they arrived at the lakebed, at the point where it met the base of the rock pyramid.

They panned their flashlights over the surface of the island pyramid, to reveal *hundreds* of images cut into the rocky surface. They were mainly standard Egyptian carvings: hieroglyphics and images of pharaohs shaking hands with gods.

'Jack,' Astro said into his facemask mike, 'we've got carvings. Lots of them.'

Pooh Bear waved a portable GPR—ground-penetrating radar—device over the image-riddled wall. Kind of like an X-ray, it could detect hollows and voids behind the surface of the wall. 'Here! Got a void behind this carving!'

Astro shone his flashlight onto the suspect section of wall, and found himself illuminating a carving he'd seen before:

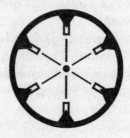

The symbol for the Machine.
'We should've known,' he said. 'Found it.'

Astro and Pooh Bear then quickly set about affixing a peculiar tent-like device over the point where the lake floor met the wall of the pyramid island, covering the carving of the Machine.

Shaped like a cube, the tent-like device was a portable variable-aperture United States Navy submarine docking door—a gift to West from the Sea Ranger.

Normally used to join submersibles to submarines, it was a rubber-walled docking unit that operated like an airlock: once you affixed it in place, sealing the edges, you filled it with air—inflating it like a balloon and expelling any water from it—thus providing a dry 'docking environment' between two submerged points.

There were removable entry holes in each of the cube's six sides, and at the moment one of these—on the upper side of the docking unit—was connected to the tube that snaked back up to the Zodiacs.

Once the unit was in place, its corner points bolted to the lake floor and to the pyramid island itself, Jack started an air pump, filling the tube and the docking unit with air.

The docking door inflated quickly and suddenly the way was clear to climb down its tube—perfectly dry— and access the wall of the ancient pyramid island.

*

Jack climbed down the rubber tube, gripping its inbuilt ladder holds, slowly descending into Lake Nasser.

He carried a full-face scuba mask but did not wear it. It was a precaution, just in case the docking door collapsed or otherwise unexpectedly filled with water. He also held the cleansed First Pillar in a chestpack. On his head he wore his trademark fireman's helmet.

He came to the bottom of the entry tube and stood— thanks to the air-filled docking unit—on the floor of Lake Nasser. His boots stepped down into an inch of water, water that formed a suction-layer against the bottom of the tent-like docking unit.

The exposed flank of the pyramid island stood before him, rocky and uneven and glistening wet.

Carved symbols covered it, a kaleidoscope of images in which the carving of the Machine was easily lost.

But there was no discernible door in the wall. Nothing but carving after carving after carving.

Jack gazed at the symbol for the Machine.

It was a fairly large carving, about the size of a manhole. And the six rectangles in it depicting the six Pillars seemed to be lifesized, the same size as the Pillar in Jack's chestpack.

Unlike all the others, however, the uppermost rectangle in the carving was *indented*, recessed into the image.

'A keyhole,' Jack said aloud.

He removed the Pillar from his chestpack, held it against the recessed rectangle.

It was an exact match for size.

'You'll never know if you don't try . . .'

And so he reached forward with the Pillar and pressed it into the rectangle—

—and immediately *the entire circular carving* turned on its axis, rotating like a wheel, and retreated into the wall, revealing a dark round tunnel beyond it.

Jack stepped back in surprise, still gripping the Pillar.

'*Jack? You okay down there?*' Zoe's voice asked in his ear.

'Am I ever,' he said. 'Come on down. We're in.'

The Tunnel of Sobek

The tight tunnel beyond the round entry hole was slick with wetness. A dripping noise echoed from somewhere within it.

Gripping an amber glowstick in his teeth and guided by the light on his fireman's helmet, Jack belly-crawled for about five metres down the claustrophobic tunnel before he came to its first obstacle: a huge Nile crocodile, easily an eighteen footer, blocking the way and grinning at him from a distance of three feet.

Jack froze.

The thing was enormous. A great fat prehistoric beast. Its fearsome teeth protruded from the edges of its snout. It snorted loudly.

Jack shone his helmet flashlight down the tunnel past the big croc, and saw others beyond it, maybe four more lined up in single file down the length of the tight little tunnel.

There must be some other entrance, Jack thought. *A crevice somewhere above the waterline that the crocodiles have slithered in through.*

'Hey, Jack?' Zoe said, arriving in the tunnel behind him. 'What's the hold-up?'

'A large animal with a whole lot of teeth.'

'Oh.'

Jack pursed his lips, thinking.

As he did so, Zoe came up behind him and shone her flashlight past him. 'Oh, you have got to be kidding me.'

Then abruptly Jack said, 'It's too cold.'

'What?'

'It's too early in the day for them, their blood's still too cold to be a threat.'

'What are you talking about?' Zoe asked.

'Crocodiles are cold-blooded. For a croc, especially a big one, to perform any kind of athletic act, it needs its blood to be warmed up, usually by the Sun. These guys are scary, sure, but it's too early in the morning for them, too cold, so they're not gonna be capable of big aggressive movements. We can crawl past them.'

'Now you really are kidding.'

At that moment, Pooh Bear and Wizard arrived behind them.

'What's the problem?' Pooh Bear asked.

'Them,' Zoe jerked her chin at the line of large crocodiles before them. 'But don't worry, Captain Courageous here thinks we can crawl by them.'

Pooh Bear's face went instantly white. 'Cr-crawl by them . . . ?'

Wizard gazed at the crocs, nodding. 'At this time of day, their blood will still be very cold. The only thing they could really do right now is bite.'

'Biting is what worries me,' Zoe said.

Jack checked his watch. It was 5:47 a.m.

'We've got no choice,' he said. 'We've got twenty-five minutes to get to the Vertex and that means getting past these guys. I'm going in.'

'Er, Huntsman,' Pooh Bear said. 'You know . . . well . . . you know I'd follow you anywhere. But I'm . . . not good with crocs at the best of times and this is—'

Jack nodded. 'It's okay, Zahir. No one's completely fearless, not even you. You sit this one out. I won't tell anyone.'

'Thank you, Huntsman.'

'Zoe? Wizard?'

He could see that they were thinking similar thoughts.

Zoe eyed the tunnel determinedly. 'You can't do this alone. I'll be right behind you.'

And Wizard said, 'I've worked my whole life to see what lies beyond those crocs. I'll be damned if they'll stop me.'

'Then let's do it,' Jack said.

Crawling through the darkness, he came to the first croc.

The great reptile made him look tiny, puny.

As Jack's face came level with it, the croc opened its massive jaws, revealing every single one of its teeth, and emitted a harsh belching grunt in warning.

Jack paused, drew in a deep breath, and took the plunge, crawling past the thing's jaws and shimmying around the side of the animal, sliding up against the curved wall of the tunnel.

His eyes came level with the croc's—and Jack saw that those eyes, cold and hard, were watching him every inch of the way.

But the creature did not attack. It did nothing but shuffle on its claws.

Jack wriggled past it, his cargo pants brushing up against the bulging belly of the beast, and he could feel the flabby give of its abdomen, and then suddenly he was alongside its spiky tail, past it.

Jack let out the breath he'd been holding.

'I'm past the first one,' he said into his headset mike. 'Zoe, Wizard. Come on through.'

The Stairs of Atum

In this manner, Jack, Zoe and Wizard slithered down the long tight tunnel, squeezing on their bellies past the five gigantic Nile crocodiles.

At the end of the tunnel, they emerged at the top of a square stone well equipped with a staircase that delved down into darkness.

The stairs bent back and forth as they dived down the well-shaft. On the walls of each landing were thousands of hieroglyphs, including more large carvings of the Machine's wheel-like symbol.

Jack descended the first flight of steps and came to the first landing . . .

. . . where the Machine symbol in the wall retreated inwards by some unseen mechanism and revealed a wide gaping hole behind it, a hole that could contain any kind of deadly liquid . . .

. . . but then the Pillar in Jack's hand glowed slightly and the hole instantly resealed itself.

Jack exchanged a look with Wizard.

'Doesn't look like you get past these traps without the Pillar in your possession.'

'Not without great difficulty,' Wizard agreed.

Down the stairs they climbed, winding back and forth.

At every landing, the wheel-like symbol for the Machine opened but then closed again when it sensed the Pillar in West's hand.

Down and down.

Wizard counted the stairs as they went, until at last they came to the bottom, where the stairs stopped at a great stone archway—tall and imposing, twenty feet high. It opened onto dense blackness.

Wizard finished his count. '267.'

Jack stepped into the archway, staring out into the blackness beyond it. A light breeze struck his face, cool and crisp.

He sensed a large space before him, so he pulled out his flare-gun and fired it into the black.

Fifteen flares later, he just stood there in the archway, his mouth open in wonderment.

'Now that's a sight you'll remember for a long time,' he breathed.

The Hall of the Machine

The twenty-foot-high archway in which Jack stood looked microscopic compared to the space that opened up below it.

The archway stood at the summit of an immense mountain of stone steps—five hundred of them, maybe more—steps that descended to a flat-floored hall that was easily four hundred feet tall and five hundred wide. The colossal collection of stairs stretched for the entire width of the hall, from wall to wall, an enormous mountainside of perfectly square-cut steps.

The ceiling of this mighty subterranean hall was upheld by a forest of glorious columns, all of which were carved in the colourful Egyptian fashion, with brilliant red-blue-and-green lotus leaves at their tops. There must have been forty such pillars, all in regular rows.

'Just like the temple of Rameses II at Karnak . . .' Wizard breathed.

'Maybe the temple of Rameses was a replica built in honour of this,' Zoe said.

Standing at the top of the great flight of stairs, Jack felt like he was standing in the topmost row of a football stadium, gazing down upon the field far below.

And there was one other thing.

Down in the hall, *there was no fourth wall opposite the stair-mountain.*

Indeed directly opposite the huge staircase, past the forest of ornate columns, was nothing at all: the polished floor of the hall simply ended abruptly at a sharp edge, a rail-less balcony five hundred feet wide, essentially a great viewing platform that looked out over an even larger space of more darkness.

But from their vantage point at the top of the staircase, Jack and the others couldn't see what lay inside this larger space, so they descended the stairs, looking like ants against the gargantuan hall.

They were halfway down the stairs when Jack saw what lay in the larger space.

He stopped dead.

'We're gonna need more flares,' he breathed.

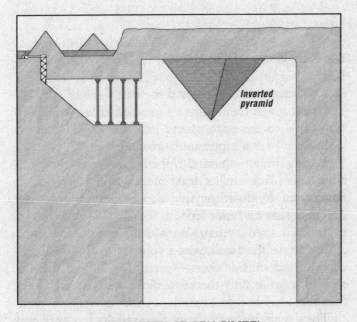

THE VERTEX AT ABU SIMBEL

The First Vertex of the Machine

Jack, Wizard and Zoe crossed the vast floor of the hall, passing through the forest of superhigh columns, before they came to the edge of the hall, the point where it looked out over a larger underground void.

A gargantuan abyss dropped away before them. Deep and black and at least a thousand feet wide, it plummeted to unfathomable depths, into the densest darkness Jack had ever seen.

And mounted over it, suspended from the flat stone ceiling above the abyss, was a colossal pyramid—hanging inverted, upside-down—perfectly cut and, by the look of it, of exactly the same dimensions as the Great Pyramid at Giza. It looked beyond ancient, beyond anything mankind could hope to build. Its flanks blazed with a lustrous bronze sheen.

Jack was reminded of the Pyramide Inversée at the Louvre in Paris—the beautiful upside-down glass pyramid that hung over a smaller one. Made famous in the blockbuster novel *The Da Vinci Code*, its construction was shrouded in both Masonic and neo-pagan myth.

He also thought of the Hanging Gardens of Babylon, built as they were into a giant natural stalactite in a great cavern in southern Iraq, and it struck him that perhaps the Gardens were built in homage to this.

Either way, the incredible size of the pyramid dwarfed the hall in which Jack, Wizard and Zoe stood, the hall which until now had seemed so gigantic.

'Jack. Zoe. Meet the Machine,' Wizard said.

Jack checked his watch.

It was 6:02 a.m. The Jovian equinox would be at 6:12.

They'd made good time.

His radio squawked.

'*Huntsman, you still alive down there?*' Pooh Bear asked anxiously.

'We're in. We've found the Machine.'

'*Sky Monster just called. He's picked up a large force of land vehicles heading this way from Aswan. Over a hundred vehicles coming in behind the tourist coaches.*'

'ETA?' Jack asked.

'*An hour, maybe less.*'

Jack did some calculations in his head. 'We can be gone by then. Just.'

As Jack spoke into the radio, Zoe and Wizard examined the walls of the hall.

They were literally covered in images—thousands and thousands of beautiful and intricate carvings.

Some they recognised, like the Mystery of the Circles, the circular symbol for the Machine, and even the layout of Stonehenge was there. But others were completely new:

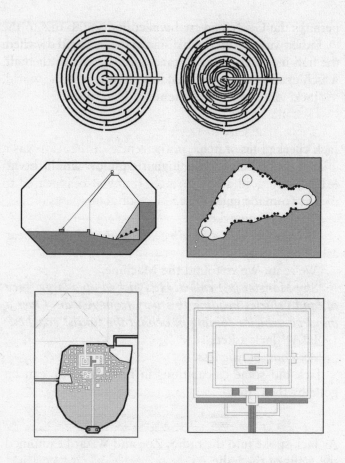

Zoe quickly pulled out a high-res Canon digital camera and started clicking away, trying to capture as many of the images as she could.

'That's Ur,' Wizard exclaimed, pointing at the second-last image.

'It is?' Zoe said.

'It's the layout of the ancient city of Ur, in Mesopotamia. Ur famously had two walled harbours, one to the west, the other to the north—you can see both of them clearly in the carving. Until the Great Pyramid was built, the Ziggurat at Ur was the tallest building in the world. And do you know what the word "Ur" means?'

'Tell me.'

'Light. The City of Light.'

Taking pride of place in the centre of the wall was a huge polished obsidian plaque. Every carving in it was edged with gold and its ornate frame also appeared to be cut from a single square piece of gold:

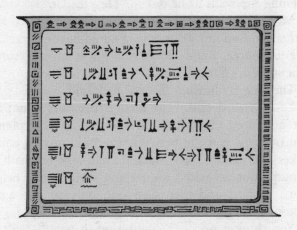

'Oh my God, the six vertices . . .' Wizard breathed. 'That symbol repeated on the left, an inverted triangle surmounting a rectangle, is Thoth for "vertex". This carving is a description of *all six* vertices. I'll have to get Lily to decipher it.'

Zoe snapped several photos of the plaque, then stared at the incredible hall around them and the gravity-defying pyramid suspended above the abyss.

'Wizard, who could build a place like this?' she asked. 'Not ancient man. Not even modern man could do something like this.'

'This is true,' Wizard said. 'So who could? Extra-terrestrial visitors? Some think so—over 70 per cent of people believe that the Earth has been visited by aliens at some point in history. And if they exist, perhaps aliens did visit our planet and build these structures. But I don't subscribe to that view.'

'What do you think?'

'He thinks men built them,' Jack said, joining them, scanning the walls as he did so. 'Hey, it's Ur.'

'Men?' Zoe frowned. 'But I thought you agreed that neither modern nor ancient man could have—'

'I did agree. But I didn't rule out a race of *super*-ancient men,' Wizard said.

'The past civilisation theory,' Jack said.

'Yes,' Wizard said. 'The theory that ours is not the first advanced civilisation to flourish on this planet. That over the eons, in between asteroid impacts, comet strikes and deadly Dark Stars, human-type beings have on numerous occasions risen above their animal neighbours, thrived and then died out, only to rise again millions of years later.'

'You think a previous civilisation of *people* built all this?' Zoe asked.

'Yes. A highly advanced human civilisation, far more advanced than we are today. Why, did you notice how all the doors and steps we have passed through to get here have *all* been suited to our size and stature? This is not coincidence. That an *alien* culture would build *human*-sized steps would be an astronomical co-incidence. No, this structure—this wonderful structure—

was built by human hands a long, *long* time ago.'

'Humans who despite their advancements couldn't save themselves from extinction,' Zoe pointed out.

'Maybe something else killed them,' Jack said. 'While they were building this, a rogue asteroid might have wiped them out.'

Wizard nodded. 'A lot can happen in a hundred million years. Entire species can emerge, evolve, thrive and become extinct in that time. By contrast, modern *Homo sapiens* is only 100,000 years old. And hey, at least the people who built this Machine were trying to save themselves from the future return of the Dark Star.'

'Wizard, sorry to interrupt, but would you mind taking a look at this.' Jack had moved to the edge of the balcony and was gazing at the colossal inverted pyramid through a pair of binoculars.

The peak of the upside-down pyramid hovered level with their balcony, but it was still three hundred feet— about ninety metres—away.

'The peak isn't pointed,' he said, handing the binoculars to Wizard. 'It's flat at the summit.'

'Like the Great Pyramid was?' Zoe said.

'Sort of, but smaller. Much smaller,' Wizard said. 'About the size of . . .' he looked at the Pillar in Jack's hands ' . . . that.'

'So how do we get over there to place it?' Zoe asked.

'I'm guessing the same way we got in here,' Jack said, pointing to the floor at his feet.

Zoe looked down—and saw the symbol for the Machine engraved into the marble floor beneath Jack's boots. Again, the rectangles in it were lifesized.

Jack placed the cleansed Pillar into the rectangular slot nearest to the abyss.

No sooner had it slotted into place than a deep rumbling could be heard.

Jack snapped left, then right, but couldn't see any obvious source of the sound. Wizard and Zoe did the same.

And then Jack saw it.

Saw a great narrow bridge emerging from the wall of the abyss *directly below him*. It folded upward as it emerged from the wall, like a drawbridge that folds *up* into place not down, a long rail-less stone bridge.

Accompanied by the great rumbling, it rose up and up until with a loud boom it stopped perfectly in front of West, a great leaping tongue of stone that formed a half-bridge stretching out over the abyss from his feet all the way to . . . the inverted summit of the pyramid.

'Nice . . .' Jack said.

Gripping his cleansed Pillar, Jack West Jr stepped out onto the bridge, absolutely tiny against the vastness of the hall, the abyss and the colossal pyramid.

The sheer rock-walled abyss below him seemed almost bottomless, disappearing into infinite black.

Jack tried not to think about it and kept his eyes fixed forward as he approached the gigantic bronze pyramid.

Wizard and Zoe watched him every step of the way.

Then Jack came to the end of the bridge, to the summit of the upside-down pyramid . . .

. . . just as the clock struck 6:11 a.m.

Up on the surface of the lake, the first rays of dawn were creeping over the horizon.

Alby had set up his telescope on the surface of the pyramid-shaped island, just above the two bobbing Zodiacs.

He was bent over the eyepiece when he called, 'Saturn has just risen over Jupiter! The gap is coming . . . *now!*'

Jack's watch ticked over to 6:12.

After all the grandeur of the hall and its staircase and the great pyramid and the vast abyss, Jack found it odd that the peak of the massive structure could be so small when seen up close—

Suddenly the pyramid began to hum.

It was a low *thrumm*—a deep and powerful vibration that resonated throughout the entire cavern.

Jack's eyes went wide.

'*Captain West,*' came Alby's voice on the radio. '*The Titanic Rising has just begun. You now have approximately one minute to lay the Pillar.*'

'Thanks,' Jack replied. 'Somehow I had the feeling it'd begun.'

Standing at the very end of the elongated bridge, high

above an abyss of indeterminate depth, he examined the summit of the thrumming bronze pyramid.

As he'd noted from the balcony, the massive pyramid did not end at a sharp triangular point. Rather, it was flat. The great structure ended in a very small square-shaped flat section barely a handspan wide, as if its tiny capstone had once upon a time been sliced off.

Set into this square summit was an equally square hole—one which, Jack saw immediately, matched the size of his Pillar.

'Wizard?' he said into his radio. 'Any final thoughts? There's no ceremonial thing I have to do?'

'*Not that I know of,*' Wizard replied. '*Just insert the Pillar into the pyramid.*'

'Okay then . . .'

Jack took a final glance at his watch. It was still 6:12 a.m.

Then, gripping his Pillar with both hands, standing high above a bottomless abyss far beneath the surface of the world, he inserted the cleansed Pillar into the matching hole in the pyramid.

The Pillar slotted into the pyramid . . .

. . . and instantly lodged inside it, half-in/half-out of the pyramid, firmly locked in place.

The ominous thrumming ceased instantly.

Silence hung in the air.

Jack held his breath.

Then—*bam!*—the clear diamond Pillar, now lodged in the peak of the pyramid, *blazed* to life, glowing with intense white light.

Jack reeled away, shielding his eyes.

The blinding white light illuminated the entire cavernous space around him, showing Jack for the first time just how deep the abyss below him was. It was unimaginably huge, its sheer walls plunging down beyond even the reach of the blazing light of the Pillar.

But then, with a great thunderboom, a thick column of laser-like white light blasted downward from the Pillar and shot down the shaft-like abyss, rocketing toward the core of the Earth.

Jack couldn't watch it properly—it was just too bright.

And then with startling suddenness, the laser retreated back up into the Pillar and the pyramid, and just as quickly as it had sprung to life, the event was over, and the cavern was dark again—save for the pathetic light of Jack's amber flares.

Uncovering his eyes, Jack peered up at the massive pyramid, staring in awe at the ancient mechanism.

Then he saw the Pillar.

It was *pulsing* with light, its liquid core throbbing with a soft luminous glow.

And then, slowly, gradually, a strange kind of text began to appear on every surface of the Pillar—white symbols apparating on all of the Pillar's glass-like surfaces.

Jack recognised the symbols instantly.

The Word of Thoth.

The mysterious language found in Egypt and decipherable only by the Siwan Oracles: Lily and her twin brother, Alexander.

Then he recalled the reward that went with the placing of the first Pillar.

Knowledge.

These symbols conveyed some kind of wisdom, highly advanced wisdom.

Knowledge that nations would kill for.

He reached out to grab the Pillar. No sooner had he touched it than—*shnick*—there was a soft slicing noise and the pyramid's clamping mechanism released the Pillar into his hands, now glowing with its pristine-white Thoth symbols.

Jack examined it, and immediately noticed that a small pyramidal section of the Pillar had been removed, excised, from its upper end.

Jack looked up in wonder—and saw that the great inverted bronze pyramid was now whole again. Somehow, during the dazzling lightshow, it had taken a section of the diamond Pillar *as its capstone*, thus completing its perfect triangular shape.

'*Nice . . .*' Jack said, gazing down at the newly formed pyramidal void in his Pillar.

'Wizard,' he said into his mike. 'This is serious shit . . .'

'*Don't I know it.*'

Jack tucked the glowing Pillar into his rucksack. 'Well,' he said, 'all things considered, that was really kinda painless.'

'*Yes, which is most unusual for us—*' Wizard began, only for his radio signal to cut off abruptly and be replaced by a long droning tone.

Jack's blood turned to ice. This wasn't a simple loss of signal. That would produce static or hash. Tone meant something else.

He turned and saw Wizard at the edge of the balcony, holding his hands out, palms up. Beside him, Zoe was waving Jack over hurriedly.

Jack dashed back across the bridge, holding his rucksack like a football under his arm, keying his radio as he ran. 'Astro! Lily! Alby! You guys still on the air?'

No reply.

Only the flat monotone.

He reached Wizard and Zoe. Wizard gazed at the Pillar nestled in the rucksack. Zoe, however, went straight up to him.

'Jack. All our comms have just been jammed. Someone else is here.'

They rose out of the lake on every side of the two Zodiacs—armed men in black wetsuits and scuba gear, brandishing MP-5 submachine-guns.

Twelve of them. Frogmen.

'Shit!' Astro cursed. 'The moving sonar signal from before. It wasn't a croc. It was a man.'

'Quiet, you,' the lead frogman said evenly, his accent all Eton. 'Guns down and put your hands in the air.'

Astro and Pooh Bear complied.

British troops, Astro thought. *Probably SAS or Royal Marines*. He spun to glare at Iolanthe, but her face was a mask.

The British frogmen clambered up into the Zodiacs, their black wetsuits dripping, their guns glistening.

Pooh Bear instinctively pushed Lily and Alby behind him.

The lead frogman went to Iolanthe, removed his mask and rebreather. He was young, square-jawed, with a pockmarked face. 'Lieutenant Colin Ashmont, ma'am. Royal Marines. We've been waiting for you. And, as ordered, monitoring Captain West's radio signals till we heard the Pillar had been placed.'

'Good work, Lieutenant,' Iolanthe said, striding over to stand with the British frogmen. 'West is down there with two others. The old man, whom we need, and the woman, whom we don't.'

She handed Ashmont her headset mike, just as he switched off the jamming device on his hip.

He spoke into the mike. 'Captain Jack West. This is the Royal Marines. You have no escape. You know it and we know it. Bring out the Pillar.'

'*Go fuck yourself*,' came the reply from the radio.

Ashmont smiled. Then he looked at Lily and Alby as he spoke again: 'Bring out the Pillar, Captain, or I start killing the children. The boy first.'

'*Okay. We're coming.*'

Minutes later, Iolanthe, Ashmont and three of his men stood inside the docking unit suctioned to the base of the rocky island, staring down the pipe-like tunnel filled with Nile crocodiles.

At the other end of the tunnel stood Jack, Zoe and Wizard.

'Send the old man out with the Pillar!' Ashmont called.

'What's your name, soldier?' Jack said evenly.

'Ashmont. Lieutenant. Fifth Regiment, Her Majesty's Marines.'

'You threatened my little girl and her friend, Lieutenant Ashmont. I'm gonna make sure you die *hard* for that.'

'You don't scare me, Captain West,' Ashmont replied haughtily. 'I've heard of you and I know your kind. Some may think you're good, but to me you're loose, undisciplined, reckless. Just another wild animal from a *colony* that should be kept on a tighter leash. I've a mind to kill the boy just on principle. Now send the old man through with the Pillar or I give the order.'

Jack handed his rucksack to Wizard, who then proceeded to shimmy down the crocodile-infested tunnel for the second time that morning.

Again, the big crocs grunted in protest, but they did not attack.

As Wizard crawled down the tunnel, Jack called, 'Iolanthe. I'm disappointed.'

'Sorry, Huntsman,' she replied. 'Blood is thicker than water, especially royal blood.'

'I'll remember that.'

At length, Wizard emerged from the hole at the end of the tunnel and stepped out in front of the three gun-toting Royal Marines.

Ashmont snatched the rucksack from him, saw the glowing Pillar within it, handed it to Iolanthe.

'Up, old man,' he jerked his chin at the ladder leading back up to the boats.

Wizard protested: 'But—'

'Move!'

Reluctantly, Wizard ascended the ladder.

Standing at the tunnel's entrance, Iolanthe gazed down it, seeing West and Zoe at the far end. She held the Pillar in her hands, brushing the new pyramid-shaped hollow in one end of it with her fingers.

'Enjoy your tomb, Captain,' she said.

Then she pressed the solid end of the glowing Pillar into the rolled-back symbol of the Machine at the entrance and immediately the manhole-sized symbol rolled back into place, sealing the ancient tunnel with a resounding *boom*, locking Jack and Zoe inside.

Iolanthe, Ashmont and the other Royal Marines climbed back up into the Zodiacs.

Once they were all up, Ashmont broke the seal on the docking unit, and it instantly flooded, covering the entrance to the subterranean system with water again.

Then he pushed Lily and Wizard onto the first Zodiac, leaving Alby, Pooh Bear and the American, Astro, on the second one.

The British lieutenant deferred to Iolanthe. 'What about them?'

'We keep the girl and the old man. The others we don't need.'

'So be it,' Ashmont growled. Then he promptly cuffed Pooh, Astro *and* Alby to their Zodiac, cut the ropes anchoring their boat to his and to the island, and then—*blam!-blam!-blam!*—fired three shots into its rubber sides.

Lily screamed at the gunshots.

The second Zodiac instantly began to deflate . . . and sink . . . with Pooh Bear, Astro and Alby handcuffed to it!

The many crocodiles that had lurked in wait in a wide circle around the two boats now began to stir. Unlike the ones inside the cool interior of the island, these crocs were alert, awake and mobile.

'Perhaps you'll be lucky and drown before the crocs take you,' Ashmont said. 'Otherwise, I hope your death is not too frightening.'

'When it comes, I certainly hope yours is,' Pooh Bear retorted. 'Bastard.'

'Alby!' Lily screamed, her eyes filling with tears.

Alby himself was petrified, turning this way and that, looking from his sinking boat to the wide circle of crocs.

'Farewell,' Ashmont said.

Then he gunned the engine of his Zodiac and sped off into the dawn across Lake Nasser, heading back for the docks at Abu Simbel, leaving Pooh Bear, Alby and Astro to their fate.

Water began to dribble in over the sides of the sinking Zodiac.

Standing on the sinking boat, cuffed to it, Alby felt like a passenger on the *Titanic*: unable to stop his craft's inexorable sinking and destined to die on it very soon.

'Okay,' Pooh Bear said between anxious breaths. 'What would Huntsman do? He'd have some kind of extra oxygen tank hidden on his belt, right? Or a blow-torch to cut through these cuffs.'

'We're out of both,' Astro said drily.

Pooh thought of the small amount of C-2 plastic explosive he kept concealed in his beard-ring, but no, it was too powerful for his handcuffs. It'd blow his hand off in the process.

A large croc splashed nearby, whipcracking its tail.

'How you doing, kid?' Astro said to Alby.

'Scared out of my mind.'

'Yeah, I'm feeling about the same,' Astro replied.

Water began to gush in over the edges of the deflating boat, *pouring* in, and the whole boat began to sink faster.

The water came up to Alby's knees, then his thighs.

They would go under any moment now.

A sudden splashing nearby made Alby spin and he turned round in time to see a huge crocodile come launching out of the water at his face, jaws wide, making a lunge for him—only for a booming gunshot to ring out and the croc fell in mid-lunge, lashing and spasming, shot in the eye by Astro.

'Holy *shit* . . .' Alby breathed. 'Oh-my-God, oh-my-God . . .'

The water level was at his waist now.

The boat was nearly fully under, tilting dramatically in the water.

Pooh Bear came alongside Alby. He ripped off his facemask and handed it to Alby, despite the fact it had no oxygen tank attached to it. 'Here, put this on. It might give you more time. I'm sorry, lad. I'm sorry we couldn't do more for you.'

Then, with a final inward rush, the crippled Zodiac filled fully with water and went under . . .

. . . taking Pooh Bear, Astro and Alby down with it.

Underwater.

Holding his breath, Alby felt the Zodiac pulling him downward by the wrist. As he fell through the murky haze, he could just make out the wall of the rocky island nearby.

Crocodiles lurked at the perimeter of his vision, hovering in the void, just watching the Zodiac's slow freefall.

Then in ultra-slow-motion the Zodiac hit the bottom, kicking up silt and one of the crocs moved in.

It glided through the water, propelled by its thick tail, zeroing in on Alby, jaws opening as it approached, and Alby screamed a soundless underwater scream as it rushed at him and—

—stopped.

Stopped dead, three inches from Alby's face.

Its snarling teeth were halted right in front of Alby's bulging eyes, and it was only then that Alby saw the great big K-Bar knife—Pooh Bear's knife—that had been lodged up into the soft underside of the crocodile's lower jaw.

Pooh Bear had reached over with his free hand and stabbed it up through the creature's jaw, just in time.

But then Alby saw the big man's eyes—they were wide open and bloodshot, running out of air. That lunge, it appeared, had been Pooh Bear's last act on this Earth. He visibly sagged.

Then a second croc advanced from the other side, again coming for Alby, the smallest prey, and this time Alby knew there was no escape. Pooh was done. Astro was too far away.

The crocodile zoomed in toward him, jaws opening, charging.

Running out of air and now totally out of heroes, Alby shut his eyes and waited for the end.

But the end didn't come.

There was no explosion of pain or slashing of teeth.

Alby opened his eyes—to see Jack West, wearing scuba gear, wrestling with the gigantic crocodile, rolling and struggling; the croc bucking and snapping.

And then suddenly someone jammed a scuba regulator to his mouth and Alby sucked in glorious air. Zoe hovered beside him in the water, also scuba-equipped.

Then she dashed to the limp Pooh Bear's side and inserted the regulator into his mouth. He came to life instantly. She moved on to Astro.

As for the fight between Jack and the crocodile, it was now a rolling struggle, hidden amid a cloud of roiling bubbles.

Then all of a sudden, Alby saw the croc bite down hard on Jack's left hand—only to see, two seconds later, Jack *extract* his hand from the great beast's jaws!

And just as Alby recalled that Jack's left hand was made of metal, he saw the crocodile's head explode underwater and spontaneously become a cloud of red. As it bit him, Jack must have left a grenade in its mouth.

At that moment, Zoe fired a shot through Alby's handcuff and did likewise with Pooh's and Astro's bonds and then Jack was right beside him, sharing his regulator, and Alby found himself being guided to the surface, somehow alive.

They broke the surface together and swam for the rocky island, where Jack pushed Alby up the slope, clear of the waterline, until he could lie safely on the less-steep upper surface.

Pooh and Astro were pushed up next, then Zoe and last of all, Jack, keeping a watchful eye on the crocs— but thankfully, most of them were preoccupied with eating the corpse of their now-headless comrade.

Jack lay on the island, sucking in great heaving breaths.

'How did—how did you get out?' Alby gasped.

'There were crocs in the entry tunnel,' Jack said. 'They'd got in by another entrance on the other side, a small cleft in the rock that was probably created by a tremor sometime. We came out through there.'

Jack propped himself up on his elbow, looked back out over the lake. 'Did they head back for Abu Simbel?'

'Yeah,' Alby said.

'They took Lily?'

'And Wizard. Are you angry, Mr West?'

West clenched his teeth. 'Alby, angry doesn't even begin to describe how I'm feeling right now.' He keyed his radio. 'Vulture! Scimitar! You copy?'

His radio remained silent. No reply.

'I say again! Vulture, Scimitar! You guys still at the dock?'

Again there was no reply. Just silence on the airwaves.

Jack swore. 'Where the hell have they got to?'

At the same time this was happening, Lieutenant Colin Ashmont's stolen Zodiac was arriving back at the docks not far from the great statues of Abu Simbel, flanked by two smaller inflatable speedboats—which had been inflated out on the lake and were now filled with the other eleven members of his squad of Royal Marines.

The first convoy of tourist coaches was just now arriving in a carpark not far from the docks.

Tourists of all nationalities piled out of the buses— German, American, Chinese, Japanese—and they variously stretched their legs and yawned.

Ashmont shoved Lily and Wizard out of the Zodiac, pushing them toward a couple of white Suburbans with tinted windows parked nearby. Iolanthe led the way, striding quickly, all business, carrying West's rucksack with the Pillar inside it.

As Lily and Wizard were guided toward the two British Suburbans, some of the tourists from the nearest bus came closer.

They were classic Japanese tourists—four older men with Nikon cameras slung from their necks and wearing bulky camera vests and sandals with white socks.

One of the Japanese called to Ashmont: 'Halloo, sir! Excuse me! Where statues?'

Ashmont, now wearing a T-shirt over his wetsuit,

ignored the man and walked right past him.

Lily wanted to shout to the Japanese men, to scream—

—but then she saw the first Japanese man's eyes follow Ashmont, glinting with purpose, and she suddenly realised that something was very, very wrong here.

The four old Japanese tourists were arrayed around Ashmont's cars and team in a perfect semi-circle.

Heart thumping, Lily scanned their faces, and saw only steely eyes and grim expressions.

And then, fleetingly, she saw the forearm of one of the Japanese men . . . and beheld a *tattoo* on it, a tattoo she had seen before, a tattoo of the Japanese flag with a symbol behind it.

'Tank . . .' she said aloud. 'Oh, no. Oh, *no* . . . Wizard! Get down!'

She threw herself into the bewildered old professor, tackling him around the legs, felling him just as the Japanese 'tourist' nearest to Ashmont opened his photographer's vest to reveal six wads of C-4 strapped to his chest. Then the kindly little old man thumbed a switch in his palm and he exploded.

Four shockingly violent blasts ripped through the air as all four of the Japanese suicide bombers just *disappeared* in identical outward sprays of smoke, fire and body parts.

The windows of every car in a twenty-metre radius blew out simultaneously, showering the area with glass.

Ashmont was hit hardest by the blast. He was flung into the side of his Suburban with terrible force and dropped to the ground like a rag doll.

Three of his men, those closest to the Japanese suicide bombers, were killed instantly. All the others were hurled every which way.

Iolanthe was further away and thus more sheltered from the blast—she was only thrown back fifteen feet by the concussion wave, where she hit the ground hard, banging her head, knocked out cold.

Tumbling to the ground on top of Wizard, Lily felt a wave of searing heat hit the back of her body—like a slap to her bare skin—then she smelled something burning, but the sensation didn't last long, because an instant later, she blacked out.

In fact, the only person to survive the attack completely unscathed had been Wizard—thanks to Lily's last-second tackle—which put him below the blast-zone.

His ears ringing, he raised his head, to see Lily lying on top of him, her shirt on fire!

He wriggled out from under her and quickly used his jacket to extinguish her flaming shirt. Then he picked her up—unconscious and limp—and stood there open-mouthed amid the carnage: smoke, the damaged cars and the bloody remains of Ashmont's Royal Marines.

There came a shrill scream, and Wizard spun.

The *real* tourists in the *real* buses nearby had seen the horrific blasts and, fearing a terrorist incident like the one that had occurred at Hatshepsut's Mortuary Temple in 1997, stampeded back into their coaches.

Wizard's eyes swept the area and landed on Iolanthe and the rucksack on the ground beside her.

Carrying Lily on his hip, Wizard raced over to Iolanthe's body and scooped up the rucksack with the Pillar inside it. Then he swung into one of Ashmont's Suburbans, gunned the engine and sped out of the lot.

'Sky Monster! Sky Monster!' Wizard yelled into his radio as he sped away from Abu Simbel, heading south. He had a clear signal. Ashmont's jamming device must have been destroyed in the suicide blasts.

'*Wizard! Where've you been! I've been trying to contact you guys for the last twenty min—*'

'Sky Monster, it's all gone sour!' Wizard blurted. 'The British blindsided us and then got blindsided themselves! Now Lily's out cold and Jack was sealed inside the shrine and Alby, Pooh Bear and Astro were left to die in the lake with the crocodiles! Oh, Alby—'

'*Alby's fine,*' another voice came in over the airwaves. Jack's voice.

*

Jack was walking quickly around the far side of the pyramidal island, skirting its lower edge, followed by the others.

'He's with me. So are Pooh, Astro and Zoe. We're all safe. What happened, Wizard?'

Wizard's voice said, '*Four men, Japanese, just blew themselves up near Ashmont's escape cars at the dock. It was an ambush. They were waiting. It was like they wanted to destroy the Pillar. I'm in one of the British escape cars now, heading south, away from the town.*'

'What about Iolanthe and the Pillar?'

'*She was knocked to the ground, so I took the Pillar. Not sure if she's dead or not.*'

'Okay,' Jack said. 'I want you to get as far away from here as you can, to a spot where Sky Monster can grab you. Sky Monster, Stretch: we need you to give us a boat-drop so we can get back to the shore and catch up with Wizard—'

Sky Monster's voice came in. '*Er, Huntsman, I don't think that's going to be possible—*'

Circling in the sky high above Abu Simbel, Sky Monster peered down at the vast body of Lake Nasser and the highway leading into the town from the north. Stretch sat in the co-pilot's seat beside him, also gazing down at the landscape.

'—This is what I've been trying to tell you,' Sky Monster said. 'It's why I've been trying to get in contact. That *second* convoy we saw earlier is now only about three miles out from the town, approaching fast from the north and it's *not* just comprised of tourist coaches. The coaches are cover. It's a military convoy: rapid-strike cars, armoured jeeps, Humvees and troop trucks. My guess, it's the Egyptian Army—tipped off by someone. They're gonna hit your town in about four minutes.'

Sky Monster and Stretch looked down at the highway coming from the north, a thin ribbon of black overlaid upon the dull yellow of the desert.

There they saw the convoy speeding along it.

Tourist coaches led the way, kicking up a tailcloud of dust behind them as they hit the shoulder of the highway, a cloud that concealed dozens of military vehicles: trucks, Humvees, and machinegun-mounted jeeps. All up, the convoy looked like it possessed about fifty vehicles and maybe three hundred men.

'This is seriously deep shit,' Sky Monster breathed.

Jack said, 'Okay then. The plan stays the same. Wizard, you run: get out of here, take the highway and head south for the Sudanese border. Sky Monster can scoop you up somewhere down there. We'll follow as best we can and try to catch up.'

'*Okay . . .*' Wizard said doubtfully.

Sky Monster said, '*Huntsman, standby. I'm sending you two packages. Couple of early Christmas presents.*'

From his rocky island, Jack looked up to see the dark shape of the *Halicarnassus* bank around in the dawn sky.

Then he saw the big 747 swing low, barely a hundred feet above the lake, and as it roared by something dropped from its rear loading ramp—something with a parachute attached to it, arresting its fall. Perfectly released, the speeding object landed with a great splash about fifty yards out from Jack's rocky island.

As soon as it hit the water, the object sloughed its outer casing and inflated rapidly—revealing itself to be a brand-new Zodiac complete with outboard engine.

'Merry Christmas,' Jack said.

Minutes later, he and the others were skimming across the surface of Lake Nasser, heading back for the western shore.

They hit land a few miles south of the massive statues of Abu Simbel, at a remote fishermen's dock.

No sooner had the Zodiac slid to a halt on the decrepit boat-ramp than a second parachute-equipped pallet from the *Halicarnassus* landed lightly on the desert floor a few hundred yards in front of them.

Sitting on the pallet was a compact Land Rover Freelander four-wheel drive—donated to the *Halicarnassus* by the British at Mortimer Island—stripped and modified for military work.

And sitting at the wheel was Stretch.

'Need a ride?' he said.

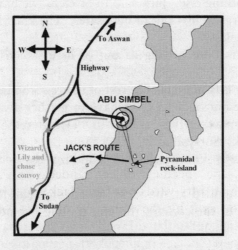

The Freelander's tyres squealed as the little four-wheel drive shot off the mark.

Jack sat in the passenger seat while Stretch drove. Piled into the back were Astro, Alby, Pooh Bear and Zoe—nestled amid a pile of guns and Predator rocket launchers that Stretch had brought along.

Jack tried his radio again, 'Scimitar! Vulture! Come in!' No reply. They were meant to be covering the dock, Jack thought, but Wizard had made no mention of them in his report of the suicide attack. Scimitar and Vulture were suspiciously absent without leave.

The little Freelander sped across the desert, kicking up a dustcloud behind it, heading for the blacktop highway leading south.

On that highway, Jack and the others could see the chase at hand: Wizard's lone white Suburban out in front of the convoy of Egyptian Army coaches, jeeps, trucks and Humvees.

'If nothing else,' Jack said to Stretch, 'we have to get that charged Pillar out of here safely. The knowledge on it is priceless.'

'What about getting *us* out of here safely?' Stretch asked.

'Only Lily matters. The rest of us are secondary. If we can't get out ourselves, we have to get her away. She's more important than any of us.' He offered Stretch a wry look. 'Sorry, buddy.'

'Nice to know where I stand in the scheme of things.'

Jack nodded at the scene ahead of them: 'See that last bus in the convoy, the one trailing behind all the others.'

'Yeah . . .'

'I want it.'

Wizard drove frantically.

He gripped the steering wheel of his stolen Suburban with white knuckles, anxiously swinging his eyes between three sources: the road in front of him, the convoy of pursuers behind him, and the passenger seat next to him—in which Lily lolled lifelessly, swaying with every bump in the road, her eyes closed, bloody scratches on her face.

The chase cars were catching up, filling his rearview mirror. Two fearsome-looking Humvees with gun turrets on their backs were about to pull up on either side of his Suburban.

'Sky Monster!' he yelled. 'Where are you!'

'*Here!*'

Voooooom!

Without warning, the enormous black underbelly of the *Halicarnassus* thundered low over the top of Wizard's car and landed on the highway in front of him, its rear loading ramp folding open as it did so . . . right in front of Wizard's speeding car.

'*Okay! I'll slow a little! Bring yourself on board!*' Sky Monster's voice called.

The big black 747 rolled along the desert blacktop at a cool 130 km/h, its wings stretched out over the dusty shoulder, speeding out in front of the collection of cars on the roadway.

Wizard floored the Suburban.

It leapt forward, heading directly for the yawning rear ramp of the jumbo.

At which point, the two Humvees behind it opened fire.

Bullet sparks exploded all over the Suburban and the plane, even in the hold up inside the loading ramp.

The rear and side windows of the Suburban shattered. Wizard ducked, shielding his face.

But he remained focused on the ramp of the *Halicarnassus*.

The Suburban began to wobble and slide, but he held her tight and with a final thrust on the gas pedal, he took the plunge and lunged at the ramp . . . and hit it perfectly . . . and swooped up into the rear hold of the *Hali* where he slammed full tilt into the forward wall!

The Suburban jolted to a halt, safely inside.

'Oh my goodness, I did it . . .' Wizard exclaimed.

'*Jesus, Wizard, you did it!*' Sky Monster said. '*Man, I thought you were going to miss by a metre! Nice driving, Fangio . . .*'

Wizard turned to check on Lily and he saw her eyes open weakly.

'Hi there. Nice to see you awak—'

He was cut off as their car was jolted violently, hit from behind by one of the Egyptian Humvees that had itself charged up the loading ramp after them!

Wizard was thrown forward, then he snapped round and saw the intruder.

Instinct kicked in.

He jammed the Suburban into reverse and hit the gas.

The Suburban lurched backwards and slammed into the unsuspecting Humvee, shunting it *back down the ramp* and out of the plane, back into the sunshine, where the hapless Humvee hit the road and, its brakes locking, jack-knifed sideways and tumbled into a roll. Two chase cars managed to avoid it before a third car— a big troop truck—hit it square in the side and finished both of them off.

'Sky Monster!' Wizard called from the hold. 'Pull up that ramp and go!'

'*On it, Wiz!*'

The *Hali*'s engines roared louder, firing up for

take-off. At the same time, the loading ramp came up and through the slowly-closing aperture, Wizard saw the chase convoy—an angry body of heavily armed vehicles.

But then just as the ramp was about halfway closed, he saw the convoy split in the middle and allow a Humvee to come to the front: a Humvee with a rocket-launcher pod mounted on its back.

The Humvee fired—a single lethal rocket streaking out of its pod, and Wizard's eyes boggled at the thought that the rocket might shoot inside the hold and go off, but instead the missile banked away to the side, darting out of Wizard's sight.

He sighed with relief. A miss.

Only to realise a sickening moment later that it wasn't a miss at all.

For right then he heard one of the *Hali*'s two starboard engines get hit.

It was a direct hit—the missile slammed into the *Hali-carnassus*'s outer starboard engine, causing it to blast out in a thousand pieces and spew a thick horizontal column of black smoke.

'*Fuck me sideways!*' Sky Monster yelled, flicking switches, dumping fuel that could be ignited by the exploded engine and cutting all excess lines so that the fire didn't spread to the tanks inside the wing.

He looked out his starboard cockpit window. The engine was a tangled mess of twisted metal and smoke. He'd have to jettison it. Take-off was still possible, but with only three engines it would be a whole lot harder: they'd need a longer runway.

The damage had been done.

The plane slowed.

And the chase convoy pounced.

It was an incredible sight.

A 747 jumbo jet racing down a vast desert highway, pursued by a horde of military vehicles—Humvees, jeeps, trucks and coaches—all of them rushing along at well over 100 kilometres an hour, like a pack of hyenas chasing down a wounded water buffalo.

When they got in range, the chase convoy attacked.

Naturally, their first strategy was to fire at the *Hali*'s tyres, but the big plane had a set of kevlar guards shielding them and the bullets just pinged away.

So the chasers adopted a second, more ruthless option.

The first chase truck rushed forward and swung in under the left-hand wing of the *Hali*, where it threw off its canvas roof to reveal a platoon of fully armed Egyptian special forces troops.

They wasted no time employing a standard plane-storming technique—they danced up onto their truck's driver's cabin and from there leapt up onto the wing at its lowest point, at the spot where it met the *Halicarnassus*'s fuselage.

Sky Monster watched helplessly from the cockpit. 'Oh, damn, damn, damn.'

He went to the window on the other side and saw *an entire bus* of soldiers swing in under the armpit of the starboard wing with more men climbing up through a hatch onto its roof, readying themselves to storm that wing.

'Shit, shit, shit . . .'

Wizard arrived in the cockpit with Lily. 'What's going on?'

'We've lost engine four and now they're boarding us via the wings!' Sky Monster said. 'And we have no defence against that! They're like fleas I can't shake.'

'You have to do something . . . !'

'Wizard, I don't know of any pilots who've been in this kind of situation before! I'm adapting the best I can!'

'Can we take off?'

'Yes, but we'll need a hell of a long runway,' Sky

Monster started swinging the *Halicarnassus* wildly left and right.

On the wing outside, the Egyptian troops staggered and struggled for balance, grabbing for handholds, one of them dropping off the wing with a shout and falling to the road below.

But they soon got their balance, and the bus under the starboard wing began unloading more troops.

The *Halicarnassus*—speeding along the desert highway, unable to take off—was under siege.

In the cockpit, Wizard clumsily unfolded a map. 'This highway straightens out in about four kilometres into a long unbroken stretch about three kilometres long. But after that it twists and turns through hills all the way to the Sudanese border.'

'Then that's our runway,' Sky Monster said.

'Our *only* runway.'

Sky Monster was still staring anxiously out the starboard window. 'Wizard, you think you can drive this for a few minutes?' he said, standing suddenly.

'Drive?' Wizard blanched. 'I don't even drive a *car* very well, Sky Monster.'

'Well it's time to learn. Here, pay attention, I'll show you how . . .'

About a mile behind the desperate scenes on the *Hali*, the last bus in the Egyptian military convoy drove quietly in its allotted place, everyone on board it keenly watching the spectacular goings-on up ahead.

They never noticed the little Land Rover Freelander—now driven by Pooh Bear—swing onto the highway behind it, never noticed it creep right up close to its rear bumper, never noticed the three figures of West, Stretch and Astro clamber out onto the bonnet of the Freelander and climb up the ladder attached to the back of the big coach.

The three small figures then danced along the roof of the speeding coach, pausing briefly to drop two of Astro's knock-out-gas grenades through a hatch.

A moment later—as all the occupants of the bus passed out and the coach began to veer off the bitumen, West lay on his belly and reached down, unlatching the safety catch on the coach's forward door and swung himself inside, followed by his two comrades-in-arms.

Inside the bus, wearing his lightweight half gas-mask, West pulled the unconscious driver out of the driver's seat and took the wheel.

He scanned the road ahead: beyond the convoy, he saw the wounded *Halicarnassus* lumbering along, spewing black smoke from its right wing, and bearing bad guys on the inner segments of both wings.

Astro examined the rest of their bus. It was filled with slumped-over soldiers, all of them low-level infantrymen.

'They're Egyptian Army,' he said, grabbing the uniform of the nearest trooper.

'Like a lot of African countries, sometimes Egypt's army is up for hire,' Jack said. 'If you've got enough dough and the right contacts, you can buy yourself some local muscle for a day or two. The question is: who's paying for Egypt's services today? Now, if you don't mind, it's time to clear the road and get those bastards off our plane. Stretch, I don't need this windshield anymore.'

Stretch stepped forward and fired a burst from his submachine-gun into the windshield. It shattered and dropped from view. Wind rushed in.

'Gentlemen,' Jack said, removing his gas-mask. 'Tyres.'

With wind now blasting into his bus, West gunned it, lifting his coach to over 140 km/h and bringing it forward through the convoy, at the same time as Stretch and Astro fired their guns out the open front windshield, blasting the rear tyres of the other buses in the convoy.

The tyres of the other buses punctured loudly and caught off guard, they fishtailed crazily, skidding off the roadway and onto the sand shoulder while West's bus shot past them, moving ever forward.

After four such bus crashes, one of the Egyptian Humvees noticed West's rogue bus and it turned its turret-gun on Jack—just as Stretch nailed the Humvee with a Predator missile. The Humvee exploded, lifting completely off the ground before flipping and rolling in the dust.

Another jeep saw them and brought its gun around, only for West to ram it with his bus, sending the jeep spinning off the road like a toy.

'Pooh Bear!' he called into his radio. 'Stay in our shadow! We'll shield you all the way to the *Halicarnassus*'s loading ramp!'

At the wheel of the Freelander, Pooh Bear shouted, 'Roger that!'

Beside him, Zoe and Alby peered out at Jack's stolen coach and at the vehicles of the enemy convoy ahead of them.

They were now only about sixty metres behind the *Halicarnassus*—on which they could see about a dozen armed men, six on each wing and gathering at the wing-doors. Four more buses and a couple of Humvees stood between them and the fleeing 747, all of the enemy cars hovering at the flanks of the plane, tucked under its wings.

They heard Jack in the stolen coach calling over the radio: '*Sky Monster! Come in! We need you to open the rear ramp!*'

But, oddly, there was no reply from Sky Monster.

At that very same moment, the Egyptian troops on the left-hand wing of the *Halicarnassus* managed to get its wing-door open. They flung it wide—

Boom!

The first Egyptian trooper was blown off his feet by a massive shotgun blast.

All the other troopers dived for cover as they saw the enraged figure of Sky Monster standing inside the doorway, shucking a Remington twelve-gauge, readying it for the next shot.

'Get off my plane, yer ratbastards!' the hairy-faced New Zealander shouted. Unseen by him, his radio earpiece dangled uselessly off his ear—dislodged in his desperate scramble to get down here from the cockpit.

At the same time back up in the cockpit, Wizard drove the speeding plane—terribly—but right now any driver was better than none.

'Damn it,' Jack swore. 'I can't get hold of Sky Monster, so I can't open the ramp.'

He stared up at the *Halicarnassus* from his speeding bus, trying to figure out another way to board it, when suddenly Astro leaned forward and said, 'May I make a suggestion?'

As he spoke, he pulled an unusual weapon from a holster on his back and offered it to Jack.

Seconds later, Jack and Astro found themselves again standing on the roof of their speeding coach, only this time they were looking up at the gigantic tailfin of the *Halicarnassus* looming directly above them.

Astro held his unusual weapon in his hands.

It was a weapon peculiar to the elite of the United States Marine Corps, the Force Reconnaissance Marines: an Armalite MH-12A Maghook.

Looking like a twin-gripped Tommy gun, a Maghook was a pressure-launched magnetic grappling hook that came equipped with a 150-foot length of high-density cable. It could be used either as a conventional grappling hook—with its claw-like anchor-hook—or as a magnetic one, with its high-powered magnetic head that could attach to sheer metallic surfaces. The 'A' variant was new, smaller than the original Maghook, about the size of a large pistol.

'I've heard of these, but never seen one,' Jack said.

'Don't leave home without it,' Astro said, firing the Maghook up at the tailfin of the *Halicarnassus*. With a puncture-like *whump*, its magnetised hook soared into the air, trailing its cable behind it.

The hook slammed into the *Hali*'s high tailfin and held, suctioned to the great steel fin with its magnet, holding firm.

'Now hold tight,' Astro said as he handed Jack the Maghook and pressed a button on it marked 'RETRACT'.

Instantly, Jack was whisked up off the roof of the

speeding bus, reeled upwards by the Maghook's powerful spooler.

He came level with the tailfin of the *Halicarnassus* and swung himself onto one of its flat side-fins. Then, safely on the plane, he grabbed the Maghook again and prepared to throw it back down to Astro, so that he could come up after—

But Astro never got a chance to follow Jack: at that moment, his bus was hit from the side by one of the Egyptian coaches, a great thumping blow that knocked Astro off his feet and almost off the roof entirely.

Driving the bus, Stretch swung to look right . . . and found himself staring into the angry eyes of the driver of the other coach.

The driver raised a Glock pistol at Stretch—

—just as Stretch drew a Predator RPG launcher in response, holding it like a pistol, and fired.

The RPG blasted through his automatic door, smashing through the glass, and drilled into the rival bus. An instant later, the Egyptian bus travelling alongside his coach lit up with blazing white light before bursting like a firecracker into a million pieces.

Inside the *Halicarnassus*, Sky Monster was standing guard at the open port side wing-door, the wind whipping around him, with his shotgun levelled and ready to fire at anything that dared poke its head through the doorway.

Abruptly, two troops on the port wing slid across his view, and he fired but missed, they were too fast, and for a moment he wondered what they had been trying to do—their movement hadn't achieved anything, when suddenly it dawned on him that it *had* done something: it had captured his attention.

Almost immediately, the *starboard* side wing-door behind him was blown inward and stormed by Egyptian SF troopers.

More raging wind rushed into the cabin.

One, then two, then three troopers charged in, AK-47s up and ready to shred the totally exposed figure of Sky Monster—

Blam!-blam!-blam!

Multiple gunblasts filled the cabin.

Sky Monster was ready to collapse under a hailstorm of bullets, but it was the three intruders who fell, their bodies exploding in fountains of blood.

As they dropped to the floor, Sky Monster spun and saw who had shot them: Jack, standing on the *port* wing, his Desert Eagle smoking. He must have fired over Sky Monster's shoulder from behind.

Sky Monster sighed with relief, only to see Jack's expression turn to one of horror, 'Monster! Look out!'

Sky Monster spun, bewildered, to see one of the three fallen Egyptians, hit but not dead, whip up a pistol with a bloodied hand and aim it at him from point-blank range. The Egyptian pulled the trigger—just as from out of nowhere a speeding blur of brown whooshed past him and in the blink of an eye the Egyptian was gunless.

It was Horus.

Jack's little falcon—who'd remained on board the *Hali* during the mission at Abu Simbel—had snatched the gun from the attacker's bloody fingers!

Jack stepped past Sky Monster and kicked the shocked Egyptian out the starboard doorway and suddenly there was silence in the cabin, a brief moment of respite.

Horus landed on Jack's shoulder, presenting him with the Egyptian's pistol. 'Good work, bird,' Jack said, striding back to Sky Monster and replacing the hairy pilot's earpiece in his ear. 'If *you're* down here, who's driving?'

'Wizard.'

'Wizard can hardly ride a bicycle,' Jack said. 'Get back up top, I need you to open the rear ramp—we have to get the others on board. I'll cover the entrances down here.'

'Jack, wait! I have to tell you something! We're gonna run out of road soon! With only three engines we need a longer runway to take off and this stretch of road coming up is the last chance we've got.'

'How soon till we hit it?'

'Couple of minutes, at the most. Jack, what do I do if . . . if not everyone gets on board in time?'

Jack said seriously, 'If it comes to that, you get Lily, Wizard and that Pillar out of here. That's the priority.' He clapped Sky Monster on the shoulder. 'But hopefully you won't have to make that call.'

'Roger that,' Sky Monster said, bolting back up the stairs toward the upper deck.

After their first failed attempt, the Egyptians now doubled their efforts to storm the 747: two more buses swung under the *Halicarnassus*'s smoking right wing, travelling in single file, one in front of the other, disgorging armed men who ran across the roofs of both buses before leaping up onto the wing.

Where they were met by Jack.

Bent on one knee, half hidden in the wing-door and blasted by speeding wind, Jack fired away at the onslaught of invading troops.

But just as he took down one man, another would appear in his place.

He couldn't keep this up for long, and with a quick glance over his shoulder, he saw a bend in the highway up ahead. Beyond it was—

—the long straight strip of highway.

Their last chance of escape.

Better do something fast, Jack . . .

Bullets slammed into the doorway above him and he saw the next wave of Egyptian assailants—and to his horror saw that these guys carried lightweight armoured shields, like the ones riot police use, complete with little peepholes in them.

Shit.

Blam! He fired—and the first attacker to appear

on the wing dropped, hit in the eye, shot *through* the peephole.

This is getting totally out of hand, he thought.

But then he saw the road behind him and a look of total despair fell across his face.

His enemy's reinforcements had arrived . . .

. . . in the form of six American Apache helicopters thundering low over the highway from the direction of Abu Simbel, blasting through the heat haze. Beneath them was another armada of military vehicles, this time American vehicles.

'I guess we know who's paying now,' he breathed as the lead chopper loosed two Hellfire missiles in his direction. 'Sky Monster—!'

Sky Monster charged into the cockpit of the *Halicarnassus* and slid into the captain's chair, hitting 'LOADING RAMP OPEN' as he did so.

The rear loading ramp of the *Hali* instantly lowered, kicking up sparks as it hit the fast-moving roadway.

Then Jack's voice exploded in his ear: '*Sky Monster! Deploy decoys, now, now, now!*'

Sky Monster hit a button marked 'CHAFF DECOYS'— and immediately two firecracker-like objects shot out from the *Hali*'s tail, springing up into the air.

The first Hellfire missile hit one of the decoys and exploded harmlessly high above the speeding *Halicarnassus*.

The second missile—confused by the decoys, but not completely suckered—shot right past them and slammed into the roadway next to the 747's right wing—causing the entire plane to shudder wildly and almost taking out the two Egyptian special forces coaches laying siege to that wing.

It was chaos. Total chaos.

And in the midst of all this mayhem, the plane and its chasers took a final bend in the road and swung onto the last straight stretch of highway in Egypt.

Things were happening everywhere now.

Sky Monster yelled into his radio: 'People, whatever you're gonna do, do it soon, because we're about to run out of road!'

As his bus took the final bend behind the *Halicarnassus*, Stretch saw a third Egyptian bus swing unseen beneath the plane's left wing with men on its roof.

'Pooh Bear!' he called to the Freelander behind him. 'You'll have to make your run for the ramp by yourself! I have to get that bus!'

'*Got it!*' Pooh Bear replied.

Stretch peeled off to the left, powering forward, leaving Pooh's Freelander thirty yards directly behind the now-open loading ramp of the *Halicarnassus*.

Speeding wildly, Stretch's bus rammed into his opponent, causing it to fishtail wildly, the enemy bus's tyres slipping off the bitumen and onto the rubble shoulder, where it lost all grip and control, and it flipped horribly . . . and rolled . . . *an entire bus* tumbling over and over in a great cloud of dust and smoke and sand.

Pooh Bear gunned his Freelander—with Zoe and Alby still in it with him—accelerating hard, his eyes fixed on the loading ramp of the *Hali*.

The little Freelander skimmed along the highway, gaining on the plane, when suddenly Alby called, 'Look out!' and Pooh yanked on the steering wheel just in time to avoid a kamikaze-style lunge from an enemy Humvee on the right.

The Humvee missed them by millimetres and went careering off the road, bouncing away into the dust.

'Thanks, young man!' Pooh shouted.

At that moment, Zoe's cell phone rang. Thinking it'd be Wizard or one of the others, she answered it with a yell, 'Yeah!'

'*Oh, hello,*' a soft female voice said pleasantly from the other end. '*Is that you, Zoe? This is Lois Calvin, Alby's mother. I was just calling to see how everything was going there on the farm.*'

Zoe blanched. 'Lois! Er . . . hi! Things are going . . . great . . .'

'*Is Alby there?*'

'Wha—huh?' Zoe stammered, trying to process the weirdness of receiving this call at this moment. In the end, she just handed the phone to Alby. 'It's your mother. Please be discreet.'

A missile whooshed by overhead.

'Mom . . .' Alby said.

Zoe didn't hear the other end of the conversation, only Alby saying, 'We're out in the east paddock in a jeep . . . I'm having a great time . . . oh yeah, we're keeping busy all right . . . Lily's good . . . I will . . . yes, Mom . . . *yes*, Mom . . . okay, Mom, bye!'

He hung up and handed the cell phone back.

'Nice talkin', kid,' Zoe said.

'My mom'd have kittens if she knew where I was now,' Alby said.

'So would my mother,' Pooh Bear growled as he pulled the Freelander right in behind the *Halicarnassus* and readied to zoom up its ramp when—*bam* they were hit with terrible force from the left, by another Humvee that none of them had seen.

The Freelander was thrown violently to the right, out of alignment with the *Hali*'s ramp, and it slammed up against the broad flank of one of the two Egyptian buses attacking the plane's starboard wing, pinned against it by the Humvee.

'Blast!' Pooh Bear shouted.

On the right wing of the *Halicarnassus*, Jack was still doing battle with the oncoming Egyptian forces—firing hard, with Horus hovering nearby—when he saw the Freelander bounce into view from underneath the tail of the speeding 747, the little 4WD being squeezed up against one of the Egyptian buses by a far bigger Humvee.

His first thought, strangely, was of Alby—Lily's friend; Lily's loyal little friend—and how he was still in the Freelander, and suddenly in a strange disconnected corner of his mind, Jack knew that Alby's destiny was connected to Lily's, that he somehow sustained her, gave her strength, and in that moment Jack knew that he couldn't let anything happen to the boy. Zoe and Pooh Bear, they could take care of themselves, but not Alby.

And so he acted.

'See you later, bird,' he said to Horus. 'Any cover you can provide would be appreciated.'

Just then two more Egyptian troopers tried to mount the starboard wing—both of them bearing riot shields—

at the exact same moment that Jack charged out from his cover *onto* the wing, shot both of them through their eye-slits and in one clean move scooped up one of the dead men's shields and leapt *down* . . . onto the roof of the first Egyptian bus driving along beneath the wing!

There he was met by no less than seven Egyptian special forces troops, momentarily shocked to see him, one lone man, attacking *them*.

At which point Horus rushed into their midst, talons slashing, slicing three deep claw-marks across the first soldier's face and unbalancing the second.

It gave Jack the moment he needed, for he wasn't planning on staying on that roof for long.

Holding the riot shield in one hand, he pivoted quickly and dropped off the bus's leading edge, dropping down in front of its windshield—attaching the grappling hook of Astro's Maghook to the forward edge of the roof as he fell.

He swung down in front of the speeding bus's windshield—completely shocking its driver—but continued downwards, dropping the kevlar shield underneath him as he hit the speeding roadway, using it as a bodyboard, and *disappeared* under the bumper of the big coach!

Down the length of the bus Jack slid—*under* it—lying on his back on the riot shield, using the Maghook's rope to control his slide.

As he went, he grabbed his Desert Eagle and fired it into every vital mechanical part he could see: axles, electronics, brake cables, fluid hoses—so that just as he popped out from underneath its rear bumper, the Egyptian bus started to veer wildly, out of control, off the highway and away from the plane.

But Jack's wild slide wasn't finished yet.

The second Egyptian bus—the one Pooh's Freelander was pinned against—was tailing the first one, so under *that* bus Jack went, still sliding on his shield.

As he went under the second bus, he hit a button on his Maghook, causing it to reel in quickly.

Free-sliding under the second bus, he could see the speeding wheels of the Freelander only a few yards away and, beyond them, the larger tyres of the Humvee—so as he slid, Jack extended his gunhand sideways and fired it *through* the wheels of the Freelander, hitting the tyres of the Humvee, puncturing them.

The Humvee instantly lost control and skidded away—but not before two of the Egyptian troops on it had leapt aboard the Freelander, attacking Pooh Bear.

Despite the fact that he was wrestling with two men, Pooh Bear pulled the Freelander away from the bus and once again aimed it at the rear loading ramp of the *Halicarnassus,* now with a clear line at it.

Zoe leaned forward to help Pooh with his two attackers, but as she did the Freelander swayed wildly: if they gunned it now, they'd hit one of the loading ramp's struts and crash terribly.

Pooh Bear seemed to realise this, too. And he grabbed hold of the two men assailing him and in a fleeting moment locked eyes with Alby and Zoe.

'Get away from here,' he growled.

And then, before they could stop him, Pooh Bear leapt from the speeding Freelander, *taking the two stunned Egyptian troopers with him!*

They landed on the roadway together, rolling and

tumbling—although Pooh had made sure that his attackers took the brunt of the fall.

Alby spun to watch them recede back down the highway while Zoe climbed into the driver's seat and took the wheel—now with a clear run at the loading ramp.

Zoe floored it.

The Freelander hit the ramp at phenomenal speed, leaping up into the hold and skid-smashing into the white Suburban already parked there, but at last safe and inside.

From his position underneath the second Egyptian coach, still sliding on the riot shield, Jack had seen Pooh Bear whip back down the roadway with his two attackers; he'd also just seen the Freelander shoom up into the hold of the *Hali*.

Abruptly something cut across his view: the side of a bus, with its forward door open, travelling right alongside him.

Jack whipped up his gun—only to see Astro appear in the open door of this new bus, lying on its steps on his belly. 'Jack! Give me your hand!'

Thirty seconds later, Astro was hauling Jack out from under the Egyptian coach and up into his stolen bus, where Stretch was still at the wheel.

After he hefted Jack up, Astro deftly attached a magnetic explosive charge to the Egyptian bus and yelled 'Clear!'

Stretch pulled them a safe distance away as the charge detonated and the entire side of the Egyptian bus just blew off it.

Suddenly Sky Monster's voice came through Jack's earpiece: '*Huntsman! Where the hell are you! In about ten seconds I have to power up or else we're not going to be able to take off!*'

Jack looked forward at the plane, and the realisation hit him: *it was too far away*. He, Stretch and Astro could never get to it in time.

Then a dull echoing *boom* caught his attention and he spun to look back behind him—and saw another Hellfire missile heading down the highway, chasing the fleeing plane.

'Monster,' he said. 'We can't catch you.'

'*What?*'

Both Stretch and Astro heard this, too, and they exchanged a look.

Then Lily's voice came over the line: '*No, Daddy! We'll wait for you—*'

'No, honey. You have to get away. I'll find you, Lily. I promise. But trust me, *you have to get away from here*. We're not as important as you are. *You* have to survive. You, Zoe, Wizard and Alby—you have to continue this mission and find the Second Pillar and place it in the Second Vertex. Call the twins, use their help. This is your mission now. I love you. Now Sky Monster, go.'

He clicked off the radio and turned to Stretch: 'Stop the bus.'

Having heard everything Jack had said, Stretch just glanced questioningly at him.

'Sideways. Across the road. Now,' Jack said.

Stretch did so, bringing the bus to a skidding squealing halt across the centre of the highway, blocking the road completely.

The *Halicarnassus* powered off down the blacktop,

disappearing into the heat haze, speeding up.

'And now, gentlemen,' Jack said, '*run*.'

Jack, Stretch and Astro abandoned the bus, racing across the road and diving into the sand just as it was hit by the incoming missile intended for the *Halicarnassus*.

The bus exploded—a billowing fireball that mushroomed into the sky, raining twisted metal everywhere.

Covered in sand, blood and sweat Jack looked up to see the *Halicarnassus* rushing away to the south, getting smaller and smaller, until eventually, slowly and painfully, it lifted off into the sky, carried by its three remaining engines.

Within a minute, a half-dozen American-manned Humvees skidded to simultaneous halts around him. The six Apaches patrolled the air overhead, kicking up a sandstorm of their own.

Jack stood, dropping his weapons and raising his hands behind his head as the first soldier—an American trooper—strode up to him and wordlessly smashed him in the face with the butt of his gun and instantly Jack saw nothing but black.

At the K-10 base on Mortimer Island, six SAS troopers stood guard outside a small building at the edge of the complex, grim sentries standing in the pouring rain.

Inside the outbuilding, the Terrible Twins, Lachlan and Julius Adamson, were working away at adjoining computers.

Lachlan talked as he typed, 'You know that 5:12:13 right-angled triangle that connects Stonehenge to the Great Pyramid at Giza? Its right-angled corner actually touches an island not far from here, Lundy Island—'

Suddenly Julius leapt back from his computer and punched the air. 'I've got it! I've got the Second Vertex!'

He kicked back his chair to allow his brother and Tank Tanaka to see his monitor. On the screen was a digital photo of one of the trilithons at Stonehenge, taken during the lightshow:

Surrounding this image was a collage of satellite images of southern Africa, maps of the Cape of Good Hope, and even one window opened onto Google Earth.

Julius smiled, pointing at the number '2' at the bottom of the trilithon. 'It's near Table Mountain.'

'In Cape Town?' Lachlan said.

'Are you sure?' Tank said.

'Positive. It's about three miles to the south of Table Mountain,' Julius said. 'In the hills and mountains there. The whole area is densely forested, uninhabited, and very difficult to get to. I *am* the master!'

He grinned triumphantly just as Tank's cell phone rang. He stepped aside to answer it, saying a muffled, 'Hello? Ah, konichiwa . . .'

Lachlan said to Julius, 'You do realise this doesn't mean you're in any way *superior* to me. No. 2 was an easy one. The outline of Africa was obvious. I'm still just trying to figure out where the coastline for No. 3

actually is. It doesn't match any known coastline on the Earth today.'

In the corner, Tank frowned at his phone. 'Oh?'

Julius clasped his hands behind his head mock-smugly. 'Maybe I can give you some tutoring in topographical analysis sometime, dear brother. Hey, you know, that could be my call-sign: *Analyser*.'

'Sure. And we can shorten it to *Anal*. You better send that location to Jack and Wizard, Anal. They'll be pleased. Oh, and while you're at it, tell Lily I found her backpack in the observation room. She must've left it behind in the rush to leave.'

'Rightio,' Julius tapped some keys, then cheerily hit 'SEND'.

As he did so, Tank ended his call with a curt, 'Yoroshii, ima hairinasai,' and hung up.

He walked back over to the twins.

'Hey, Tank,' Julius said. 'What do you think about the call-sign *Analyser* for me?'

Tank smiled sadly. 'That would seem most appropriate, young Julius.'

'So who's coming in?' Lachlan asked Tank.

'What?'

'You said it on the phone just now, "Yoroshii, ima hairinasai." It means, "Okay, you may come in now."'

Tank frowned. 'You speak Japanese, Lachlan?'

'A little. I once dated a Japanese science major—'

Julius scowled. 'You didn't date her! You corresponded with her in a chatroom!'

Lachlan blushed. 'There was a connection there, Anal. Which means it qualifies as dating—'

Abruptly, the door to their study slammed open and one of their British SAS guards was hurled

into the room by a wave of silenced gunfire
phwat-phwat- phwat-phwat-phwat-phwat!

Blood sprayed the walls and all over Lachlan's glasses.
The corpse of the SAS guard hit the floor with a loud
thud.

Then the study was stormed by six black-clad men,
all moving low, with perfect balance and posture,
and all holding MP-5SN silenced submachine-guns
pressed to their shoulders in the special forces way,
their goggle-covered eyes looking straight down the
barrels.

As five of the intruders covered the twins, the leader
of the team went straight over to Tank and removed his
goggles, to reveal a young Japanese face.

'Professor Tanaka, we have a chopper outside. What
about these two?'

Two guns cocked next to the twins' heads.

Lachlan and Julius froze, holding their breath.

For a long moment Tank eyed the two brilliant young
men, as if he was deciding their fate: whether they lived
or died.

At last he said, 'They can still be of much use. We
take them with us.'

And with that, Tank swept out of the study, walking
with purpose, leading the way. The twins were shoved
from the building after him at gunpoint and as they
stepped out into the pouring rain, they passed the bodies
of their SAS guards, all dead, all shot in the head.

AIRSPACE OVER AFRICA

Belching smoke from its wounded starboard engine, the *Halicarnassus* limped through the African sky. The landscape below it was an undulating carpet of lush green hills.

They had been flying for nearly two hours since their dramatic escape from Abu Simbel and were now flying over Uganda in eastern Africa. Their current plan was to head for their old station in Kenya and regroup.

Zoe and Wizard entered the cockpit, where Sky Monster sat alone, flying the plane. Lily and Alby were downstairs, sleeping after their exciting morning.

'You rang?' Zoe said.

'Got good news and bad news,' Sky Monster said. 'Which do you want first?'

'The good news,' Wizard said.

'Okay. A message just came in from England, from the twins. Something about the Second Vertex.'

Wizard leapt to a nearby computer and scanned the message. 'Cape Town. Table Mountain. Oh, those boys are talented. Good work, boys. Good *work!*'

Zoe turned to Sky Monster. 'And the bad news?'

'We're almost out of fuel and Kenya just became a no-go zone.'

'What!'

'How so?'

'About ten minutes ago I started picking up aerial signals running north–south grid patterns up and down the Kenyan–Ugandan border. *Perfect* north–south runs, which means computer-driven planes, which means unmanned aerial drones. Predators.'

'But only the US and the Saudis have Predator drones—' Wizard began.

'The fuel situation,' Zoe said. 'How much longer can we stay in the air?'

Sky Monster grimaced. 'I had to dump a lot back on that highway when our engine got hit. I figure we got enough fuel to reach Rwanda. Another hour at the absolute most. Then we'll be on fumes.'

'We're going to have to land in Rwanda?' Zoe said.

'We can land or we can crash,' Sky Monster said. 'Either way, we're going to be on the ground somewhere in Africa within the hour.'

Zoe exchanged a look with Wizard.

Wizard said, 'We have seven days to get to the Second Vertex. But we need to find the Second Pillar first, and Iolanthe said it still resides with the Neetha tribe in the Democratic Republic of the Congo. We'll need a chopper at some point, but we can make it to the Congo going overland through Rwanda.'

'*Overland through Rwanda*?' Zoe said. 'I hate to remind you, Max, but Rwanda is still classified as *the* most dangerous place on Earth, with the Congo a close second.'

Wizard grabbed a map of central Africa and unrolled it on the cockpit's console:

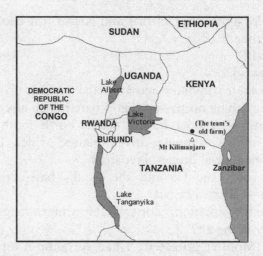

Sky Monster said, 'We're here, over Uganda, just north of Lake Victoria.'

Wizard pointed at the vast southern regions of the Democratic Republic of the Congo—taking up the whole left-hand side of the map. 'The DRC's nearly all jungle. Dense jungle. Few roads, no runways for a 747 anyway. Maybe we can steal a chopper in Rwanda, the UN left dozens of supply depots there.'

'We're gonna need help,' Zoe said. 'Supplies, language, local customs. Solomon?'

Wizard nodded. 'Solomon. I'll call him at the farm in Kenya. See if he can hightail it to Rwanda with supplies and anything else he can muster.'

Sky Monster added, 'See if he can bring some jet fuel while he's at it. I don't want to abandon my plane in Rwanda. She deserves more than that.'

Zoe saw the look on Sky Monster's face—to abandon his trusty plane in one of the wildest countries in Africa hit him hard.

But then he said, 'Go on, you guys. Better grab whatever you're going to take with you, because in about forty-five minutes, we're going down.'

FIFTH ORDEAL
THE DARK CONTINENT

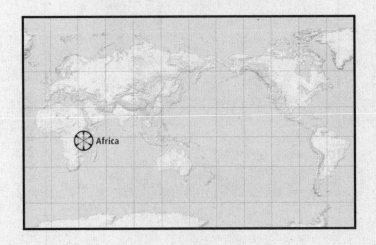

AFRICA
11 DECEMBER, 2007
6 DAYS TO THE 2ND DEADLINE

WOLF'S MINE

SOMEWHERE IN AFRICA
11 DECEMBER, 2007, 1800 HOURS

Darkness, silence, peace.

Then a blinding flash of violent pain in his right hand jolted Jack West awake.

His eyes shot open—

—and he found himself lying on his back on a large slab of stone, at the base of a deep square-shaped pit, with his arms spread wide . . . and a large black man hammering a thick nail into his right palm!

The man brought his mallet down again, and to Jack's horror the nail now went *all the way through* the flesh of his palm and into a small block of wood buried in the stone beneath it. Blood splattered from the wound.

Jack began to hyperventilate.

He snapped to look at his left arm, only to discover that it had already been nailed down into another block sunk in the slab—his mechanical left hand still wore its leather glove. His legs were tied down.

It was then that the full horror of the situation hit him.

He was being crucified . . .

Crucified on his back against a slab of stone, at the bottom of a pit in God-only-knew-where.

Still breathing fast, he scanned the pit around him. It was deep, about twenty feet, with sheer rock walls, and the world beyond its rim appeared dark, lit by firelight, like a cave or a mine of some kind.

Then the muscular black man hammering his hand into the stone called, 'He is awake!' and four men appeared up on the rim of the pit, gazing down into it.

Two of the four Jack didn't recognise: they were a pair of American soldiers, the first a bulky young trooper with wide unblinking eyes, the second a compact Asian-American wearing Marine fatigues.

Jack did know the third man. He was Chinese, older, and had furious eyes. It was Colonel Mao Gongli of the People's Liberation Army, whom Jack had last seen in Laozi's trap system, gagging on the contents of a smoke grenade. Jack vaguely recalled pistol-whipping Mao as he'd run past him there, breaking his nose.

The fourth man, however, was a man Jack knew very well, and he figured (correctly) that the two younger troopers were his lackeys. Blond-haired and blue-eyed, the fourth man was an American colonel who went by the call-sign *Wolf*. Jack hadn't seen him in years and was quite happy with that.

Wolf gazed down at Jack—helpless on his back, nailed to the pit floor—with a peculiar look on his face.

Then he smiled.

'Hello, son,' he called.

'Hello, father,' Jack said.

The man standing above him was Jack West Sr.

Jonathan West Sr—Wolf—gazed down at his son from the top of the pit.

Behind him, unseen by Jack, lay the workings of an enormous underground mine. In it, hundreds of emaciated Ethiopians stood on ten-storey-high scaffold towers, toiling with picks and shovels at great walls of dirt, clearing centuries of hard-packed grit from what appeared to be a collection of ancient stone buildings.

'*Isopeda isopedella*,' Wolf said slowly, his voice echoing in the vast mine.

Jack didn't reply.

'The common huntsman spider,' Wolf said. 'A large-bodied, long-limbed spider native to Australia. Similar to the tarantula in size and general notoriety, it's known to grow to sizes in excess of fifteen centimetres.'

Still Jack said nothing.

'But despite its fearsome appearance, the huntsman spider is not a lethal spider. In fact, it is not dangerous at all. A bite will cause no more than transient local pain. It is a fake, a fraud. An animal that attempts to mask its general ineffectiveness with the appearance of size and power, much like you. I never liked your call-sign, Jack.'

A bead of sweat trickled down Jack's forehead as he lay on his back at the bottom of the pit.

'Where are my friends?' he asked, his throat coarse and dry. He was thinking of Stretch, Pooh Bear and Astro—all of whom had failed to escape after the chase from Abu Simbel.

At that moment, Wolf guided Astro into view beside him. Jack saw the young American Marine through blurry eyes. He seemed okay and, importantly, he *wasn't* wearing any handcuffs. He said nothing, just looked down coldly at Jack.

Had Astro been with Wolf all along? Jack thought. It had always been a possibility. But no, he thought he'd picked Astro as a good man, loyal. He couldn't have been a plant.

'What about the other two?'

'Never mind their fate,' Wolf said. 'They will certainly outlive you, but not by much. We were talking about the flaws in your chosen call-sign, son.'

'I didn't choose it. You don't choose your own call-sign.'

Wolf looked away.

'How is your mother?' he asked suddenly. 'No matter how hard I try, I just can't seem to find her. It's as if she doesn't want me to locate her.'

'I can't imagine why,' Jack said.

To explain what had gone wrong with his parents' marriage meant understanding Jack's father.

Powerful physically and brilliant mentally, John West Sr was an intellectually vain man, convinced of his superiority in all matters. As a strategist, he was unrivalled in the US, his methods were bold, vicious and, most of all, successful. These accomplishments only bolstered his sense of omnipotence.

But when this viciousness seeped into his marriage

and took violent form, Jack's mother had left Jack Sr and, infuriating him further, divorced him in an Australian court—*an Australian court*.

After that, Jack's mother had disappeared and now resided in the remote town of Broome in a distant corner of Western Australia, not far from Jack's farm. It was a location that only Jack and a few others knew.

Wolf shrugged. 'She's of no importance right now. But when this is all over, I'm going to make a point of finding her.'

'If only she could see us now . . .' Jack said.

'You did well to better Marshall Judah in your race to find the Seven Ancient Wonders,' Wolf said. 'He was smart, Judah. Although did you really have to throw him into the engine of a jet plane?'

'At least I didn't crucify him.'

Wolf's face went hard. 'Judah worked for me. Just as, once upon a time, you could have worked for me. In the end, his failure, while regrettable, was not total. Tartarus was just the beginning. A far larger mission— the repelling of the Dark Star and the acquisition of its rewards—is now at hand. And as we both know, the Power of Tartarus was nullified recently by our mutual enemies, the Japanese Blood Brotherhood.'

Jack didn't know this, and the look on his face must have shown it.

Wolf grinned. 'You didn't know? About the counter ceremony they performed at the autumnal equinox, at the second Great Pyramid beneath Easter Island, the geographical opposite of Giza? Some of us want to rule the world, Jack, others like you wish to save it, others still, like our honour-obsessed Japanese friends, wish to end it.

'It was they who flew that plane into the Burj al Arab in Dubai, trying to destroy the Firestone. It was they who ambushed the British Marines near the dock at Abu Simbel with their suicide bombers. Death does not frighten them. Indeed, like their kamikaze forebears, a glorious self-sacrificing death is the ultimate honour.'

Jack grimaced in pain, nodded at Mao. 'So are America and China in this together? The Chinese attack on my farm. The torture of Wizard in China by that asshole.'

Mao visibly stiffened. Wolf was the picture of calm.

'Sadly, I do not formally represent America any-more,' Wolf said. 'After Judah's failure with the Seven Wonders, the Caldwell Group was cut loose by the Administration. But our influence still runs deep in the halls of power and in the military, especially in the Army and the Air Force. We will certainly outlast this Administration.

'No, our small group of concerned patriots feels that consecutive American governments have not taken America far enough in its role as the only remain-ing superpower on this planet. America needs to rule this planet with an iron fist, not with diplomacy or conciliation. We do what we want. We do not ask permission.

'As for China, well, it is no secret that the Chinese wish to rise in the world, to be respected as the behe-moth that they are. The Caldwell Group's relationship with them is mutually beneficial. We have much to offer each other—we have information; they have muscle.'

Jack called to Mao, 'Hey, Mao. He'll cut your throat as soon as he's used you.'

'I will take that chance, Captain West,' Mao replied

coolly. 'You are lucky he won't let me cut yours right here and now.'

'So who're they?' Jack jerked his chin at the two men beside his father.

Wolf indicated the Asian-American first. 'This is Switchblade, United States Marines, but now on loan to the CIEF.'

The CIEF, Jack thought grimly. *Technically, it was the Commander-in-Chief's In Extremis Force, but in reality it was the Caldwell Group's private army.*

Wolf then threw an arm around the larger man with him. 'And this young man, Jack, this is your half-brother, my other son, Grant West. Army Special Forces, and also now CIEF. Call-sign: *Rapier.*'

Jack assessed the wide-eyed young man standing next to his father. Big, burly and intense, Rapier just glared back at him, not blinking. Judging by his age, Jack figured Rapier had been born while Wolf had still been married to Jack's mother—another reason to dislike his father.

'He's not unlike you, Jack,' Wolf said, 'talented, driven, resourceful. But in many ways he is also an improvement on you: he's a better soldier, a more disciplined killer. He is also obedient, although perhaps this can be attributed to his higher level of breeding.'

'Just what you always wanted,' Jack said, still grimacing with pain. 'Your very own attack dog. So what's with all this?' He indicated his position. 'Couldn't you just shoot me?'

Wolf shook his head. 'Oh, no. No, no, no. You see the man beside you, Jack? The one who just nailed you to that slab? He is an Ethiopian Christian, as indeed, you are now in Ethiopia.'

Ethiopia?

'Ethiopia is a curious country,' Wolf mused, 'with an equally curious mix of faiths. Christianity is unusually strong here, brought here in the Middle Ages by the Templars. The well-known Churches at Lalibela are testimony to their presence. And did you know that according to some legends, Ethiopia is the final resting place of the Ark of the Covenant, spirited here directly from Solomon's Temple.

'Islam is practised in some areas, but most curiously, there exists in this country an underclass of Jewry. Like many Jewish populations elsewhere in the world, they are horribly persecuted by the other faiths.

'In fact, in this mine, most of our slave-miners are Ethiopian Jews. Our guards, however, are Ethiopian *Christians*, and here lies the meaning behind your means of execution.

'Our guards are most devout in their Christianity, Jack. Indeed, at Easter every year, they choose one of their own to play the Christ and they crucify him in much the same manner as you are now crucified. To die in such a manner is a great honour.'

Jack felt a chill run through him.

'My guards fear me,' Wolf said, 'as they should. They guard well because they fear the consequences of failure. Likewise, all the guards in this mine are aware that you are my firstborn son. For me to kill my firstborn in such a way strikes fear into their very hearts. I am like God himself—subjecting my own son to this, the most cruel of deaths. Your death will make me a god in their eyes.'

'Great,' Jack rasped.

As he spoke, he noticed the Ethiopian hammer-holder

scuttle up a ladder cut into one wall of the pit, hurriedly escaping from it.

For Wolf wasn't finished. 'Note the stone slab on which you lie, my son. It is one of dozens that have been dropped into that pit over the last three hundred years. Right now, you lie on layer upon layer of previously crucified Ethiopian Christians. You will not die from the crucifixion—crucifixion is notoriously slow, sometimes taking up to three days. No . . .'

At that moment, Jack heard an ominous grinding noise and suddenly a large flat stone slab was dragged across the corner of the pit's upper rim, pushed on rollers by a team of Ethiopian guards. The square-shaped slab perfectly fitted the dimensions of the deep square pit.

' . . . you will be crushed, and thus become another layer in these people's remarkable faith.'

Jack's eyes went wide.

The square stone slab was now halfway across the pit's opening.

They were going to drop it into the pit.

They were going to drop it into the pit now.

Holy shit.

This was happening too fast.

Jack began to breathe faster. He looked all around himself, and he beheld his right hand, bloodied and nailed to the slab beneath him.

The slab beneath him: the thought of it made him sick, picturing all the previously crucified Ethiopian men lying immediately below him, crushed between dozens of piled-up slabs.

'Goodbye, Huntsman,' Wolf intoned, as the slab cut him off from Jack's view. 'You really were a good soldier, a true talent. Believe me when I say that it's a terrible shame. We could have fought together and we would have been unbeatable. But now, because of the choices you've made, like the spider of your namesake, you must be crushed. Goodbye, my son.'

The slab came fully across the pit, and as Jack shouted, 'No!' the team of Ethiopian draggers withdrew the wooden rollers holding it poised above the pit and suddenly the great slab fell, fell a full twenty feet—down into the pit, its hard edges skimming against the pit's walls, down toward Jack West Jr—before it hit the bottom with a shocking *boom* that echoed throughout the mine.

Wolf gazed down at the stone slab that had just crushed his son to death. The slab had landed askew, as it did when it landed on a human body. Over the coming days it would slowly sink down further on Jack West Jr's body, flattening it.

Then with a shrug Wolf turned on his heel and walked toward the gantry elevator that led out of the mine. Mao, Rapier and Switchblade followed.

Astro, however, did not.

He wobbled on his feet, drugged and dazed, held up by two Ethiopians who had been out of Jack's sight.

'Father,' Rapier said, indicating Astro. 'What do we do about him?'

Wolf stopped, gazed at Astro for a moment. 'A futile gesture from our enemies back in the US—a pitiful play from a weak-willed Administration that has thrown its lot in with these pathetic small nations. But there can be no evidence we killed American servicemen. Take him with us. When he recovers his senses, he gets a choice: he either joins us or he dies.'

'What about the other two?' Switchblade said softly. 'The Israeli sniper and Anzar al Abbas's fat second son.'

Wolf paused a moment. 'The Israeli is still upstairs?'

'Yes.'

'There is a considerable bounty on his head. Sixteen million dollars. The Mossad put it up after he refused to obey their orders at the Hanging Gardens. His fate is sealed: we return him to the Old Master and claim the reward. Sixteen million dollars is sixteen million dollars. Then that vengeful old bastard Muniz and the Mossad can torture him for as long as they like.'

'And Abbas's second son?'

Wolf looked back out over the grim mine complex.

On the other side of the vast space, against the far wall, hung a small medieval cage, suspended above a wide pool of simmering liquid.

Imprisoned inside this cage, hanging ten feet above the dark pool, was Pooh Bear.

He was dirty, bloodied and bruised from his tumble along the highway in Egypt, but alive. His hands were spread wide, held by manacles that were themselves attached to the bars of the cage.

The liquid in the pool beneath him was a mix of water and arsenic. While this wasn't technically a gold mine, occasionally the miners found traces of gold in the walls and they used the arsenic-infused liquid to separate it from the earth. They also used it to punish anyone caught hiding gold on his body—thieves would be lowered, inside the cage, into the pool where they would drown in the thick black liquid.

To the guards' great surprise, Wolf and his people didn't seem to care for the gold that was found and they happily allowed the guards to keep any that was unearthed by the slave-miners.

No, Wolf and his minions cared for something else, something that according to an ancient legend lay buried somewhere within the tower-like stone structures that bounded the walls of the mysterious subterranean complex.

Wolf gazed at the pathetic figure of Pooh Bear, dangling in his cage above the deadly pool.

'Let the guards sacrifice him to their god. He is of no use to anyone anymore.'

And with those words, Wolf left.

He came to the gantry elevator, where he was met by two figures standing in the shadows there.

One of them stepped forward.

It was Vulture.

'American,' he said slyly to Wolf. 'My government grows impatient. You arrived at Abu Simbel too late and the Pillar got away. You knew our bargain: we get the First Pillar—with its reward—and you get the second one.'

'I know the bargain, Saudi,' Wolf said. 'You will get the First Pillar, but not before we have our hands on the Second. I know you, Vulture. I also know your methods: you've been known to abandon your allies when your ends have been achieved but not theirs. And I want to know for sure that I have your allegiance for the entirety of this mission. The First Pillar is not in our possession right now—Max Epper has it—but it is easily acquired. It's the Second that poses a more immediate problem.'

'Why?' Vulture said.

'Captain West's plane was last seen heading south into Africa. They're going for the Second Pillar, among the Neetha tribe in central Africa. But the Neetha are elusive.'

Vulture said, 'Epper thinks he can locate them.'

'So if we find him, we find the Neetha and their Pillar. This should suit the House of Saud, Vulture, for when we catch up with Epper, we get your Pillar. This is why you're going to help me now: call your government and get them to open their treasury and offer every African nation between Sudan and South Africa whatever it costs to hire their army and cover every road, river and border in central Africa. With Huntsman dead and Wizard on the run, it shouldn't be hard to find him. It's time to shut them down.'

Wolf then stepped into the gantry elevator and accompanied by Mao, Rapier and Switchblade, whizzed up the side of the mine, leaving Vulture and his companion there. He exited the complex at ground level via an earthen doorway seventy metres above the floor of the great cave.

As they strode out of the mine, Switchblade whispered to Wolf, 'Will the knowledge of Epper be enough to find the Neetha?'

Wolf kept walking. 'Max Epper is the world's leading authority in this field, and his conclusions thus far have matched our own. Should he stumble or die, it will be of little concern, we have our own studies to fall back on. Plus we have our own expert on these matters to aid us.'

Wolf stepped out into daylight—passing several more Ethiopian guards on the way—to behold, seated and smiling in the back of his car, Miss Iolanthe Compton-Jones, Keeper of the Royal Personal Records of the United Kingdom, last seen unconscious on the docks at Abu Simbel.

Vulture and his companion remained at the base of the gantry elevator on the floor of the mine. Vulture's companion had requested a few additional moments here before they left.

The two of them strode across the mine floor and stopped before the lone cage suspended above the pool of arsenic.

Pooh Bear stood in the tiny medieval cage with his hands manacled, looking like a captured animal.

From his cage, he had not been able to see Vulture and his companion talking with Wolf at the elevator—so when he suddenly saw them approaching now, he mistook their presence for a rescue.

'Brother!' he cried.

Vulture's companion—Scimitar, Pooh's older brother—gazed up at Pooh Bear impassively.

Pooh Bear shook his bars. 'Brother, quickly, set me free! Before they return—'

'They will not be returning,' Scimitar said. 'Not for some time anyway. Not until this mine yields its secret.'

Pooh Bear froze, stopped shaking his bars.

'Brother, are you not here to release me?'

'I am not.'

Scimitar strolled over to the pit in which West had

been killed, idly looked down into it, saw the great slab that had crushed Jack West.

He walked back over to the arsenic pool. 'Brother, you have always had a fatal flaw. You ally yourself with the weak. Even as a schoolboy in the playground you defended the scrawny and the frail. This appears noble but it is ultimately foolish. There is no future in such a course.'

'And what strategy do you champion, *brother*?' Pooh Bear said, anger now in his voice.

'I side with the strong,' Scimitar said, his eyes dead. 'I do so for the good of our family and our nation. There is no *future* in your alliance with the small nations of the world. Yours is a childish dream, the stuff of fairy tales and children's stories. Only an alliance with the powerful, with those who will rule, will be of any benefit to the Emirates.'

'So with your skulking Saudi friend here you side with these renegade Americans?'

'The American colonel and his Chinese allies are useful to us at the moment. Wolf uses the Chinese, the Chinese are most assuredly using him, and we use both of them. This arrangement has its dangers, but still it is better than your coalition of minnows.'

'I'd rather be in a coalition of minnows than a coalition of bandits,' Pooh shot back. 'Remember, brother, there is no honour among thieves. When things go awry, your allies will not remain by your side. They will abandon you in a second.'

Scimitar gazed steadily at Pooh Bear, genuinely curious. 'You value these people?' A nod at the pit: 'The tragic Captain West? The Israeli Jew who is right now being sent to face the Mossad? The vulgar daughter of the Siwa Oracle—a girl who presumes it is her right to learn and who disgraces you by addressing you with the name of a fat cartoon character?'

'They have become my family, and now I realise that they are more family to me than you.'

'There is no honour in living this way, Zahir. It is a slap in the face to every tradition we hold dear. Muslims do not befriend Jews. Girls do not go to school. Nor do they address Muslim men with comical nicknames. The world I shall make will reimpose tradition. It will restore the old notions of honour. You clearly have no place in such a world, which is why you must die.'

'At least I die for my friends. You, my brother, will surely die alone.'

'I see.' Scimitar looked down at the ground. 'So be it.' He began to walk away. 'Out of respect for our father, I shall tell him that you died honourably, Zahir, shielding my body from an enemy bullet. I will not allow him to be shamed by your death. I leave you to the savages.'

Then, with Vulture beside him, Scimitar departed via the gantry elevator, shooting up out of the mine.

'Do as you will, my brother,' Pooh Bear said after him. 'Do as you will.'

And thus Pooh Bear was left alone in the vast underground mine, suspended in a medieval cage above a pool of foul liquid, not forty metres from the pit where his good friend, Jack West Jr, had met a violent death at the hands of his own father.

Tiny against the vast scale of the mine, abandoned by his own brother, and now totally alone in the darkness, Pooh Bear began to weep.

KIBUYE PROVINCE, RWANDA
11 DECEMBER, 2007, 2335 HOURS

Hammered by pouring rain, out of gas and using only three of its engines, the *Halicarnassus* made an unseen landing on a stretch of highway in the remote south-western Rwandan province of Kibuye.

Once the 747 was down, its rear ramp yawned open and out of it zoomed the Freelander—with Zoe, Wizard and the kids on board. They took with them Wizard's laptop computer, a multi-frequency radio scanner, some jerry cans filled with petrol and a couple of Glocks.

Thirty minutes earlier, a call had gone out to Solomon Kol in Kenya. Ever knowledgeable about the local hazards and safe meeting points, Solomon had instructed them to link up with him at an abandoned United Nations repair depot, number 409, on the outskirts of the Rwandan town of Kamembe, located in the south-westernmost province of the country, Cyangugu.

Sky Monster, however, did not go with the others.

He stayed with his beloved plane, alone, now wearing twin holsters on his waist and a shotgun on his back. He was going to remain with the *Halicarnassus* and wait for some companions of Solomon's who were to bring him some jet fuel, enough to limp over Lake Victoria to the old farm in Kenya when the aerial patrols were called off.

And so as the Freelander sped away, Sky Monster stood beneath the giant *Halicarnassus*, alone in the Rwandan hills.

In the distance, something howled.

Wizard, Zoe, Lily and Alby sped along a remote Rwandan highway.

As Zoe drove, Wizard kept the radio scanner on, searching the airwaves for transmissions.

Soon after they left the *Halicarnassus*, the scanner picked up a military signal instructing all government forces to be on the lookout for a compact Land Rover just like theirs, carrying passengers just like them: a blonde woman, an old man with a beard, perhaps a third male, and two children.

Zoe swore. Unmanned drones patrolling the air over Kenya. Rwandan forces combing the country for them. It felt like every bad guy in Africa was on their tail.

This wasn't altogether untrue.

She didn't know that twelve hours previously, on instructions from Vulture, a series of multi-million-dollar wire transfers had fanned out from the treasury of the Kingdom of Saudi Arabia into the bank accounts of a dozen desperately poor and hopelessly corrupt African regimes. Each transfer was accompanied by a message:

Find a black Boeing 747 that was expected to make an emergency landing somewhere in central Africa. On it would be at least two Western fugitives: an old man with a long white beard, a woman with pink-tipped blonde hair, and possibly a third man, a pilot from New Zealand. With them would be two children: an Egyptian girl, also with pink in her hair, and a little black boy with glasses.

Any African nation that partook in the search would receive $50 million simply for their efforts.

To the country that *found* the fugitives and captured the old man and the little girl alive would go an additional $450 million.

Thanks to a half-*billion*-dollar price on their heads, they really did have a dozen African regimes hunting them in the most dangerous place on the planet.

Africa.

In this age of GPS satellites and rapid air travel, it's easy to say the world is small, but it is Africa that shows what a lie such a statement is.

Africa is *big* and despite centuries of exploration, much of its jungle-covered central region remains untrampled by modern man. Its outer territories—like Nigeria with its oil and South Africa with its diamonds—have long ago been plundered by European nations, but the unforgiving nature of the interior has defied Western penetration for over five hundred years.

With isolation comes mystery, and the mysteries of Africa are many.

Take, for instance, the Dogon tribe of Mali. A primitive tribe, the Dogon have known for centuries that the star Sirius is in fact a *trinary* system: it is accompanied by two companion stars invisible to the naked eye, stars known as 'Sirius B' and 'Sirius C'. Western astronomers using telescopes only discovered this fact in the late 20th century.

In their ancient verbal legends, the Dogons also state that stars are in fact *suns*, an astounding thing for a primitive tribe to know.

Exactly how the Dogon people know what they know is one of Africa's great mysteries. The thing is, they are not the only African tribe to possess unusual and ancient secrets.

In the middle of the vast and dark landmass of Africa is the tiny country known as Rwanda.

Hilly and jungle-ridden, it is barely 200 kilometres wide and would fit easily inside the state of Connecticut, one of America's smallest states.

Of course, the world now knows of the 800,000 Tutsis massacred by ethnic Hutus in the space of a month in 1994—an orgy of obscenely violent killing in which the murderers used machetes and nail-studded clubs called *masus*. In one month, ten per cent of Rwanda's 7.5 million people were wiped off the face of the Earth.

Less well-known however is the plight of the *survivors* of the genocide: the many Tutsis who were not killed had their arms cut off by the machete-wielding Hutus. Today it is not uncommon to see half-armed or one-armed locals quietly going about their daily farmwork.

Desperately poor, decimated by an unprecedented bloodletting, and with nothing to sell that the world wants, Rwanda has been cast aside as an ugly example of the worst of human nature.

In an already dark continent, it is a black hole.

That night the Freelander stood parked behind an abandoned church in the south of Kibuye Province, covered in branches and a filthy tarp.

The church near it was a frightening sight.

Bullet holes and dried blood covered its walls. In the decade since 1994, no one had even bothered to clean it.

Zoe stood at the back of the building, peering out into the darkness, gripping an MP-5. Wizard and the kids sat inside the church.

'During the genocide, the Tutsis fled to churches like this,' Wizard explained. 'But often the local priests were in league with the Hutus and their churches became cages into which the villagers willingly ran. The priests would keep the Tutsis inside with promises of safety, while at the same time notifying the dreaded Hutu patrols. A patrol would show up and kill all the Tutsis.'

The kids stared at the bloody bullet holes in the walls around them, imagining the horrors that had happened in this very room.

'I don't like this place,' Lily said, shivering.

'So, Wizard,' Zoe said from the doorway, deliberately changing the subject. 'Tell me something. What does all this really mean? When all the Pillars and sacred stones and underground vertices are stripped away, what's this mission about?'

'What's it all about?' Wizard said. 'The Apocalypse, Judgement Day, the end of the world. Every religion has an apocalypse myth. Whether it's the coming of the four horsemen or a great day on which everyone is judged, ever since humans have walked this planet, they have had the idea that one day it will all end badly.

'And yet—somehow—we have been provided with this test, this test of tests, this system of vertices built by some advanced civilisation in the distant past that will allow us to avert this terrible end, *if* we are up to the challenge. Which reminds me: Lily, can you have a look at this, please?'

Wizard grabbed Zoe's digital camera and clicked through to a photograph she'd taken at the First Vertex, one of the golden plaque they'd seen on the main wall there:

'Can you translate those lines?' he asked Lily.

'Sure,' Lily said. 'Looks like a list, a list of . . . do you have a pen and paper?'

Scanning the image of the plaque, she quickly jotted down a translation. When she was done, it read:

1st Vertex	*The Great Viewing Hall*
2nd Vertex	*The City of Bridges*
3rd Vertex	*The Fire Maze*
4th Vertex	*The City of Waterfalls*
5th Vertex	*The Realm of the Sealords*
6th Vertex	*The Greatest Shrine of All*

'It's a description of all six vertices . . .' Zoe said.

Wizard said, 'And thus perhaps the clearest description of the immense challenge we face.'

'A city of bridges? A fire maze?' Alby whispered. 'What's a fire maze? Geez . . .'

It got Wizard thinking, too. 'Lily, can you grab the Pillar, please, the one that was charged at Abu Simbel?'

Lily extracted the Pillar from its rucksack.

It still looked extraordinary—no longer cloudy but clear, with its luminescent central liquid and the mysterious white writing on its glass-like exterior.

'Do you recognise the writing?' Wizard asked her.

Lily peered at the Pillar closely . . . and her eyes widened.

She spun to face Wizard.

'It's a variety of the Word of Thoth,' she said. 'A very advanced variety, but it's Thoth for sure.' She scanned the white writing closely.

After a minute she said, 'It seems to be a mix of instructions, diagrams and symbols grouped into formulas.'

'Knowledge . . .' Alby said.

'Exactly,' Wizard said. 'The reward for successfully placing the First Pillar in the First Vertex. The other rewards are *heat*, *sight*, *life*, *death* and *power*. Those formulae you see on this charged Pillar are some kind of secret knowledge being handed down to us from the builders of the Machine.'

Lily grabbed another sheet of paper, started copying down the writing on the Pillar. Then, joined by Alby, she began translating it.

Zoe came beside Wizard and nodded at the two children: 'They're holding up well.'

'Yes. It's important to keep their spirits up, because this is going to get scary.'

'Scarier than the Rwandan genocide stories you've been telling them?'

Wizard went red. 'Oh. Yes. Mmmm.'

'Doesn't matter. Listen, I got something else that's bothering me,' Zoe said.

'What?'

'You.'

'Me? What about me?' Wizard asked, confused.

Zoe was looking at him in a strange almost amused way. Then in answer she held up a toiletry bag, and extracted from it some scissors and a razor.

'Oh, no, Zoe . . .' Wizard protested weakly. 'No . . .'

Ten minutes later, Wizard again sat with the children, only now he was beardless and his usually long shock of white hair had been shaved bald.

He looked completely different; thinner, more gangly.

'You look like a shorn sheep,' Lily giggled.

'I liked my beard,' he said sadly.

Lily tittered again.

'All right, Lily,' Zoe said, holding up the scissors. 'Take a seat in the barber's chair. Your turn.'

'*My* turn?' Lily's face went white.

Five minutes later, she sat beside Wizard, head also bowed, with her own hair cut dramatically short, the pink tips long gone.

Now Wizard chuckled.

Alby did, too. 'Lily, you look like a boy . . .'

'Shut up, Alby,' Lily grumbled.

'Sorry I had to do that, little one,' Zoe said, reaching around to grab her own hair. 'Wanna cut mine for me?'

Lily did so, sadly snipping off the pink end-tips from Zoe's shoulder-length blonde hair—undoing the work they had performed together in happier times. When she was done, Zoe looked like a short-haired punk rocker.

'Come on, it's time we all got some sleep,' Zoe said. 'Wizard, you have the first watch. I'll take the late shift.'

With that they each found a space on the floor, and with Wizard standing guard at the back door, curled up to sleep inside the isolated Rwandan church, a place that stank of death.

Lily woke with a startled gasp to find a hand smothering her mouth.

It was Zoe.

'Stay still, we're in trouble.'

With frightened eyes, Lily peered around her. They were still in the abandoned church. Near her, Alby was crouched on the floor, not daring to make a sound. Wizard was nowhere in sight. Through a dirty cracked window, Lily saw the dim blue glow of pre-dawn—

A figure crossed the window.

A black man wearing camouflage fatigues, a helmet, and carrying a machete.

'They arrived a few minutes ago,' Zoe whispered.

Wizard arrived at Zoe's side, staying low. 'There are four of them and they have a technical parked at the side of the building.'

A technical was the name of a truck common in Africa, a large pick-up with a machine-gun mounted on its open rear tray.

Wizard said, 'Their uniforms are old. Probably ex-Army soldiers that the government couldn't afford to pay, now a rape gang.'

In the wasteland that Rwanda now was, rape gangs prowled—human predators looking for women and children in isolated farmhouses and villages. They were known to terrorise whole towns, sometimes for a week at a time.

Zoe pursed her lips, then said: 'You take the kids and wait by the back door. Get ready to make a run for that technical.'

'The technical?'

'Yes.' Zoe stood, her eyes fixed and focused. 'We need a new car anyway.'

Several minutes later, the leader of the rape gang rounded the front corner of the church.

Skinny but muscled, he was dressed in ragged Army fatigues with his shirt open at the front. His helmet, however, was not standard military—it was a vivid sky-blue helmet with 'UN' written in large white letters on it; a gruesome prize that was highly regarded by the thugs of Rwanda: at some time, this man had killed a UN peacekeeper.

The lead rapist crept onto the wooden porch of the church, gripping a machete in his fist—

'Looking for something?'

He spun, to see Zoe standing in the front doorway of the derelict church.

At first, the man was stunned at what he saw: a woman, a *white* woman. Then his eyes narrowed with evil intent. He called to his comrades in Kinyarwanda.

The other three came running from their truck and when they saw Zoe, they formed a loose ring around her.

Zoe tapped her foot on the floorboard—the signal for Wizard and the kids to leave via the back door—and then stepped forward, into the middle of the ring of rapists.

What happened next happened very fast.

The leader of the gang lunged at Zoe—just as Zoe, moving with lightning speed, punched him hard in the throat.

The leader dropped to his knees, gagging, at which point, the other three attacked—but in a flurry of moves, Zoe kicked one in the mid-section, snapping his ribs, broke another's nose with a vicious elbow, and hit another, baseball-style, with the second man's machete, square in the groin. He screamed wildly as he fell.

It was all over in seconds, and when it was done, the four Rwandans lay writhing on the ground beneath the standing figure of Zoe.

'You got off lightly,' she said as the technical skidded to a halt nearby, now driven by Wizard with the kids in the back.

She took the gang's machetes and their leader's Army shirt—plus his UN helmet—then she leapt aboard the technical and it roared away into the dawn.

Later that morning, Zoe and the others sped into the province of Cyangugu in their stolen technical.

Zoe drove, now wearing the Army shirt she had taken from the rape gang leader, while beside her, Wizard sat tall wearing the UN helmet, giving them the appearance of a senior UN official being driven around the country by his female driver.

The carcasses of militia jeeps lay beside the road, their wheels and tyres long since stripped. A distressing number of one-armed women cooked outside their homes. Children splashed in open sewers. Local men lay passed out on doorsteps, drunk before noon.

One such fellow, Zoe noticed, had a dirty cell phone clipped to his belt.

The untraceable phone was quickly acquired and as they neared the town of Kamembe, Lily tried Jack's cell phone number. Putting the call on speakerphone, the others listened, too.

The phone rang once . . .

Click.

'Hello . . . ?' It sounded like Jack.

'Daddy!' Lily exclaimed.

'*No, this is not your daddy, Lily. But it's a pleasure to meet you at long last. I'm your grandfather, Jonathan West Sr, and I regret to inform you that I killed your daddy two days ago. Thank you for calling, though. Now my people can triangulate your position.'*

Lily jammed down on the 'END CALL' button, her face white with shock.

Zoe exchanged a look with Wizard. 'They killed Jack . . .'

She grabbed the phone from Lily and tried Pooh Bear's and Stretch's numbers, but both calls went straight to voicemail—for whatever reason, their phones were off.

'Jonathan West Sr . . .' Wizard breathed. 'The Wolf. Good God, he's in charge. And now he knows where we are . . . which means he'll figure out we're going after the Neetha.'

Zoe looked away, her mind buzzing.

Jack is dead, and we're out here in the middle of Africa, alone and hunted . . .

Beside her, Lily stared into space, blank-eyed. Then she started sobbing, deep aching wrenching sobs. Alby put his arm around her.

'We can't give up,' Wizard said softly but firmly. 'Jack wouldn't want us to give up. We have to stay focused and find the Neetha and the Second Pillar.'

Zoe was silent for a long time, her mind still racing. In one fell swoop, she'd learned the man she loved was dead and a great responsibility had fallen on her shoulders— the Neetha, the Pillars, keeping Lily and Alby safe—and she wasn't sure she could handle it. She wanted to cry, too, but knew she couldn't in front of the others.

Then Lily spoke and Zoe blinked back to the present.

'I'm sorry,' Lily said. 'I didn't mean to let them know where we are—'

'Don't be sorry, honey,' Zoe said kindly. 'We all wanted to call him.'

Lily looked at Zoe, tear-streaks on her cheeks. Zoe returned her gaze, and then Lily dived into her arms and burst out crying again, clutching Zoe tightly.

As they embraced, Zoe looked out at the road ahead of them.

The jungle-covered mountains of the Congo loomed over the western horizon. The Congo was far more rugged than Rwanda, more densely forested, more impenetrable.

Somewhere in there were the Neetha, a mysterious tribe known for their deformed faces and wanton savagery, the guardians of the Second Pillar.

And now, alone and without Jack, Zoe had to find them.

Around two that afternoon they arrived at the outskirts of Kamembe, where they quickly found the abandoned UN depot they were after.

It looked like a dump. The depot's ten-foot-high chain-link fence was broken in several places and near an old gate was a battered sign: UNITED NATIONS— DEPOT 409: AIRCRAFT REFIT AND REFUEL.

Through the fence, Zoe saw a few fuel trucks mounted on bricks, their tyres and vital parts long gone, and a couple of rusty old Huey helicopters that no longer possessed any landing skids.

A man stepped out from behind the nearest chopper. A very tall black man.

Zoe whipped up her gun—

'Zoe? Is that you?' he said.

Zoe heaved a sigh of relief and for the first time in days, smiled.

There, emerging from behind the rusty old chopper, was Solomon Kol.

Solomon had two porters with him, carrying fuel cans on poles across their shoulders.

'These are my friends,' Solomon said. 'They have fuel for your plane. We have been here since early morning and were starting to wonder if you had been waylaid by bandits.'

'Almost,' Wizard said.

'We also have food,' Solomon smiled.

'Oh, Solomon,' Zoe said, 'we are so glad to see you.'

They sat and ate inside the fenced UN depot.

'A friend of mine has a Fokker, for dusting crops. He flew us in this morning, dropping us off a few miles to the east of here,' Solomon said. 'There were rumours in the villages we passed through of an announcement over the government radio network. It spoke of a vast reward to the person or persons who found a group of white fugitives believed to be in Rwanda. Our enemies have cast a wide net for you and they summon the common people to aid them—'

'Hey! I think I've got it . . .' Alby said suddenly.

He had been sitting apart from the others, still examining the charged First Pillar.

It had become something of an obsession for him, figuring out what the Pillar's glowing symbols meant. With Wizard and Lily's help, he knew what some of them stood for, but now he'd made another connection.

'What is it, Alby?' Wizard said.

Alby held up the oblong glass-like Pillar with its pyramidal void at one end. He showed its four long sides. All contained the glowing white writing.

'See this side, with the spiderweb-like matrix on it. This matrix is actually a variety of *carbon* matrix—an extremely complex interconnection of carbon atoms, far more complex than anything we have today.'

'Meaning?' Lily asked.

'Carbon forms the basis of diamonds, the strongest substance on Earth. Carbon-fibre, too, is superstrong but light—fighter aircraft and racecars use it to reinforce their cockpits. Strong and light. Titanium, steel, they're strong but they're heavy. This matrix, however, is something else: a carbon-based alloy that's unbelievably strong yet incredibly light.'

'Technical knowledge . . .' Wizard breathed. 'It's technical knowledge.'

'Have you deciphered any of the other sides?' Zoe asked.

'Partially. This one here seems to be a representation of the star Sirius and its two companion stars. The second companion star is shown as a zero-point field, the same stuff that our Dark Star is made of.'

'Nice to know this may happen elsewhere in the universe,' Wizard commented.

'The next side of the Pillar is even wilder,' Alby said. 'It, well, it seems to be an explanation of the Universe Expansion Problem.'

'Goodness . . .' Wizard's eyes widened. 'Are you sure?'

'The *what* expansion problem?' Lily asked.

Wizard explained. 'It's commonly accepted that our universe is expanding. The problem faced by astrophysicists and theoreticians, however, is that it should be expanding faster than it actually is. This has caused scientists to conclude that there is a *negative energy* or force somewhere out there holding the universe together—binding it, so to speak—and thus slowing its expansion. The discovery of the physical components of this negative energy would win you the Nobel Prize tomorrow.'

Lily smiled at Alby. 'Better start writing your speech.'

'I don't think finding an ancient Pillar and reading it counts as *discovering* anything,' Alby said.

'The point is,' Wizard said, 'these are incredible things to know; incredible *knowledge*. Alby's discovery is essentially *the* explanation for the state of balance in our universe; the so-far inexplicable balance that exists between a universe that has been expanding since the Big Bang yet which is held in perfect check by a counteracting force. This is momentous. Advanced knowledge being passed down to us by an exceedingly generous prior civilisa—'

A scream pierced the air, echoing out over the hills. A completely random scream.

There was a momentary silence as they all looked out into the Rwandan countryside. Alby's discovery had briefly made them forget where they were.

When all was silent again, Wizard said, 'I'll be very interested to know what the last side of the Pillar says. Good work, Alby, you've done *very* well. Jack always said you were a special one. Lily's lucky to have a friend like you.'

Alby beamed.

Zoe had observed the entire exchange with interest—focusing on these problems and puzzles was a good way to keep their minds off the loss of Jack. She leaned forward, 'So if this is *knowledge*, what is the next reward, *heat*?'

All eyes turned to Wizard.

'Something similarly advanced, I assume. But somehow different from pure knowledge like this. I once knew an American academic who was interested in the Ramesean Stones, a fellow at MIT named Felix Bonaventura.

'Bonaventura was mostly interested in the second reward. He interpreted *heat* to mean energy, an energy source of some kind, since all our known sources of energy require the production of heat: coal, steam, internal combustion, even nuclear power. But if one could produce heat or motion without the need for *fuel*, one would have an unlimited supply of energy.'

'Are you talking about perpetual motion?' Alby said in disbelief.

'That's exactly what Bonaventura thought the second reward was,' Wizard said. 'The secret of perpetual motion.'

Zoe said, 'It'd be something China would kill for. It's choking on its own coal-based pollution.'

'Same for America,' Alby said. 'It wouldn't need Middle Eastern oil any more.'

'The whole world would change,' Wizard said. 'The Saudis and their vast oil reserves would no longer be needed. Coal would be useless. Why, warfare as we know it would be transformed. Did you know that by the end of World War II, the Nazis were using horses and carts because they'd run out of petrol? As a reward, pure *heat* would certainly be a world-changing one.'

Throughout the afternoon, Solomon and Zoe set about repairing one of the Hueys in the UN compound. Unlike the trucks, the choppers' engines were more or less intact, and where one of them was missing parts, they could mostly scavenge matching parts from the other.

Late in the afternoon, Solomon came over from the chopper, wiping his hands on a rag. 'Ladies and gentlemen. Your helicopter is ready.'

Wizard stood. 'Then let's go find the Neetha.'

DEMOCRATIC REPUBLIC OF THE CONGO

The rusty old UN Huey helicopter soared low over the jungle-covered mountains of the eastern Congo, still without any landing skids.

Zoe flew, with Wizard beside her, flipping between a tangle of maps, notes and his laptop computer.

'A few years ago I got Jack to do some research on the Neetha,' he said, finding a certain page in his notes:

NEETHA TRIBE
- *Remote tribe from Democratic Republic of the Congo/Zaire region; warlike; much-feared by other tribes; cannibals;*
- *Congenital deformities in all members, variety of Proteus Syndrome (bony growth on skull, similar to Elephant Man);*
- *Found by accident by HENRY MORTON STANLEY in 1876; Neetha warriors killed seventeen of his party; Stanley barely escaped alive; years later, he tried to find them again, but could not locate them.*
- *Possibly the same tribe encountered by the Greek explorer HIERONYMUS during his expedition into*

central Africa in 205 B.C. (Hieronymus mentioned a
tribe with terrible facial deformities in the jungles
south of Nubia. It was from the Neetha that he stole
the clear spherical <u>orb</u> that was later used by the
Oracle at Delphi.)

- BEST-KNOWN EXPERT: DR DIANE CASSIDY, Anthropologist from USC. But her whole 20-man expedition
went missing in 2002 while searching for the Neetha
in the Congo.

- Cassidy found this cave painting in northern Zambia
and attributed it to ancestors of the Neetha:

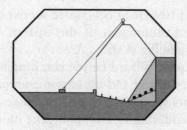

- Seems to depict a hollowed-out volcano with
the Delphic Orb at the summit but its meaning is
unknown.

'Hey, I've seen that painting!' Zoe said. 'It was
at . . .'

'It was at the First Vertex,' Wizard said. 'Which
suggests a clear connection between our quest and
the Neetha. The key, however, is Hieronymus,' he
clicked through the database on his laptop. 'Hieronymus . . . Hieronymus . . . Ah, here it is!'

He'd found the entry he was after: a scan of an
ancient scroll, written in Greek.

'What's that?' Lily asked.

'It's a scroll that was kept at the Library of Alexandria, a scroll written by the great Greek teacher and explorer, Hieronymus.'

Years before, Wizard and Jack had uncovered a vast collection of scrolls in the Atlas Mountains—a collection which, it turned out, was that of the fabled Alexandria Library, long believed to have been destroyed when the Romans burned down the famous Library. After months of careful scanning, Wizard had managed to load all the scrolls onto his various computers.

'Hieronymus was a truly exceptional man. Not only was he a great teacher, he was also an explorer beyond comparison, the Indiana Jones of the ancient world. He taught alongside Plato at the Academy, teaching no less a student than Aristotle himself. He was also the man who stole the Delphic Orb from the Neetha and took it back to Greece, where the Oracle at Delphi later used it to foretell the future.'

'The Delphic Orb?' Zoe said as she flew. 'You mean the Seeing Stone of Delphi? One of the Six Sacred Stones?'

'Yes,' Wizard said. 'Hieronymus stole it from the Neetha, but from what I've studied of him, he always intended to return it. That was why he wrote this scroll—it's a set of instructions detailing the location of the Neetha, so that the Orb could one day be returned.'

'Was it ever returned?' Alby asked.

'After they saw its power, the Greeks didn't want to give it back,' Wizard said, 'but late in his life Hieronymus crept into the Oracle's temple-cave, grabbed the Seeing Stone and fled from Greece by boat. He stopped in Alexandria—where he deposited these scrolls, written in Greek and Latin, at the Library—before he headed south into Africa. He was never seen again.' Wizard turned to Lily. 'Think you can translate this scroll?'

She shrugged. It was in Latin and Latin was easy for her. 'Sure. It says:

AT THE VALLEY OF THE ARBORIAL GUARDIANS
AT THE JUNCTION OF THE THREE MOUNTAIN STREAMS
TAKE THE SINISTER ONE
THERE YOU WILL ENTER THE DARK REALM
OF THE TRIBE THAT EVEN GREAT HADES FEARS.'

'"The tribe that even great Hades fears"?' Zoe said. 'Charming.'

Solomon said, 'The Neetha have a reputation so fearsome it has become myth; many Africans use tales of Neetha bogeymen to frighten young children: cannibalism, human sacrifice, killing their young.'

'Takes more than a scary story to frighten me off,' Lily said in her best adult voice. 'So what's the "Valley of the Arborial Guardians"? That seems to be the starting point.'

'Arborial means trees,' Alby said. 'The tree guardians?'

Wizard was clicking through more entries on his computer. 'Yes, yes. I've seen a reference to just such a valley before. Here it is. Ah-ha . . .'

Lily leaned over, and saw on his screen the title page of a book, an old 19th-century pulp-fictioner called *Through the Dark Continent* by Henry Morton Stanley.

'Stanley wrote many books about his expeditions in

Africa, most of them pure romantic rubbish,' Wizard explained. 'This one, however, detailed his genuinely remarkable trip *across* the African continent, from Zanzibar in the east to Boma in the west. Stanley departed from Zanzibar with a caravan of 356 people and, over a year later, emerged at the Congo River estuary near the Atlantic with only 115, all of them on the verge of starvation.

'Over the course of his journey, Stanley recounted numerous gunbattles with native tribes, including one particularly gruesome skirmish with a tribe that resemble the Neetha. Immediately *before* that battle Stanley recounted travelling through an isolated jungle valley in which the trees had been carved into marvellous statues, towering statues of men, some of them over seventy feet high.

'Such a valley has never been found, an unfortunate fact which has only added to the overall historical opinion that Stanley made up most of his adventures.'

'So . . .' Zoe prompted.

'So, I believe Stanley was telling the truth; he just got the details of his route wrong—something he did quite a lot. That's why no one's ever found this valley. But if we can reconstruct Stanley's *actual* route from landmarks and land formations mentioned in his book, we just might get lucky.'

'Can't say I've got a better plan,' Zoe said.

'Me neither,' Lily said. 'Let's do it.'

The Congo.

Formerly known as Zaire but renamed the Democratic Republic of the Congo in 1997, the Congo is the third-largest country in Africa, almost as big as India. Yet only three per cent of its vast land area is cultivated, meaning 97 per cent of the Congo is pure jungle, much of which remains unexplored to this day.

It is a brutal land—from the dangers of the mighty Congo River; to dense jungles teeming with snakes and hyenas; not to mention the chains of active volcanoes in the wild south-east—the dark heart of the Dark Continent.

Following Wizard's directions, Zoe took them south.

They flew for three days, stopping occasionally at abandoned UN depots to steal food and helicopter fuel, until they entered the least populated area of the country—perhaps the entire continent—the Katanga Plateau in the deep south.

Dotted with volcanoes, mountains and lush river valleys, it was as spectacular as it was remote. Giant waterfalls plummeted from mountain clefts. Fed by constant humidity, the layers of mist that shrouded the valleys remained in place all day long.

As she flew, Zoe keyed her radio scanner so that it continuously monitored all frequencies, military and commercial, allowing her to keep track of any radio activity in the area: Congolese Army patrols, UN people and maybe . . .

'—*Wolf, this is Broadsword. Just picked up a rogue signal south of Kalemie. Huey signature. Could be them*—'

'—*Check it out*—' Wolf's voice replied.

Wolf's people were close behind.

Then, late on the third day, after following a dozen false leads, Wizard spotted a mountain that had been mentioned by Stanley in his book, a mountain with twin waterfalls.

'That's it!' he called excitedly over the roar of the rotors. 'Zoe! Cut south-westward!'

Zoe did so, bringing the chopper low over a densely forested river valley that was itself fed by three small fast-flowing mountain rivers.

'Bring us down at the junction of the rivers,' Wizard called.

They landed on the riverbank, the strutless Huey landing lightly on its belly. Then, cautiously, they stepped out of the chopper.

It was Lily who spotted them first.

'Now *that* is cool . . .' she breathed, gazing at the nearby jungle.

Alby came up beside her. 'What—oh my . . .'

His jaw dropped.

There in front of them, stretching away into the hazy mist, was a forest of enormous trees.

Ghostly grey in colour, they soared to a height of two hundred feet, their interlocking upper leaves forming a canopy through which the Sun couldn't penetrate.

But it was their *trunks*—their wide, huge trunks—that seized the children's attention.

Each gigantic trunk, dozens of them, rank upon rank, all at least thirty feet in diameter, had been beautifully carved into the shapes of *men*.

Some depicted old chiefs, others warriors and priests. All were stern in appearance, fierce, warlike.

And they were old, *really* old. The great trees were faded with age and strangled by countless vines, vines that seemed to constrict around the figures like giant coiled snakes. The figures stretched away into the mist, an army of sentries standing guard over time itself.

The air was still, the dense jungle silent.

Wizard came up alongside Lily, put a hand on her shoulder.

'The Valley of the Arborial Guardians,' he said softly.

'So where do we go now?' Solomon asked.

Alby had Zoe's digital camera slung around his neck. He raised it and took a series of quickfire photos of the incredible carved forest.

Wizard recited Hieronymus's scroll: '"At the valley of the Arborial Guardians/At the junction of the three mountain streams/Take the sinister one." It seems pretty clear. We proceed to the junction of the three streams near here and take the sinister fork.'

'The sinister one?' Solomon said.

Lily smiled. 'I don't think it's supposed to be scary, Solomon. In ancient Latin, *sinister* or *sinistra* means left. We take the left-hand tributary.'

*

While the others were staring in awe at the huge carved forest, Zoe was exploring the riverbank upstream.

Something had caught her eye about fifty yards in that direction and she wanted to see what it was.

She came around a bend in the river . . .

. . . and stopped dead in her tracks.

'Oh, *shite*,' she breathed.

No fewer than thirty riverboats lay before her, crumpled and broken, half-sunk in the river. Derelict boats of various types and ages. Some were recent designs, others were World War II-era patrol boats, others older still: 19th-century modular riverboats of the kind used by Henry Morton Stanley. There were even a couple of semi-destroyed seaplanes and one crippled helicopter with the insignia of the Angolan Army on it.

Zoe froze.

It was a collection of vehicles that had arrived at this place and never left.

'Shite. We just walked into a trap.'

She spun, calling, 'Lily! Wizard! Get back to the chopp—'

It was at that moment, however, that their helicopter exploded.

The explosion echoed throughout the valley.

Wizard, Solomon and the kids all spun as one to see the chopper burst out in a massive fireball.

Zoe came running back along the riverbank, staring at the flaming wreck of the Huey.

Then a branch snapped on the opposite bank and she whirled to see a dark figure slither out of the water and disappear into the foliage.

A native.

Then it hit Zoe.

The Neetha *had* been found over the centuries, probably on many occasions. By explorers, by accident, even by one Angolan patrol, it seemed. But if an outsider who found the tribe *never got away* to tell the world about them, then the Neetha would forever remain the stuff of legend.

And what better way to distract a recently arrived visitor than with these spectacularly carved trees—the great statues absorbed the visitor's attention while the tribe's saboteurs sank their boat or disabled their chopper.

And now they've trapped us, too, Zoe thought.

'Christ,' she said. 'How could I have been so—oh, damn.'

They emerged from the foliage at the base of the

huge carved trees: dark-skinned tribesmen, their faces covered in harsh white warpaint, their yellow eyes blood-shot. Foul bony growths protruded from their foreheads and jaws, giving them a gruesome, less-than-human appearance.

Proteus Syndrome, Wizard thought. *Deformities caused by diet and worsened by years of inbreeding.*

There were maybe sixteen of them and they held bows and guns in their hands. They crept forward in a low manner, cautious but strong.

As they approached from all sides, Zoe, Solomon and Wizard instinctively formed a circle around the two children.

'I think our search is over,' Solomon whispered. 'It appears the Neetha have found *us*.'

SIXTH ORDEAL
THE TRIBE
HADES FEARS

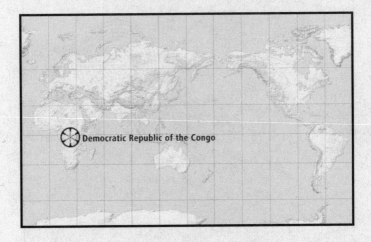

Democratic Republic of the Congo

DEMOCRATIC REPUBLIC OF THE CONGO
14 DECEMBER, 2007
3 DAYS TO THE 2ND DEADLINE

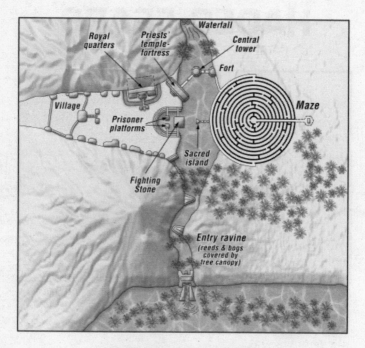

THE REALM OF THE NEETHA

THE REALM OF THE NEETHA

KATANGA PROVINCE, CONGO

Surrounded by Neetha warriors, Zoe and the group were force-marched up the left-hand river-fork—a winding walk through dense foliage and past some rocky rapids. At one point in their journey, Wizard tripped on a root and fell; he rose to his knees only to find a knife pressed against his throat, a Neetha guard gripping him in the apparent belief it had been an escape attempt.

'Quwanna wango,' the Neetha man hissed. Wizard froze as his captor slowly pressed the blade against his throat, drawing a thin line of blood. Zoe and the others all held their breath . . . but abruptly the guard released Wizard with a rude shove. No one else lost their footing after that.

As night fell, they came to a great cliff that rose high above the jungle.

A large crack in the otherwise solid natural wall loomed before them, a dramatic ravine perhaps twenty metres wide.

Plugging the base of this ravine was an imposing man-made structure—a huge stone fort lit by flaming torches and constructed of enormous cube-shaped boulders. Hundreds of sharpened elephant tusks flanked a steep stone stairway that led up to the structure, all pointing aggressively outwards.

The only gap in the fort was a great gateway at its base. At least twenty feet high, it was built in the shape of an animal's jaws bared wide. A fast-flowing river gushed out from its lower half and tumbled down a canal in the centre of the stone stairs—so that there seemed to be no actual footway that allowed access through the gateway.

Ten Neetha warriors manned a platform in front of the gate. With them, snarling and grunting and straining on leashes, were hyenas.

'Tamed hyenas?' Zoe breathed in horror as they climbed the stairs.

Wizard whispered, 'Hieronymus claimed that the Neetha used hyenas as hunting dogs, but his claims were dismissed as fanciful. He said they rear hyenas from cub-age and train them using a terrible system of beatings and starvation.'

Solomon hissed, 'If a hyena could be tamed, it would be an incredible asset. Their sense of smell is second to none. You could never hope to escape a pack hunting you.'

'A trap back at the river. Destroyed boats and planes. Hyenas as guard dogs,' Zoe said. 'What the Hell have we got ourselves into?' She gripped Lily's hand a little more tightly.

They came to the great gate at the top of the stairs. One of the sentries there blew a horn and suddenly a wooden bridge fitted with steps was lowered from inside the arch structure. It slotted into place so that it straddled the flowing river rushing out from the gate's yawning mouth.

Dwarfed by the terrible archway, surrounded by their fearsome guards, Zoe and her team stepped onto the drawbridge and disappeared inside the gate, entering the realm of the Neetha.

They emerged inside the ravine.

Sheer vertical cliffs rose dramatically on either side of them, soaring up toward the sky.

At the top of the ravine, four hundred feet overhead, the trees of the rainforest had been deliberately bent, forced to grow inwards so that they formed a canopy *over* the ravine, blocking it from outside view. To an observer flying overhead, the ravine—already hidden between three extinct volcanoes—would have been indistinguishable from the sea of green jungle above it.

During the daytime, Zoe figured, dappled light would shine through the canopy, but right now, thin shafts of moonlight cut through it, illuminating the gorge in a haunting blueish glow.

As she gazed up at the enormous walls, Lily saw that they possessed a strange kind of movement: a constant trickle that flowed down the uneven rock-walls, feeding the clumps of twisted vines that had attached themselves there. Among the snake-like vines were all manner of real snakes, speckled African rock pythons, black mambas, and various others slithering in and out of every available orifice.

'Do you *see* them?' she gasped.

Alby nodded vigorously, terrified. 'Yuh-huh.'

The ravine before them stretched away into misty darkness, twisting and bending, blocked in places by stone forts that prevented an intruder from moving in a straight line.

Likewise, the gorge's base was made up of difficult-to-pass substances.

Mostly, it was just water, a flowing stream which ultimately flowed out through the gate. But along the way, this stream passed through two dense reed-fields, three mud-ponds, and one foul stinking bog inhabited by several semi-hidden Nile crocodiles.

As the group emerged from the great gate, the lead guard blew another horn and a huge cogwheel at one of the forts upstream was turned by a slave-gang. Without warning, a series of stone platforms that had previously been hidden beneath the waters of the stream rose from beneath the waves right in front of Zoe's team, instantly providing a zig-zagging walkway that allowed one to proceed up the ravine unhindered.

'These people are most able,' Solomon said, 'for a tribe of cannibals untouched by civilisation.'

'Just untouched by *our* civilisation,' Wizard said.

'Wizard,' Zoe whispered, 'what's going to happen?'

Wizard stole a glance at the children, made sure they couldn't hear. 'We're marching to our deaths, Zoe,' he said. 'The only question is how long the Neetha keep us alive before they eat us one severed limb at a time.'

But then he was shoved onward by the guards and thus they progressed through the dark ravine, passing the various fortifications until they turned a final bend and emerged into a wider space, lit by grim firelight.

'God in all creation . . .' Wizard breathed as he beheld the realm of the Neetha.

THE REALM OF THE NEETHA

They had come to a point where their ravine met another smaller one—a T-junction of two ravines nestled between three extinct volcanoes—and suddenly they found themselves in a *very* wide space.

A broad lake lay in the middle of what could only be described as an ancient village built into the walls of the giant ravine-junction.

It looked like nothing they had ever seen.

Dozens of stone stuctures dotted the walls of the junction, some at dizzying heights, and they ranged in size from small huts to a large freestanding tower that rose up from the waters of the lake itself.

Ladders led to the upper huts while swooping ropebridges crisscrossed the minor ravine to the left, connecting the structures.

For Zoe, it was the bridge-building skills of these people that was most remarkable: ropebridges; the concealed stone bridges that she had walked on from the main gate; she even saw a series of *drawbridges* giving access to the tower out on the lake.

'Wizard,' she said, 'did these people—'

'No. They didn't build this place. They just moved in. Like the Aztecs did at Teotihuacan.'

'So what civilisation did?'

'I imagine the same one that built the Machine.

Would you look at that . . .'

They'd stepped out onto the main square of the town and Wizard was gazing off to the right, out over the lake.

Zoe turned. 'At what—'

She cut herself off.

An incredible structure lay across the lake.

It was utterly immense, literally carved out of the cone of the extinct volcano that lay on the far side of the ravine.

It looked like a modern stadium, an enormous circular arena. A series of round walls could be seen inside it—a maze of some sort. And rising up out of the very centre of the circular maze like the needle on a sundial was a superthin yet superhigh stone *staircase* easily ten storeys high.

Made of hundreds of steps, the thin staircase was wide enough for one person only and had no rail, and it rose precariously to a squat trapezoidal doorway built into the rockface on the far side of the maze.

The challenge was clear: only if you made it to the centre of the maze could you ascend this mysterious staircase.

There was one other thing that Zoe noticed about the village area: there was a small triangular island located out in the middle of the lake, in the exact centre of everything, as if it were the focal point of the entire ravine-junction.

Erected on this little island was a bronze tripod-like device that looked to Zoe like some ancient kind of inclinometer.

And on a pedestal next to the 'inclinometer', raised for everyone in the village to see, were two very sacred objects:

A smoked-glass Pillar and a beautiful crystal orb.

Wizard saw them, too, and he inhaled sharply. 'The Second Pillar *and* the Seeing Stone.'

They weren't able to stare at the little sacred island for long, however, for just then their guards brought them to a deep semi-circular pit off the main square: in it were two square granite platforms that rose twenty feet above the pit's muddy base.

Down in the mud, looking up at Lily and Alby with unblinking eyes, prowled two large crocodiles.

Two drawbridges thunked into place and the group was shoved at sword-point onto the granite slabs: the two girls on one, the two men and Alby on the other. Each tower-like platform was about ten feet from the edge and seven feet from each other, so escape was impossible. Both bore frightening axe-marks and bloody scratches on their surfaces.

The drawbridges were removed.

A crowd had gathered around the platforms—curious Neetha townsfolk, all of them possessing bony growths on their faces, and all staring at the captives, murmuring animatedly among themselves.

But then the whispering ceased and the crowd split as a series of flaming torches cut through their ranks, and an official party emerged.

Twelve men, led by a great obese fellow whose animal-skin outfit was covered in weapons, skulls and ornaments. His fleshy face was disgusting, covered in growths. Among the weapons on his belt, Wizard saw a 19th-century Winchester rifle.

The chief of the tribe. Bearing the weapons and skulls of those his line had vanquished over the centuries. Good Lord . . .

Seven younger men escorted the chief, all standing tall and proud.

Probably his sons, Wizard thought.

The other four men in the leadership group were different: *three* were clearly warriors; lean and muscly, with fierce eyes and warpainted faces.

The fourth and last man, however, was just bizarre.

He was old and gnarled, hunched, with the worst facial growths of any of them. He too had a warpainted face and he possessed the most terrifying eyes Wizard had ever seen in his life—this hunched old man had diseased yellow irises that stared crazily at both everything and nothing.

He was the warlock of the Neetha.

Their belongings were emptied in front of the warlock.

Watched by the chief, the warlock rummaged through their stuff, before with a cry he held aloft the clear First Pillar.

'*Neehaka!*' he yelled.

'Neehaka . . . ooh, neehaka . . .' the crowd murmured.

'*Neehaka bomwacha Nepthys! Hurrah!*'

Wizard didn't have a clue what was being said.

But then, from the other slab, he heard Lily say: 'He's speaking the language of Thoth. Speaking it. "Neehaka" is *nee*, "The First" and *haka*, "Great Pillar". The First Great Pillar. *Bonwacha* means infused or impregnated. "The First Great Pillar has been infused by Nepthys."'

'Nepthys is another name for the Dark Star,' Wizard whispered. 'Its Greek name.'

Then the warlock extracted the Philosopher's Stone

and the Firestone from Lily's pack and his eyes went even wider.

He shot a look at Wizard and barked a flurry of phrases.

Lily translated timidly. 'He wants to know how you came upon the great tools of cleansing.'

'Tell him, "After much study and many years of searching",' Wizard said.

In a frightened voice, Lily conveyed this.

The warlock inhaled sharply and muttered something, his eyes remaining wide.

Lily said to Wizard, 'He's surprised that I can speak Thoth. He finds this prophetic. He is a warlock and he thinks that you must be one also—'

A shout from the warlock silenced her.

Then the warlock turned suddenly and called for someone. Again the crowd parted, and now a woman stepped forward from the back of the group.

When she saw her, Lily gasped.

So did Wizard.

It was a white woman, perhaps 55 years of age, with grey-blonde hair and an elfish face that seemed beaten down, worn. She was dressed like the other Neetha women, in a leather hide and with primitive jewellery.

Wizard breathed, 'Dr Cassidy? Dr Diane Cassidy?'

The woman looked up sharply at his words, as if she hadn't heard English in a long, long time.

The warlock barked at Cassidy, and instantly she bowed her head.

So this was what had become of Dr Diane Cassidy, expert on the Neetha. She had found the lost tribe and in return they had enslaved her.

The warlock spoke curtly with Cassidy.

Lily listened to their exchange. 'He's calling her "the Great Chief's Eighth Wife". He mustn't trust me. He wants her to translate.'

The warlock spun and gazed angrily at Wizard, speaking harshly and quickly.

Diane Cassidy translated slowly and softly in English: '*The great warlock, Yanis, desires to know if you have come here to steal the Pillar of the Neetha?*'

'Oh no,' Wizard said. 'Not at all. We have come here to beseech you for the use of your Pillar, to borrow it in our quest to save the world from the Dark Star, the one your warlock calls *Nepthys*.'

Dr Cassidy translated.

The warlock reeled at the response, shocked beyond measure. When he spoke, he spat.

Cassidy translated: '*Yanis says that Nepthys rules as he pleases. Such is his divine right. Who are you to deny Nepthys his will?*'

Wizard said, 'I am one of a small few who wish to save our world.'

The warlock spat again.

'*Yanis says if Nepthys wishes to destroy this world, then that is what Nepthys will do. It is our privilege to be alive when he unleashes his godly power. Yanis will speak with you no more.*'

And with that the warlock swirled on the spot and stormed off, taking all of their belongings—including the Firestone, the Philosopher's Stone and the First Pillar—with him.

Lily and the others were left to sit on their bare stone platforms for the rest of the evening: waiting, helpless, fearful.

The warlock had retreated to a large fortress-like building to the north of the platforms which backed onto the central lake.

Fitted with dozens of outward-pointing elephant tusks, this temple-fortress was guarded by four white-painted priests bearing spears. A few also wore guns on their hips.

Wizard said, 'Warrior-monks. The finest Neetha warriors join the holy class. There they receive special training in fighting and the art of stealth. Hieronymus once said that by the time you discovered a Neetha priest had hunted you down, your throat would already have been cut.'

Throughout the evening, the townsfolk gathered to gawk at the mysterious prisoners, gazing curiously at them as if they were animals in a zoo.

The children eyed Alby with particular curiosity.

'What are they saying?' Alby said, unnerved.

'They're wondering about your glasses,' Lily said.

The women pointed at Zoe, whispering among themselves. 'Because of your cargo pants and short hair, they're not sure if you're a woman or a man,' Lily said.

But then some men came and the Neetha women and children scattered, and the atmosphere around the platforms changed.

The men were clearly persons of standing in the tribe and they gathered before Lily and Zoe's platform, pointing and gesticulating at them like horse traders. Clearly the biggest fellow among them was the leader of the group, and the rest his entourage.

'What are they saying?' Wizard asked, concerned.

Lily frowned. 'They're talking about Zoe and me. The big one is saying that he doesn't want Zoe, since she has most likely already been touched, whatever that means—'

Without warning, the biggest Neetha man shouted at Lily and spoke quickly.

Lily was taken aback. She shook her head and said, 'Ew, no. *Niha*.'

The cluster of Neetha men instantly fell into a huddle of intense muttering and whispering.

'Lily,' Wizard said. 'What did he just ask you?'

'He asked if I had a husband. I said no, of course not.'

'Oh, dear,' Wizard breathed. 'I should have anticipated this—'

He was cut off as the big fellow laughed loudly and marched back to the largest house in the village, followed by his entourage.

'What was that about?' Lily asked Zoe.

'I don't think you want to know,' Zoe said.

Late in the night, sometime long after midnight when all the villagers were sleeping, Lily awoke to see a procession of warrior-monks led by the warlock cross the lake via the drawbridges and, holding flaming torches aloft, head for the large circular maze on the other side.

One of them, Lily saw, carried the Firestone reverently, with outstretched arms. Another carried the Philosopher's Stone with equal veneration. Behind him, a third warrior-monk carried the First Pillar.

Lily noticed that Zoe was already awake—she'd been keeping watch. They hissed to Wizard and the others on the second platform, waking them.

They all observed the warlock break away from the larger group and stride out onto the sacred triangular island in the centre of the lake, via a stone bridge that rose from beneath the rippling surface. There the Delphic Orb and the Second Pillar sat proudly on their stone pedestal.

With great reverence, the warlock lifted the Delphic Orb from its pedestal and handed it to one of his monks, who dashed off to rejoin the procession.

The warlock stayed on the island, where he was joined by the two monks bearing the Philosopher's Stone and the Firestone.

Lily and the others then watched in awe as, with great solemnity, the warlock placed his people's Pillar—the Second Pillar—inside the Philosopher's Stone.

When the Firestone was set atop it, a familiar white flash flared from within the Philosopher's Stone, and when the warlock removed the Neethas' Pillar from it, the Pillar was no longer hazy and cloudy. Its rectangular glass body was perfectly clear.

Cleansed.

The warlock looked like a man who had seen his god.

The ceremony complete, he replaced the Second Pillar on its pedestal. As for the Firestone and the Philosopher's Stone, he handed them to his monks and while he remained on the sacred island, they took them—along with the First Pillar—into the maze.

About twenty minutes later, the warrior-monks with the Firestone, the Philosopher's Stone and the First Pillar emerged on the narrow flight of stone steps that rose out of the centre of the maze.

'They know how to get through . . . ?' Lily said, confused.

'Mazes like this were common in the ancient world,' Wizard said. 'The labyrinth of Egypt; the palace at Knossos. But such mazes are not designed to be impenetrable. Each possesses a secret solution and so long as you know the solution, you can pass through a given maze quite quickly.'

Zoe said, 'Most often, only royalty or royal priests knew the solution. It's a cunning way to keep your treasures safely hidden from the commoners.'

The monks climbed the great staircase and then disappeared inside the trapezoidal doorway at its summit, entering some kind of inner sanctum where the two stones—the Firestone and the Philosopher's Stone—and the First Pillar would be kept safe and secure.

Low chanting followed. The fires of their torches danced.

Then, a few minutes later, a speck of firelight appeared in the *sky* through a carefully cut gap in the tree canopy that covered the ravine—it appeared at a spot directly above the inner sanctum. One of the monks must have climbed up an internal shaft and emerged at the very summit of the volcano two hundred metres aloft.

Suddenly—*whap!*—the speck of firelight was replaced by a completely otherworldy purple glow.

'It's the Orb,' Wizard whispered. 'They must have taken the Firestone up to the summit, too. They've placed the Orb atop the Firestone and unleashed *its* special power.'

'And what is that?' Solomon asked.

'The ability to see the Dark Star,' Alby answered solemnly. 'Look.'

He pointed over at the warlock, still standing on the triangular island—only now the gnarled old man was bent over the inclinometer there, peering through an eyepiece on it, an eyepiece that was angled straight up at . . . the purple glow of the Delphic Orb high up on the volcano's summit.

'It's a *telescope*,' Alby said. 'A tubeless telescope like the kind Hooke built in the 1600s. A telescope doesn't necessarily need a tube, only two lenses, one at the bottom and another at the top, set at the right focal length. Only this tubeless telescope is huge, the size of that volcano.'

'A telescope designed for one purpose,' Wizard said. 'To see the Dark Star.'

As if on cue, the warlock howled with delight, his eye locked to the eyepiece.

'*Nepthys!*' he cried. 'Nepthys! Nepthys!'

Then he intoned something in his own language.

Lily listened then translated. '"*Great Nepthys. Your loyal servants are ready for your arrival. Come, bathe us in your deadly light. Rescue us from this earthly existence.*"'

'This is bad . . .' Zoe said.

'Why?'

'Because this warlock has no intention of saving the world from the Dark Star. He *wants* it to come. He *wants* it to unleash its zero-point field on the Earth. More than anything, this man *wants* to die at the hands of his god.'

Lily again fell asleep, but just before dawn, something else happened.

It was many hours after the warlock and his monks had concluded their nocturnal activities by returning their people's sacred objects to their usual places: the Delphic Orb and the (now cleansed) Second Pillar were returned to the pedestal on the triangular island, alongside the ancient inclinometer. After that, the priests had retired to their temple-fortress and the village was still—a stillness that had prevailed until Lily was woken by a series of small objects pelting her body.

'Huh?' she looked up with bleary eyes . . .

. . . to see a young Neetha man tossing pebbles at her.

She sat up.

He was perhaps twenty years old and short, and if you could have removed the growth on his left temple, he would have qualified as a fresh-faced youth.

'Hello?' he said tentatively.

'You speak our language?' Lily asked, stunned.

He nodded. 'Some. I am student of chief's eighth wife,' he said slowly, articulating each word carefully. 'She and I both oppressed in tribe, so speak much. I have many asks for you. Many asks.'

'Such as?'

'What is your world like?'

Lily cocked her head, looking at this Neetha youth more closely, and she softened. Amid all the fierce trappings of this ancient warrior tribe was the most universal kind of individual, a gentle and curious young man.

'What is your name?' she asked.

'I am Ono, seventh son of High Chief Rano.'

'My name is Lily. You speak my language very well.'

Ono beamed with pride. 'I am keen student. I enjoy to learn.'

'Me, too,' Lily said. 'I'm good with languages. Yours is a very old one, you know.'

'This I know.'

Ono, it turned out, was a *very* curious young man who had many questions about the outside world.

The concept of flight, for example, intrigued him. As a younger man he had helped disable a seaplane down at the carved forest. After the unfortunate people in the plane had been taken away and eventually killed and eaten, he had examined the plane for hours. But try as he might, he hadn't been able to figure out how such a heavy object could fly like a bird.

Likewise, he had a radio—Zoe's radio, taken from their belongings—and he asked Lily how such a device could enable two people to speak over great distances.

Lily did her best to answer his questions, and the more she talked with him, the more she found Ono to be not only curious but sweet and kind.

'Can you tell me about your tribe?' she asked.

He sighed. 'Neetha have long history. Power in tribe rests on, how you say, balance between royal family and priests of Holy Stone.

'My father chief because family strong for many

years. Strong chief respected by Neetha. But I think my father brute. My brothers brutes, too. Large of body but small of mind. But here, strong get all they desire—healthy women, first food, so strong continue to rule. They beat the weak and take from them: animals, fruit, daughters.

'But warrior-priests *also* have power because they guard maze. Inside their fortress, from very young age, them study and learn spells and also fighting arts so when come of age, emerge as killers.'

Lily eyed the dark temple-fortress nearby. With its high battlements, tusks and folding drawbridges, it looked fearsome.

She asked, 'Is their fortress the only way to get to the maze and the sacred island?'

Ono nodded. 'Yes. Over centuries, ruling clan and priest class find it . . . beneficial . . . to honour each other's power. Royal family orders people to honour priesthood, while priests approve royal marriages and support ruling clan by punishing any person who attacks royal.'

'What's the punishment for attacking a royal?' Lily asked.

'One is sentenced to the maze,' Ono said, looking out at the massive circular structure across the lake. 'Animals lurk in it. Sometimes accused is hunted in there by priests; sometimes by dogs; other times, condemned man is left to roam maze until starve or take own life in despair. No man ever escape maze.'

Ono looked off sadly into the distance.

'Sweet Lily. I am not strong. I small, but have keen mind. But keen mind mean nothing here. Disputes settled on Fighting Stone,' he nodded at a large square stone platform that sat between Lily's slab and the triangular island on the lake. 'I could not hope to defeat my brothers in fight, so I reduced to shadow life. Life in my tribe is not happy life, Lily, even when you chief's seventh son.'

Ono bowed his head, and Lily looked kindly at him.

But then abruptly something clinked somewhere and Ono stood.

'Dawn comes. Village awakes. I must go. Thank you for talk, sweet Lily. I sorry for you, for day ahead of you.'

Lily sat upright.

'The day ahead of me? What do you mean?'

But Ono had already dashed away, disappearing into the shadows.

'What about the day ahead of me?' she said again.

Morning came.

Shafts of sunshine lanced down through the tree canopy above the Neetha gorges as a large crowd gathered around the two prisoner platforms.

The enormous warrior who had previously assessed Lily and Zoe now stood before the assembled crowd. Beside him stood the fat Neetha chief, looking proud and approving of what was to come.

The big warrior addressed the crowd in a loud booming voice that Lily translated quietly:

'Subjects of the High Chief Rano, our great and noble king, champion of the maze, conqueror of white men and owner of a white woman, listen to my words! As the first-born son of our glorious chief, I, Warano, seeking to follow in my illustrious father's footsteps, claim this white woman!'

Lily's eyes boggled. *What?*

This ugly Neetha man was claiming Zoe.

'Unless another among you dares challenge me for her, I will, now and at this moment, take her to my bed and consider her my wife!'

The crowd remained silent.

No one, it seemed, dared to challenge this mountain of a man.

Lily spotted Ono in the back of the crowd, saw him

bow his head sadly. She also spied Diane Cassidy, and saw her turn away in horror, covering her mouth.

Then Lily turned to Zoe—only to see that Zoe's face was as white as a sheet.

Lily frowned, confused.

She spun again and this time saw that all the Neetha women in the crowd were pointing at *her*, looking her up and down and nodding approvingly.

And then it hit her.

This man wasn't claiming Zoe.

He was claiming *her*.

Lily's blood froze.

The crowd was still silent. The chief's eldest son eyed her lustfully, his mouth opening slightly to reveal foul yellow teeth.

His wife? But I'm only twelve! her mind screamed.

'I will fight you for her,' a voice said evenly, in English, invading Lily's thoughts.

She turned.

To see Solomon standing up on his platform, tall, thin and gangly, yet firm and noble in his stance.

'I will resist your claim,' he said.

The chief's first son—Warano—turned slowly to face Solomon. Clearly, he had not expected any challengers. He assessed Solomon from head to toe before snorting derisively and shouting something loudly.

Cassidy translated. 'Warano says, "So be it. To the Fighting Stone!"'

Planks were laid out and Warano and Solomon strode across them, out onto the Fighting Stone—the wide square platform at the edge of the central lake.

This platform was lower than the prisoner slabs, barely a foot above the surface of the water. Several large crocodiles lay at its edges, ever watchful.

The Neetha villagers swarmed to take their places on the steps flanking the Fighting Stone, to watch the bloodsport.

Two swords were tossed onto the Fighting Stone.

Lily watched in horror as Solomon picked up his blade—he held it all wrong, as though he had never swung a sword in anger in his life, which so far as Lily knew, was probably true.

Warano, on the other hand, twirled his sword easily and fluidly in one hand: seasoned and experienced.

Ono appeared beside Lily's platform, spoke across the ten-foot gap. 'This madness. Even if thin man beat Warano, he be sentenced to maze for killing royal son. Is your friend skilled fighter?'

Lily's eyes were filling with tears. 'No.'

'Then why does thin man challenge Warano for you?'

Lily couldn't answer. She just gazed out at Solomon, standing out on the Fighting Stone on her behalf.

Zoe answered Ono's question. 'Where we come

from, sometimes you stand up for your friends, even when you can't win.'

Ono frowned. 'I see no sense in this.'

At that moment, a great drum was struck and the obese chief of the Neetha assumed his place in a royal box overlooking the Fighting Stone and called, 'Fight!'

It would be the most horrific spectacle Lily had ever seen.

Warano lunged at Solomon with a flurry of powerful blows, and Solomon—gentle Solomon, kind Solomon, who had bounced Lily on his knee as a baby—parried them as best he could, staggering back toward the edge of the Fighting Stone.

But it was clear this was a total mismatch.

Wide-eyed and venomous, with five crashing blows, Warano disarmed Solomon and then without so much as a blink, ran him through, the bloody blade of his sword protruding from Solomon's back.

Lily gasped.

Solomon dropped to his knees, skewered by the sword, and he looked over at Lily, locking eyes with her, uttering, 'I am sorry, I tried,' a moment before Warano sliced his head from his body.

Solomon's corpse slumped to the ground, headless.

The crowd roared.

Tears flowed down Lily's cheeks. Zoe clutched her to her chest, holding her tight. Wizard and Alby just stood on their slab, watching in abject horror.

Warano raised his fists in triumph, his eyes insane, before casually using Solomon's body to wipe the blood off his blade.

Then he kicked the body off the Fighting Stone, leaving the crocs to fight over it.

'Are there any other challengers!' he roared. 'Does anyone dare oppose me now!'

The crowd of natives cheered.

Lily sobbed.

But as she did so, in a distant corner of her mind, she heard a strange voice coming from Ono's radio saying, '—*picked up a residual heat signature about a half-hour ago. Just found it. Looks like a downed Huey, UN markings. Near a strange-looking forest. Sending you my co-ordinates now, sir—*'

The cheering died down and suddenly there was silence around the Fighting Stone.

Long silence.

The only sound was the foul crunching of the crocs tearing Solomon's body apart.

'So there is no one then!' Warano shouted again, quickly translated by Cassidy. 'Excellent! I shall take my new woman and enjoy her . . . !'

But then someone spoke.

'I challenge you.'

This time it was Zoe.

The response from the assembled Neetha said it all. They had never seen anything like this.

A *woman* challenging a royal son.

They murmured animatedly, aghast.

'Unless the chief's son is too cowardly to do battle with a woman,' Zoe said.

Sensing the moment, Diane Cassidy immediately translated Zoe's words for the others and the crowd went into total apoplexy.

Zoe shouted to Warano, adding the sweetener. 'If he defeats me, this Warano can have two white wives.'

When Cassidy translated this, Warano's eyes lit up like lightbulbs. To own a white woman might have been the ultimate status symbol, but to own *two* . . .

'Bring her to me!' he called. 'After I beat her, I shall keep her, but as a master keeps a dog.'

Zoe was released from her platform and she strode down the long plank that gave entry to the Fighting Stone.

Once on the Stone, the plank was withdrawn and she faced off against the giant Warano.

Wearing only a singlet, cargo pants and boots, she wasn't exactly big. But her lean muscular shoulders, glistening with sweat, contained a wiry strength.

Standing before the Neetha chief's number one son, the top of her blonde head came level with his shoulders. The great black warrior loomed over her.

He kicked Solomon's sword across to her, saying something derisive in his own language.

'Is that so?' Zoe picked up the sword. 'But I don't think you've ever met a woman like me before, asshole. Let's dance.'

With a roar, Warano lunged forward, swinging his sword in a crushing downward motion that Zoe parried away with some difficulty before sidestepping out of the way.

Warano stumbled and turned, snorting like a bull.

He engaged Zoe again, raining a flurry of blows down on her, only for Zoe to desperately deflect each one, her sword vibrating terribly with each thunderous hit.

Warano was obviously stronger, and he seemed to gain confidence with every volley of blows he unleashed. Zoe was doing all she could to defend herself, so much so that she hadn't even been able to attack once. This, it seemed to the assembled Neetha, would be easy.

But as they continued to fight—as Zoe continued to parry all of Warano's lunging blows—it soon became apparent that it wasn't going to be so easy at all.

Five minutes became ten, then twenty.

As she watched the fight tensely, Lily could see Zoe just weathering the storm, blocking blows and then retreating and waiting for the next flurry.

And gradually, Warano's attacks became slower, more laboured.

He was sweating profusely, tiring.

And Lily began to recall a movie she'd watched with Zoe once—a documentary about a boxing match between Muhammad Ali and George Foreman in Africa. Foreman had been bigger, stronger and younger than Ali—but Ali had just weathered his punches for eight whole rounds, letting Foreman grow tired in the process, and then Ali had pounced—

Zoe pounced.

As Warano lunged wearily in another attack, quick as a flash, Zoe dodged out of the way and plunged her short-bladed sword into his fleshy throat, right through his Adam's apple, all the way up to the hilt.

The big man froze where he stood.

The entire crowd gasped.

The chief leapt to his feet.

The warlock turned to his priests and nodded. Some priests dashed away.

Warano wobbled unsteadily on the Fighting Stone—alive but incapable of movement, speechless on account of the sword lodged in his throat, his bulging eyes staring incredulously at her, at this woman—this *woman*!—who had somehow bested him.

Zoe just stood in front of the paralysed giant, looking him right in the eye.

Then, slowly, she took his sword from his useless right hand and held it in front of his horrified eyes.

She addressed the crowd: 'That sword in his throat is for all the little girls this man has "married" over the years.'

Diane Cassidy translated in a quiet voice.

The crowd watched in stunned silence.

'And this is for the friend of mine he killed today,'

Zoe said, grabbing the grip of the sword lodged in Warano's throat and gruesomely pushing on it, driving him back toward the edge of the Fighting Stone, where he fell, landing on the very edge.

Zoe then kicked his useless legs out over the rim, allowing Warano to watch in paralysed terror as the nearest crocodile saw them. With a fearsome lunge, the croc launched itself out of the mud and brought its jaws down on Warano's feet with a crunching sideways bite.

A second croc joined in, and before he was dragged into the muddy pool, Warano got to *watch* as the two crocodiles ripped two of his limbs from his body, literally eating him alive.

His blood washed across the Fighting Stone before the crocs took him under and the muddy waters were still once again.

'Holy fucking shit,' Alby gasped, breaking the stunned silence that followed.

The chief stood in his box, speechless with rage. His firstborn was dead, killed by this woman.

But the warlock beside him still had his wits about him. He called out in his native tongue, shouting in a shrill voice.

Diane Cassidy translated: 'A member of the royal clan has been slain! All know the punishment for such an outrage! The murderer must face the maze.'

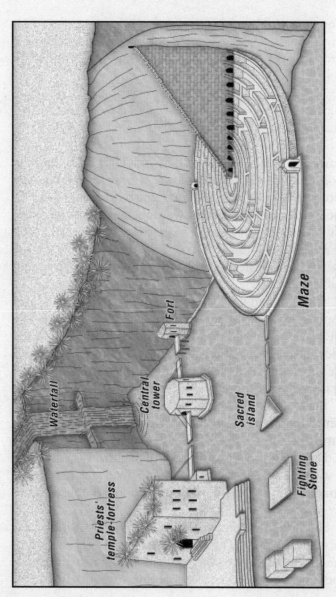

ZOE'S CHALLENGE: THE MAZE

Planks were thrown down onto the Fighting Stone and Zoe was suddenly surrounded by warrior-monks. She dropped her sword and was immediately shoved at spear-point off the Stone toward the temple-fortress, the only point of entry to the giant maze on the other side of the lake.

The warlock stood beside Zoe at the gate to the temple-fortress.

'This woman has taken royal blood!' he called. 'Her sentence shall be as follows: she will be condemned to the maze, where she will be hunted by dogs. Should the gods in their eternal wisdom allow her to emerge from the other side alive and unscathed, then it is not for us to deny the great gods their will.'

'Such an old conceit,' Wizard spat. 'Since she can't escape the maze, the gods will be assumed to have sanctioned her death. It's like dunking a woman accused of witchcraft in a river and saying if she drowns, she's *not* a witch. It's a no-win situation for her and an all-win situation for the priest who claims a connection with the divine.'

Standing at a discreet distance, Diane Cassidy said formally to Zoe, 'The maze has two entrances, one to the north, another to the south. It also has many dead-ends. Both entrances have separate routes that lead to the centre. You will be thrown in at the northern end—a few minutes later, four warrior-monks with hyenas will enter behind you. To live, you must navigate your way to the centre of the maze and from there, successfully negotiate the southern half to the south entrance. That is the only way to survi—'

The warlock barked something at Zoe. Cassidy translated: 'The warlock asks if you have any final requests.'

Zoe gazed out from the gate of the temple-fortress. She looked out at Lily and Wizard on their platforms, their eyes wide with horror, and at Alby as well—when suddenly she spotted something hanging from Alby's neck.

'As a matter of fact, I do have a request,' she said.

'Yes?'

'I would like one of my group to accompany me in the maze: the boy.'

Wizard and Lily both blurted, '*What?*'

Alby pointed at his own chest. 'Me?'

Diane Cassidy frowned with surprise, but relayed Zoe's words to the warlock.

The warlock glanced at the little figure of Alby and, apparently seeing no danger in him, nodded his assent.

Alby was taken from his prison platform and led to the steps of the temple-fortress, where he joined Zoe.

'Zoe . . . ?'

'Trust me, Alby,' was all she said as the gate to the temple-fortress rumbled open, lifted on chains.

Just before the two of them were led inside it, Zoe called back to Lily: 'Lily! Keep listening to your friend's radio!'

'Huh?' Lily said.

But by then the great gate to the temple-fortress had rumbled ominously shut behind Zoe and Alby.

Two mighty drawbridges were lowered into place and they crossed them, arriving at the edge of the vast circular maze, looking back at the village; at Lily and Wizard on their platforms; at the villagers on the amphitheatre-like seating around them; and at the sacred island with the Orb and the Second Pillar displayed on it.

A snarling noise made them turn.

Four warrior-monks emerged from a cage dug into the wall nearby, holding four large spotted hyenas on leashes.

The dog-like animals heaved and strained—they seemed starved, just for occasions like this—and they barked and snapped, saliva spraying from their jaws.

'Tell me again why you brought me along,' Alby whispered.

'Because you can read maps better than I can.'

'Because I can what?'

'And because you have my digital camera around your neck,' Zoe said, looking at him meaningfully, 'and my camera holds the secret to this maze.'

'How?'

Before Zoe could answer, they were brought to the northern extremity of the maze and the entrance there: a wide arch set into the outermost stone ring.

The stonework of the wall itself was remarkable—a marble-coloured rock without any visible joins or seams. Somehow the superhard igneous stone had been cut and smoothed into this incredible configuration, work that was far too advanced for a primitive African tribe.

The warlock addressed the crowd across the lake, calling loudly: 'Oh mighty Nepthys, dark lord of the sky, bringer of death and destruction, your humble servants commend this taker of royal blood and her companion to your maze. Do with them as you will!'

With that, Zoe and Alby were thrust through the archway and into the maze, the ancient labyrinth from which no accused had ever emerged alive.

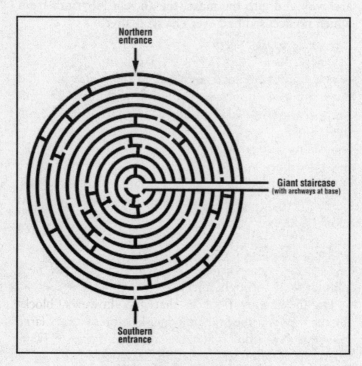

THE MAZE OF THE NEETHA

The Maze of the Neetha

A heavy door boomed shut behind them and Zoe and Alby found themselves standing in a superlong open-topped white-walled corridor that curved away in both directions.

Looming above the maze's ten-foot-high walls, rising out of its very centre, was the spectacular stone staircase that led up into the volcano, into the priests' inner sepulchre. Right now ten warrior-monks stood on the staircase, guarding the inner sanctum in the unlikely event Zoe and Alby got to the centre.

They had three choices.

Left, right or—through a yawning gap in the next circular wall—straight ahead.

On the muddy floor in that gap, however, blocking the way, was the foul decaying skeleton of a very large crocodile that hadn't quite made it out of the maze. Half-eaten, the skeleton still had rotting flesh on it.

What on earth ate a crocodile? Alby thought.

Then it hit him.

Other crocodiles. There are other crocodiles in here . . .

'Quickly, this way,' Zoe said, dragging Alby left. 'Give me the camera.'

Alby extracted the camera and gave it to her. As they ran, Zoe clicked through its stored photos, clicking back through their African adventure—shots of the Neetha's carved tree forest, of Rwanda, and then of Lake Nasser and Abu Simbel and . . .

. . . the shots Zoe had taken at the First Vertex.

Images of the immense suspended bronze pyramid leapt off the camera's little screen, and then shots of the *walls* in the Vertex's massive pillared hall, including the picture of the golden plaque.

'That one,' Zoe said, showing it to Alby. 'That's the one.'

He looked at the photo as they hurried down the long curved passageway:

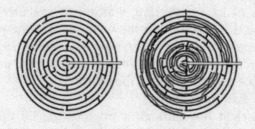

The photo showed two curious circular images intricately cut into a rockwall. Images of a maze. *This* maze. One image showed the maze empty, while the other showed two routes through it, one from the north, the other from the south, both ending at the centre.

Alby shook his head. With its ten concentric rings and the straight narrow staircase branching from its centre out to the right, it certainly *looked* like their maze . . .

'That warlock and his priests probably have this

exact carving somewhere,' Zoe said. 'That's how they alone know how to successfully navigate the maze.'

'Zoe! Wait! Stop!' Alby shouted, halting suddenly.

'What?'

'According to this, we've gone the wrong way!'

'Already?'

Peering at the camera's tiny screen, they checked the carving showing the route through the maze. They had gone immediately left, racing around the outermost circle of the maze—

'We should have jumped over that crocodile carcass and taken the next circle,' Alby said. 'Look. This route only leads to a bunch of dead-ends. Quickly! We have to go back before they release the hyenas!'

'Glad I brought you along,' Zoe smiled.

Back they ran, arriving at the huge entry gate and again they saw the half-eaten crocodile carcass. They hurdled it.

'*Now* we go left,' Alby directed.

Left they went, running desperately around the curving alleyway.

They saw the high staircase looming above them, coming nearer, saw a semi-circular archway in its base, allowing them to run under it if they wished.

'No!' Alby called. 'Go right, into the next circle!'

Bam!

A banging noise echoed throughout the maze.

It was closely followed by the barking of the hyenas and the rapid splashing of paws on mud.

'They just let the dogs in,' Zoe said.

Through the maze they ran.

Dashing down its long curving alleyways, often hearing the hyenas over the walls.

Occasionally, they came to a pit filled with dank, stinking water and inhabited by a crocodile or two. Human remains were often nearby; crocodile skeletons, too, of those reptiles that hadn't made it out before they'd starved.

These they skirted or jumped, not daring to slow down—although on one occasion, Zoe grabbed a long, thick croc bone from one of the skeletons.

They kept running.

All the while, the central staircase came nearer.

'Zoe,' Alby asked. 'What are we gonna do if we get out of here? Won't they just kill us some other way?'

'Not if what I think is going to happen happens,' Zoe said. 'I needed to buy us some time. That's why I took so long to kill that asshole prince.'

Alby was shocked. 'You *deliberately* took that long? Why? What's going to happen?'

'The bad guys are going to arrive.'

'I thought the bad guys already had us.'

'The badder guys, then. The ones who chased us out of Egypt and killed Jack. They're almost here. And when they arrive and attack the Neetha, that's our chance. That's when we want to be out of this maze and ready to run.'

Out in the main village, Lily sat alone on her high stone platform. Ono sat across from her, as close to her as he could.

Abruptly, the radio around his neck squawked.

'—*Ground Team Leader, this is Wolf, come in.*'

'—*This is Ground Team Leader. What is it, sir?*'

'—*Switchblade, be alert. While you and Broadsword have been rubbernecking at those big carved trees, we've spotted some heat signatures coming your way. Human signatures, about a dozen of them, and they're sneaking up on your choppers from the east.*'

'—*Thanks for the heads-up, sir. We'll handle it. Switchblade, out.*'

Lily turned to Wizard on the other platform. He'd heard it, too.

'Wolf's men . . .' he said. 'They're almost here . . .'

Zoe and Alby plunged deeper into the maze, racing down its long bending passageways with Alby directing and Zoe looking out for danger. Curiously, as she ran, she also dragged her crocodile bone against the wall, scraping it harshly.

The staircase in the centre gradually came nearer and just after they hurried through one of the ten archways cutting through its base, they suddenly found themselves in a perfectly round space fitted with *two* entrances and, momentarily shocking them both, the base of the narrow staircase itself.

They were in the centre of the maze.

Alby gazed up the superhigh staircase. Its steps stretched up and away from him into the lofty heights of the hollowed-out volcano, wide enough only for one person at a time and without any kind of safety rail. Fierce-looking warrior-monks bearing spears and guns stood along its length.

At the base of the stairs, in the exact centre of the

entire maze, stood an ornate marble podium. Carved into it was a list of some sort, written in the Word of Thoth:

Given the podium's central position, Alby figured the carvings on it were important, so he quickly snapped off some photos before Zoe yanked on his hand. 'Come on, we have to get through the second half, and we still have those dogs on our tai—'

A blur of brown knocked her off her feet, tearing her away from Alby.

Alby fell backwards, his mouth falling open as he saw the massive animal straddling Zoe.

A hyena.

The thing was *huge,* with foul brownish fur, matted and speckled, and the signature stunted hind legs of the hyena.

But it was alone. The pack must have split up in their hunt.

Zoe rolled underneath the snarling jaws of the hyena. Then she slammed it with her boot into the marble-like wall of the maze and the animal yelped. But it instantly pounced back at her, jaws bared—only to impale itself on the now sharpened crocodile bone held in Zoe's outstretched right hand.

Zoe extracted the weapon, allowing the lifeless hyena to slump to the floor.

Alby stared. 'This is hard core . . .'

'Fuckin'-A it is,' Zoe said, already on her feet again. 'I bet your mother wouldn't want to see you doing this. Let's go.'

Out in the village, again Lily heard a message over Ono's radio:

'—*Rapier, this is Switchblade. Neutralised the bogeys who were sneaking up on our chopper. Natives. Nasty. They were trying to sabotage the chopper. We've found the entrance to their base—due east of the carved forest; a fortified gate of some sort; heavily guarded. Gonna need some more men.*'

'—*Copy that, Switchblade. We're on the way, coming in on your signal.*'

Lily looked up in horror.

With Zoe and Alby in the maze, and her and Wizard trapped on their platforms, Wolf's men were arriving at the main gate and were about to storm the realm of the Neetha.

Desperate running through the maze.

Zoe and Alby didn't dare stop. Now they were making their way through the southern half of the maze, heading away from the central staircase.

They encountered more muddy croc pits, a few deep holes, and even more human remains.

Halfway across, a second hyena caught up with them, but Zoe smashed it in the face with a crocodile skull, using the skull's teeth as a multi-edged blade that pierced the side of the snarling hyena's head. The hyena howled and skulked off, blood all over its face.

They kept running, until after a time, brilliantly guided by Alby, they entered the outermost circle of the maze and charged around its long sweeping curve until they came to a high archway just like the one through which they had entered the maze.

The southern entrance.

Zoe halted twenty yards short of it. 'We don't want to leave the maze too early,' she said. 'We have to wait for the time to be just right.'

'And when will that be?' Alby asked.

Just then, right on cue, the distinctive blast of a grenade explosion echoed out from somewhere in the Neetha ravine system.

'Now,' Zoe said. 'The badder guys just arrived.'

Wolf's rogue CIEF force stormed the main gate of the Neetha, led by the Marine trooper named Switchblade and a Delta man named Broadsword and supplemented by no less than a hundred Congolese Army troops bearing AK-47s.

Essentially *bought* with Saudi money, the Congolese soldiers were there literally as an army for hire, and Switchblade used them as such, as front-line fodder.

He hurled them at the main Neetha defences in the mouth of the ravine—a series of booby traps and hidden positions that took out a point man or two, but which were soon nullified by the sheer number of advancing troops.

Some of the Neetha guards had guns—but most of them were old and poorly maintained, and they were no match for the modern weapons of the invading force.

And so Wolf's force advanced through the ravine system, killing Neetha defenders on every side. The Neetha fought fanatically, giving away nothing, fighting to the bitter end. Many Congolese troops were killed, either by gun or by arrow, but their numbers were too great and their techniques too good, and soon they were spilling out onto the main village square.

*

As the invasion of the ravine system began, pandemonium broke loose all around the prisoner platforms.

The villagers—until then eagerly awaiting the results of the hunt in the maze—had scattered. So too the royal clan members, taking up their weapons.

Any warrior-monks who had remained near the platforms quickly dashed to the safety of their temple-fortress, crossing its first drawbridge and taking up positions in their holy tower—the four-storey structure situated out on the lake, halfway between the temple-fortress and the opposite shore.

As for Lily and Wizard, they were simply left on their platforms.

They could only watch helplessly as explosions and gunfire rang out from the ravine, growing louder and closer.

But then Lily saw some movement on the other side of the lake.

She saw the warlock and two monks dash out to the triangular island in the middle of the lake and scoop up the three sacred items sitting there: the Delphic Orb, the Second Pillar and the inclinometer-like sighting device.

Then they turned and bolted for the opposite shore, arriving at a narrow path next to the maze's outer wall just as—

—Zoe and Alby dashed out along the same path, racing out from the shadows at the southern end of the maze!

Lily almost cheered. *They'd got through the maze . . .*

A struggle ensued, with Zoe disarming the two warrior-monks before jamming the butt-end of a spear into the warlock's face, felling him, knocking him out cold.

Lily then watched as Zoe and Alby snatched up the three sacred objects and—

Clunk!

Lily turned at the sudden sound.

And saw Ono standing opposite her platform, holding a plank vertically, as if he was ready to lay it down across the void to her platform. Diane Cassidy stood similarly near Wizard's platform, also with a plank in hand.

They both held rather old-looking pistols in their spare hands.

In the chaos all around them—Neetha warriors rushing to the defences, exploding grenades, wild gunfire—the prisoner platforms were being ignored.

Ono said quickly, 'Young Lily! There is escape tunnel hidden within priesthood's island tower! I will show you . . . if you take us with you.'

'Deal,' Lily said.

Ono didn't understand the word.

'Yes, yes,' Lily said quickly. 'We'll take you with us.'

Clunk! Clunk!

Both planks thunked loudly into position on the two platforms and Lily and Wizard dashed off them, free at last.

As they ran toward the temple-fortress of the priesthood, Wizard saw Zoe and Alby on the other side of the lake, running in the same direction, carrying the island's sacred objects.

'Zoe!' he called. 'Get to the central tower! The priests' tower! It's an exit!'

'Got it!' Zoe yelled.

No sooner had she spoken than a great explosion blasted out above the huge waterfall at the northern end of the Neetha ravine.

The awning of bent-over trees concealing the ravine there spontaneously erupted in flames, and burning branches and tree-trunks rained down onto the lake below, falling a full four hundred feet.

Then with a terrific roar, two CIEF Black Hawk helicopters swooped down through the opening that had been created, hovering perfectly—noses up, tails down—directly above the priests' island tower!

They were modified Black Hawks known as Defender Armed Penetrators, or DAPs—although the only modifications they possessed were in the amount of weaponry they carried. These choppers were armed to the teeth with guns, rocket pods and missile launchers.

Rockets shot out from the two DAPs, hitting every one of the Neethas' strategic defensive positions. Stone towers were blown to pieces. Warriors were hurled into the lake. Obstacles in the main entry ravine were blown clear out of the water, allowing the Congolese foot-soldiers to pour into the village unopposed.

The priesthood's temple-fortress was also hit by a rocket from above.

In a single instant, flames flared from every one of its narrow stone windows, and a moment later its huge armoured doors flew open and burning warrior-monks came spilling out of it, rushing down the steps and hurling their flaming bodies into the lake . . . where the flames were doused, but where the ever-patient crocodiles lay waiting.

Screams. Splashing. Thrashing.

'This is our chance,' Wizard said. 'Inside! Now!'

With Lily, Ono and Cassidy behind him, he rushed for the temple-fortress, ducking arrows and dodging bullets—

—only to be blocked at the steps of the temple-fortress by three unexpected players: the obese chief of the Neetha and two of his sons, all of them brandishing pump-action shotguns, aimed right at Wizard's fleeing group.

The chief barked some angry words at Ono and Cassidy, and they immediately lowered their little pistols.

'What'd he say?' Wizard whispered.

'He says that we cannot leave,' Cassidy said. 'He says that I am his, that he owns me. When this is all over he says he will teach me a lesson in his bedroom, and that he will thrash Ono to within an inch of his worthless life.'

Cassidy glared at the chief.

'There will be no more lessons in your bedroom,' she said flatly, defiantly, just as she whipped up her pistol and fired it twice—expertly—into the foreheads of the two royal sons.

Both men dropped, the backs of their skulls bursting with blood, dead before they hit the ground.

Stunned, the chief whipped up his own shotgun, only to find himself already staring into the barrel of Diane Cassidy's pistol.

'I've been waiting five years for this,' she said.

Blam!

The bullet went through the Neetha chief's nose, breaking it on the way into his brain, causing a massive geyser of blood to splatter all over his face.

The fat ruler collapsed onto the steps of the temple-fortress, his body sliding down them, his cracked-open skull oozing brains.

The King of the Neetha was dead.

Diane Cassidy stared down at his body with a mix of disgust and bloody triumph.

Wizard scooped up the fallen chief's shotgun and grabbed Cassidy's hand. 'Come on! Time to go.'

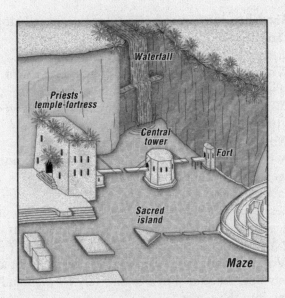

The Drawbridges and the Tower

Wizard's group hurried through the temple-fortress of the Neetha priesthood.

It was like running through a gothic freakshow.

Bloody skeletons hung from torture devices, steaming pots of foul liquids simmered, ancient inscriptions lined the walls.

They hurried up some stairs and came to a long drawbridge that led to the central tower out on the lake. A second matching drawbridge stretched out from the tower itself, meeting with their lowered bridge in the middle.

'This way!' Ono said, rushing out onto their drawbridge.

The group raced across it.

But when they were halfway across, a call stopped Wizard dead in his stride.

'*Epper! Professor Max Epper!*'

Wizard turned . . . to see Wolf standing down near the Fighting Stone, looking directly over at him.

'We found you, Max! You knew we would! You can't win this! My son couldn't, so how can you?'

Wolf held up something for Wizard to see:

A battered and worn fireman's helmet, bearing the badge: 'FDNY Precinct 17'.

Jack's helmet.

Beside him, Wizard heard Lily gasp as she saw it.

'I watched him die, Epper!' Wolf called. 'My own son! You're all out of heroes! Why keep running?'

Wizard instinctively clenched his teeth. 'Not completely out,' he said softly, taking Lily by the hand and racing into the tower.

On their side of the lake, Zoe and Alby were also heading for the central tower inside the priests' enclave.

They were rushing along a narrow lakeside path toward a small fort nestled up against the ravine-wall when a new wave of Wolf's men entered the ravine, this time from the north, from above the waterfall.

They came abseiling down the cliffs there on drop-ropes, two dozen Congolese and American troops, covered by one of the Black Hawks.

Alby was gazing up at this new wave of attackers when suddenly a Neetha warrior-monk popped up into view on the roof of the little fort in front of him and fired—of all things—an Angolan RPG up at the Black Hawk!

The RPG hit its mark, and hovering above the lake, the Black Hawk exploded, blasting apart. Bleeding smoke, it nosedived into the water, landing with a massive splash not far from the tower.

'Jesus, I think these Neetha guys have kept every weapon they've ever found,' Zoe said.

As the Black Hawk crashed, the warrior-monk who'd fired the rocket ducked from sight, probably to reload.

His disappearance gave Zoe and Alby the opening they needed to race to the cliff-side fort, dash inside it and climb its internal stone stairs.

One floor up, they came to a stone half-bridge stretching out from the fort toward the central tower. Mounted on several stone columns, this half-bridge was designed to meet the island tower's eastern drawbridge when it was fully lowered—as it was now.

As they looked out across this double-bridge, they spotted Wizard standing in the doorway to the tower, waving them over.

'This way! Hurry!' he yelled as, without warning, the drawbridge in front of him began to rise.

Wizard seemed perplexed. He wasn't doing it. Someone else was.

'Run!' he called.

'*Run!*' Zoe said to Alby.

She and Alby dashed out into open space, gunfire and explosions ringing out all around them, an RPG zooming past them, its smoketrail slicing through the air before it slammed into the cliff-side fort behind them and detonated. The fort erupted. Rocks and debris flew every which way.

But the RPG-firing warrior-monk who had been on its roof had already got out of there—and he came charging out of the little fort behind Zoe and Alby, also seeking to cross the double-bridge and get to the tower.

The drawbridge was rising—one foot above the leading edge of the half-bridge. Two feet . . . three . . .

Zoe and Alby were almost at it.

The monk was sprinting hard behind them.

Zoe and Alby got there as the rising wooden drawbridge rose four feet above the gap. Zoe quickly picked up Alby and hurled him at the rising bridge's edge.

Alby flew through the air and thudded chest-first into the leading edge of the drawbridge. The hit winded him but he got a handhold, and held on, half-bent over the edge of the rising bridge.

With Alby safely on the drawbridge, Zoe jumped for it herself, leaping from the end of the stone half-bridge, arms outstretched, and she caught the edge of the drawbridge with her fingertips and exhaled a sigh of relief.

Until the warrior-monk behind her also leapt for the drawbridge and, since he could no longer reach it, caught *her* by the waist!

Zoe was jerked downward, yanked by the extra weight, but she held on, her fingers going white as they gripped the edge of the ascending drawbridge.

Ever rising, the drawbridge passed through 20 degrees, 30, then 45 degrees . . .

Bent over the leading edge of the rising bridge, clutching the Second Pillar in one hand, Alby saw Zoe beneath him, struggling with the warrior-monk. He shifted awkwardly, juggling the Pillar, so that he could get into a position to help her . . .

. . . when—*thunk!*—without warning the whole huge drawbridge stopped with a violent lurching jolt that sent the unbalanced Alby flying clear off its upper edge and tumbling down its length, heading *into* the tower!

Alby rolled down the steep drawbridge, trying his best to keep hold of the Pillar. But at the very bottom of his fall, he landed heavily on the stone base of the half-raised drawbridge and the Pillar popped from his grip and bounced away from him, through the tower and out onto the *other* drawbridge, the one that stretched back toward the village.

Alby watched in horror as the glass-like Pillar came to rest out on the other drawbridge, right at the point where it joined with the matching drawbridge that folded out from the temple-fortress.

'Alby!' a voice called.

He turned, and saw Wizard standing at the bottom of a flight of stone steps that burrowed down into the floor to his right. Lily was with him.

But then Alby heard more voices, and he looked out at the Pillar just in time to see, appearing inside the temple-fortress beyond it, some heavily armed Congolese Army men led by an Asian-American US Marine.

The Pillar lay exactly halfway between them and Alby.

A pained shout from Zoe made Alby spin on his knees. He saw her fingers at the top of the half-raised drawbridge. Saw them slipping slowly out of view . . .

This is all happening too fast, his mind screamed. *Too many choices, too many variables. Escape with Lily, grab the Pillar or help Zoe . . .*

And suddenly everything went silent and time slowed for Alby Calvin.

In the silence of his mind, Alby faced his choice.

Of his three options, he could do two.

He could make it to the Pillar and get back to Wizard and Lily in the tower—but he couldn't do that *and* help Zoe. If he took this option, Zoe would drop into the croc-filled lake and die.

Or he could help Zoe and, with her, join Wizard and Lily—but that would mean leaving the Pillar to these intruders. And that could have *global* ramifications.

Global ramifications, he thought.

The Pillar or Zoe.

One choice could potentially save the world. The other would save a single life: the life of a woman who was dear to him and to those he cared about, Lily, Wizard and Jack West.

It's not fair! he thought angrily. *This is not a choice a kid should have to make! It's too big. Too important.*

And so Alby made his choice.

A choice that would have far-reaching consequences.

Time sped up again and Alby leapt to his feet and ran *back* toward the half-raised drawbridge, toward Zoe.

He scrambled up the sloping wooden bridge, clawing at it with his fingernails. He came to Zoe's fingers, hooked over the edge, just as they slipped a final time—

—and he caught one of her hands with both of his, leaning back with all his strength to hold her.

Below him, Zoe snapped to look up, a new look of hope leaping across her face. Then, knowing that one of her hands was secure, she used her other hand to loosen the grip of the warrior-monk hanging from her belt and wrenched him free of her.

The warrior-monk screamed as he fell away from her, landing with a splash in the water below before several large reptilian shapes converged on him and took him under.

Then, with Alby's help, Zoe hauled herself up and over the edge of the drawbridge.

'Thanks, kid.'

'We really have to go,' he said.

They slid together on their butts down the sloping drawbridge, landing on their feet inside the tower—just in time to see the Congolese Army men reach the Pillar on the other drawbridge and bring it to the attention of Switchblade.

'Damn. The Second Pillar . . .' Zoe breathed.

Alby swore under his breath, but he'd made his choice.

'This way,' he said firmly, pushing Zoe down the stone steps inside the tower, to the spot where Wizard and Lily waited with Ono and Diane Cassidy.

Lily called, 'Quickly! There's an escape tunnel down here. Come on!'

Alby made to follow Zoe down the steps, but it was right then that the most unexpected thing of all happened.

He got shot.

He'd been about to follow Zoe down the stairs when suddenly something *slammed* into his left shoulder, spinning him, hurling him three feet backwards, into the nearby wall.

Alby slumped to the base of the wall, dazed, in shock, his left shoulder burning in a way that he'd never felt before. He looked down at it to discover that the entire shoulder was awash with blood.

His blood!

He saw Zoe down at the base of the stairs, saw her try to come for him, but it was too late—the Congolese Army men and the Asian-American Marine were now entering the tower—and Wizard had to pull Zoe back down the stairs and into the escape tunnel down there.

Leaving Alby just sitting there against the stone wall, dumbstruck, bloodied and horrified, and now at the mercy of the US Marine coming toward him.

Dark, wet and narrow, the escape tunnel led northward.

Through its tight confines they ran, Ono leading the way, holding a flaming torch above his head. He was followed by Lily and Diane Cassidy, with Wizard and Zoe bringing up the rear.

'Oh, God! Alby!' Zoe cried as she ran.

'We had to leave him!' Wizard said with surprising firmness.

'I think he got hit—'

'Wolf can't be so evil as to kill a small boy! And we had to get away! We have to protect Lily. What did you manage to get from the sacred island?'

'We grabbed the Orb and its sighting device, but we lost the Second Pillar!' Zoe said. 'Alby saved me instead! Wolf's men got it before they got him!'

Wizard kept running hard. 'After he's done with the Neetha, Wolf and his rogue army will now have both Pillars, plus the Firestone and the Philosopher's Stone! They'll have everything they need to perform the ceremony at the Second Vertex *and* at every other vertex to come! This is a disaster!'

They dashed up a long flight of stone steps and came to a concealed stone doorway cut into a small cave, the end of the escape tunnel.

Emerging from the cave, they found themselves on the banks of the wide jungle river that fed the Neetha waterfall.

To the south, three volcanoes loomed over a seamless green valley—except for a newly opened hole in the canopy, the Neetha's ravine was completely hidden by the jungle.

Shouts and gunfire made them whip around.

About a hundred yards from the cave, another battle was being waged on the riverbank.

Two Congolese Army pilots were desperately defending a large seaplane from about thirty Neetha warrior-monks. The seaplane—or more correctly, 'flying boat'—was a very old model, a Soviet rip-off of the classic Boeing 314 'Clipper'.

Big and bulky, with an upper flight deck and a lower passenger cabin, it had four wing-mounted propeller engines and a huge bulbous belly that sat low in the river. Cheap and old, knock-off Clippers like this one were common in those parts of Africa where the only landing strips were rivers.

Right now this Clipper was literally crawling with Neetha warriors. They were scaling its flanks, jumping on its wings, standing on its nose and hammering its cockpit windshield with clubs.

Zoe stepped up alongside Wizard, seeing the activity going on all over the big seaplane.

Wizard saw her eyes narrow. 'You're not thinking . . .'

'You bet I am,' she said, taking the chief's shotgun from him.

*

Thus while the plane's two Congolese pilots fired their guns wildly, defending their plane against the many Neetha attackers, five figures swam silently and unnoticed around the tailfin of the floating plane, around to its open side and to the entry door there.

Zoe led the way, climbing up out of the water and reaching for the door.

She pulled it open—only to be confronted by a yellow-toothed Neetha warrior-monk, looming over her! He whipped up his bow . . . just as, one-handed, Zoe brought up the shotgun and blasted the monk out of the way.

A minute later, still brandishing the chief's shotgun, she hustled into the upstairs cockpit, just in time to see the plane's Congolese co-pilot get yanked bodily out of the smashed forward windshield, screaming as he went.

Two Neetha monks hacked into the poor man right there on the nose of the plane. When they were done, the two murderers crouched to enter the cockpit, only to find themselves looking straight down the barrel of Zoe's gun.

Boom! Boom!

The two monks went flying off the nose of the plane, sailing down into the river.

Zoe slid into the pilot's seat while the others piled in behind her. With Ono beside him, Wizard stood guard at the top of the spiral staircase that led down to the lower passenger deck, covering the stairs with an AK-47 he'd picked up downstairs.

'Can you fly this thing?' Lily asked Zoe.

'Sky Monster's been giving me lessons.' Zoe scanned

the dizzying array of dials in front of her. 'It's not *that* much different to a helicopter . . . I think.'

She punched the ignition switch.

The big seaplane's four turboprop engines roared to life.

Its remaining pilot—firing vainly from the shore-side doorway—was taken completely by surprise as the big Clipper's propellers began to rotate and then blur with speed.

His surprise was his undoing.

For as he turned at the sound, he was struck by six arrows from his Neetha opponents and he fell from the doorway—and as the plane began to move away from the shore, the ten or so remaining Neetha warrior-monks assailing it from the riverbank went rushing en masse up the gangway before the gangway itself fell away into the water behind the departing plane.

Wind blasted in through the shattered cockpit windshield as Zoe jammed forward on the collective and felt the plane surge beneath her.

The waves of the river started to rush beneath the bow of the seaplane, getting faster and faster, until suddenly they fell away and Zoe had them airborne.

She smiled with relief. 'Dear God, I think we made—'

Gunfire from the cabin made her turn.

Wizard was firing his AK-47 at the Neetha warrior-monks trying to enter the upper deck via the stairs.

They were practically suicidal in their assault—hurling themselves over their dead, shrieking and screaming, trying to fire arrows if they could.

If she could have seen her plane from the outside, Zoe would have been shocked: several Neetha men were still on its roof, clambering forward on their bellies toward the open cockpit.

At the same time, two more warriors on one wing were preparing to—suicidally—throw a thick net into one of the propellers. They threw the net . . . and with a great mechanical jerk, the thick rope got hopelessly entangled in the propeller . . . and with a blast of black smoke, that engine seized completely!

The entire aeroplane banked wildly at the unexpected loss of power and the two Neetha men were thrown off the wing and went plummeting to their deaths.

Zoe spun in her seat just in time to see them flail off the wing. She wrestled the plane back level.

'What is *wrong* with these people!' she shouted.

Diane Cassidy answered: 'They guard the location of their realm with rabid fanaticism. If, by his death, a Neetha warrior can prevent an intruder from escaping, then he is assured a place in heaven.'

'So our escape plane is infested with suicidal fanatics,' Zoe said. 'Wonder—'

Gunfire cut her off. Oddly distant gunshots.

'Wizard!' she called.

'It's not me!' Wizard shouted back from the stairs. 'They've stopped trying to storm the upper deck. A moment ago they all just went downstairs.'

More distant gunshots.

And suddenly Zoe saw another of her wing-mounted engines explode with belching black smoke, its propellers stopping.

Then she realised what was going on.

'Oh, *Jesus*. They're firing at the engines from the side doors. They're going to bring us down that way.'

'If they don't ignite all the fuel in the wings beforehand!' Wizard called.

More distant gunfire.

'Shit, shit, shit . . .' Zoe said.

Gripping the pilot's control yoke, she could feel the plane becoming less responsive.

There's no way out of this, she thought. *You can't stop someone intent on bringing your plane down this way.*

'We're screwed,' she said aloud.

As if in answer to her comment, her radio abruptly crackled.

'*Zoe! Is that you in the Clipper? It's Sky Monster!*'

'Sky Monster!' Zoe grabbed a headset. 'Yes, it's us! Where are you?'

'*I'm right above you,*' came the reply.

As the big Clipper seaplane soared over the jungle, an even larger plane swung in low above it, descending from a higher altitude.

The *Halicarnassus*.

'*Sorry it took me so long to get here,*' Sky Monster said. '*Had to go via Kenya!*'

'How did you find us?' Lily asked.

'We'll discuss that later!' Zoe said. 'Sky Monster, we've got a bunch of angry passengers downstairs who are trying to bring our bird down from the inside! We need extraction, pronto!'

'*Roger that. I see you got no windshield. Are you all mobile?*'

'Yes.'

'*Then let's do a dog-sniffer. Zoe, power up to 400 knots and then send everyone over.*'

'Gotcha.'

'What's a dog-sniffer?' Lily asked.

'You'll see,' Zoe said, turning sharply.

More gunshots were echoing out from downstairs.

The two planes flew over the Congo jungle in formation, the massive 747 looming above the smaller Clipper seaplane.

Then the *Halicarnassus* powered forward in front of
the Clipper and, with its rear loading ramp open, lowered itself in front of the seaplane's smashed cockpit.

From her position inside the Clipper's cockpit, Zoe saw
the *Hali*'s enormous tail section lower into place in front
of her, filling her field of vision.

Its rear loading ramp yawned before her, bare metres
in front of her own plane's nose cone.

'Okay, Sky Monster!' she yelled in her mike. 'Hold
her there, I'll bring us forward and send everyone
over!'

Zoe then powered up and edged the seaplane closer
to the *Halicarnassus*'s rear ramp, until the Clipper's nose
was literally scraping against the edge of the ramp.

Then she yelled, 'Okay! Wizard, grab Lily, Ono and
Dr Cassidy, and go!'

Wizard didn't need to be told twice.

He quickly slid up over the cockpit dashboard and
stood out on the nose of the Clipper, in the battering
wind, *between the two flying planes!*

He pulled Lily, Ono and Cassidy out after him, and
after a few hurried steps across the nose of the Clipper,
they hopped up onto the rear ramp of the *Hali* and
found themselves standing in the relative calm of the
747's rear hold.

This left Zoe alone in the cockpit of the seaplane.

She hit autopilot and left the controls, sliding up and
out onto the nose cone just as the Neetha managed to
hit another of her engines and it exploded and the entire
plane lurched wildly.

Too far gone to go back now, Zoe jumped, diving

for the *Hali*'s rear ramp at the exact moment that the seaplane beneath her just fell away, banking downward at an extreme angle.

Zoe landed awkwardly, her forearms banging on the edge of the ramp, her fingers clutching for a hydraulic strut but missing, and to her utter horror she felt herself drop off the edge of the ramp and fall into the wide blue sky . . .

. . . at which point no fewer than *three* sets of hands grabbed her outstretched arms.

Wizard, Lily and Ono.

All three of them had seen her leap from the flailing seaplane, seen her clasp the hydraulic strut with one hand, and then seen her grip begin to falter.

And so all three of them had lunged to her rescue, diving for her outstretched hands at the same time.

Now they held her, together, while far beneath Zoe the pilotless Clipper seaplane veered wildly downward and—with its cargo of fanatical Neetha warrior-monks—crashed into the forest, exploding in a great billowing fireball.

Wizard, Lily and Ono hauled Zoe up into the hold while Diane Cassidy closed the rear ramp. The ramp thunked shut and they all sat there for a moment on the floor in the wonderful silence of the hold.

'Th-thanks guys,' Zoe gasped.

'You're thanking us?' Wizard said in disbelief. '*You're* thanking *us*? Zoe, did you *see* yourself these last few days? You killed a warrior on the Fighting Stone, you deciphered an unconquerable maze, you flew a Neetha-covered plane out of Hell and almost died to make sure we all got off it safely.

'Honestly, Zoe, I've never seen anything like it. What you've done was *extraordinary*. Jack West Jr is not the only out-and-out hero I know. When he was gone, you stepped up to the plate. You're an absolute wonder.'

Zoe bowed her head. She hadn't even thought about what she'd done. She'd just done it.

Lily gave her a huge hug. 'You were awesome, Princess Zoe. Five-star *girl* power. Grrrr!'

And for the first time in days, Zoe smiled.

Back at the Neetha village, through sheer force of arms, Wolf's people had taken control of the town.

Neetha villagers and warrior-monks were gathered together on their knees, bound with flex-cuffs and guarded by Congolese Army men.

Switchblade came striding over to Wolf.

'Sir, we have it,' he said proudly, stepping aside to reveal the Delta man, Broadsword, who held the Second Pillar.

Wolf's eyes sparkled at the sight. He took the cleansed Pillar and held it reverently in front of his face.

'We also found this young gentleman,' Switchblade shoved Alby forward, clutching his wounded shoulder. 'Name's Albert Calvin. Says he's a friend of Jack West's daughter.'

Wolf eyed the little boy before him and snuffed a laugh. 'Tend his wound. He comes with us from here.'

Switchblade went on: 'Rapier's up in the inner sanctum above the maze. He says he's found the Firestone, the Philosopher's Stone and the First Pillar, all laid out on altars. He's bringing them down.'

'Splendid,' Wolf said. 'Splendid. The Neetha took them from Max Epper. This is turning out to be an excellent day.'

He turned suddenly to Switchblade. 'What about the

Orb, the Delphic Stone?'

'It's gone, sir. As are Professor Epper and his group.'

Wolf snorted. 'Alive or not, Epper won't be happy. Because he knows that we now have every trump card in the deck: the first two Pillars, the Philosopher's Stone *and* the Firestone.'

'There's one more thing, sir,' Switchblade said.

'Yes?'

Switchblade nodded to someone, and from the crowd another prisoner was brought forward.

Wolf's eyebrows arched in surprise.

It was the warlock of the Neetha.

The gnarled old man's hands were cuffed, but his eyes blazed with rage.

'And just how can *you* help *me*?' Wolf said, knowing the old shaman couldn't possibly understand him.

To his surprise, the old man answered him. But he didn't speak in Thoth. Rather, he spoke in a language that Wolf recognised: Greek, classical Greek.

'*The Second Corner of the Machine,*' the warlock drawled in slow but perfect Greek. '*I have seen it. I will take you there.*'

Wolf leaned back in surprise, a sly smile forming.

'Switchblade, Broadsword. Fire up the choppers and call our people in Kinshasa. Tell them to prep a plane for Cape Town. It's time to get our fucking reward.'

As the *Halicarnassus* soared south-eastward in glorious peace, Zoe and the others joined Sky Monster in the seated area immediately behind the cockpit.

Ono and Diane Cassidy were introduced and Sky Monster explained what had happened to him since they'd left him in Rwanda.

'After Solomon's boys arrived with some start-up fuel, I flew to the old farm in Kenya and gave my baby a full check-up and refuel, even had a brand-new engine mounted.'

'You keep spare jet *engines* there?' Zoe asked.

'I might've . . . found . . . some in my travels and kept them for a rainy day,' Sky Monster said bashfully. 'Anyway, I've been tracking every aerial scramble in central Africa, and sure enough, earlier today, I spotted these Congolese guys on the satellite scanner—in some Clipper transports and escorted by a few US choppers—all heading to this region. Figured they'd found you, so I tagged along from a distance. Then when I saw you take off in the other direction, I figured it could only be Zoe flying.'

'Ha-de-ha-ha,' Zoe said.

Sky Monster said, 'Hey, where's Solomon? I gotta thank him for sending that fuel.'

Zoe shook her head.

'He died defending me,' Lily said, her eyes downcast.

'Oh,' Sky Monster said softly. 'And Alby?'

'Don't even ask,' Zoe said, rubbing her temples, clearly still dealing with that issue. 'Hopefully he's not dead, too.'

She glanced at Lily as she said this, and their eyes met. Lily said nothing.

While they talked, Wizard tapped away on a computer, posting an encoded message on the *Lord of the Rings* messageboard he, Lily and Jack used for such communications. If Jack was somehow alive, he would check in on the messageboard eventually.

'You think Daddy's still alive?' Lily said, moving behind Wizard as he typed. 'Even after that man showed us his helmet?'

Wizard turned to face her.

'Your father's a very resilient fellow, Lily. The most resilient, stubborn, brilliant, loyal, caring and difficult-to-kill man I know. As far as I'm concerned, Jack West isn't dead until I see his unmoving body with my own eyes.'

This didn't seem to encourage Lily.

Wizard just smiled. 'We must always retain hope, little one. Hope that our loved ones are alive, hope that good will prevail over evil in this epic conflict. In the face of powerful opponents and overwhelming odds, hope is all we have.

'Never lose it, Lily. Deep in their hearts, bad people like Wolf have no hope and so they replace it with lust: lust for dominance, for power—and if they ever gain that power they're only happy because now everyone else is as miserable as they are. Always have hope, Lily, because hope is what makes us the good guys.'

Lily looked at him. 'That Wolf man said on the phone before that he's my grandfather, Daddy's father. How can Daddy be so good and Wolf be so bad?'

Wizard shook his head. 'That I cannot explain. The path a person takes in life is often determined by the strangest, most incidental things. Jack and his father are alike in many ways: both are fiercely determined and incredibly intelligent. Only Jack acts for others, while his father acts for himself. Somewhere in their lives, they each *learned* to act in these ways.'

'What will I be like then?' Lily asked nervously. 'I want to be like Daddy, but it seems that's not guaranteed. I don't want to make the wrong choice when it matters.'

Wizard smiled at her, tousled her hair. 'Lily, I cannot ever imagine you making the wrong choice.'

'And now that Wolf man has got Alby,' Lily said.

'Yes,' Wizard said. 'Yes—'

At that moment, something pinged in the cockpit and Sky Monster went to check on it. Two seconds later, he shouted: '*What in the name of . . . ?*'

Zoe and the others raced into the cockpit to see what had upset him.

They found Sky Monster pointing at a satellite aerial map of southern Africa.

Dozens of little red dots filled the air above the northern border of South Africa. Many more blue dots flanked the western coast just off Cape Town.

'What is it?' Zoe asked.

'See all those dots,' he said. 'The red ones represent military aircraft, the blue ones warships. And there's a repeating message coming in over all frequencies: the

South African Air Force has blockaded South African airspace to all foreign air traffic—military and commercial. At the same time, their Navy's formed a perimeter around Cape Town, Table Mountain and half the Cape of Good Hope.'

He pointed to a few white-coloured dots on the ocean south of the Cape. 'Those white dots, they're the last civilian craft that were allowed in about an hour ago. Judging from their transponders, they're South African-registered fishing trawlers returning from the Indian Ocean. They're the last ones they've let back in. Now all the sea lanes are closed.'

'But we have to get to Cape Town by tomorrow night,' Zoe said.

Sky Monster swivelled in his seat. 'I'm sorry, Zoe, but we can't do that, not without getting shot down. Our enemies have completely shut us out. They musta bought off the South African government with a boat-load of cash. I hate to be the one to say this, but we can't get to Cape Town.'

SEVENTH ORDEAL

THE SECOND VERTEX

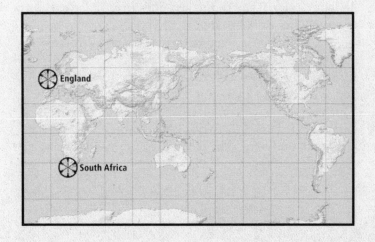

ENGLAND–SOUTH AFRICA
11 DECEMBER, 2007
6 DAYS TO THE 2ND DEADLINE
(4 DAYS EARLIER)

ENMORE MANOR,
LAND'S END, ENGLAND
11 DECEMBER, 2007

Lachlan and Julius Adamson sat gloomily in the locked library of Enmore Manor, a secluded estate in the far south-west of England near Land's End.

The blinking red light of a super-sensitive motion-tracking unit gazed down at them, tracking their every movement, telling their Japanese captors that they were still where they were supposed to be.

They sat with Lily's backpack and nothing else. Only her toys remained in the pack—everything else they had of worth had been taken by the Japanese.

Every now and then, their captors came for them and got them to explain some diagram on their computer or some email that Wizard had written about the Machine.

Tank Tanaka was always polite but curt, his eyes hard and cold, fixed on a purpose that the twins simply couldn't comprehend.

Only once did Lachlan shake him from his trance. 'Yo, Tank! Why are you doing this, man! What about your friends, like Wizard and Lily?'

Tank rounded on him, his eyes flaring. 'Friends?

Friends! The notion of friendship is nothing compared to the rank *humiliation* of a nation. In 1945 my country was dishonoured, not just beaten in battle, but beaten like a dog before the whole world. Our Emperor, sent to us by God himself, the last in the longest line of kings on this planet, was belittled in front of the entire world. This was a slur that no Japanese has ever forgotten.'

Julius said, 'But Japan is strong again. One of the richest and most advanced countries in the world.'

'Robots and electronics do not rebuild honour, Julius. Only vengeance does. I have studied this Machine for twenty years, all the while with vengeance on my mind. In their hearts, all Japanese agree with me, and they will all rejoice when our vengeance is made manifest.'

'But they'll be *dead*,' Julius said. 'If you succeed, all life on this planet will be extinguished.'

Tank shrugged. 'Death is not death when you take your enemy with you.'

A few times when Tank was out, their Japanese guards conversed in the twins' presence, assuming that as *gaijin* the twins did not understand Japanese.

On one such occasion, as he typed on his computer for them, Lachlan, listening discreetly, snapped up.

'What is it?' Julius whispered.

'They're saying that they just got word from "their man in Wolf's unit", some guy named Akira Isaki?'

'Isaki?'

'Whoever he is, he's not loyal to Wolf. He's working for these assholes. He just called in and told them—oh, shit—that Jack West is dead and that Wolf is now heading for the Congo, going after the Second Pillar. This

Isaki will report back when that's over and tell our guys whether they have to move or not.'

'Huntsman's dead?' Julius said. 'You think it's true?'

'I don't know what to think. But I do know this: our time is limited. It's time we flew the coop.'

Twelve hours later in the dead of night, one of the Japanese guards came to check on them.

A sensor had detected that one of the windows in the library had been breached, but the motion tracker still showed the twins to be in the library, moving very little, probably sleeping.

The Japanese guard opened the library door, and stopped dead in his tracks.

The library was empty.

The twins were gone.

The only moving object: Lily's little robot dog, Sir Barksalot, stomping up and down on his little metal legs, barking soundlessly at the dumbstruck Japanese guard.

The alarm was sounded and the grounds lit up with floodlights, but by the time Tank and his men had searched the area for the twins, they were already sitting in the back of a pick-up truck speeding east, heading far away from Land's End.

'So where do we go now?' Julius asked, the wind whipping his hair.

Lachlan grimaced in thought. 'There's only one place I can think to go.'

MINE COMPLEX
SOMEWHERE IN ETHIOPIA
11 DECEMBER, 2007

At the same time Zoe was guiding her group through the wilds of the Congo, and the twins had been making good their escape from Tank's Japanese Blood Brotherhood at Land's End, Pooh Bear was languishing in the mysterious Ethiopian mine, suspended above the arsenic pool in his medieval cage.

Six hours after the shocking death of Jack West—and since his own brother, Scimitar, had left Pooh to die—the working day came to an end and the Ethiopian Christian guards in charge of the mine shepherded the Ethiopian Jewish miners into their subterranean quarters—dirt-walled caves with planks for beds and rags for blankets. Mouldy bread and a soup-like gruel was served up for food.

Once the slave-miners were safely locked away, the thirty or so Christian guards gathered around the arsenic pool and stared up at the imprisoned Pooh Bear.

Torches were lit.

Chants were intoned.

A great drum was hammered.

A full-sized Christian cross was erected and set alight.

Then the tribal dancing began.

Once the cross was burning, all the other torches were extinguished, so that it was the only light source in the vast cavern—it lit up the great underground space with a haunting orange glow that bounced off the stone towers half-buried in the mine's high dirt walls.

Pooh Bear looked out from his cage in horror. His time, it seemed, had come. He shot a sad look at the deep pit about thirty metres from the arsenic pool, the pit in which Jack had met his end.

Then, with a clunking jolt, Pooh Bear's cage suddenly began to *descend* toward the steaming pool on its chains. At the edge of the pool, a pair of Ethiopian guards were slowly uncranking a spooler, lowering the cage.

The other guards began chanting quickly. It sounded like the Lord's Prayer, in Latin, and uttered feverishly fast: '*Pater Noster, qui es in caelis, sanctificetur nomen tuum . . .*'

The cage descended.

Pooh Bear shook its bars.

'*Pater Noster, qui es in caelis, sanctificetur nomen tuum . . .*'

Pooh's cage was only ten feet above the simmering pool of black liquid.

'*Pater Noster, qui es in caelis, sanctificetur nomen tuum . . .*'

Nine feet, eight feet . . .

Pooh Bear began to feel the heat of the pool, the hot steam rising all around him.

'*Pater Noster, qui es in caelis, sanctificetur nomen tuum . . .*'

The chanting continued.

The dancing continued.

The drum kept booming.

And Pooh Bear's cage kept lowering.

As his cage descended, Pooh's eyes flashed from the simmering pool below him to the surging throng of chanting-and-dancing guards and then over to the blazing cross towering over them all—and somewhere in the middle of the hellish scene, over the booming of the drum, he thought he heard another sound, a kind of banging noise, but he couldn't see where it had come from and he dismissed it.

'*Pater Noster, qui es in caelis, sanctificetur nomen tuum . . .*'

The pool was only three feet beneath him now, its steaming fumes engulfing him. Sweating profusely, with death approaching and no avenue of escape, Pooh Bear began to pray.

The heavily muscled Ethiopian guard who had hammered Jack West to his horizontal cross was now leading the sacrificial ceremony, banging on the great drum with gusto.

His eyes widened with delight as Pooh Bear's cage came to within a few feet of the deadly pool.

Now he hammered harder on the drum, heightening the frenzy of the crowd—just as a thick masonry nail came flying through the air from out of nowhere *and lodged squarely in his right eye*, driving a full six inches back into his brain, killing him instantly, throwing him to the ground, and abruptly ending the beating of the drum.

Everything stopped.

The dancing, the chanting, the movement. Even the men lowering Pooh Bear's cage stopped their cranking.

Silence.

The crowd of guards turned.

To behold a man standing at their rear, beside the blazing cross, fearsomely illuminated by its firelight, a terrifying figure literally covered in his own blood—it was on his face, on his clothes, and most obviously, on the rag wrapped around his wounded right hand.

Newly risen from the dead, from beneath a great stone slab at the base of a deep stone pit, it was Jack West Jr and he was pissed as Hell.

If the killing of Jack West by his own father had raised comparisons to Christ in the minds of the fundamentalist Ethiopian Christian guards, now his resurrection chilled them to the core.

That he had already silently disarmed four of their number during their wild dancing and now held a gun in his good hand only served to make them believe even more that this man had God-like abilities.

Except for one thing.

Jack West Jr was not a merciful god.

It had taken Jack six hours, six long hours of careful shifting and excruciatingly painful movements to get himself out.

Blocking the fall of the stone slab had been frightening enough.

As the great slab had been slid across his pit, Jack had thought quickly: the only thing he possessed that could possibly withstand the weight of such a slab was his titanium forearm.

And so, at the very moment the slab had slid across the top of his pit, he had clenched his teeth and yanked with all his strength on his nailed-down artificial left hand.

It shook the nail slightly, but on the first pull, he did not pull it loose.

The slab fell into his pit—

—just as he yanked on the nail again, and this time, his metal hand came free, nail and all, and as the huge stone slab fell down into the pit, Jack planted his false arm perpendicular to his body, made a fist and tucked his legs up against his side as—*clang!*—the full weight of the slab hit his metal fist, crushing two of its fingers, but the arm held and the irresistible force of the slab met the immovable object of Jack's upraised titanium forearm.

The leading face of the slab came to a stunning halt a centimetre from Jack's nose and to anyone looking down at it, it would have appeared that he had been completely crushed by the great stone slab.

Jack, however, had his legs squeezed to the left of his body while his head was facing right, his right hand still nailed to the floor, itself only centimetres away from the face of the slab above it.

From there, all he needed was courage, strength and time—courage to grab, with his real right hand, the nail sticking through it; strength to form a fist around the head of the nail and jimmy it from the block beneath it; and time to do so without tearing his own hand apart or dying from shock.

Three times he passed out from the strain, blacking out for he didn't know how long.

But after a couple of hours of this agonising sequence of jimmying and yanking, he finally dislodged the masonry nail and got his right hand free.

Deep hyperventilating gasps followed as he then used his teeth to extract the nail from his bloody right palm.

Clenched in his jaws, the nail came free and blood

issued from the hole in his palm. Jack quickly unlooped his belt from his trousers and with his teeth created a tourniquet.

At which point, he promptly blacked out again, passing out for an entire hour this time.

He woke to the sounds of chanting, dancing and drums.

'*Pater Noster, qui es in caelis, sanctificetur nomen tuum . . .*'

Now he had to deal with the issue of the slab on top of him.

All he needed was one crack in it, and he found it near where his right hand had been nailed down.

Into this crack he jammed a chewing-gum-sized wad of C-2 plastic explosive—the high-impact low-radius explosive he kept in a compartment in his artificial arm for use in enemy doorlocks in case of capture.

The C-2 went off—the distant bang Pooh would hear—and a long fatal crack snaked up the length of the slab, breaking it perfectly in two. The partial slab to Jack's right fell flush to the floor of the pit, providing a narrow aperture through which he could squeeze.

After some careful wriggling, he was all but out, save for his artificial left arm, which still held the other side of the slab off the ground.

A tough predicament—there was no way he could lift the half-slab off his titanium arm. So he did the only thing he could.

He simply unlatched the forearm section of his false arm from the bicep section and rolled out.

And so Jack stood at the base of the pit, with one full arm and one half arm, to the sounds of chants and drumbeats—only now he was free.

Another wad of C-2 cracked the section of slab above his artificial forearm, releasing it, and Jack quickly reattached it and tied a rag tightly around his wounded right palm.

Then he climbed the ladder in the wall of the pit and commenced his own one-man war against the guards of his father's mine.

Jack stood before the crowd of guards looking like Death incarnate.

His eyes were bloodshot and a ring of his own blood was caked around his mouth, blood from the masonry nail he had wrenched from his own hand with his teeth.

But he was still just one man against thirty.

It was then that he brought his spare hand into view. In it was a fire extinguisher, grabbed from over by the gantry elevator.

With a sudden blast of white carbon-dioxide, he fired the extinguisher into the burning cross, and it went out, plunging the mine into darkness.

Absolute black.

The guards panicked, started shouting. Then there came the sound of many feet shuffling, moving, and—

—*Bam!*—

—the mine's dim emergency lights came on, revealing Jack standing in exactly the same position as before, beside the cross . . .

. . . only now an army stood behind him.

An army of several hundred slave-miners that he had released from their underground quarters before confronting the guards.

The looks on the faces of the slaves said it all: hatred, anger, *vengeance*. This would be a battle without mercy to avenge their horrific treatment, to even the score for months, years of slavery.

With a piercing cry, the crowd of slave-miners rushed forward, attacking the guards.

It was a slaughter.

Some of the guards tried to get their guns from a nearby rack, but they were intercepted on the way, crash-tackled to the ground and stomped to death. Others were grabbed by many hands and hurled into the arsenic pool.

A few tried to flee for the gantry elevator—the only exit from the mine—but they were set upon by several dozen slave-miners waiting there with nail-studded planks. They were clubbed to death.

Within minutes, all the guards were dead and the mine was eerily silent in the dim emergency lighting.

Jack quickly set about releasing Pooh Bear from his cage. Once he was free and standing on solid ground, Pooh gazed at Jack in horror.

'By Allah, Jack, you look like shit.'

Bloody and filthy and weary beyond all human endurance, Jack smiled a crooked smile. 'Yeah—'

Then he fainted into Pooh Bear's arms.

Jack awoke to the wonderful sensation of warm sunlight on his face.

He opened his eyes, to find himself lying on a cot in a guardhouse just inside the upper entrance to the mine, sunshine slanting in through the window.

A fresh bandage was on his right hand and his face had been washed. He also wore crisp new clothes: some traditional Ethiopian robes.

Squinting, he stood and padded out of the guardhouse.

Pooh Bear met him in the doorway.

'Ah, the warrior wakes,' Pooh Bear said. 'You'll be happy to know we now own this mine. We took out the upper guards with the help of the miners—who, it should be said, were most enthusiastic in assailing their captors.'

'I'll bet,' Jack said. 'So where are we in Ethiopia?'

'You're not going to believe it.'

They stepped out of the office and emerged in bright sunshine.

Jack took in the surrounding landscape.

Dry, barren brushland, with rust-coloured soil and treeless hills.

And dotting the hollows of some of those hills were structures—stone *buildings*—exquisitely carved buildings, each easily five storeys tall, that had been hewn from solid rock and which were sunk inside massive stone-walled pits. It was as if they had been cut out of the living rock.

One of the buildings, Jack saw, was carved in the shape of an equal-armed cross, a Templar cross.

'You know where we are?' Pooh Bear asked.

'Yes,' Jack said. 'We're in Lalibela. These are the famous Churches of Lalibela.'

'Our mission is in tatters, Huntsman,' Pooh Bear said sadly.

It was a short time later and the two of them were sitting in the sunshine, with Jack nursing his injured right hand. Around them, the freed slave-miners variously left, ate or plundered the upper offices for clothes and booty.

'We've been scattered to the winds,' Pooh went on. 'Your father sent Stretch back to the Mossad, intent on collecting the bounty on his head.'

'Aw, shit . . .' Jack said. 'And did I see Astro go off with Wolf?'

'Yes.'

'*Timeo Americanos et dona ferentes*,' Jack muttered.

'I don't know, Jack,' Pooh said, 'From what I could see, Astro didn't seem, well, himself. And during our mission, he struck me as a fine young man, not a villain. I wouldn't rush to judgement on him.'

'I've always valued your opinion, Zahir. Consider judgement suspended, for the moment. What about Wolf?'

'He set off after Wizard, Zoe, Lily and Alby, to find

the ancient tribe and get the Second Pillar.'

'The Neetha . . .' Jack said, thinking.

He stared out into space for a moment.

Then he said, 'We have to catch up with Lily and the others. Make sure they get that Pillar and get it to the next vertex in time.'

'You need rest,' Pooh Bear said, 'and a doctor.'

'And a panel beater,' Jack said, touching the two half-crushed metal fingers on his mechanical left hand.

Pooh Bear said, 'I say we head for our old base in Kenya, the farm. There you can get you some medical attention and re-arm yourself. Then you can set out from the farm for the central regions of the continent.'

'*I* can?' West said. 'What about *we* can?'

Pooh Bear looked at him closely. Then he looked away into the distance. 'I will be leaving you at the farm in Kenya, Huntsman.'

Jack remained silent.

'I cannot leave my friend to suffer in the cells of the Mossad,' Pooh Bear said. 'The Mossad do not forget a slight. Nor do they forgive those agents who disobey their orders. Even if the world is to end, I will not leave Stretch to die a cruel death in a dungeon. He would not let such a fate befall me.'

Jack just returned Pooh Bear's gaze. 'I understand.'

'Thank you, Jack. I shall get you to Kenya and there we shall part.'

Jack nodded again. 'Sounds like a plan—'

Just then, however, a delegation of about a dozen Ethiopian Jews approached them. The leader of the delegation, a dignified-looking man, held a bundle in his hands, wrapped in dirty hessian cloth.

'Excuse me, Mr Jack,' he said humbly. 'As a gesture

of thanks, the men wanted to give you this.'

'What is it?' Jack leaned forward.

'Oh, it is the stones your father had us digging for,' the man said matter-of-factly. 'We found them three weeks ago, we just didn't tell him or his evil guards that we had. So we hid them and kept digging as if the stones had never been found, awaiting salvation, awaiting you.'

Despite himself, Jack shook his head and grinned. He couldn't believe this.

'And since you set us free,' the leader said, 'we would like to present the holy stones to you, as a token of our thanks. We think you a good man, Mr Jack.'

The leader of the Jewish slave-miners handed Jack the hessian bundle.

Jack maintained eye-contact with the leader as he took it. 'I sincerely thank you for this. I also apologise to your people for the cruelty of my father.'

'His acts are not yours. Be well, Mr Jack, and should you ever need aid in Africa, send for us. We will come.'

And with that, the delegation left.

'Well, I'll be,' Pooh Bear said. 'No good deed really does go unrewarded . . .'

Beside him, Jack gently unwrapped the hessian cloth, to reveal two stone tablets, each the size of a manila folder, and clearly ancient, and both inscribed with half a dozen lines of text, written in the Word of Thoth.

'The Twin Tablets of Thuthmosis,' Jack breathed. 'God damn.'

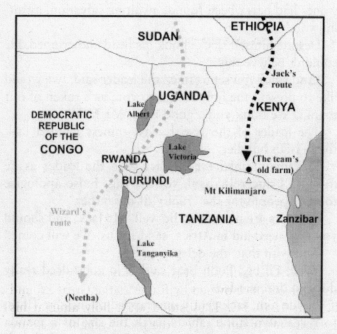

THE SEPARATION OF THE TEAM

KENYAN SAVANNAH

12 DECEMBER, 2007

FIVE DAYS TO THE 2ND DEADLINE

Jack and Pooh Bear sped across the vast Kenyan savannah in an old truck they'd stolen from the mine at Lalibela.

Pooh Bear drove while Jack sat in the passenger seat, gazing at the two ancient tablets.

'Huntsman. What are those things?'

Staring at the tablets, Jack said, 'You wouldn't believe me if I told you.'

Pooh gave him a look. 'Try me.'

'Okay. The Twin Tablets of Thuthmosis are a pair of stone tablets once owned by Rameses the Great around the year 1250 BC. They stood on a holy altar at his favourite temple in Thebes, the most valuable treasure of his reign. But they were taken from Rameses late in his life, stolen from the temple by a renegade priest.'

'I confess I have not heard of these tablets before,' Pooh Bear said as he drove. 'Should I have?'

'Oh, you've heard of them. Only you've heard them called by their other name. You see, the Twin Tablets of Thuthmosis are more commonly known as the Ten Commandments.'

'The Ten Commandments!' Pooh Bear exclaimed. 'You can't be serious. The two carved stone tablets containing God's laws handed to Moses at Mount Sinai?'

Jack countered, 'Or how about two carved stone tablets containing crucial ancient knowledge stolen by *an Egyptian priest* named Moses from the Ramesseum at Thebes and spirited to Mount Sinai after making his escape from Egypt.

'And, while we're being precise about it,' Jack added, 'according to Egyptian sources, the two tablets only contain five commands, not ten—the tablets are identical, containing the same text. Whether God sent them to Moses on Mount Sinai or whether Moses just revealed them to his followers for the first time on Mount Sinai, is open to question.'

'It is?'

'Well, let me ask you: who was Moses?'

Pooh Bear shrugged. 'A Hebrew peasant, abandoned by his mother to the rushes, who was found by the queen and raised as the brother of . . .'

' . . . Rameses II,' Jack finished. 'We all know the story. That Moses lived during the time of Rameses the Great is likely. That he was a Hebrew is *unlikely*, since "Moses" is an Egyptian name.'

'The name "Moses" is Egyptian?'

'Yes, in fact, strictly speaking it's only *half* a name. "Moses" means "born of" or "son of". It is normally combined with a theoriphic prefix pertaining to a god. So Rameses—or spelled another way, "Ra-moses"— means "Son of Ra".

'As such, it is highly unlikely that "Moses" was actually the name of the man we call Moses. It'd be like calling a Scotsman *Mc* or an Irishman *O'* without adding the family name—McPherson, O'Reilly.'

'So what was his name then?'

'Most modern scholars believe that Moses' full name was *Thuth*moses: the son of Thoth.'

'As in the Word of Thoth?'

'The very same. And as you and I know very well, Thoth was the Egyptian god of knowledge. Sacred knowledge. This has led many scholars to deduce that the man we call Moses was in fact a member of an Egyptian priesthood. More than that, he was a very influential priest: a gifted orator, a charismatic leader of people. Only there was a big problem. He preached a heretical religion.'

'Which was?'

'Monotheism,' Jack said. 'The idea that there is only one god. In the century before Rameses ascended the throne of ancient Egypt, Egypt had been ruled by a peculiar pharaoh named Akenaten. Akenaten has gone down in history as the one and only Egyptian pharaoh to preach monotheism. Naturally, he didn't last long. He was assassinated by a group of holy men, aggrieved priests who had been telling Egyptians for centuries that there were many gods to worship.

'But. If you look at the Biblical Moses, you'll see that he preached a very similar idea: one almighty God. It's very probable that Moses was a priest of Akenaten's new religion. Now, think about it, if this charismatic priest were to come upon a pair of stone tablets carved by an advanced prior civilisation, don't you think he might use them to augment his preaching, to say to his followers, "Look at what God in his wisdom sent you! His immutable laws!"'

'You realise that if you're right, Christian Sunday

schools will never be the same again,' Pooh Bear said. 'So what has all this to do with some remote stone churches in Ethiopia?'

'Good question. According to Biblical history, the Ten Commandments were kept in the Ark of the Covenant, the *arca foederis*, inside a special vault deep within the Temple of Solomon. Now, in the movies, Indiana Jones found the Ark in the ancient Egyptian city of Tanis, but according to the people of Ethiopia, Indy was wrong.

'The people of Ethiopia have claimed for over 700 years that the *arca foederis* has resided in their lands, brought there direct from the Temple of Solomon by European knights in the year 1280 AD, the same European knights who built the Churches of Lalibela. Seems the Ethiopians were right.'

'So if the tablets *don't* contain the ten ultimate laws of God, what's written on them?' Pooh Bear asked.

Jack gazed at the engraved writing on the two tablets in his lap. 'What the tablets contain is just as important: they contain the words of a ritual that must be performed at the sixth and last vertex of the Machine, when the Dark Star is almost upon the Earth. The Twin Tablets of Thuthmosis contain a sacred text that will save us all.'

They drove south through Kenya, zooming along its highways until at last they crested a final hill and their old base came into view—a large farmhouse not far from the Tanzanian border. On the distant southern horizon, the cone of Kilimanjaro rose majestically into the sky.

And standing on the porch of the farmhouse waiting for them, were two white men.

One wore a black T-shirt, the other a white one.

The shirts read: 'I HAVE SEEN THE COW LEVEL!' and 'THERE IS NO COW LEVEL!'

The twins.

Horus was perched on Lachlan's forearm. She squawked with delight when she saw Jack and flew directly to his shoulder.

'When we got here this morning,' Julius said, 'your little friend was waiting.'

'That's one loyal bird you've got there,' Lachlan said.

'Best bird in the world,' Jack said, grinning at the falcon. 'Best bird in the world.'

They headed inside the farmhouse.

'We've got a lot to tell you—' Lachlan said as they walked, but Jack just held up his finger and went into his old study.

There he prised open a floorboard and extracted from under the floor a shoebox filled with wads of US dollars and an Australian SAS first-aid field kit.

Jack grabbed a syringe from the kit and loaded it with a drug called Andarin—'Superjuice' as the men of the SAS liked to call it. Andarin was a potent mix of adrenaline and high-grade cortisol. It was a battle drug, designed to mask pain and provide an adrenal kick, and thus get a badly wounded soldier—as Jack was now—through a hostile engagement.

Jack injected it into his arm and instantly blinked. 'Ow, that's powerful stuff.' He apologised to the twins: 'Sorry, gentlemen. Just needed something to keep me standing till this is over. Now, tell me everything.'

They settled in the lounge room of the empty farmhouse, and there the twins blurted out everything they'd learned over the last week.

They informed Jack of the location of the Second

Vertex: to the south of Table Mountain in Cape Town, South Africa.

They told him about Tank Tanaka and his Japanese brotherhood's avowed mission to avenge their national disgrace in World War II—through mass global suicide. They also mentioned their golden piece of knowledge: that this Japanese brotherhood had infiltrated Wolf's CIEF force with one of their own, a man named Akira Isaki.

While they'd waited at the farmhouse for someone to arrive, the twins had hacked an American military database and discovered that there was indeed a US serviceman named A.J. Isaki—Akira Juniro Isaki—a Marine who had been seconded to the CIEF.

Lachlan said, 'Isaki was born in America in 1979 to a Japanese-American couple who—'

'—by all accounts were very lovely people,' Julius added.

'Thing is,' Lachlan said, 'his *grandparents*—his paternal grandparents—were purebred Japanese and during the Second World War, they were imprisoned in a Californian internment camp—'

'Very nasty, those camps. Black spot in American history . . .'

'But when baby A.J.'s parents were killed in a car crash in 1980, A.J. Isaki was brought up by his grandparents—'

'His now bitterly resentful pure-blood Japanese grandparents, members of the Blood Brotherhood. A.J. joined the Marines, was steadily promoted to Force Recon, and was ultimately seconded—upon his own application—to the CIEF in 2003.'

'His call-sign,' Lachlan said, 'is Switchblade.'

'Switchblade,' Jack said, vaguely recalling the Asian-American Marine whom Wolf had introduced to him back in the Ethiopian mine, when Jack had been nailed down at the base of the pit. He asked, 'You guys still online?'

Julius cocked his head. 'Is the starship *Enterprise* powered by dilithium crystals? Of course we're online.'

He handed his laptop to Jack.

Jack tapped some keys. 'We've got to find out if Wizard and Zoe got the Second Pillar from the Neetha. Hopefully, they've left a message for me on the Net.'

He brought up the *Lord of the Rings* chat-room, punched in his username—STRIDER101—and password.

A new screen came up, and Jack scowled. 'Nothing.'

No message awaited him.

Wizard's message would not arrive on the notice-board for another three days.

Lachlan said, 'Jack, there's one more thing.'

'What?'

'Since we got here we've been scanning the military frequencies, searching for news of you or the others. Over the last twenty-four hours, a whole bunch of African nations have scrambled their air forces. There's also been a spate of air traffic lockdowns in the south of the continent: first Zimbabwe and then Mozambique, then Angola, Namibia and Botswana. No commercial air traffic allowed. Someone's cutting off all the air corridors to South Africa.'

Jack thought about that. 'The next vertex is underneath Table Mountain in Cape Town, you say?'

'A little to the south of it, yes,' Lachlan said.

'We have to get there,' Jack said, suddenly standing.

'We have to get there before the deadline.'

'What do you mean?' Julius asked.

'The way I see it, there are two ways this thing can pan out—one, Wizard, Lily and Zoe get the Pillar and get to Cape Town; which means they're going to be arriving in Cape Town with enemies hot on their heels. They'll need us there.'

'And second?'

Jack bit his lip.

'The second option is worse. It's that Wolf gets the Pillar and heads for Cape Town with it. If he sets it in place, that's fine by me—it saves the world for a little longer. But as you've just said, Wolf's CIEF team has been compromised by the Japanese Blood Brotherhood. At least one member of his team, this Switchblade, is a traitor—and he does *not* want to see the Pillar set in place at all. He wants to destroy the world, to erase Japan's shame. And if Switchblade is part of Wolf's Cape Town team, then he's going to make sure they *don't* successfully lay the Pillar.'

'Which would be very bad,' Lachlan said.

'End-of-the-world bad,' Julius said.

'Yeah,' Jack said. 'So, either way, we have to get to Cape Town, to help Wizard or—and I can't believe I'm going to say this—to help Wolf.'

Julius asked, 'But how do we get to South Africa within four days and *not* do it by air?'

Jack gazed out the window.

'There's one man I know who might be able to help us, but we haven't a moment to lose.' He stood up. 'Come on, gentlemen. We're going to Zanzibar.'

That evening, Jack stood on the tarmac at Nairobi International Airport, about to board a chartered private plane, a little Cessna that he'd paid for wholly in cash, adding a grand to ensure that no questions were asked.

The Kenyan pilot took the money without so much as a blink. Such payments weren't uncommon for people travelling to Zanzibar.

As the twins boarded the plane, Jack remained on the tarmac with Pooh Bear.

'I guess this is it,' he said.

'It's been an honour and a privilege to serve with you, Jack West Jr,' Pooh Bear said.

'The honour has been mine, my friend.'

'When you see Lily again, please give her my love.'

'I will.'

'I am sorry I cannot go with you from here. But I just can't leave Stretch to—'

'I understand,' Jack said. 'If I could, I'd go with you.'

They stared at each other for a long moment. Then as if he was struck by a thought, Jack reached down and unstrapped his bulky wristwatch. He handed it to Pooh. 'Here. Take this. It has an SOS distress beacon, a GPS locater. If you get in trouble, press the button and I'll know where you are.'

Pooh Bear took the watch and put it on. 'Thank you.'

Jack regarded Pooh for a moment, then he stepped forward and embraced the Arab tightly.

'Good luck, Zahir.'

'Good luck to you, too, Huntsman.'

And then they separated and Jack watched as Pooh Bear walked purposefully off the runway, and as he stood there by the steps of his plane, Jack wondered if he would ever see his friend again.

ZANZIBAR

OFF THE COAST OF TANZANIA

13 DECEMBER, 2007, 2345 HOURS

4 DAYS TO THE 2ND DEADLINE

It was almost midnight when Jack and the twins arrived in Zanzibar in the Cessna.

Zanzibar.

A small island off the east coast of Africa, in the 19th century it had been the haunt of pirates, slave traders and smugglers; a decadent and lawless hideaway for those with little respect for the law.

In the 21st century, little had changed.

Except for the glitzy waterfront hotels that serviced tourists on their way home from Kilimanjaro, Zanzibar largely retained its centuries-old seaminess: modern-day pirates lurked in back-alley drinking holes while South African fishermen frequented the many gambling dens and brothels, engaging the services of cut-price African native girls in between blackjack hands. Old pirate caves on the island's ferocious eastern coast were still used.

It was to this ferocious eastern coast that Jack and the twins headed in a crappy old Peugeot rental car, heading for a long-abandoned lighthouse on a remote headland.

They passed through a barbed-wire gate and drove

up a long overgrown driveway to the front door of the lighthouse.

Not a soul could be seen anywhere nearby.

'Are you sure about this?' Lachlan asked nervously. He fingered the Glock pistol that Jack had given him.

'I'm sure,' Jack said.

Stopping the car, he got out and walked over to the main door of the lighthouse. The twins followed him, eyeing the waist-high ring of uncut grass that encircled the structure's base.

Jack rapped on the door three times.

No answer.

The door did not open.

No sound but the crashing of the waves.

'Who are you!' an African-accented voice demanded suddenly from behind them.

The twins whirled. Lachlan whipped up his gun.

'Lachlan, no!' Jack leapt forward and pushed the gun down.

The move saved Lachlan's life.

They were surrounded.

Somehow, as they'd stood at the base of the lighthouse, no less than ten Tanzanians—all with deep black skin and all wearing navy-blue military fatigues and armed with brand-new M-16 assault rifles—had crept up on them. Absolutely soundlessly.

Jack recognised the leader of the group.

'Inigo, is that you? It's me, Jack. Jack West. These are my friends, Lachlan and Julius Adamson, a couple of Net-jockeys from Scotland.'

The Tanzanian did not acknowledge Jack's introduction at all.

He just glared at the twins.

'Net-jockeys?' he said, frowning fiercely. 'Computer persons?'

'Y-yes,' Lachlan said, gulping.

The Tanzanian was still frowning darkly. He had a line of raised traditional markings on his forehead.

'You play *Warcraft* on Internet?' he demanded.

'Er, yeah . . .' Julius said.

The African pointed at their 'COW LEVEL' T-shirts. 'The cow level. You play computer game, *Diablo II*?'

'Well . . . yes . . .'

Abruptly the leader's dark frown became a broad smile, showing a mouthful of enormous white teeth. He spun to face Jack:

'Huntsman, I have heard of this cow level, but for the life of me, I just cannot get to it!' He turned to the twins: 'You two will show me how to find it, you . . . *cow* boys!'

Jack smiled.

'Nice to see you, too, Inigo. But I'm afraid we're in a bit of a hurry. We need to see the Sea Ranger immediately.'

They were taken into the lighthouse, where instead of going up, they went down—first through a dusty old cellar and then through a storage basement. In this storage basement was a hidden staircase that went even further down, delving deep into the headland before emerging in a giant cave at sea level.

Sometime in the distant past—probably by pirates in the 1800s—the cave had been fitted with two wooden docks and some cabins. More recently, the Sea Ranger had installed generators, lights and some concrete extensions for the docks.

Taking pride of place in the centre of it all, tied up to one of the docks with its conning tower soaring high, was a Kilo-class submarine.

Jack had been here before, so he wasn't surprised by the rather impressive sight.

The twins, however, were gobsmacked.

'It's like the Batcave . . .' Lachlan said.

'No, better . . .' Julius agreed.

A winding river-like passage led out to the ocean, and halfway along it, a movable breakwater protected the cave from the rough seas outside. Exit from the cave could only be achieved at high tide—at low tide, jagged rocks would be exposed along the winding passage.

J.J. Wickham stood waiting on the dock at the base of

the stairs: former US Navy XO, brother-in-law of Jack West Jr, the Sea Ranger.

He and Jack embraced. They hadn't seen each other since that New Year's Eve party in Dubai.

'Jack,' Wickham said, 'what the hell's going on? These last few days, half the African continent has gone completely nuts. The Saudis put up half a billion dollars for any country that found two people who sounded a lot like my niece and your mentor.'

'The Saudis . . . ?' Jack said aloud.

Up until now, he'd thought the Saudis had been backing *him*—by sending Vulture to be a part of his team.

Vulture, he thought. *You scheming little . . .*

It explained the blocked air corridors in the south of the continent—only the Saudis could afford to pay off whole African countries.

'The Saudis are in league with my father . . .' he said aloud.

It made sense. The Caldwell Group and the Saudis had longstanding links based on oil. And if the Second Reward—'Heat'—was what Wizard suspected it was, an unending energy source, perhaps even perpetual motion, then the Saudis had a *huge* interest in acquiring it. All this time, he hadn't just been battling against his father, he'd been fighting a *triple* threat: the Caldwell Group, Saudi Arabia and China, all allied together.

He turned to Wickham. 'It's a complicated situation that just got a whole lot more complicated. Right now, I need to get to Cape Town inside of four days, unseen, and I can't go by air. I can tell you more along the way.'

'Your father is involved?'

'Yeah.'

'Say no more,' Wickham said, already moving toward his submarine. 'Fathers-in-law can be tough, but that man was the biggest *asshole* of a father-in-law a guy ever had.'

Jack walked after Wickham. 'Our enemies'll be on the lookout for subs. You got any kind of cover?'

Wickham kept walking. 'As a matter of fact, I do.'

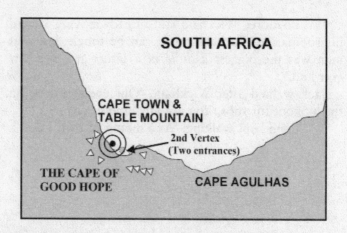

Three days later, Jack and the twins found themselves rounding Cape Agulhas, approaching the point where the Indian Ocean met the Atlantic Ocean.

Cape Town lay to the north-west, over a mountainous peninsula of wilderness, facing out over the Atlantic.

They'd made excellent time from Zanzibar, travelling halfway down the east coast of Africa on the surface of the ocean in Wickham's diesel-electric Kilo-class submarine, re-christened by him the *Indian Raider*.

The reason they could travel in this way was because of the shell Wickham had recently created to cover his 74-metre-long Russian submarine.

The upper half of an ageing South African fishing trawler—gutted of its engine and heavy machinery—had been mounted on top of the submarine. With the advent of wake-spotting satellites, Wickham had recently decided that he needed an extra level of visual protection, and had hit upon the idea of a 'shell' to mount on his sub.

Then a few months back, when a crew of drunken South African fishermen, in port on a break from a six-week cruise, had beaten one of the sweeter prostitutes in town, the Sea Ranger and his men had decided to teach them some manners.

The South African fishermen were dealt with and while they lay unconscious in a back alley, Wickham stole their boat and brought it back to his cave.

There it was stripped and gutted and hoisted on chains, ready for a mission just like this.

As the sub cruised toward Cape Town, Jack told Wickham about his epic quest so far—of negotiating a booby-trapped cavern in China; decoding Stone-henge; finding the incredible First Vertex near Abu Simbel and then engaging in a bus-vs-747 car chase in the desert.

He also told him about the Six Ramesean Stones, the Six Pillars and the Six Vertices of the Machine, and how all six Pillars had to be set in place before the arrival of the Dark Star.

At the same time, the twins were getting along famously with Wickham's crew of Tanzanian sailors, showing them some computer tricks, including guiding them to the cow level on *Diablo II*, an act which made the sailors gasp in wonder and which finally earned the twins their nicknames: *The Cowboys*.

Individually, Lachlan became *Quickdraw*, while Julius was *Gunslinger*. They *loved* their call-signs.

At regular intervals on the journey, Jack checked

the *Lord of the Rings* noticeboard for messages from Wizard, Zoe or Lily.

For three days, no messages appeared.

But then, at the beginning of the fourth and last day, as Jack forlornly signed on, he found a single message waiting for him, from the user ID: 'GANDALF101.'

Jack almost leapt out of his chair.

The message had been posted only an hour previously: a cascade of numbers; a coded message that could only have come from Wizard, Lily or Zoe.

They were alive!

He turned and quickly grabbed the collection of books he had bought at Nairobi Airport, six paperbacks and one hardback novel.

The entire *Harry Potter* collection.

Jack's code with the others was a 'book code'.

Most book codes used three digits to find words in a single book: the code '1/23/3' means 'page 1, line 23, word 3'.

For Jack this wasn't secure enough. He'd added an extra digit at the start, denoting which Harry Potter book the code was coming from.

Therefore '2/1/23/3' meant 'Book 2 (*Harry Potter and the Chamber of Secrets*), page 1, line 23, word 3'.

Jack set about decoding the message on the chatroom screen.

When he was done flipping pages in the novels, he was left with:

MISSION TO JUNGLE A DISASTER.
WOLF CAUGHT UP WITH US AND NOW HAS BOTH PILLARS,

PHILOSOPHER'S STONE AND FIRESTONE. RON TAKEN PRISONER. KINGSLEY SHACKLEBOLT DEAD.

REST OF US SAFE ON THE HIPPOGRIFF NOW, BUT SOUTH AFRICA CLOSED TO ALL AIR TRAFFIC.

OUT OF OPTIONS AND JUST HOPING YOU'RE ALIVE.

PLEASE REPLY.

Jack reeled at the message.

His worst fears had come true.

Wolf had the Second Pillar. That Wolf might lay the Pillar at the Vertex was disturbing but not disastrous: Jack only wanted to save the world from destruction, and so long as *someone* set the Second Pillar in place today, the world would be okay for another three months until the next set of four vertices required attending.

But as Jack now knew, Wolf had the suicidal Switch-blade in his team.

'Oh, this is bad,' Jack said aloud. 'This is very, very bad.'

He stared at the line 'KINGSLEY SHACKLEBOLT DEAD' and sighed. Kingsley Shacklebolt was a tall black wizard from the fifth Harry Potter book and hence their code-name for Solomon Kol.

So Solomon had been killed. *Damn.*

But worse still was the previous line: RON TAKEN PRISONER. Of course 'Ron' was code for Alby—for just as Ron was Harry Potter's best friend, so Alby was Lily's.

Wolf had Alby.

Jack rarely swore wholeheartedly but he did so now. 'Fuck.'

Consulting his *Harry Potter* books, he quickly typed out a reply, then clicked 'POST'.

His message was:

STILL IN THE GAME.

ON WAY TO CAPE TOWN WITH FRED AND GEORGE AND SIRIUS BLACK.

CAN'T RISK CALLING YOU YET. WILL CALL WHEN I CAN.

SO GLAD YOU'RE SAFE. WILL GET RON BACK OR DIE TRYING.

Hidden beneath its false shell, the *Indian Raider* powered toward Cape Town.

As it happened, it would be the very last boat in a line of about a dozen South African fishing trawlers to be allowed back into South African waters that afternoon.

Then the sea lanes were closed.

And as the sun set and Cape Town found itself shut off from the world, the night of the second deadline began.

At length, the *Indian Raider* came to the eastern coast of the Cape of Good Hope, a rugged peninsula of densely forested mountains and valleys.

Blasted all year round by biting winds from the Antarctic, and featuring many impassable gorges, it was an inhospitable place and even in the present day, uninhabited.

Nestled up against the immense bulk of Table Mountain on the other side of the peninsula was the modern city of Cape Town. Right now, two dozen South African Navy warships formed a semi-circular perimeter around the city, covering the seaward approach.

Anchored in close to the rocky coastline about a mile south of the city's last seaside residence were a few unmarked American vessels and one private cruiser with Saudi Arabian markings that had arrived several days ago.

In a diving bell beneath those vessels, CIEF troops in scuba gear were busily at work, pulling a veil of seaweed from an ancient stone doorway cut into the rockwall of the coast.

It was the main entrance to the Second Vertex.

But as Jack knew, since the Second Vertex was modelled on the layout of the ancient city of Ur—or more correctly, Ur had been based on the much-older Vertex—there was a *second* entrance, one that arrived at it from the east before bending down to meet the vertex from the north.

'It's got to be around here somewhere,' Lachlan said, eyeing the sub's GPS readout.

'I'm pinging the shore for voids and recesses,' the Sea Ranger said. 'But we have to be careful with the active sonar. If someone hears it, they'll know we're here.'

He was firing sonar signals at the underwater shoreline; those signals then bounced back to the *Indian Raider* . . . unless they disappeared inside an aperture in the rockwall.

'Sir!' a sonar operator called. 'Sonar anomaly in the coastline, bearing 351. Depth 52 metres.'

The Sea Ranger came over. So did Jack and the twins.

'Makes sense,' Julius said. 'Sea levels are a lot higher now than they would have been back then. An ancient entrance would be underwater now.'

'Let's take a look,' the Sea Ranger said. 'Fire up the outside forward camera.'

A monitor was switched on, showing the underwater world outside in ghostly night-vision green, thanks to a camera mounted on the sub's bow.

On the monitor, fish glided by, even a shark or two. Seaweed waved lazily in the current and, beyond it all, the rockwall of the coast cruised by—

'There!' the Sea Ranger said abruptly, pointing at a blurry dark spot on the screen.

Jack leaned close, and his eyes widened.

'Sharpen focus,' the Sea Ranger ordered.

The image was refined, came into clearer focus.

As it did, Jack knew they'd found it.

On the screen in front of him, partially covered by strings of twisting seaweed, was an ornate ancient doorway, huge in size, perfectly square in shape and beautifully cut out of the solid rock around it.

'Holy shit . . . we're here.'

The Eastern Entrance to the Second Vertex

The *Indian Raider* jettisoned its trawler shell and dived.

Moving slowly, the sub pushed through the veil of waving seaweed that hung down over the ancient doorway and entered the darkness beyond it.

Twin beams of light lanced through the haze from the two floodlights mounted on its bow.

On the monitor inside the conning tower, Jack saw a square-shaped tunnel stretching away into darkness, boring into the very foundations of the Cape itself.

The Sea Ranger kept his men alert, kept them driving the sub slowly and carefully, now using his active sonar without restraint.

After about fifty minutes of this slow travel Jack saw something on the monitor that he'd seen before: columns.

Great, high stone pillars holding up a flat rock-cut ceiling. And yet still the space was wide enough for the seventy-metre-long submarine to fit between them.

'This place must be enormous . . .' the Sea Ranger whispered.

'You should have seen the last one,' Jack said.

A wall of steps appeared in front of them. Just like at the First Vertex at Abu Simbel, it was an enormous mountain of steps, *hundreds* of them, all as wide as the pillared hall through which they were cruising. Only at this vertex, they went upward not downward, rising up and out of the water.

'Sir, I've spotted the surface,' the sonarman said. 'There's an opening up there, at the top of the steps.'

'Let's see what's up there,' the Sea Ranger said, swapping a look with Jack.

The *Indian Raider* rose gracefully through the spectacular underwater hall, gliding silently up past the hall's massive pillars, following the incline of the submerged super-staircase.

Then it left the hall, breaking the surface.

The *Indian Raider*'s conning tower rose silently out of a still body of water, seawater sliding off its sides.

It found itself hovering in a walled pool easily a hundred metres wide. It looked like a miniature harbour, four-sided, with walls on two sides and the ultrawide stairs rising up out of the water on the third. On the fourth side, there were some stone buildings, half-submerged.

Darkness filled the air above this mini-harbour. But a sickly yellow light peeked over the horizon at the top of the steps, illuminating the space.

It was a gargantuan cavern, the ceiling easily six hundred feet high.

The hatch on the conning tower swung open and the Sea Ranger and Jack emerged, gazing in wonder at the immense dark space around their little sub.

Wickham drew a flare gun, but Jack stopped him.

'No! Wolf's already here.'

He nodded up at the sickly yellow glow above them—the result of flares already fired elsewhere in the supercavern.

Within a few minutes, they'd rowed ashore and, with the Sea Ranger and the twins beside him and Horus perched on his shoulder, Jack stepped up the wide hill of stairs, climbing them.

When they reached the top and beheld what lay beyond them, Jack let out a gasp of astonishment.

'God save us all,' he whispered.

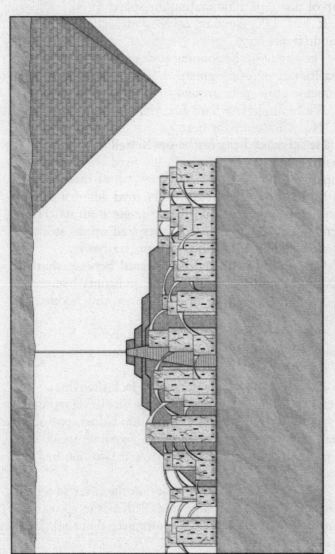

THE SECOND VERTEX

An underground city lay before him.

An entire city.

A collection of stone buildings, all of them tall and thin like towers, stretched away from him for at least five hundred metres. Bridges connected all of them— some dizzyingly high, others very low, others still were constructed of steeply angled stone stairways.

Canals of water filled the 'streets' between all these buildings, seawater that over the millennia had seeped in through the cave's two entrances and flooded the city's floor.

Dominating the forest of towers before him was a massive ziggurat, a great stepped pyramid that rose up in the very centre of the ghost city.

Exactly as it did in ancient Ur, Jack thought.

At the summit of this ziggurat was a very peculiar structure: an ultra high and very thin ladder-type object that shot up vertically from the ziggurat's peak until it hit the rocky ceiling of the cavern two hundred feet above.

At the point where the ladder hit the cavern's ceiling, a series of rung-like handholds led to the spectacular centrepiece of the cavern, a centrepiece that took Jack's breath away.

Looming off to the side of the underground city was another inverted pyramid—bronze and immense, exactly like the one Jack had seen at Abu Simbel.

It hung from the ceiling of this cavern, hovering like some kind of spaceship above the vast indoor city, easily twice the size of the ziggurat below.

From where he stood, Jack couldn't see any buildings directly beneath the pyramid—he guessed that it hung suspended above a bottomless abyss like the one at Abu Simbel had done.

But unlike the one at Abu Simbel, this pyramid was surrounded by its supplicant city, an exact twin of the ancient Mesopotamian city of Ur.

Jack wondered if all six of the vertices were somehow subtly different, unique shrines built to complement a central upside-down pyramid—Abu Simbel had a massive viewing hall looking out at its pyramid; this one had a city of spectacular bridges kneeling before it.

Suddenly, shouts and mechanical noises made Jack look up. They'd come from the other side of the cavern.

A flight of steep stone steps rose up the side of the nearest tower. Jack climbed them. Arriving at the summit of the tower, he was rewarded with a full view of the immense cavern and a glimpse of exactly where he stood in this life-or-death race.

Things didn't look good.

There, standing on a rooftop halfway across the vast cavern, having obviously got here some time ago, surrounded by the men of his quasi-private army, was Wolf.

Jack swore.

His enemies were far more advanced across the

labyrinth than he was. Once again he was starting from behind.

And then, among the group of soldiers standing immediately behind Wolf, Jack glimpsed a diminutive figure and his heart sank.

He only saw the figure for a moment, but the image lodged in his brain instantly: head bowed, left arm in a sling, right hand gripping Jack's fireman's helmet, terrified and alone, it was a small black boy with glasses.

It was Alby.

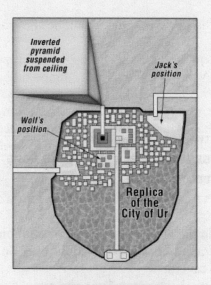

**COMPARATIVE POSITIONS
OF JACK AND WOLF'S TEAMS**

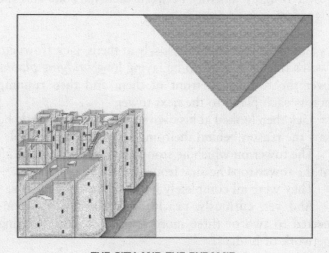

THE CITY AND THE PYRAMID

THE SECOND VERTEX

BENEATH THE CAPE OF GOOD HOPE

SOUTH AFRICA

Jack took in the monumental task ahead of him.

First he assessed Wolf's position, over on the other side of the cavern.

They must have entered via the main western 'harbour' some time ago, because they were standing on a tower roughly halfway between their harbour and the ziggurat.

A big headstart.

But as he looked more closely at them, Jack frowned. Wolf's troops seemed to be laying long *bridging planks* over the rooftop in front of them and then running across each plank to the next tower.

Jack then looked at his own situation and instantly he saw the reason behind their unusual method of travel.

The tower on which he stood had *no roof*. In fact, *all* of the tower-tops he saw from up here were roofless.

They were all completely hollow, like smokestacks.

And yet, curiously, nearly every rooftop was connected to two or three more rooftops by the dizzying network of bridges.

'Oh, man,' Jack said, realising. 'It's a huge trap system.'

Every roof that Jack could see from here was the same.

On each one there was a tongue-like platform stretching out from the leading edge of the roof to its middle, out over that tower's black hollow core.

Ringing this tongue-like platform were three smaller stepping-stone-like platforms, each situated exactly halfway between the central platform and the roof's three other edges, and each requiring a substantial jump of about five feet to land on them.

Jack examined the rooftop on which he was standing.

Carved into the stone tongue on which he stood was some text written in the Word of Thoth. On each stepping stone was a similar carving.

'How does it work?' the Sea Ranger asked.

'Question and answer,' Jack said. 'This carving here, on the tongue, is the question. You jump on the stepping stone carved with the correct answer. If you're right, the stepping stone holds your weight.'

'And if you're wrong?' Lachlan asked.

'If you're wrong, I imagine it doesn't hold your weight and you fall down the hollow of the tower.'

The Sea Ranger looked down into the black void inside the tower before them. Its walls were sheer and slick. You'd never be able to climb out, if you hadn't already landed in something deadly.

Jack said, 'I imagine the struts holding up the false stepping stones are made of a brittle material. They look strong, but they're not.'

'But you have to get *every* riddle right all the way across,' Julius said. 'Would you stake your life on your ability to answer all those riddles correctly?'

But Jack wasn't listening any more.

He was staring into space.

'Riddles,' he said aloud. 'Aristotle's Riddles . . .'

He turned sharply to the Sea Ranger. 'Have you got any sat-phones on the *Raider*, video-capable? We need to call in some expert help.'

Of course, the Sea Ranger had several satellite-phones on board the *Raider*. He even had some small helmet-mounted cameras that could be connected to them. He had them brought out.

Handing one to West, he said, 'Jack, if you put out a call on that thing, anyone in the area with even a basic scanner is going to know we're here.'

'Believe me, they'll know we're here soon enough. And if we're going to survive this, we need help.'

With that, Jack called the *Halicarnassus* on the video-phone.

When the satellite-phone console on the *Halicarnassus* suddenly started ringing, everyone on board exchanged worried glances.

Zoe picked up the phone and cautiously said, 'Hello?'

'*Zoe! It's me.*'

'Jack!'

Quick greetings were exchanged and an overjoyed Lily blurted out a brief summary of their quest through Africa before finishing with the explosive arrival of Wolf's forces at the kingdom of the Neetha and the loss of Alby and the Pillar to him.

Wizard leaned in to the mike. 'Jack. It was great to get your message. We didn't know if you were alive. But now we're in dire straits. We can't get into South Africa. We're sitting on an airstrip in the Kalahari Desert in Botswana, just north of South Africa, while Wolf has gone to the Second Vertex. Where are you?'

'*I'm at the Second Vertex,*' Jack said.

Wizard's jaw dropped.

'*And I need all of your help.*'

Moments later, Wizard, Zoe and Lily were gathered around the video-phone monitor peering at the feed coming from Jack's helmet-mounted camera.

Wizard saw the underground city and breathed, 'The city of bridges . . .' but Jack directed their attention to the carved words of Thoth on the first rooftop's tongue-like platform:

$$ \text{ЗꙅꝪ➔\♆⟩ᚲⵊ ᛉⵣᚱⵣ➔ ▮▮▮ ➔ π♋➔ᚲ} $$

'*Lily?*' Jack asked.

Lily read the text quickly.

'It says, "What is the best number of lies?"' she said.

Standing to Lily's left, Wizard frowned. 'The best number of—wait a minute . . .'

But then, from her right, Zoe said, 'Hey! I've seen that carving!'

'Where?' Wizard asked.

It was Jack who answered over the radio: '*Somewhere in the Neetha realm, I imagine. Along with a list of other carvings, carvings that looked like numbers maybe.*'

'Yes,' Zoe said. 'Yes. They were in the very centre of the maze there. Carved onto a beautiful white-marble podium. But how could you know that, Jack?'

'*Because this is one of Aristotle's Riddles,*' he said.

'Of course,' Wizard said. 'Of course . . .'

'I don't get it,' Zoe said.

Jack explained, '*At the Academy in Greece, Aristotle was Hieronymus's favourite student, the same Hieronymus who found the Neetha. It makes sense that Hieronymus told his favourite student about the Neetha and what he'd discovered there. Aristotle's*

Riddles aren't Aristotle's at all. They're Hieronymus's. Riddles that Hieronymus found during his time with the Neetha, riddles that I imagine he got someone among the Neetha to translate for him.'

'So what is the best number of lies?' Lily asked.

'One,' Wizard said. 'You know the old saying, if you tell one lie, then soon you'll find yourself telling another and then another to sustain it. But if you can tell only one, it is optimal.'

In the vast cavern of the Second Vertex, Jack checked the carvings on the three stepping stones in front of him.

'You sure about that, Wizard?'

'Yes.'

'Would you stake your life on it?'

'Yes.'

'Would you stake mine on it?'

'Er . . . well . . . I, I mean, I think . . .'

'It's okay, Max. I'm not stupid,' Jack said. 'I'm gonna wear a rope around my waist when I make the jump.'

Jack gazed at the stepping stone to his right: it bore a single horizontal slash on it. One.

The stepping stone seemed to hover above the black void beneath it. Jack still had Astro's mini-Maghook with him, so he cinched its cable around his waist and handed its launcher to Wickham.

'Here we go,' he said.

Then without another thought, he jumped, out over the void, leaping for the stepping stone to the right—

—Jack's boots landed on the stepping stone and it caught him, holding his weight.

Jack stood on the small flat stone, high above the dark hollow core of the tower beneath him.

After another leap, he was standing at the base of a long stepped bridge that soared upward to the roof of the next tower.

'Hey, Cowboys,' he called back to the twins. 'Go grab some spray paint or something from the *Raider* and then follow us, painting the correct stones as we go. Oh, and if something happens to us, you'll have to take our place, jumping across these stones.'

Lachlan and Julius both gulped. Then they raced back to the submarine to find some paint.

And so Jack made his way across the labyrinth of high bridges—leaping onto stepping stones—guided by the voices coming in over his headset, answering the riddles.

'What is the best number of eyes . . .'

'One,' Wizard's voice had answered. '*The all-seeing eye that appeared on capstones.*'

'What is the best life . . .'

'*The second life, the afterlife,*' Wizard said. '*Jump*

onto the stone saying "Two".'

He made good progress, with the Sea Ranger and the twins running after him across the bridges and over the hollow towers.

As they advanced across the dazzling bridged city, Jack looked out across the cavern, trying to gauge Wolf's progress—and to his dismay, he saw that Wolf was moving just as fast, if not faster, than he was.

Then suddenly bullets started pinging off the walls above his head.

Alerted by his radio transmissions, Wolf's men had spotted him and were now firing at him whenever they got a clear line of sight through the dense forest of towers and bridges.

Jack and the Sea Ranger came to a ledge that burrowed *inside* one of the hollow towers. Inside the tower, they were presented with another triple choice, only here there were *no* carvings at all on the three available stepping stones.

Lily quickly translated the inscription on the ledge. '*What is the direction of Death . . .*'

'*It's west*,' Wizard said, 'the direction of the setting Sun. The ancient Egyptians always thought that the Sun was born every morning in the east and died every evening in the west. That's why they always buried their dead on the western side of the Nile. The answer is "west".'

Jack jumped for the stepping stone to the west of him.

It held and he ran up the stair-bridge to the next tower, followed by the Sea Ranger.

They'd made it halfway to the ziggurat in the centre of the mini-city when suddenly they heard some shouts

and Wolf yelling, 'Okay! Switchblade and Broadsword!
It's all yours! Go! Go!'

Jack peered out around the corner of a building—and
spotted Wolf's CIEF team scampering up the stairs on
the front face of the ziggurat, looking like ants against
the scale of the structure.

Damn it, no! Jack thought.

They'd reached the ziggurat first and were now heading for the ladder that led across the ceiling to the great
pyramid.

Jack saw Wolf with his son, Rapier, and Alby on
the stairs of the ziggurat with the main cluster of CIEF
troops. Then he spotted two men dashing out ahead of
the main group, running up the ziggurat: one was Cau-
casian in appearance and wore the uniform of a Delta
operator. The second man was of Asian appearance and
wore the distinctive battle dress uniform of a Marine
Force Reconnaissance trooper.

Switchblade.

The traitor.

And so despite the fact that he was still well behind in
this race, Jack just kept going as best he could.

Never stop, he thought. *You never give up*.

Across the bridges he flew.

Up the ladder, Broadsword and Switchblade went.

Jack leapt across more riddle jumps, aided by Wizard
and Lily from afar, all the while under fire from Wolf's
men guarding the ziggurat.

Broadsword and Switchblade reached the top of
the ladder, started venturing out across the ceiling
of the supercavern, hanging from the rungs by their

hands high above the underground city.

Jack's course from the western harbour took him in a wide northward curve that passed close to the suspended pyramid. Here Jack discovered that there was indeed another abyss delving deep into the Earth directly beneath the immense bronze pyramid.

He came to a tower at the very edge of the city, one that adjoined the abyss itself—the tower's northern side actually blended perfectly with the near wall of the abyss—and from there Jack got a clear view of the pyramid itself.

He watched as the two CIEF men climbed hand over hand down a line of handrungs cut into the spine of the pyramid. Dangling high above the seemingly bottomless pit, they edged downward, moving ever closer to the pyramid's peak.

And Jack came to a horrific realisation.

He was too far away.

He was too late.

He couldn't get there in time—there was no way he could get to the ziggurat, somehow get past Wolf's men there, and then scale the ladder and the spine of the pyramid and stop Switchblade from doing whatever he planned to do.

The two CIEF men reached the inverted peak of the pyramid—and Jack watched in wonder as the Delta man named Broadsword slung a climbing harness over the last handrung and, hanging from it, used his now free hands to extract from his chestpack . . .

. . . the Second Pillar.

Cleansed and ready to be set in place.

*

On the ziggurat, Wolf also gazed in awe at the scene, his eyes glistening with delight. With him stood Rapier and Alby and the warlock of the Neetha, flanked by two guards.

Wolf's mind buzzed with the possibilities.

The reward would be his: *heat*. According to his chief researcher, the MIT professor, Felix Bonaventura, it was heat generated by the secret of perpetual motion. Energy without fuel. *Limitless* energy that could power electricity grids, aeroplanes and cars, but which would not require coal or oil or gasoline. The Saudi stranglehold on America would be broken; the entire Middle East would become irrelevant.

It was of course at that precise moment, as Wolf reached a rapture of delight, that the most unexpected thing of all happened.

For then, as Wolf watched in horror, out on the inverted pyramid's peak—while Broadsword readied the Pillar for placement—Switchblade drew a K-Bar knife and sliced it across Broadsword's throat, grabbing the Pillar from him as he did so.

Broadsword went instantly limp, blood flowing from the gaping hole in his neck and dribbling down into the abyss like a macabre waterfall.

Then Switchblade callously cut Broadsword's harness and the dying Delta operator fell from the peak of the pyramid, dropping into the fathomless void, his limp figure disappearing into darkness.

'What the fuck . . . ?' Wolf said. 'Switchblade!'

*

From his position on the nearest tower, Jack also watched as Switchblade killed Broadsword.

'Oh, God . . .' he breathed as he saw Broadsword fall.

Out on the pyramid, Switchblade now hung from his own harness, holding the Pillar in one hand. He held it up for Wolf to see and shouted, 'Welcome to the end of the world, Wolf! A world that gloried in the humiliation of my people! Now that world will be no more! Nippon was never defeated!'

'Switchblade! No!' Wolf yelled.

Switchblade snarled, 'Covetous man! You want earthly power. There is no greater power on this planet than the ability to destroy it. Now witness that power, and know that, in the end, we won the war!'

He then thrust the Pillar out from his body, his arm fully outstretched, preparing to drop it into the abyss.

'See you in Hell!' he roared.

And with those final hateful words, Switchblade dropped the cleansed Second Pillar into the abyss.

Switchblade let go of the Pillar—at the exact moment that someone came thudding into him, swinging on a rope of some kind.

It was Jack, hanging onto the end of Astro's Maghook, *having swung across from his tower, two hundred feet away!*

With nothing else to call on, he'd fired the Maghook's magnetic head into the side of the pyramid and hoped to God that the structure had magnetic properties.

It did, and the bulbous magnetic head stuck fast against the pyramid and Jack swung—a long swooping arc over the bottomless abyss, an absolutely astonishing two-hundred-foot swing—arriving at the peak *just as* Switchblade yelled his final insult to Wolf and released the Pillar . . .

. . . which Jack caught . . .

. . . a nanosecond before he *slammed* into Switchblade himself and stopped abruptly, becoming entangled in the insane Marine's harness! Clutching desperately for a handhold, he was forced to release the Maghook and it swung back toward the city, leaving him clinging to Switchblade at the peak of the pyramid.

Switchblade was furious. His eyes blazed with rage at this intrusion on his triumph.

He punched Jack hard in the face, a withering blow,

and Jack recoiled sharply, his helmet-camera dislodging from his head. It plummeted down into the abyss, cartwheeling wildly. As he was flung backwards by the blow, Jack only just managed to keep hold of the Pillar with his right hand while clinging to Switchblade's chest-harness with his left.

Hanging on desperately, he looked up into Switchblade's eyes . . .

. . . and saw that the Japanese madman wasn't finished.

Switchblade glared at Jack as he began to unclip the central buckle of his harness.

'Oh, you're not . . .' Jack said.

He was.

He was going to drop them both into the abyss!

'We're both going to die anyway!' Switchblade yelled. 'Might as well die now!'

And with those words, he managed to unclip the buckle—just as Jack made a final lunge, yanking himself up Switchblade's body, reaching with his outstretched arm for the peak of the pyramid—and in the very instant that the buckle unclasped and they both dropped together, *he jammed the Pillar into its slot in the summit of the pyramid* and then fell, with Switchblade but no longer holding the Pillar, dropping away from the pyramid's peak, watching it get smaller and smaller as the sheer walls of the abyss closed in around him.

And thus Jack West Jr and the fanatic named Switchblade fell down into the abyss beneath the inverted pyramid of the Second Vertex of the Machine, an abyss that for all anyone knew went all the way to the centre of the Earth.

As the two tiny figures disappeared into the dark abyss beneath the pyramid, the great structure's mysterious mechanism came loudly and spectacularly to life.

First there was heard an ominous thrumming, then a deafening thunderboom that shook the entire supercavern. Then a dazzling laser-like beam of light lanced out from the pyramid's apex, shooting down into the abyss, before a moment later it sucked back up into the pyramid's peak.

Silence.

The combination of the ancient spectacle and the fall of Switchblade and Jack hit the various spectators in different ways.

Wolf.

At first, he'd been shocked by the reappearance of Jack, but he regathered quickly and after the lightshow he dispatched Rapier to go and grab the now-charged Pillar from the pyramid and thus garner the reward, the secret of perpetual motion.

Once the Pillar was retrieved and in his hands, Wolf swept out of the underground city.

Someone asked him what they should do with the boy, Alby, and he cast a dismissive wave.

'Leave him here,' he said before striding out with his

men, leaving Alby alone, on top of the ziggurat in the middle of the city.

The Sea Ranger and the twins.

They just stood motionless on the roof of the tower from which Jack had swung only moments before.

The Sea Ranger stared at the scene, digesting what had just happened.

The twins stood with their mouths agape. Horus, who had been sitting on Lachlan's shoulder, flew off toward the abyss.

'He did it . . .' Lachlan breathed. 'He fucking-A did it. He set the Pillar in place.'

Julius shook his head. 'The guy is frigging SuperJack.'

'You can say that again,' the Sea Ranger said, glancing around them.

None of them had seen Alby through the labyrinth of buildings.

'Come on, gentlemen,' Wickham said. 'We can't stay here. We have to get back out that entry tunnel before Wolf's buddies send a destroyer to seal it off. Come on.'

They hustled back to the *Indian Raider*.

'What about Horus?' Lachlan said as they moved.

'That bird's destiny is with Jack,' Wickham said grimly. 'Always has been.'

Alby.

Standing alone on the summit of the ziggurat in the middle of this vast underground space, abandoned by his captors and with darkness descending all around him as their flares began to fade, he felt the most profound sense of aloneness.

The sight of Jack West plummeting from view had shocked him to his very core—till now Jack had seemed indestructible, incapable of dying, but now he was gone, swallowed by the great abyss, dead.

And with that thought, a cold horror swept through Alby's body as he realised that he was going to die here, in this huge dark cave, alone.

Standing there on the ancient ziggurat in the encroaching darkness, clutching Jack's helmet, he softly began to cry.

Wizard, Zoe, Sky Monster and Lily.

They saw it happen on their video-phone monitor.

Watching it all first from Jack's helmet camera and then from the camera that Lachlan had been wearing, they watched in horror as the ultra-tiny figures of Jack and Switchblade fell away from the tip of the immense pyramid, dropping down into the abyss, before they both disappeared from sight.

'*Daddy* . . . *!*' Lily cried, leaping at the screen. '*No! No, no, no* . . . !'

'Jack . . .' Zoe's eyes filled with tears.

'Huntsman . . .' Wizard whispered.

Sky Monster pointed at the screen. 'Look, he laid the Pillar before he fell! He did it! The crazy bastard did it . . . !'

But then an alarm siren blared out in the cockpit and Sky Monster went to check on it and he called, 'Zoe! Wiz! We have incoming South African aircraft! F-15s! We have to get out of here!'

Despite their tears, Zoe and Wizard hurried off to man the wing-guns, leaving Lily staring at the monitor—alone, frozen and stunned—sobbing deep wrenching sobs and searching for some sign, any sign, that her father was alive but knowing in her heart that he could not possibly be.

'Oh, Daddy . . .' she said again. 'Daddy . . .'

Then the *Halicarnassus* powered up and they took to the air, flying north this time, away from southern Africa, fleeing yet again, uncertain and unnerved by the knowledge that now without any shadow of a doubt, they faced the remaining challenges of their quest—the placing of the last four Pillars in March of 2008—alone, without Jack West Jr.

THE END
of
The Six Sacred Stones

ACKNOWLEDGEMENTS

Writing a novel can be a somewhat solitary experience—you spend months alone at the keyboard, lost in the world you have created. I happen to find this enormously fun, which is why writing novels is the best job in the world for me.

But when you decide to write a book with ancient Chinese characters and Japanese military language in it, you have to call for help, and this is where I get to thank those many people who helped me along the way.

As always, my wife **Natalie** is the first to read my stuff and her comments still manage to be both insightful and gentle. Having read all my books in draft stage plus all my screenplays, she's now really quite an experienced manuscript reader!

To my good friend, **John Schrooten,** who (again) read this one while sitting in the M.A. Noble Stand at the SCG while waiting for the cricket to start. The cricket commenced and he just kept on reading, so that was a good sign! Great friend, great guy.

For technical support, I am indebted to **Patrick Pow** for getting the ancient Chinese scripts from China; and to **Irene Kay** for putting me in touch with Patrick.

For the Chinese language tips, my thanks go to

Stephanie Pow. Likewise, since I know no Japanese, I have to thank **Troy McMullen** (and his wife and sister-in-law!) for their help!

I read many books while researching *The Six Sacred Stones*—from works about space and zero-point fields, to more esoteric books about Stonehenge and other ancient places. I'd like to make special mention, firstly, of the works of **Graham Hancock**, which I just love and would recommend wholeheartedly to anyone who wants to view global history from an unconventional point-of-view; and secondly, a little gem of a book called *Stonehenge* by **Robin Heath** (Wooden Books, Glastonbury, 2002). It was in this book that I first saw the theory that connects Stonehenge to the Great Pyramid through a series of right-angled triangles.

I must also send out my heartfelt thanks to **Peter and Lorna Grzonkowski** for their very generous donations to the Bullant Charity Challenge—the twins in the novel, **Lachlan and Julius Adamson**, are named after their nephews.

Likewise, **Paul and Lenore Robertson**, two long-time supporters of my work and another couple who do an enormous amount for charity, for their donation at not one but two ASX-Reuters Charity Dinners! Paul, I hope you don't mind that I made you a smooth-talking double-crossing bad-guy CIA agent!

And last of all, I thank **The WAGS**, a great group of guys with whom I play golf on Wednesday afternoons, for their generous donation on behalf of **Steve Oakes**, the leader of this motley crew. In return for their kind donation to charity, I named a character at the start of this book after Oaksey . . . and promptly riddled him with bullets. As the boys say, no one likes to see that, but such are the dangers of having a character named after you in a Matthew Reilly book!

To everyone else, family and friends, as always, thank you for your continued encouragement.

Matthew Reilly
Sydney, Australia
September 2007

MATTHEW REILLY DISCUSSES
WRITING *THE SIX SACRED STONES*

SPOILER WARNING!

The following interview contains SPOILERS from *The Six Sacred Stones*. Readers who have not read the novel are advised to avoid reading this interview as it *does* give away major plot moments from the book.

Let's get straight to the biggest question of all: how could you end The Six Sacred Stones *with Jack West Jr falling into a bottomless abyss?!!!*

Okay, okay! Yes, I figured this might be an issue, and this is certainly the best place to talk about it. (Hey, I think the interview at the end of *Scarecrow* saved me from countless emails about what I did in that book!)

When I sat down to write *The Six Sacred Stones*, I asked myself, 'How can I make this book totally *different* from the others? What can I do that will be completely unexpected?'

My answer: come up with the biggest, boldest, most

outrageous novel yet with the biggest, boldest, most outrageous cliffhanger *ending* imaginable, one in which the fate of the hero literally hangs in the balance at the end of the book (and as those who have read my other books will know, I love a good cliffhanger). This worked out very well when it became apparent to me that the story I had come up with (involving six pillars being placed at six vertices) was going to be too big to achieve in one book . . . so the cliffhanging ending is merely the midway point of a larger adventure. I've often ended chapters with dire cliffhangers, just think of this as a huge chapter-end!

Jack may well get out of his terrible predicament—and indeed one method for his survival has been inserted into the book (and no, it's not Horus)—the fun is waiting to find out how. The way I see it, it's a bit like waiting for the next season of a TV show that has ended on a cliffhanger. So in the end, I apologise to everyone for making you wait in such an awful way, but I promise it will be worth it!

Seven Ancient Wonders *and* The Six Sacred Stones *have seen an increase in the scale of your books (solar rays, dark stars, vast ancient structures). What exactly are you trying to achieve with this series?*

What I am trying to achieve is really quite simple: I want to create a *Lord of the Rings*-style epic set in our world, in the present day.

I want it to be a story that is part adventure and part myth in which a small group of seemingly powerless characters struggle against the mighty and all-powerful.

There is another reason for it, too, one that is purely for me as an author. In his Introduction to *The Lord of the Rings*, J.R.R. Tolkien wrote of his prime reason for writing that tale: 'The prime motive was the desire of a tale-teller to try his hand at a really long story that would hold the attention of readers, amuse them, delight them, and at times maybe excite them or deeply move them.'

Same here.

I just wanted to try my hand at a really big epic story: a grand sweeping adventure that spans the globe, that looks out at the Sun and space itself, that examines the mysterious ancient places scattered around our planet, and in which—most importantly of all—the protagonists, in the course of carrying out thrilling feats of heroism, endure profound tests of their character.

So in contrast to the Shane Schofield/Scarecrow books, which bring back the same hero in separate adventures, the story begun in *Seven Ancient Wonders* and continued in *The Six Sacred Stones* is actually one big story (indeed, this is why the sections titled 'A Girl Named Lily' begin with 'Part III' in this book, Parts I and II having appeared in the earlier novel).

Tell us about some of the 'mysterious ancient places' that appear in this book and why you chose them?

I love ancient places and ancient things—from the pyramids to the Rosetta Stone, I can just gaze at them all day long—especially when they defy explanation.

Having explored the Great Pyramid and its fellow 'Wonders' in *Seven Ancient Wonders*, I decided to focus on some of my other favourite ancient places in this book, among them Stonehenge, Abu Simbel and the Three Gorges region of the Yangtze River in China (there are, of course, many others that I love just as much, but I'm keeping them for the next book!). I have visited all three of these places.

First, Stonehenge. Seriously, pictures don't do it justice. Those stones are *huge*! And the stuff about coastal lichens being on their surfaces is true—it is weird and unexplained!

Abu Simbel is simply colossal, bigger than you can possibly imagine, and built for the same reason the men of Gondor built the Argonath in Tolkien's *The Fellowship of the Ring*: to tell encroaching neighbours, 'Look at how powerful we are in Egypt! Don't even think of crossing these borders unless you can deal with the people who built this monument!' And it's all the better that the UN rebuilt it brick-by-brick to save it from the waters of the Aswan Dam.

Finally, the Three Gorges of China. These are simply beautiful. Natalie and I visited them in 2006, solely to research this book. A side-trip into the gorges of the Shennong River (lush, green, misty and narrow) system really crystallised my mental image of the flooded rural hamlet where Wizard finds the entrance to Laozi's trap system.

Can you tell us about the covers of these books? They're very different to your previous jackets.

I love the covers for *Seven Ancient Wonders* and *The Six Sacred Stones*.

The artwork on them was done by a very talented Australian artist named Wayne Haag (he also did the wonderfully atmospheric aircraft-carrier image on *Hell Island*). You won't be surprised to find out that Wayne's background is actually in films; he did some of the awesome matte painting work in *The Lord of the Rings* movies and *The Fifth Element*. I met Wayne when he and a colleague of his approached me about making films of my books, in particular, *Ice Station*. Suffice to say, I wasn't in a position to make *Ice Station* then, but I thought that Wayne could do some awesome book covers.

His picture of Jack West abseiling into an Egyptian chamber for the jacket of *Seven Ancient Wonders* blew me away. I wasn't sure he could top that, but then he did The Mystery of the Circles for this book and proved that he certainly could.

What else have you been working on? How is the Contest **movie coming along?**

Earlier this year, I sold a TV script called *Literary Superstars* to Sony, who successfully licensed it to the US TV network, ABC.

It's a half-hour comedy set in, of all places, the publishing industry. I figured that after ten years in the book world, I'd acquired many funny tales, so I decided to put them into a TV show. The heroine is not an author, though, but a publicist who promotes authors for a publishing house.

The script led a charmed life through Hollywood, going from my agents to Darren Star (producer/creator of *Sex and the City*), to Sony, to the lovely actress Jenna Elfman, and then to ABC. For a while there, I was flying back and forth from Sydney to Los Angeles to do meetings with studio and network executives; which was all pretty exciting. We shoot the pilot later this year, so my fingers are crossed that it gets picked up.

This has meant that I've put my ambitions for a *Contest* movie on hold for a while—after all, you have to run with the show that's actually getting made.

One question that many fans are asking is: will we be seeing Shane Schofield again in the near future?

Yes, Scarecrow is a character that my fans really do love—especially after what I put him through in *Scarecrow*. And, in all seriousness, I thank my readers for allowing me to venture into other stories and write about other heroes (believe me, as an author, it is possible to get pushed into writing about the same character over and over again). When, one day, I look back on my career as a novelist, I'd like to see an array of stand-alone books and different series, from the Schofield and Jack West series, to the (current) stand-alones of William Race and Stephen Swain and who knows who else.

That said, having taken a break from Scarecrow, I *am* rather keen to write about him again, and a new idea featuring him has started to form in my mind. So as I write the sequel to *The Six Sacred Stones* (after all, I can't leave Jack West falling down that abyss forever!), I'll be fleshing out this idea that I have for a new Scarecrow novel with the hope that it will be the next book I write after that. I should add that I also have lots of kids demanding *Hover Car Racer II*!

(Oh, and for those who missed it in 2005, *Hell Island*—the short novel that I wrote for the Books Alive initiative—features Scarecrow and is now available again in stores across Australia and New Zealand.)

Any final words?

As always, I just hope you enjoyed the book; that it took you away from your world for a few hours or a few days and entertained you in the way a good roller-coaster should. And rest assured, I'm already typing feverishly away on the next one . . .

Best wishes and see you next time!

M.R.
Sydney, Australia
September 2007

BIBLIOGRAPHY

I've never actually included a bibliography in one of my books before, but with this novel I thought I might, since it delves into so many different fields of study (from ancient Egypt and China to the African slave trade, to space and zero-point fields, to the intricacies and history of diamonds). As an author of fiction, I have to be the proverbial jack-of-all-trades and master of none—I readily admit that I am no expert in astronomy or astrophysics, but I do my best to read as widely as I can so that my characters can be.

I have not divided this bibliography into principal or lesser sources—some might only have provided me with information on a single point in my novel, but that makes them no less valid to my mind; after all, it might have been a big point—nor is it in any particular order of importance. It is simply here so that readers who have an interest in certain aspects of the book might like to read further.

Sources

Deidre Chetham, *Before the Deluge: The Vanishing World of the Yangtze's Three Gorges* (New York, Palgrave Macmillan, 2002)

Peter Hessler, *River Town: Two Years on the Yangtze* (New York, HarperCollins, 2001)

Duncan Steel, *Rogue Asteroids and Doomsday Comets* (New York, John Wiley & Sons, 1995)

Dava Sobel, *The Planets* (London, Fourth Estate, 2005)

Stephen W. Hawking, *A Brief History of Time* (London, Bantam Press/Transworld, 1988)

Gordon Thomas, *Gideon's Spies: The Secret History of the Mossad* (New York, St Martin's Press, 1999)

Bill Bryson, *A Short History of Nearly Everything* (London, Doubleday, 2003)

Robin Heath, *Stonehenge* (Glastonbury, Wooden Books, 2000)

John North, *Stonehenge: A New Interpretation of Prehistoric Man and the Cosmos* (New York, The Free Press, 1996)

Robert Guest, *The Shackled Continent* (London, Macmillan, 2004)

Adam Hochschild, *King Leopold's Ghost* (London, Macmillan, 1999)

Hugh Thomas, *The Slave Trade: The History of the Atlantic Slave Trade 1440–1870* (New York, Simon & Schuster, 1997)

Giles Milton, *White Gold: The Extraordinary Story of Thomas Pellow and North Africa's One Million European Slaves* (London, Hodder & Stoughton, 2004)

Peter Watson, *A Terrible Beauty* (London, Weidenfeld & Nicolson, 2000)

The Seventy Wonders of the Ancient World, edited by Chris Scarre (London, Thames & Hudson, 1999)

The World's Last Mysteries, Reader's Digest (Sydney, Reader's Digest Services, 1978)

Ian Balfour, *Famous Diamonds* (London, William Collins & Sons, 1987)

Robert Bauval, *Secret Chamber* (London, Century, 1999)

Graham Hancock, *Underworld* (London, Michael Joseph/ Penguin, 2002)

Graham Hancock, *The Sign and the Seal: A Quest for the Lost Ark of the Covenant* (London, William Heinemann Ltd, 1992)

Graham Hancock, *Fingerprints of the Gods* (London, William Heinemann Ltd, 1995; London, Century, 2001)

Michael Baigent, Richard Leigh and Henry Lincoln, *The Holy Blood and the Holy Grail* (London, Jonathan Cape, 1982; London, Century, 2005)

Michael Baigent and Richard Leigh, *The Elixir and the Stone* (London, Random House, 1997)

Peter Marshall, *The Philosopher's Stone* (London, Macmillan, 2001)

Christopher Knight and Robert Lomas, *Uriel's Machine* (London, Century, 1999)

Lynn Picknett and Clive Prince, *The Stargate Conspiracy* (London, Little, Brown & Co, 1999)

Manly P. Hall, *The Secret Teachings of the Ages* (New York, Jeremy P. Tarcher/Penguin, 2003 edition; original text, 1928)

Craig Unger, *House of Bush, House of Saud: The Secret Relationship Between the World's Two Most Powerful Dynasties* (London, Gibson Square Books, 2004)

www.panmacmillan.com